THE RIVEN REALM

By

H A Culley

Book three of the Saga of Wessex

Published by

Orchard House Publishing

First Kindle Edition 2020

Text copyright © 2020 H A Culley

TABLE of CONTENTS

PLACE NAMES

Note: In my last series of novels I used the modern names for places in Anglo-Saxon England as some readers had said that my earlier novels were confusing because of the use of place names current in the time about which I was writing. However, I had even more adverse comments that modern names detract from the authentic feel of the novels, so in this series I have reverted to the use of Anglo-Saxons names.

Abergafenni (Welsh)	Abergavenny, Wales
Ægelesthrep	Aylesford, Kent
Afne	River Avon
Afon Wysg	River Usk (Welsh)
Alba	Scotland
Basingestoches	Basingstoke, Hampshire
Baðum	Bath, Somerset
Bedaforde	Bedford, Bedforshire
Berncestre	Bicester, Oxfordshire
Berrocscīr	Berkshire
Biceilwæd	Biggleswade, Bedfordshire
Buccascīr	Buckinghamshire
Cæstir	Chester, Cheshire
Cantwareburh	Canterbury, Kent
Casingc Stræt	Watling Street
Cent	Kent
Cicæstre	Chichester, West Sussex
Cilleham	Chilham, Kent
Cippanhamme	Chippenham, Wiltshire
Cocheham	Cookham, Berkshire

Cynuit	Countisbury, Devon
Dyfneintscīr	Devon
Danmǫrk	Denmark
Dēvā	River Dee
Dofras	Dover, Kent
Dornsæte	Dorset
Dumnonia	Cornwall
Dyflin (Viking name)	Dublin, Ireland
Ealdredes Geat	Aldersgate, City of London
Earninga Stræt	Ermine Street
Ēast Hlenc	East Lyng, Somerset
Ēast Seaxna Rīce	Essex
Eforwic	York, North Yorkshire
Englaland	England
Escanceaster	Exeter, Devon
Eveshomme	Evesham, Worcestershire
Flēot	River Fleet in London
Frankia	France and part of Germany
Frisia	Most of the Netherlands
Fŏsweg	Fosse Way (Roman road)
Freumh	Frome, Somerset,
(also the name of the River Frome)	
Glestingaburg	Glastonbury, Somerset
Glowecestre	Gloucester, Gloucestershire
Guilforde	Guildford, Surrey
Hæfen Kernow	Porthcurno, Cornwall
Hamtunscīr	Hampshire
Hamtun	Northampton, Northamptonshire
Hamwic	Southampton, Hampshire
Herewic	Harwich, Essex
Honfleur, Frankia	Honfleur, Northern France
Hreopandune	Repton, Derbyshire

Hrofescæster	Rochester, Kent
Hwicce	Part of Mercia
(most of Gloucestershire and Worcestershire)	
Íralandes Sǽ	The Irish Sea
Íralond	Ireland
Isca Augusta (Roman name)	Caerleon, South Wales
Lambehitha	Lambeth, South London
Lindesege	District of Lindsey, Lincs
Lundenwic/Lundenburg	London
Mann	Isle of Man
Meregate	Margate, Kent
Midweg	River Medway
Monez	Isle of Anglesey
Norðmanndi	Normandy, France
Norþweg	Norway
Orkneyjar	The Orkney Islands
Oxenaforda	Oxford, Oxfordshire
Neen	River Nene
Norþ-sǽ	North Sea
Pedredan	River Parrett
Pegingaburnan	Pangbourne, Berkshire
Poole Hæfen	Poole Harbour, Dorset
Portcæstre	Portchester, Hampshire
Readingum	Reading, Berkshire
Sæfern	River Severn
Sandtun	No longer exists
Sceapig	Isle of Sheppey, Kent
Scirburne	Sherborne, Dorset
Sidyngbourn	Sittingbourne, Kent
Silcestre	Silchester, Hampshire
Snæland	Iceland
Somersaete	Somerset

Stanes	Staines-upon-Thames, Surrey
Sudwerca	Southwark, South London
Sūð-sǣ	English Channel
Sūþrīgescīr	Surrey
Suth-Seaxe	Sussex
Suttun	Plymouth, Devon
Swéoland	Sweden
Sveinsey	Swansea, South Wales
Tamiseforde	Tempsford, Bedfordshire
Temes	River Thames
Thon	River Tone
Tōfecæstre	Towcester, Northamptonshire
Tomtun	Tamworth, Staffordshire
Tunbrige	Tonbridge, Kent
Uisge	River Great Ouse
Verulamacæster	St. Albans, Hertfordshire
Wælingforde	Wallingford, Oxfordshire
Waras	Ware, Hertfordshire
Watsforde	Watford, Hertfordshire
Wealas	Wales
Werhām	Wareham, Dorset
Whitlond	Isle of Wight
Wiltunscīr	Wiltshire
Winburne	Wimborne Minster, Dorset
Wintanceaster	Winchester, Hampshire
Witenestaple	Whitstable, Kent
Ynys Enlli	Bardsey Island, off Gwynedd, North Wales
Ytene	River Itchen

List of Principle Characters

Historical figures are in bold.

Ælfred – King of Wessex

Ælfnoð – Abbot of Cantwareburh

Æscwin – The elder son of Leofflæd and Jørren, also the name of Jørren's eldest brother, the Thegn of Cilleham in Cent

Æthelflaed – Eldest daughter Ælfred and Ealhswith, later Lady of the Mercians

Æthelhelm – The late King Æthelred's elder son

Æðelred – Mercian nobleman, later Ealdorman of Mercia

Æthelwold – The late King Æthelred's younger son, a contestant for Ælfred's throne

Acwel and Lyndon – Two of Jørren's hearth warriors

Ajs and Ecgwynna – Alric's children

Alric – Jørren's other brother

Arne – A Norse captive who became Jørren's body servant

Asser – Bishop of Wintanceaster

Bjarne – A former ship's boy on a longship hailing from Swéoland, now the Sæ

Hereræswa (admiral) of Wessex

Bryhthelm – One of Eadda's warriors, employed to teach Edward swordsmanship

Cei – A former slave belonging to Jørren's family, now the captain of the fortress of

Dofras

Ceolwulf II – King of Mercia after Burghred, puppet ruler installed by the Danes

Cináed – A Pict enslaved by Vikings, now one of Jørren's hearth warriors

Cissa - Ealdorman of Berrocscīr

Cuthfleda – Jørren's elder daughter

Cynbald – Hereræswa of Mercia

Drefan – Ealdorman of Wiltunscīr, later also Hereræswa of Wessex

Dudda – Ealdorman of Sūþrīgescīr

Eadda – Former Hereræswa of Wessex, later Edward's military tutor

Eadwig – Master shipbuilder at Hamwic

Ealhswith – Ælfred's Mercian wife and Lady of Wessex

Eafer – A feral boy who became Jørren's body servant

Eadred – Ealdorman of Dyfneintscīr

Ecgberht – The brother of Leofflæd, Jørren's first wife

Edward – The elder son of King Ælfred and the Lady Ealhswith

Eomær – One of Jørren's hearth warriors

Eohric – Guðrum's son, later King of East Anglia

Erik Barkse – Danish Jarl who held Lundenwic

Ethelred – Archbishop of Cantwareburh

Guthild – Alric's wife, daughter of a former Ealdorman of Hamtunscīr

Guðrum – Danish King of East Anglia, now known as Æðelstan

Håkon – Danish jarl in command of Lundenwic

Heardwig – Ealdorman of Suth-Seaxe

Heardwig Geonga – His eldest son

Hilda – Jørren's second wife

Jerrik– A Jute, Bjarne's deputy and commander of the eastern fleet

Jørren – The protagonist and narrator, Ealdorman of Cent and Hereræswa of Wessex

Nerian – Ealdorman of Somersaete

Oswine - Jørren's stepson

Othilia – A girl from Cæstir, later Jørren's body servant under the name of Gebeor

Pæga – Thegn of Sandtun, Cent

Plegmund – Abbot of Cantwareburh after Ælfnoð's death, later archbishop

Redwald – The reeve of Silcestre, one of Jørren's vills

Rinan – As a boy he saved Jørren's life at Ethundun, now one of his hearth warriors

Sexmund – Eadda's son

Sherwyn and Rowe – Sons of Redwald

Sigehelm – A thegn from Cent

Wolnoth – A Northumbrian, now one of his hearth warriors

Tescelin – A Frankish shepherd

Tidwold – One of King Ælfred's priests.

Tunbehrt – Former Ealdorman of Hamtunscīr, now an exile

Uhtric and Leofwine – Two urchins

Wealmær – One of Jørren's hearth warriors, later captain of his warband

Wilfrið – Captain of Jørren's skeid, the Saint Cuthbert

Wulfhere – Former Ealdorman of Wiltunscīr, now a fugitive

Wulfthryth – King Æðelred's widow and Ælfred's sister-in-law

Ywer and Kjestin – Jørren's twin children

GLOSSARY

ANGLO-SAXON

Ætheling – literally 'throne-worthy. An Anglo-Saxon prince

Avantail - a curtain of chainmail attached to a helmet to cover the throat and neck

Birlinn – a wooden ship similar to the later Scottish galleys but smaller than a Viking longship. Usually with a single mast and square rigged sail, they could also be propelled by oars with one man to each oar

Bondsman – a slave who was treated as the property of his master

Braies – Underwear similar to modern undershorts. Worn only by males.

Bretwalda – Overlord of some or all of the Anglo-Saxon kingdoms

Burh - fortified settlement

Byrnie - a tunic of chain mail, usually sleeveless or short sleeved

Ceorl - Freemen who worked the land or else provided a service or trade such as metal working, carpentry, weaving etc. They ranked between thegns and villeins and provided the fyrd in time of war

Cyning – Old English for king and the term by which they were normally addressed

Ealdorman – The senior noble of a shire. A royal appointment, ealdormen led the men of their shire in battle, presided over law courts and levied taxation on behalf of the king

Fyrd - Anglo-Saxon army mobilised from freemen to defend their shire, or to join a campaign led by the king

Gesith – The companions of a king, prince or noble, usually acting as his bodyguard

Hearth Warriors - Alternative term for members of a Gesith

Hereræswa – Military commander or general. The man who commanded the army of a nation under the king

Hide – A measure of the land sufficient to support the household of one ceorl

Hideage - A tax paid to the royal exchequer for every hide of land.

Hundred – The unit for local government and taxation which equated to ten tithings. The freemen of each hundred were collectively responsible for various crimes committed within its borders if the offender was not produced

Pallium - an ecclesiastical vestment bestowed by the Pope upon metropolitans and primates as a symbol of their authority

Reeve - a local official including the chief magistrate of a town or district, also the person manging a landowner's estate

Sæ Hereræswa – Commander of Ælfred's navy

Seax – A bladed weapon somewhere in size between a dagger and a sword. Mainly used for close-quarter fighting where a sword would be too long and unwieldy

Settlement – Any grouping of residential buildings, usually around the king's or lord's hall. In 8th century England the term town or village had not yet come into use

Shire – An administrative area into which an Anglo-Saxon kingdom was divided

Shire Reeve – Later corrupted to sheriff. A royal official responsible for implementing the king's laws within his shire

Skypfyrd – Fyrd raised to man ships of war to defend the coast

Thegn – The lowest rank of noble. A man who held a certain amount of land direct from the king or from a senior nobleman, ranking between an ordinary freeman or ceorl and an ealdorman

Tithing - A group of ten ceorls who lived close together and were collectively responsible for each other's behaviour, also the land required to support them (i.e. ten hides)

Wergeld - The price set upon a person's life or injury and paid as compensation by the person responsible to the family of the dead or injured person. It freed the perpetrator of further punishment or obligation and prevented a blood feud

Witan – Meeting or council

Witenaġemot – The council of an Anglo-Saxon kingdom. Its composition varied, depending on the matters to be debated. Usually it consisted of the ealdormen, the king's thegns, the bishops and the abbots

Villein - A peasant who ranked above a bondsman or slave but who was legally tied to his vill and who was obliged to give one or more day's service to his lord each week in payment for his land

Vill - A thegn's holding or similar area of land in Anglo-Saxon England which would later be called a parish or a manor

VIKING

Bóndi - Farmers and craftsmen who were free men and enjoyed rights such as the ownership of weapons and membership of the Thing. They could be tenants or landowners. Plural bøndur.

Byrnie - a tunic of chain mail, usually sleeveless or short sleeved

Helheim – The realm in the afterlife for those who don't die in battle

Hersir – A bóndi who was chosen to lead a band of warriors under a king or a jarl. Typically they were wealthy landowners who could recruit enough other bøndur to serve under their command

Hirdman – A member of a king's or a jarl's personal bodyguard, collectively known as the hird

Jarl – A Norse or Danish chieftain; in Sweden they were regional governors appointed by the king

Mjolnir – Thor's hammer, also the pendant worn around the neck by most pagan Vikings

Nailed God – Pagan name for Christ, also called the White Christ

Swéoþeod – Swedes, literally Swedish people

Thing – The governing assembly made up of the free people of the community presided over by a lagman. The meeting-place of a thing was called a thingstead

Thrall – A slave. A man, woman or child in bondage to his or her owner. Thralls had no rights and could be beaten or killed with impunity

Valhalla – The hall of the slain. It's where heroes who died in battle spend the afterlife feasting and fighting

LONGSHIPS

In order of size:

Knarr – Also called karve or karvi. The smallest type of longship. It had 6 to 16 benches and, like their English equivalents, they were mainly used for fishing and trading, but they were occasionally commissioned for military use. They were broader in the beam and had a deeper draught than other longships.

Snekkja – (Plural snekkjur). Typically the smallest longship used in warfare and was classified as a ship with at least 20 rowing benches. A typical snekkja might have a length of 17m, a width of 2.5m and a draught of only 0.5m. Norse snekkjas, designed for deep fjords and Atlantic weather, typically had more draught than the Danish type, which were intended for shallow water.

Drekar - (Dragon ship). Larger warships consisting of more than 30 rowing benches. Typically they could carry a crew of some 70–80 men and measured around 30m in length. These ships were more properly called skeids; the term drekar referred to the carvings of menacing beasts, such as dragons and snakes, mounted on the prow of the ship during a sea battle or when raiding. Strictly speaking drekar is the plural form, the singular being dreki or dreka, but these words don't appear to be accepted usage in English.

HISTORICAL NOTE

ABOUT DANISH MERCIA, EAST ANGLIA & NORTHUMBRIA

In 874, following their winter stay in Repton, the Great Heathen Army drove Burghred, the Mercian king, into exile in Rome and conquered Mercia. They placed a thegn named Ceolwulf on the throne but he had no real power. According to Ælfred the Great's biographer, Asser, the Vikings then split into two bands. The Danes went north to subdue a revolt in Northumbria for a time but returned in 877 to partition Mercia. The west of the kingdom went to Ceolwulf, whilst in the east the Five Boroughs began as the fortified burhs of five Danish armies who settled in the area and introduced Danelaw, their native laws and customs.

Each of the Five Boroughs was ruled as a Danish Jarldom, controlling lands around a fortified burh, which served as the centre of political power. These rulers were probably initially subject to their overlords in the Viking Kingdom of Jorvik (Saxon Eforwic and modern York) and cooperated militarily in alliance with the rulers of their neighbouring lands. In addition to the Five Boroughs there were also a number of large Danish jarldoms to the south which existed in a similar fashion, but independent, fashion. Their jarls looked toward East Anglia, rather than Northumbria, for leadership.

The Five Boroughs were based around (Saxon names, modern names in brackets):
- Lindocolina (Lincoln)
- Snotengaham (Nottingham)
- Deoraby (Derby)
- Ligeraceastre (Leicester)
- Steaneforde (Stamford)

The other independent jarldoms in the remainder of the Danelaw were based around:
- Huntandun (Huntingdon)
- Grantebrycge (Cambridge)
- Snotengaham (Northampton)
- Bedaforde (Bedford)
- Tamiseforde (Tempsford)

After 878 Guðrum (baptised as Æthelstan after his defeat at Ethundun) ruled as King of East Anglia, the boundaries of which corresponded roughly to those of the modern counties of Norfolk, Suffolk and Essex.

The Danish Kingdom of Yorvik (York) - ruled in 882 by Guthfrith, a Christian Viking - consisted of the southern half of the former Saxon Kingdom of Northumbria and extended from the Rivers Mierce (Mersey) and Hymbre (Humber) in the south to the River Tes (Tees) in the North.

The land between the Rivers Tes and Tuede (Tweed) was called Bernicia and was an independent

and dumped him on the ground. The boy was shaking with fear but his aim had been true. However, the effort required to draw and fire had tired his arms.

The second horseman stopped chasing the girl and, drawing his sword, changed direction towards the two boys. Rowe was about to flee but he couldn't bring himself to abandon his brother as the latter fumbled drawing another arrow from his quiver. The only weapon that Rowe had was a dagger which his father had given him two months ago on his tenth birthday.

It was his most treasured possession and it was a finely balanced weapon. Ever since he'd been given it he'd practiced throwing it and he thought that he was now reasonably proficient. However, his only target to date had been a circle drawn on the timber wall of his father's stables.

In his haste and fright, Sherwyn had dropped the arrow and the horseman was nearly upon them. Rowe took a deep breath and threw the dagger. It flew through the air and struck the horse in its right eye. Admittedly the boy had been aiming for its chest but blinding it in one eye was even better. The stallion reared up in pain and its rider fell backwards over its hind quarters. He hit the ground hard and lay there badly winded.

The horse galloped off shaking his head, trying to dislodge the thing it its eye. It didn't get far before it slowed and then fell to its knees before rolling over and expiring. By then the unhorsed rider was trying to get to his feet. Sherwyn thought of making a run for it but the sobbing girl reached them at that point and collapsed on the ground in relief. He plucked another arrow from the quiver and this time his hands didn't shake. He drew back, the muscles in his arms and shoulders protesting at the effort, and let fly just as the man stood upright.

The leather armour he was wearing did nothing to halt the flight of the arrow at that range and it struck the middle of his chest. He fell backwards and lay still.

'The other man's coming,' Rowe shouted in panic.

Sherwyn looked to where his brother was pointing and saw that the first warrior had regained his feet, despite the arrow in his shoulder, and was heading towards them, sword drawn and yelling expletives. What he was saying puzzled the boy. He'd assumed that they were Danes, although they weren't wearing the wide woollen wrappings around their lower legs which were favoured by the Vikings; both men were wearing narrow ribbons criss-crossed in a diamond pattern typical of Anglo-Saxon men. The fact that the man was swearing at them in English confirmed that the raiders were indeed Saxons.

'Come on, my arms are too tired to use the bow again, Sherwyn said urgently. 'He's wounded and will soon weaken. We're going to have to make a run for it.'

'What about mother and father?' Rowe almost wailed, appalled at the prospect of leaving his parents behind.

Sherwyn gestured towards Silcestre where black smoke was now rising into the sky from those buildings that had been set alight.

'I'm sorry, Rowe. I fear that there is nothing we can do. They wouldn't want us to throw our lives away needlessly. Besides we need to get her to safety.'

The younger boy nodded miserably and helped the girl to her feet. She was sobbing uncontrollably and, although Rowe felt pity for her, she needed to pull herself together, and quickly. He did the only thing he could think of; he slapped her across the face.

'Stop it, I know it's tough, but we need to get moving, unless you want to stay here and become the plaything of those raiders?'

The girl looked indignant and for a moment Rowe thought that she was going to hit him back, but then she nodded and he looked around for Sherwyn. His brother came loping back to him carrying four things: Rowe's dagger, a heavy purse of coins and hacksilver taken from the dead man, and his weapons: a sword for himself and a seax for Rowe.

By now the wounded warrior was less than a hundred yards away. Sherwyn picked up his bow and the three of them started to run towards the trees. By the time they had reached the wood the man had given up the chase and was heading back towards Silcestre. With one final look at the burning settlement, the trio headed towards Basingestoches, the next vill to the south.

Chapter One

WESSEX

Autumn 882

I was visiting the king's new burh at Wælingforde when the messenger from Basingestoches found me.

My name is Jørren from Cilleham in Cent and I was the ealdorman of that shire, although Wælingforde is in Berrocscīr, not Cent. I was here in my capacity of King Ælfred's hereræswa. One of my responsibilities was the defence of Wessex and to that end the king was building a large number of burhs, or walled settlements, with a permanent garrison in case of future invasions by the Danes.

Hopefully they had learnt their lesson at Ethundun four years previously when their leader Guðrum had been soundly defeated, losing over two thirds of his army in the process. Although he had signed a treaty with Ælfred, had been baptised with the Christian name of Æðelstan, and had been recognised as the King of East Anglia, I still didn't trust him. In any case, there were numerous other bands of Vikings all over what used to be the north-eastern half of Mercia. We knew of at least ten more or less independent Danish enclaves, each ruled by a jarl. Those in the five boroughs in the north of Mercia owed some sort of allegiance to the Viking who ruled

Northumbria but the others were a law unto themselves.

When the messenger told me that my vill of Silcestre had been sacked I thought those responsible must be the Danes, but the messenger said that the two boys who had escaped were positive that they were Saxons.

'Who are these two boys? How can they possibly tell Dane from Saxon?' I asked, thinking that they must be mistaken.

'There names are Sherwyn and Rowe, the sons of Reeve Redwald,' he replied.

Then it hit me. Redwald was one of my oldest friends. He had joined Cei and I seventeen years ago when I was a callow boy of thirteen searching for my older brother Alric, who had been captured by the Danes. If Silcestre had been pillaged and burnt, then the likelihood was that Redwald and his wife were dead. Moreover, I knew the two boys well and had seen them grow up. If they were certain that the raiders were Saxons, then they must have good reason for thinking so.

'Where are the boys now?' I asked.

'At your vill of Basingestoches, lord.'

It made sense. My only other vill outside of Cent was a mere eight miles south of Silcestre.

I had a permanent warband of seventy warriors but in these peaceful times – or so I had thought – I had only brought my gesith, my hearth warriors, with me whilst touring the kingdom to inspect progress on the burhs before winter set in. The rest of my warband were split between my hall at

Cantwareburh and the mighty fortress of Dofras on the south east coast of Cent. It was also where King Ælfred's eastern fleet was based.

The boys had said that there were over a score of the Saxon raiders and I only had an escort of eight warriors with me. However, they were all experienced young men ranging in age from eighteen to late twenties; all except for their captain, Wealmær, who had just turned thirty one. I would back them against twice their number of Danes, let alone rogue Saxons.

The thegn who owned Wælingforde and several of the surrounding vills pressed me to take some of his warband with me but I declined. They were worthy men, no doubt, but they didn't have the training or experience that my men had. Besides, they were needed at Wælingforde to continue the training of the thousand man garrison of this vital stronghold on the River Temes. The garrison were all ceorls from the fyrd and they had a lot to learn yet before they would be a match for the Danes.

As I came out of the thegn's hall I stopped at the top of the steps and studied my hearth warriors as they waited patiently on their horses in the light drizzle of a late September morning. Their captain Wealmær was the third to hold the post, his predecessors having died in battle. Like two others, Sæwine and Wolnoth, he was a Bernician who had joined me after the fall of Northumbria to the Danes in 866.

Three others were from Wessex: Acel and Lyndon were both twenty three and had been with me since they were boys; the third, Rinan, was the youngest of my men. He had saved my life at Ethundun when he was just fourteen and I had found him later living wild in the forest, having lost his family during the battle.

The other two were Cináed, a Pict who I had rescued from thraldom on a Norse longship, and Eomær, the son of a charcoal burner who had elected to join me when I was a fugitive from the Danes in Mercia several years previously.

They were all good men and, despite their diverse backgrounds, they were as tightly knit a group of warriors as you could hope to meet. We had shared numerous battles and skirmishers together and each would have given his life to protect one of the others. Moreover each was proficient with bow, sword and spear and could fight as well mounted as they could on foot.

The last member of my escort was my body servant, Eafer. When I first met him a few years ago he'd been a feral boy who had been living wild before he fell in with a group of outlaws. I'd spared his life and he became my servant after Eomær, who had been fulfilling that role, became a warrior. Eafer was now seventeen and I was thinking of replacing him so that he could join my hearth warriors. He was loyal and a fierce fighter but any decision about his future would have to wait.

I mounted my horse, a magnificent grey stallion I had named Scur – meaning Storm – and we set off for Silcestre, some twenty odd miles to the south.

The settlement had an air of desolation about it. The walls still stood intact but the raiders had removed the gates and tried to burn them. Because it had been a Roman fort, there were four sets of gates – to the north, east, south and west. It would have been better for defence if I'd decided to brick three of them up, but I thanked the Lord now that I hadn't. At least some of my people might have escaped the slaughter via the other three exits.

It had started to rain as we approached Silcestre and that added to the gloomy atmosphere of the place. We rode in through the north gates and were immediately confronted by dead bodies: men, women, children and even babies. The dogs, rats and birds had feasted on them and I blamed the inhabitants of Basingestoches for not having come to give them a Christian burial as soon as they had heard about the raid. However, I knew I was being unfair; they would have been worried about their own safety with raiders on the loose.

It took us the rest of the day to bury the dead in the graveyard beside the burnt out church. There was nowhere to shelter from the persistent rain and so I decided to leave Silcestre for now and head south to Basingestoches for the night. I wasn't looking forward to telling Sherwyn and Rowe that their father, mother and two sisters were all dead.

I interrogated the boys about the raiders but they could add little to what the messenger had told me, except that Sherwyn said that he had glimpsed a banner as the raiders rode into Silcestre. He said that it was a black flag with what looked like a white horse on it. It was the banner of the Ealdorman of Wiltshire and that confirmed to me that the raiders had been Wulfhere's men.

When he had betrayed King Ælfred to the Danes during the Christmas celebrations at Cippanhamme nearly five years ago, the king, our families and I had been lucky to escape to the marshes of Athelney. After Guðrum's subsequent defeat at Ethundun Wulfhere had disappeared and he was rumoured to be hiding in Danish Mercia. Now it appeared he had re-emerged and was busy stirring up trouble in Wessex, perhaps with the hope of destroying the truce between us and the Danes.

The two boys had no other kin and so I decided to take them under my wing. They were hunters in the making and I would train the elder to be a scout. Rowe was too young as yet and so I would send him to the monastery at Cantwareburh to be educated for the next couple of years. They would hate being separated but I couldn't think what else to do with the younger boy. As for the girl, I paid the reeve to foster her until a suitable husband could be found.

I needed to tell the king what was happening but first I needed to ascertain if any of the residents of Silcestre had survived and, if so, help them to re-build the settlement. One thing was certain; the gates wouldn't be left open and unguarded ever again.

†††

'You're not certain it was Wulfhere?' Ælfred asked after I'd briefed him about the attack on Silcestre.

'Not certain, no cyning, but it seems likely that it was him. Who else would fly that banner? The new ealdorman uses the white horse, but on a green background.'

'There are two things I don't understand. If it was Wulfhere, why did he just attack Silcestre? We haven't had reports of any other settlements being raided. And why would he advertise it was him by flying his old banner?'

'I suspect that the answer to both questions is the same. He wanted to target me and to let me know it was him. Perhaps he hopes that I will go into Mercia after him and thus upset the Danes. It's in his interest to stir up trouble between us. At the moment he's an exile with no land and therefore no means of paying his men.'

'You think that he wants the Danes to invade again and thereby be granted back his old lands by them?'

'It must be a possibility. They're not going to give him an estate in Mercia. They want all the land they can get to reward their own warriors.'

'I think you may be right. The question is; what do we do about it? We can't let him get away with raiding Wessex but we can't go into Mercia after him.'

'Not officially, no, but perhaps I could send a few men disguised as Danes to try and find his whereabouts?'

'What good would that do?'

'Well, we could then watch him and the next time he comes south into Wessex we could set an ambush.'

'What if these men, dressed as Danes or not, get caught?'

'They won't, they are expert trackers and scouts; but if they should fall into the wrong hands they could say that they were looking for Wulfhere to join him.'

'Very well, Jørren. Go ahead, but if it goes wrong, on your head be it.'

What I didn't tell the king was that I intended to be one of the men going north into Danish Mercia.

My inclination was to take all my hearth warriors with me but it is more difficult for a dozen men to move stealthily than for a few to do so. Furthermore, we would have to pretend to be traders so as not to attract too much attention and that meant travelling as a small group. In the end I decided to take Wolnoth, Eomær, Rinan and also Eafer, not because I needed a body servant but because he was as skilled a tracker as anyone. After we returned – or perhaps I should say if we returned – I would invite him to join my hearth warriors.

However, I had already been away from my wife and the children for longer than I had said. After all the nagging I got the last time I was away without Hilda knowing what had happened to me I didn't intend to suffer the same fate again. When we had fled from Cippanhamme to Athelney and disappeared for five months Hilda had been frantic with worry. Not only were two of the children I had with my first wife and I missing, but so was her young son Oswine.

Now we had had a child of our own, a daughter called Æbbe, born two years ago.

After my meeting with Ælfred in Wintanceastre, we rode the thirty miles to Portcæstre. A fleet of the king's longships was based there under the command of one of my former hearth warriors, Bjarne. He was originally from Swéoland and I had captured him in battle after killing his father. Despite that he had proved to be one of most loyal warriors and one with a good knowledge of the sea. Now he was the Sæ Hereræswa; the commander of Wessex's warships.

Portcæstre was an old Roman fort which defended the inner harbour off a much larger harbour with only a narrow access out to sea. It lay immediately north of the Isle of Whitlond and was an ideal base from which to patrol the coastline from Dyfneintscīr in the west to Suth-Seaxe to the east.

It had been the first of King Ælfred's new burhs to be completed and it now had a garrison of over a thousand men when all the longships were in harbour, which admittedly wasn't often for much of the year. At least half were out on patrol most of the time from spring to autumn. However, now that the Viking raiding season was coming to an end, most were back in harbour.

One of those which rode at anchor was the Saint Cuthbert, a large skeid propelled by forty oars a side and capable of carrying forty warriors in addition to the rowers and the rest of the crew. We set sail the following day accompanied by a knarr loaded with our horses. I wanted to take Scur but he was a fierce stallion, not the sort of horse a merchant would own.

Instead I selected a dun coloured mare called Frith, meaning peace.

Our voyage was uneventful, for which I was grateful. Not only was there the risk of encountering Viking ships but this was the start of the season when gales were all too common. Several times in the past I'd come close to losing my ship in the storm-tossed waters along this coast.

I had mixed feelings as the mighty fortress of Dofras hove into view, sitting high above the settlement around the harbour. Of course, I was glad to be home and looked forward to being reunited with Hilda, and to seeing my children again, but I was dreading telling my wife that I was about leave again to go north into Mercia.

By the time that we'd docked it was dusk but someone had obviously told Hilda that I'd returned because she rode down to the quay accompanied by the children whilst the horses were being unloaded.

Hilda dismounted and came towards me. Much as I wanted to embrace her, I was conscious of the amused onlookers around us and I had to be satisfied with giving her a chaste kiss on the cheek. The children greeted me dutifully, which made me think that I needed to spend more time with them. We had grown apart in recent years, mainly because I was away so much.

The only ones missing were my eldest son, Æscwin, who was a novice monk in the monastery at Cantwareburh and my stepson, Oswine, Hilda's son by her first marriage, who was a king's page at Wintanceaster. I had hoped to see him whilst I was there but I was told that he was with the king's son, the Ætheling Edward. They and several of Edward's friends were being taught to read and write by the monks at Winburne in Dornsæte as part of their education.

I looked at my other children, reflecting how lucky I was to have them. My eldest child was Cuthfleda, who was now fourteen. Hilda had been badgering me about her betrothal but I knew that she didn't want to get married; not yet at any rate. She relished her freedom too much. She would much rather be out riding or hunting than following more appropriate pursuits like embroidery or learning how to manage a household. In that she was very much like her mother, my first wife, Leofflæd. Like her she was a good archer as well.

Beside her stood the twins, whose birth had killed Leofflæd. At first I had blamed them for her death, but they were her offspring and I had grown to love them as much as my other children. They had just turned eight and, apart from being different sexes, looked identical rather than fraternal. Their characters were quite different though. Ywer was a mischievous imp, always in trouble for some misdemeanour, whereas his sister Kjestin was more like Hilda than her real mother.

Then there was the daughter I'd had with Hilda: two year old Æbbe. She was too young yet to have a definite character but she was the spitting image of her mother.

It was only then that I noticed something. Perhaps it was the way that I sensed that Hilda was dying to tell me something but that made me look at her more closely. Then I noticed she looked a little larger around the waist than she had when I had left three months previously. She didn't have to tell me that she was expecting again. I groaned inwardly. Of course I was delighted, but it would make leaving her with winter not far off that much more difficult.

There was a feast to welcome me home that evening. However, the atmosphere was somewhat frosty on the high table. Hilda had not taken the news that I was about to leave her again at all well. In fact, it would be fair to say we had a blazing row.

In contrast Cuthfleda was excited and had wanted to come with me. Her argument was that her mother had joined me as a warrior at about the same age. It was true, although Leofflæd had been a year or so older, but the circumstances were completely different. We were shadowing the Great Heathen Army at the time seeking to rescue my brother Alric, who had been taken captive by them.

Leofflæd's parents had been killed by the Danes and she and her brother had asked to join us. As they had provisions we had desperately needed at the time, I'd agreed. She turned out to be one of my best warriors and I'd fallen in love with her. To Cuthfleda her mother was a role model but their respective situations were quite different. When I'd refused her request to join me she'd flown into a rage.

'It's time you were betrothed,' I told her at the height of our row.

'I'm never getting married, unless you can find me someone who'll let me join their warband!' she retorted defiantly.

She retreated into a sulky silence and so I ignored her for the rest of the evening. I pretended that her outburst hadn't bothered me but, in truth, I was at my wit's end. Hilda often accused me of spoiling her and pandering to the wildness of her nature too much. Perhaps she was right but I was damned if I would see my daughter forced into an unhappy marriage.

Hilda evidently thought that I should have disciplined Cuthfleda. She sat beside me huffily picking at her food and not really eating much. Much to her annoyance I spent most of the evening talking to Jerrik, Bjarne's deputy, who sat next to me, and to Cei who sat on my wife's other side.

Cei commanded the fortress' garrison and was my oldest companion and friend. He'd been a slave on my brother's vill when I persuaded him to accompany me when I set off in search of Alric all those years ago. He was a Briton from Wealas and there was a deep distrust amongst the Anglo-Saxons for his kind. I would have liked to have given him further preferment but I knew that wouldn't be a good idea, especially as Æðelred had been defeated by the King of Gwynedd in the north of Wealas at the Battle of Conwy the previous year. Feelings against the Britons of Wealas were running high as a consequence.

I'd been puzzled as to why Æðelred had invaded at the time. When the puppet king of Mercia, Ceolwulf II, had died the kingdom's witenaġemot had elected Ealdorman Æðelred as Lord of Mercia. Of course that meant nothing in the east of the country as that was firmly under the rule of various Danish jarls, but he did control the west and south from Cæstir in the north to near Lundenwic in the south east.

For some time the Britons of Gwynedd had raided all along the border with Mercia and Æðelred had decided to put a stop to it, so he led an expedition along the north coast of Wealas only to be heavily defeated at Conwy. It was an error of judgement.

His defeat seriously weakened his position and cost him a lot of warriors that he could ill afford to lose. Consequently, he had recently signed an accord with Ælfred. Wessex would come to the aid of western Mercia if needed, which kept the Danes in check, and in return Æðelred recognised him as overlord and swore never to call himself King of Mercia.

Thus Cei, although respected as a man, was nevertheless tainted by his origins and had to content himself with being the captain of my fortress. He had never married although, judging by the calf eyes that some of the prettier female slaves kept making at him, he was far from celibate.

Once we had retired, Hilda continued to treat me with coldness until I pointed out that, if her fears were realised, this would be the last night we would spend together in bed. I didn't want to part on bad terms and, although there was an undercurrent of disapproval in the air, we did at least make passionate love twice before I left.

I promised her faithfully that I would return long before the baby was due. As this wasn't until springtime I fully expected to be back before then. However, first I needed to think about where to start the search for Wulfhere.

Chapter Two

LUNDENWIC

Early November 882

I had no idea where Wulfhere and his renegade warband might be based but I was willing to wager that it wasn't in Æðelred's part of Mercia. The nearest Jarldom immediately north of Silcestre was that of Hamtun but I doubted if he would want to be too close to the ruling jarl's hall; it would restrict his freedom of action. No, it was more likely that he would be based at a smaller vill, somewhere like Tōfecæstre, which was just inside Danish Mercia on the old Roman road called Casingc Stræt.

However, it was still a long way from Silcestre and I wondered how Wulfhere had got there without being detected. I then heard that a horse stud had been attacked near Wælingforde a few days before the raid on Silcestre. It was beginning to fall into place. If Wulfhere's base was indeed somewhere along Casingc Stræt he could have reached Lundenwic fairly quickly and then traded his horses for a ship easily enough.

Boats of all types traded along the River Temes, which formed the border between Anglo-Saxon Mercia and Wessex, and his craft would have attracted little attention. Once he'd reached the stud farm and taken the horses he would have presumably ridden south to Silcestre using little known tracks; then returned to his base the same way as he'd come.

I therefore decided to put to sea again, but not in the Saint Cuthbert; she would stand out as a ship of war and I wanted to attract as little attention as possible. The five of us set sail along the coast in the knarr, but with an escort of several longships until we reached the estuary of the River Temes safely. A few hours later we docked in Lundenwic and unloaded our horses.

Wolnoth went ashore and found a decent tavern for us to stay the night. In the morning I planned to head for Verulamacæster where there was a monastery dedicated to the martyred Saint Alban. Staying at a monastery was a risk but monks were inveterate gossips and, if anyone in Mercia had heard the whereabouts of Wulfhere, it was likely to be them.

The main room of the tavern was crowded by the time we had dumped our bedrolls in the dormitory and had a wash in the trough outside. It was a chilly evening but inside the room it was overly warm. There were braziers in two corners to add to the heat produced by so many people. Although there were holes in the wall above the braziers for the smoke to escape through, quite a lot of it stayed in the room and swirled around. I was used to some smoke in my hall but this was far worse and my eyes smarted until I got used to it. Thankfully there was a spare table by the door where the air was a bit fresher. I beckoned one of the serving girls over as we sat down.

'I wouldn't sit there,' she muttered. 'That's where Håkon and his men sit.'

'Who is this Håkon that he has a table even when he isn't here?'

'He's the most powerful jarl in Lundenwic; you don't want to get on the wrong side of him.'

I was tempted to stay where we were and confront this Jarl Håkon when and if he arrived. My pride was hurt at the thought of having to slink away to stand whilst we waited for a table to become free but I didn't want to attract attention to ourselves before our clandestine mission had even started.

So we reluctantly got to our feet and went over to the counter where the tavern keeper was dispensing tankards of ale and mead. When three men got up to leave there was a rush to grab the table but Rinan tripped a man up and in the confusion we managed to reach it first. I felt that it was all rather undignified but I realised that it was all in keeping with my assumed persona as a minor trader. For the moment I had to swallow my pride and forget that I was an important noble.

The man who Rinan had tripped up glared at us and his hand went to his dagger but his friends pulled him away. Just at that moment the door banged open. A large Dane and three companions came in and took the vacant table by the door. This had to be the feared Jarl Håkon. Suddenly I realised with a start that I recognised him. When I'd last seen him nearly a decade before he'd been Oscatel's captain.

Oscatel had been one of Guðrum's senior jarls who had taken me prisoner in Mercia several years ago and had wanted to kill me himself. However, Guðrum and the other leader of the Great Heathen Army at that time, Halfdan Ragnarsson, had wanted me kept alive, no doubt so that they could personally torture me to death. Luckily, Lord Æðelred had helped me to escape and I'd taken refuge with a family of charcoal burners until the hue and cry had died down. That was when I'd met Eomær and, when I'd left to make my way back to Wessex, he'd joined me. I'd killed Oscatel later and I assume that Håkon had then taken over command of his warband.

That had been eight years ago, when I was twenty two. The sight of Håkon brought it all back to me. If I recognised him I was certain that he would recognise me; I recalled with a shudder the way that he'd stared venomously at me in King Burghred's hall as if he wanted to tear my heart out. If he saw me now that would scupper our mission before it had even started but we couldn't leave without passing right by his table.

Håkon took a drink from his tankard and his eyes swept the room. I hastily looked down at our table to avoid catching his eye but I was afraid that I hadn't been quick enough. The next time I glanced up he was talking to one of his men and so I assumed that he hadn't spotted me. However, the man got up and left shortly afterwards. The purposeful way he'd done so made me think that he might be going to fetch more men.

'Follow the man who has just left,' I whispered to Rinan.

He was one of those who had the knack of blending into the background. Even I didn't notice him taking a circuitous route to the door. A minute later the door opened to admit another man, and one I knew only too well. It was Tunbehrt, the former Ealdorman of Hamtunscīr. He was another traitor but he wasn't in the same league as Wulfhere. His crime was failing to raise his shire's fyrd and coming to join the king before the Battle of Ethundun four and a half years previously.

Ælfred had exiled him and, as far as anyone knew, he was in Frankia. Yet here he was in Lundenwic and being greeted warmly by Håkon. I didn't know what to make of it but, whatever was going on didn't bode well for Wessex.

I hadn't noticed Rinan slip out of the door as Tunbehrt entered, nor did I spot him returning as a group of boisterous young men entered the tavern.

'It's alright,' Rinan said as he sat down, 'he's just gone outside to keep watch.'

I breathed a sigh of relief but I was troubled by the meeting at the table by the door. I was even more worried when the door opened again to admit someone else I recognised. It was Pæga, the Thegn of Sandtun in my own shire of Cent. I watched in disbelief as he also joined Håkon's table, my sense of unease growing. I didn't know Pæga well but Sandtun was an important vill on the south coast. Not only was it a sizeable fishing port with a market, but there were also salt works which provided the wherewithal to export fish elsewhere. What on earth was he doing here plotting with a Danish jarl and an exiled Wessex nobleman?

My mission was to find Wulfhere but that would have to wait. Whatever plot was being hatched was likely to be much more important.

'Wolnoth, you and Eomær get ready to follow Lord Pæga when he leaves. I want to know where he's staying.'

The two nodded and we went back to drinking mead. I had ordered a bowl of pottage for everyone and that had just been brought to the table when both Tunbehrt and Pæga got up to leave.

'Don't worry, your supper won't go to waste,' Eafer said with a cheeky grin.

He pulled the two bowls towards him as the other two got up to leave. I took the opportunity to move around the table and sit on the bench they'd vacated so that I had my back to Håkon. He didn't appear to have seen me and I wanted to keep it that way.

Shortly afterwards Rinan leaned across the table and whispered that Håkon and his men were leaving. I breathed a sigh of relief but I didn't know what to do next. I decided that fretting would do no good; I'd have to confront Pæga and get the truth out of him.

✝✝✝

When Wolnoth and Eomær returned I paid for fresh bowls of pottage for them to replace those that Rinan and Eafer had scoffed as soon as the other two had left.

'Well, where did Pæga go?'

'Back to the wharf where he boarded a boat which set off across the river,' Wolnoth said.

Although there was a bridge across the Temes from Lundewic to Sudwerca, it was narrow and there were guards at both ends; Danes on the north bank and Saxons loyal to the Ealdorman of Sūþrīgescīr at the southern end. Doubtless Pæga would prefer my counterpart in Sūþrīgescīr not to know that he had been in Danish territory.

'We followed on another ferry but there were three men with horses waiting for Pæga on the far bank,' Wolnoth continued.

The sun had set long since and most sensible men weren't abroad at night but presumably Pæga wanted to be safely back in Cent before stopping for the night. My idea of interrogating him wouldn't work, unless I returned to Cent, of course. I didn't want to do that if I could avoid it, having started on my mission to find Wulfhere. My next best chance lay in questioning Tunbehrt but I had no idea where he could be found.

I explained my dilemma to my companions and it was Eafer who came up with the solution.

'If you want to find someone, lord, offer the urchins and guttersnipes a reward for finding him. They know every last corner of Lundenwic and, armed with his description, I'm willing to wager ten silver pennies that someone will have found him by nightfall tomorrow.'

I looked doubtful but I thought it was worth staying one more day in the rat infested settlement to find out.

In fact we didn't have to wait so long. We had taken the precaution of moving taverns, both because it seemed to be Håkon's favourite drinking den and I didn't want to bump into him again, and because there was an outside chance that he might have recognised me after all and be playing a waiting game to see what I was up to.

Thankfully our new abode was less popular and there were only a couple of inveterate drinkers in the place when we sat down to a meal of bread and cheese at midday. As soon as we had started to eat a high pitched whistle attracted everyone attention to the doorway. Two urchins stood there, barefoot and wearing nothing but threadbare homespun tunics with a piece of rope around their waists. Both were as thin as the haft of a spear and were so filthy it was impossible to make out their features.

The elder one, who looked to be about twelve but might have been a couple of years older thanks to his malnourished appearance, beckoned Eafer and then the two of them disappeared before the irate tavern keeper could chase them away. Eafer and I went outside, ignoring the surprised look on the man's face as he put his cudgel back behind the table that served as a serving counter.

'You promised us a reward,' the elder urchin said in a tone that indicated that he didn't trust me at all.

'Lord, you call him lord,' Eafer said, shocked at the way that the boy had addressed me.

'Lord,' the boy added, looking as he had just swallowed something unpleasant.

'First what are your names?' I asked, trying to look benevolent, much as I wanted to cuff the insolent boy about the ears.

'Why do you want to know?' he asked suspiciously, then added 'lord' when he saw the way that Eafer was glaring at him.

'Because I will know if you are lying to me if you give me false names.'

For a moment I thought that he and the other boy were about to flee but then he shrugged.

'Very well, but first tell us how you plan to reward us,' he paused. 'Lord.'

'Fair question. You and the other boy look as if you haven't had a good meal since your mother whelped you. I will give you both a bowl of pottage in the tavern first. Then you tell me where I can find the man I'm looking for and we'll go and find him. If you are telling me the truth I'll give each of you a silver penny.'

'Two,' he replied instantly. 'Give us two silver pennies each and we have a deal.'

Eafer looked shocked at his impudence but I laughed. I was beginning to like this boy. He was evidently both resourceful and clever.

The tavern keeper refused to serve the two boys at first but when I put my hand on my sword hilt he licked his lips nervously and nodded. I tossed him a coin to pay for the meals and he caught it deftly in his fist.

'But first they need to wash,' he said. 'They stink.'

It was true the two urchins brought a miasma of urine, mud, faeces and rotting matter into the room with them. There was a cloth seller near the tavern and I sent Eomær to buy two of the cheapest tunics he could find which would fit the boys. I wasn't being

53

mean but they would have been robbed of anything finer and left naked within minutes of leaving the tavern. Meanwhile the other three carried the protesting boys outside, stripped them of their filthy rags and dumped them in the horse trough.

They used the rags to wash the worst of the grime off and Eomær gave them their new tunics to cover their emaciated nakedness. They still had a whiff of the gutter about them but at least it was bearable back in the confines of the tavern.

'What are your names,' I asked once we were seated.

'I'm Uhtric and my brother is called Leofwine,' the older urchin replied through a mouthful of food.

'Very well, Uhtric, now tell me where I can find Tunbehrt.'

For a moment he looked confused and I cursed inwardly. We had deliberately not told the boys looking for him what the former Wessex ealdorman was called; they were merely given his description, including the clothes he was wearing. There were told that he was a Saxon nobleman, which narrowed the search considerably; there weren't many of those in Danish controlled Lundenwic and thankfully Tunbehrt stood out as he was vain enough to dress as befitted his rank. He would have done better to do as I had done and worn the garb of a merchant, or even a ceorl.

'The man you were sent to find,' I clarified.

'We'll take you there,' he mumbled as he stuffed the last of the pottage into his mouth.

The two boys had probably consumed more food in the last few minutes than they normally managed to scavenge in a week or more. The speed at which they had eaten indicated just how hungry they had been.

'Right, lead the way,' I said after Uhtric and Leofwine had licked every last drop from the inside of the earthenware bowls.

The younger boy hadn't said a word since the two had appeared at the door of the tavern but now he whispered something in Uhtric's ear. His brother nodded and turned to me.

'Lord, give us one silver penny now and three when we have taken you to where this Tunbehrt is staying,' he demanded.

'That wasn't our agreement,' I told him firmly. 'Two silver pennies each when I'm satisfied that I've found the man I want to speak to.'

I had a nasty feeling that, now that they had full bellies, the two boys would disappear if I gave them any money. Either they had been lying all along or there was a reason they didn't want to go to where Tunbehrt could be found. I had suspected that the two might prove reluctant to honour their part of the bargain and had been ready for this. I nodded to my companions; Rinan and Eafer grabbed the two brothers and held them firmly whilst Eomær held a knife to Leofwine's throat. At the same time Wolnoth moved to bar the door.

'Alright, alright,' Uhtric squeaked, panic stricken. 'I'll take you there, then you give us the money, but the place is crawling with armed Danes.'

55

'Thank you Uhtric. We'll keep a firm hold of Leofwine until I'm certain you haven't misled us.'

I asked the tavern keeper for a length of rope with which we tied Leofwine's hands and hobbled his ankles so that he had to shuffle along. Eafer cut off another length and formed a noose which he put over the trembling boy's head. He took the other end and led the young lad along like a horse.

Uhtric kept giving me murderous looks but he led us through the back alleys of the settlement until we came to one of the gates leading into the abandoned old Roman city, which we called Lundenburg to distinguish it from the settlement to the west.

The Saxons might have kept clear of the ruins because of their fear of ghosts but the Danes plainly had no such qualms. They had turned the place into a fortress with timber palisades replacing those sections of the old walls which had fallen into disrepair.

We were stopped at the gate but I told the sentries in Danish that we had caught a thief who had stolen from no less a person than Jarl Håkon. We had come to claim the reward. The mention of Håkon's name was enough to gain us admittance but I did wonder how we would leave again as I had no intention of leaving Leofwine behind. However, I supposed that the two boys had got in and out of the old city before somehow so presumably they could make their own escape.

I shuddered as I walked through the largely empty streets. The whole place had an eerie feel to it. Many of the stone buildings still stood, albeit most were without roofs, but others made of brick or wattle and daub had fallen into ruin. Rats scurried hither and thither and packs of scrawny wild dogs eyed us hungrily as we passed. Those people who were abroad were armed and went about in groups. None gave us more than a cursory glance.

The buildings which were occupied, and there weren't that many, had been repaired using timber. Smoke curled up through holes in the thatched roofs but even this normal sight failed to counter the general ethos of neglect and dereliction. I knew that my companions felt the same. They glanced about them nervously and Wolnoth kept muttering prayers and clutched the crucifix about his neck.

Uhtric led us to what must have been the residence of an important Roman centuries before. Now it was a ruin but someone had used two of the surviving walls as the basis for a small hall, the other two sides being made of wooden planks. It was better constructed than many of the other buildings we had passed and I deduced that it was the hall of an important Viking. A makeshift wall of stone and timber palisade infill surrounded the place and two bored looking sentries guarded the one gate into the compound.

We had taken up a position in the ruins opposite the gate from where I could see into the courtyard. The area was strewn with debris and rubble and there was a broken fountain in the centre. As I watched a man arrived on horseback. The sentries stopped him and one went off to the hall, emerging again moments later followed by Tunbehrt. Uhtric hadn't been lying after all.

'Release Leofwine,' I whispered to Rinan.

'Here, take these. Come to the tavern again tonight and I'll give you the other two.'

I handed Uhtric two silver pennies. For a moment I thought he was going to argue but he merely nodded and the two boys disappeared in the direction of the river. I caught a glimpse of them conversing earnestly before they waded through the reed beds, ankle deep in mud, and made their way back towards the Saxon settlement to the west. So that's how they got in and out of the city without being seen, I thought. It also explained why they stank so much when they had first arrived. The mud along the river banks contained much of the detritus thrown out by the inhabitants.

The horseman had handed Tunbehrt a letter and the man stood reading it at the gate, which was foolish of him. A few seconds later we sent five arrows towards the gate. Wolnoth and Rinan hit one of the sentries in the throat and the chest and Eomær and Eafer did the same to the second guard. We spent a great deal of time practicing archery and all my men were more than proficient with a bow.

I had taken aim at Tunbehrt. Mine was the most difficult shot. I wanted him alive but I needed to incapacitate him so that he couldn't seek refuge inside the hall. My arrow struck him in the thigh and he screamed in agony. I cursed; that would alert all the Danes in the hall and any in the surrounding buildings.

Wolnoth and Eomær ran across the open ground in front of the gates and grabbed the screaming Tunbehrt. Wolnoth tapped him none too gently on the head with the pommel of his seax and he collapsed unconscious. They dragged him back to where I waited. Meanwhile the other two had run to the gate and put arrows into the first two Danes who emerged from the hall. The rest retreated inside again.

One man came out of a nearby hut to see what all the noise was about; I put an arrow through his shoulder and he beat a hasty retreat. For a moment all was quiet but I knew that all hell would break out in a moment or two. We were trapped in a Roman ruin in the heart of a fortress garrisoned by Vikings. Our chances of coming out of this alive looked slim to say the least.

✝✝✝

I cursed myself for going into this without a proper plan. The only thing I could think of was to make our way down to the river and wade through the muddy reed beds until we reached the place where the River Flēot entered the Temes. The Flēot formed the physical division between the Roman city and the Saxon settlement.

I explained my plan to the others and told them to take the limp Tunbehrt with them. I would cover them and then join them. Several protested but I cut them short.

'There is no time to argue; just do as you're told.'

They withdrew towards the river using whatever cover they could find just as several warriors erupted from the hall and a large group came down the street towards me from the north. I glimpsed Håkon leading those from the hall so I sent two quick arrows in their direction and then another at the leader of those further up the street. That gained me a moment whilst they hesitated before coming on again.

I sprinted after the others and caught them up just before the reed beds. Then I saw something I had difficulty in believing. One of the ferry boats that conveyed passengers across the Temes to Sudwerca on the south bank appeared through the reeds and ran up onto the foul smelling mud. That wasn't what surprised me the most. It was the grinning face of Leofwine in the bows beckoning us towards him.

It transpired that he and his brother had stolen the boat and had come back for us. I doubted their motives were altruistic – they were no doubt more concerned about the other silver pennies I had promised them – but I have rarely been so glad to see anyone in my life.

We dumped Tunbehrt in the bottom of the boat and pushed it back into the water before clambering aboard. Uhtric gave up the oars to Wolnoth and Eomær and moments later we had left the old city behind as we struggled westwards against the current. Half an hour later we tied the boat to the wharf a hundred yards up the River Flēot and made our way back to the tavern at dusk, washing the filth from our lower legs in a horse trough on the way.

I was tempted to stay the night but I knew that there would be a hue and cry after Tunbehrt's abduction so I sent Wolnoth to find a small cart whilst the rest of us hid the unconscious man in the stables, bribing the two men and the boys who worked there to keep their mouths shut. I left Eomær and the two urchins to guard Tunbehrt whilst the rest of us packed and then saddled our horses.

An hour later Wolnoth returned saying that he had bought a small cart but he needed a horse to pull it. He took the packhorse and disappeared again whilst I fretted at the delay. Finally he returned and we loaded Tunbehrt, bound hand and foot, into the small covered cart, together with everything that the packhorse had been carrying. We had removed the arrow whilst the man was still unconscious and washed and stitched the wound but he started shrieking at the pain as soon as he came round. We had to stuff a rag in his mouth to shut him up.

I paid Uhtric and his brother what I had promised them but they seemed in no hurry to leave.

'Can we not come with you, lord,' the older boy asked, his eyes pleading with me.

'No, I have no use for you,' I told him bluntly.

'You need someone to look after the man you captured. We could travel in the wagon and make sure he doesn't give you any trouble, if you give me a knife that is.'

'I want him alive,' I said with a grin.

'Oh, we'll make sure of that, but I know something about healing. The wound needs a poultice of bread and honey to stop it festering. The knife is just to threaten him with whilst I'm treating him.'

'You know about healing?' I asked, amazed.

'Our father was an apothecary and he taught us something of his trade before mother died and he took to gambling and drinking. He died in a drunken brawl nearly a year ago and we've been living on the streets ever since.'

I looked at the two urchins again. I had thought that they were small for their age because they had been brought up malnourished. However, it seemed that this wasn't the case.

'How old are you?'

'I'm thirteen and my brother is two years younger, but he is nearly as skilled as me at healing,' he said, evidently fearing that I might take him and leave his brother behind.

'Very well, but you had better be telling me the truth. If I find out that you have no healing skills I'll abandon you by the roadside.'

'Have no fear of that, lord,' he assured me. 'Now, we'll need water, clean cloths, bread and honey in the wagon before we leave.'

That caused a further delay and it was long after nightfall when we departed. I worried that we might be challenged as we left so I avoided Casingc Stræt and took the muddy road towards Watsforde where we could cross the river and then head north for Verulamacæster.

Chapter Three

DANISH MERCIA

November 882

Uhtric hadn't lied. Tunbehrt's wound had looked red and angry when I'd first seen it but two days later the redness had gone and the scabs forming either side of his thigh looked healthy. Tunbehrt had suffered from a fever initially, during which time all he could do was to mumble incoherently, so we camped in a wood near Watsforde until he was well enough for me to question him.

At first he remained obdurately silent and so, much as I hated doing it to a helpless and injured man, I applied pressure to his wound, which made him scream out in agony. I ignored the reproachful looks that Uhtric and Leofwine gave me. I was undoing all their hard work as several of the catgut stitches broke and the wound opened up again.

'If you tell me what you were doing talking to Håkon and Pæga I will ensure that these boys look after your wound until it's healed and then I'll put you on a ship bound for Frankia. On the other hand, if you choose to keep silent I'll make your death an extremely painful one.'

He hesitated and so I pressed down on his injured thigh once more, causing him to cry out again and beg me to stop. My hand came away covered in blood and I signalled for Uhtric to put a clean cloth on the wound. Tunbehrt sighed resignedly and I could tell that he'd decided to tell me what I wanted to know.

'Very well, there's a conspiracy to take Cent from Ælfred and include it within Æðelstan's kingdom.'

I had to think for a moment who he meant by Æðelstan. Although it had been over four years since Guðrum had been baptised and given his new name, few us ever called him by anything other than his original name.

'Is Guðrum part of this conspiracy,' I asked.

Tunbehrt looked wary and I had a feeling that he was about to lie to me, so I put my hand near his bleeding thigh again.

'Stop! Yes, he knows of it but he's keeping clear of involvement for now. The man doing the planning is Håkon. With Wulfhere's help he's mustering a force of Danes from the independent jarldoms to add to Håkon's men in Lundenwic.'

'What part are you playing?'

'I've been paid to raise a force of mercenary Frisians.'

'And Pæga?'

'He's been bribed to allow Håkon's fleet to use Sandtun as their base. We didn't think you'd expect a landing on the south coast of Cent.'

He was right; I'd expect any attack to come down the Temes and be against the north coast. Although I'd promised to free Tunbehrt and send him on his way to Frankia, he'd been foolish to tell me that his role was to recruit Frisian mercenaries. I couldn't afford to let him reach the Continent at the moment.

The next night I left the rest camping in a nearby wood whilst Wolnoth and I took the cart into the monastery at Verulamacæster pretending to be travelling merchants. The gates were closed when we got there, despite it being an hour or so before dusk. I banged on the wooden gate with the hilt of my dagger and a small window opened in the right hand gate. It was small and protected by a stout metal grill so all I could see of the porter who had opened it was the central part of his face.

'Yes, what do you want?' he asked pugnaciously.

'A bed for the night for two weary travellers,' I replied in as mild a tone as I could manage in the face of the man's aggressive manner.

His eyes darted left and right trying to see if we were indeed alone, although I doubted he could see much, given the size of the opening. A moment later I heard the sound of bolts being withdrawn and the right hand gate opened. However, it wasn't large enough to admit our cart and, after much cursing the porter opened the left hand gate as well.

I was surprised to see that the porter wasn't a monk, as was usually the case, but was what I assumed was a lay brother, although he was wearing a much worn leather over-tunic and coif. He had a seax hanging from his belt and a spear lay propped against the timber palisade inside the gate with a simple bowl helmet lying beside it.

The man was evidently a former warrior, judging by the missing fingers on his right hand and several old scars on both his arms and his face. The fact that the monks employed an old soldier to guard the gate brought home to me the fact that the monastery lay just inside the boundary of the Danish Jarldom of Bedaforde. Presumably the abbot had come to some arrangement with the local jarl but nevertheless the place was defended like a burh.

A novice monk came running and pointed to where the stables were. He waited until we had unharnessed our horse and, leaving a snivelling slave who can't have been more than eight to rub the mare down and feed her, we followed the novice across to the long hut that served as guest accommodation.

The interior was basic to say the least. The wattle and daub infill had crumbled in places, letting in the wind, and there were damp patches on the beaten earth floor indicating that the roof leaked when it rained. The straw in the palisases on the floor looked as if it hadn't been changed in ages. They had the appearance of having been flattened by much use and no doubt they would be home to a variety of lice, fleas, bedbugs and the like. We pushed them aside and lay our blankets directly on the floor.

The bell sounded for Vespers at that moment, so we joined everyone else and trudged across the courtyard to the small stone built church to hear the service always said at dusk. It wasn't a long service and we emerged into the last of the twilight and went across to the refectory to eat. This was when I hoped to hear something interesting about Wulfhere.

I sat down between two monks, both slightly corpulent in comparison to the aesthetic looking abbot, in the expectation that they would prove to be garrulous. Wolnoth made his way to a different table.

That way we doubled our chances of hearing some interesting gossip.

My hope of learning about Wulfhere's whereabouts came to naught. All that I could glean was that the local jarl and his neighbour at Tamiseforde had fallen out over a girl that they both wished to wed. Both were busy raiding each other's territory, hence the heightened security at the monastery's gates.

'I had heard that a Saxon renegade called Wulfhere has been preying on innocent merchants travelling along Casingc Stræt,' I said casually before chewing energetically on a piece of stale bread and hard cheese.

'No,' the monk to my left replied. 'No such tidings have reached us here. I don't think you need to worry. Most Danes respect travel along the road as it brings much needed trade goods into Danish Mercia.'

'Come, it's time to go across for compline,' the other monk said, heaving his bulk up from the bench.

I groaned. I was as religious as most people but I found the endless church services fundamental to a stay in a monastery wearisome. After compline – the offering up of prayers at the end of the day – we would only get a few hours' sleep before it was time to rise for the service of vigil in the middle of the night. Altogether there were nine proscribed services in a twenty four hour period, although few monasteries observed all of them.

I finally had the chance to talk privately to Wolnoth when we visited the latrines before turning in. Thankfully he been more successful than I had.

'Wulfhere has been given a vill at a place called Biceilwæd,' he said to me sotto voce as we sat companionably on the two planks suspended over the foul trench below us.

'Biceilwæd? Did you find out where it is?' I asked eagerly.

'I believe that it's somewhere along a tributary of the River Uisge, less than a day's journey south of Tamiseforde. I daren't ask more or it would have looked suspicious.'

'You were quite right. We don't want to alert people to our mission. Well done; now all we have to do is find out how we get to Biceilwæd.'

†††

I may not have known where Biceilwæd was, but I did know that Tamiseforde lay on the Roman road known as Earninga Stræt, which ran from Lundenwic to Eforwic. All we had to do was to head due east until we found it. Shortly after we set out it started to rain. It wasn't a heavy downpour, it was the type of light drizzle which had a way of finding itself into every gap between clothes and skin. I envied Tunbehrt and the two urchins who were travelling inside the covered cart as more icy cold water trickled down my back.

The cart got stuck in the mud several times before we reached Earninga Stræt, by which time we were covered in mud from pushing the cart clear. I had reservations about travelling along the ancient Roman road in the open but at least the surface was cobbled for most of its length. Where the stone surface had disappeared the hardcore underneath had more or less survived. We made better progress and a few hours later the rain stopped. The air was too cold for us to dry out but nevertheless the respite from the rain improved our spirits.

We had seen few other travellers: two monks, who blessed us as they passed; a peddler walking with a donkey laden with trinkets and other wares for sale; and a party of nobles and their hearth warriors heading south. They were Saxons, if the way that they were dressed was any indication, and I wondered what they were doing in Danish Mercia. Thankfully they ignored us and we studiously looked elsewhere as we waited by the side of the road for them to pass us.

By the time that the sky started to darken with the approach of twilight I calculated that we were still around a dozen miles south of Biceilwæd. I wasn't about to risk staying at a tavern or to pay for a space in a barn on one of the farmsteads that dotted the countryside. Most would be owned by Danes with their original Anglo-Saxon owners working as their thralls, if they were lucky enough to have survived that is.

We hid the cart in some scrub land and headed into the trees at the side of the road carrying Tunbehrt on a makeshift stretcher. Following a track made by animals, we soon reached a hollow which was close enough to a small stream to serve as our campsite for the night. We set our fire in a hollow so that the flames would be hidden from view and, of course, smoke wouldn't betray our position in the darkness. It took some time before the spark from Wolnoth's flint lit the wood shavings and, even when it did, the kindling was too wet to catch alight.

It was Leofwine who found some dry twigs under a carpet of leaves. After that we got the fire going and, although the wet wood sizzled and spat, it eventually generated enough heat for us to dry our clothes. We dined on cheese, hard biscuits and water from the stream. I took the first watch and handed over to Rinan a few hours later.

I tried to sleep but my mind kept thinking about the morrow. If Biceilwæd did turn out to be Wulfhere's lair, what should I do about it? We were too few in number to attack him, even from an ambush, and if we returned knowing his location what good would that do? We could hardly launch an attack deep into Danish territory without starting a war.

I turned it over in my mind but I could see no obvious course of action if we had indeed managed to run him to earth. Eventually, an hour before dawn, I finally dropped off to sleep. Consequently I felt groggy and drained when I was woken. Everyone else was packing up ready to leave as I climbed wearily to my feet. I was too tired to think straight, let alone come up with a workable plan now when one had eluded me all night long.

As we broke our fast with yet more hard cheese, biscuits and the brackish stream water, I decided that the first priority was to establish whether Biceilwæd was indeed Wulfhere's base. Perhaps some bright idea might occur to me once we had examined the place.

✝✝✝

I'd sent Eomær and Rinan ahead to scout whilst we hid ourselves in a copse between the road and the river. The pair had worked their way northwards along the east bank of the river using the reeds in places and the overhanging bank in others until they got close to the settlement.

'There's a settlement halfway between the river and Earninga Stræt,' Eomær told me when he and Rinan returned. 'There are two halls and a number of hovels. One of the halls is quite small and the other much larger. My guess is that one is for the thegn, or whoever owns the vill, and one for his warriors – quite a lot of them judging by its size. The hovels appear to be occupied by the slaves who work the land.'

'There are various other buildings as well,' Rinan added. 'A smithy, brewhouse, large stable block and a mill.'

I thanked them and walked away. I needed time to ponder what to do next. Then I thought of something and went back to question the two scouts.

'Did you see any sort of banner?'

They both nodded.

'There was one flying outside the smaller hall, it was black with what looked like a white horse on it,' Rinan replied.

71

I felt exultant. It was the same banner as Wulfhere had used when he was an ealdorman and which Sherwyn and Rowe had seen being flown by the raiders at Silcestre. Thinking of them reminded me that I had done nothing about looking after Redwald's sons after the death of their parents. It was an omission I would need to rectify as soon as I returned to Cent.

I asked about the numbers of warriors but neither Eomær nor Rinan had been able make an estimation. I therefore decided to go closer with Wolnoth and see for myself. We set off along the river bank an hour or so before dawn the next day so that we would be in position to observe the settlement before first light.

It had been a clear, frosty night and there was a chill mist hanging over the river at first light, so we had difficulty in seeing anything at first. We heard various noises whilst we waited: horses neighing, men laughing, talking and occasionally cursing, the jingle of harness and finally the unmistakable sound of many hooves on the frozen ground.

By the time that the weak sun burnt off enough mist for us to see clearly there was no sign of any horses, or many men come to that. A few villeins and slaves were mucking out the stables and clearing up horse droppings from outside the two halls, loading it into barrows and dumping it on the midden heap and one sentry sat on the steps of the smaller hall looking bored. Otherwise all was quiet. It was obvious that Wulfhere and his warband had left; the question was, where had he gone?

We watched the settlement for the rest of the morning. Several warriors came out of the large hall to go to the latrine and the sentry was changed twice. From what we could see there were no more than four warriors left in the settlement.

Seeing that the man on duty outside the hall was asleep and the only other warrior visible was a man sitting cleaning his weapons, I reached a decision.

An hour later we rode into the settlement and dismounted between the two halls. We had already strung our bows and it was the work of moments to knock arrows. Eafer and I aimed at the startled sentry and a second later he was dead. Eomær took care of the other man just as the other two erupted from the warrior's hall to see what was going on. They stared open mouthed as Wolnoth and Rinan shot them.

I wanted at least one left alive for questioning and they had both intended to cripple their target rather than to kill them. Unfortunately Rinan's aim was off and his arrow struck his man in the middle of his chest. Thankfully Wolnoth did better and the last of Wulfhere's men collapsed with an arrow in his thigh.

He was old and far from brave. It didn't take long before he revealed that Wulfhere was headed for Lundenwic. He had a whore that he was particularly fond of there and, although the wounded man didn't say so, I guessed that he would be finalising plans with Håkon before winter set in for the invasion of Cent in the spring.

I had learnt all that I needed to know except the proposed date for the invasion. All I had got out of

Tunbehrt was that he was to return with his Frisian mercenaries by the end of March. I assumed therefore that the Vikings' attack would come sometime in early April.

I was in two minds as to what to do. My duty was to tell Ælfred what I had found out but what I wanted to do was to return to Dofras and my family before the weather broke and the roads became impassable. Either way I needed to get back to Wessex. It was too dangerous to travel via Lundenwic again and so I decided to head back to Verulamacæster and then cross the Temes at Stanes. Once south of the river we would be back in Wessex.

Of course, I had promised to put Tunbehrt aboard a ship bound for the Continent but I hadn't said when I'd do this. He would have to remain my guest until after I'd defeated Håkon and Wulfhere. However, if the king found out about Tunbehrt's involvement in the plot, he would want to execute him. I couldn't let him know that I held him prisoner or I would be forced to break my promise to the man. He might be a traitor but he still had my word that I would spare him and that mattered to me.

I was still undecided when we finally reached Stanes, where we stayed the night. It was now the end of November and the next morning I awoke to the sound of heavy rain turning the earthen courtyard of the tavern into mud. If this kept up the roads would become nigh on impassable. If I went to Wintanceaster we might be stuck there so I decided to head east.

It was hard going until we joined Casingc Stræt at Sudwerca at the southern end of bridge over the Temes. At one point the cart got stuck and we abandoned it. Thankfully Tunbehrt's wound had healed sufficiently for him to ride the horse that had pulled the cart. I could see that riding caused him some discomfort but he deserved to suffer for what he'd done.

Unsurprisingly, neither Uhtric nor Leofwine knew how to ride, not that we had horses for them if they could have done. One rode in front of Eafer and the other with Rinan. By now both of the former urchins had adapted well to their new life and had been accepted as members of our little group by the others. It helped that they now kept themselves clean and no longer stank like a midden heap.

On the seventh of December I arrived back at Dofras to be greeted with relief by Hilda. Behind her stood a nurse holding a small baby heavily wrapped in furs. I now had another daughter. Hilda was very happy to see me safely returned and proudly showed off the baby. In all the excitement she even forgot to reproach me about my foolishness in undertaking such a dangerous mission myself.

Reluctantly I kept my promise and paid for Tunbehrt's passage on a merchant ship departing for the Frisian port of Groningen. I hoped that I had seen the last of him and that I wouldn't regret my decision to free him.

I still had to inform the king of the plot to invade Cent, of course. So much rain had fallen that I knew that sending a messenger on horseback was impossible. Thankfully, the weather out at sea wasn't bad enough to prevent a ship from venturing along the coast and, although there was always the danger of storms at this time of year, I decided that it was the most sensible way of informing Ælfred.

I didn't expect a reply to reach me for some time and so I settled down to enjoy Yuletide with my family. Thinking about how to defeat the Danes could wait for now.

Chapter Four

CENT

Spring 883

The rain poured down relentlessly on the roof of my hall at Dofras. It had been a poor winter; wet with little snow or frost to turn the liquid mud into hard earth. Despite the clean rushes laid on the beaten earth floor of the hall each day, mud soon seeped up through them and people's shoes became clogged with the stuff, even if they hadn't been outside. To venture forth to go to the latrines meant a coating of the muck up to one's knees and beyond. At least it meant that the expected invasion wasn't imminent, not in this weather.

No reply had reached me from Ælfred, not that I had expected one. I doubted if a messenger could have ridden the twenty five miles from Wintanceaster to Portcæstre, even if he decided to send a letter by sea. The port of Hamwic was half that distance away from Ælfred's capital but the River Ytene, whose valley connected the two places, would doubtless have overflowed its banks and flooded the roadway long since.

I contemplated the steady drips of water coming from where the thatched roof had rotted and, although slaves kept emptying the wooden buckets under each gap, water still ended up on the floor, adding to the mud already there. Even the fire sizzled and smoked as raindrops fell on it instead of blazing merrily. The hall reeked of wet clothes, acrid smoke and mud, adding to the general air of despondency that permeated the hall.

Such conditions tended to make everyone bad tempered, even when they were sober, and I had been forced to break up more than one fight. Both Uhtric and Leofwine had been kept busy attending to squashed noses, broken bones and, on two occasions, knife wounds.

A slave girl had even attacked one of Hilda's maids when the latter had beaten the girl harshly for some minor misdemeanour. I couldn't let a slave get away with it and so I had been forced to hang the girl as a lesson to others. She was only twelve and I loathed doing it. I blamed the maid for bullying the girl beyond bearing but Hilda had taken the maid's part. She accused me of being smitten by the slave and we had had a row, one of many that miserable winter.

The only bright spot was when we christened our daughter but the joy that brought was short lived. The baby died ten days later but mourning her loss didn't bring us closer together. In fact it drove Hilda and I further apart.

It was the tenth of March when the weather finally broke. The dark clouds disappeared and weak sunshine began to dry out the land. By now the fields should have been ploughed, fertilised and the first of the crops sown. As it was, it was nearly the end of the month before the soil was dry enough to be turned and the muck from the midden heap spread.

It was a disaster as far as I was concerned, not just because of the delay to the farming year, but because everyone was needed to work the land, even me and my hearth warriors. It wasn't that I minded hard physical labour – in fact I rather enjoyed it after such a miserable winter – but it meant that the men of the fyrd didn't have the time to train for the coming invasion. Furthermore the skypfyrd couldn't be called out to man the longships.

The one thing I could do was send a dozen of my scouts to the north coast of my shire to watch the estuary of the Temes and establish a line of beacons. If, as I expected, Håkon's fleet sailed from Lundenwic and around the coast to Sandtun, I would at least have some warning.

I had taken the precaution of arresting Pæga soon after I returned. He had readily confessed to his part in the plot in exchange for my promise to look after his wife and two daughters; nevertheless I didn't let his wife keep the vill. I fulfilled my promise by arranging for his womenfolk to join the monastery at Cantwareburh as nuns. I don't think they were very happy about it but I couldn't have cared less. They were as guilty as Pæga as far as I was concerned; they must have known what he was up to.

His reeve had been involved as well and I had hanged both men from the same tree that would later be used for the unfortunate slave girl. I confiscated the vill of Sandtun and I could have added it to many I now owned but instead I gave it to Hilda; mainly to make up for putting myself in needless danger by going to Mercia, as she saw it. However I did insist on approving her choice of the new reeve. I needed a man I could trust this time.

It was late March when the chain of beacons I had installed between Witenestaple and Dofras were lit, indicating that a sizeable fleet was sailing eastwards along the estuary of the Temes. Everyone knew what the smoke meant and, without having to be told, the ceorls dropped their ploughshares and hoes and picked up their weapons. Those who would form the fyrd headed to the mustering point at Hithe whilst those detailed for duty with the skypfyrd made for Dofras to join their longships.

I didn't have to worry that the men of Cent would still give priority to sowing their crops; they knew the fate that would await their wives and children if we lost the coming battle.

✝✝✝

It was a cold but clear day as I sat on Scur on top of the ridge above Sandtun beach and watched the cluster of sails appear on the horizon to the northeast. My elder brother, Æscwin, Thegn of Cilleham and the Shire Reeve of Cent, sat on his dappled roan stallion beside me as we gazed out to sea. As the enemy fleet drew closer I was able to make a rough estimate of their numbers. There were over eighty longships out there; that meant an army of some two and a half to three thousand Vikings. It was more than I had expected and I became concerned that I hadn't gathered enough men to oppose them.

Ælfred's messenger had finally reached me a week previously but what he had to say was of little comfort or help. He had thanked me for the information and suggested that I contacted my fellow ealdormen of Sūþrīgescīr and Suth-Seaxe to muster their fyrds to come to my aid. For a start Dudda of Sūþrīgescīr was far too worried about an attack on his own shire from across the Temes to send men into Cent, and Cynegils of Suth-Seaxe had already provided several hundred men for the skypfyrd; he was hardly likely to supply more when he faced the same problems with the late sowing of the land as we did.

Besides, there wasn't any time to muster their men and get them to where they were needed once we knew that the Viking fleet had sailed. I was well aware that many of my own fyrd from the north and west of Cent hadn't yet reached Hithe.

One solitary snekkje sat far out to sea as the enemy appeared. It was there to signal my longships waiting out of sight over the horizon. Bjarne and eleven ships from Portcæstre had sailed to join Jerrik's fleet several days ago. I had hoped for more but it was all he could man in the time available. We had half the number of ships that Håkon had but that didn't matter. Their role wasn't to defeat the Viking fleet, but to delay as many ships as they could whilst I dealt with the rest of the invading army as soon as they landed.

I hoped that Håkon, Wulfhere and the other leaders would be amongst the first ashore. If we could kill them then that should demoralise the rest and the invasion would be over before it had begun.

'I only hope that you've judged the Danes' reaction correctly, brother,' Æscwin said grimly as Bjarne's ships headed for the middle of the enemy fleet.

The first of the Viking longships turned towards the long shingle beach, then backed oars, waiting for others to join them in line. Evidently the Danes intended to land en masse. The second half of the enemy fleet turned to meet Bjarne's longships but the first forty or so ships carried on, blissfully unaware that their fleet had effectively been cut in half.

My orders to Bjarne were simple. Stay clear of the enemy craft and pepper them with arrows. If the Vikings tried to close with them, Bjarne's ships would withdraw. If the Vikings raised their shields to protect themselves, then they couldn't row as well. If they tried to row on and reach the beach then my sea-borne archers would inflict serious casualties on them before they could do so.

I didn't have time to watch further; it was time to re-join the army of Cent before the first wave of longships hit the beach. Normally I would have hidden archers on the flanks to force the enemy to bunch together but almost all my bowmen were aboard Bjarne's ships. Nevertheless, I hoped that I would still be able to spring a surprise on the Danes.

I handed Scur to one of the young horse-handlers in our camp before making my way with my brother through the settlement to where my host, such as it was, waited. The hall and huts of Sandtun lay a little way from the sea, underneath the ridge of low hills on top of which Æscwin and I had watched the oncoming invasion fleet. The salt pans were located between Sandtun and the sea. These were shallow depressions lined with some substance the Romans had made which resembled stone but was obviously man made.

They had cracked over time and the local salt-makers had repaired the cracks with the same lime mortar that masons used to fill the gaps between the stones of a building. The salt-makers filled the depressions with brine and waited for the water to evaporate, leaving behind salt. This was valued for preserving fish and meat and had made the late Thegn Pæga a rich man. Now the thegn's share of the revenue would go to Hilda.

The salt depressions themselves wouldn't serve as much of an obstacle to the advancing Vikings but we had erected a line of stakes behind each salt pan to force the enemy to bunch in the gaps between them. That was where I anticipated the main battle taking place. However, some of the fyrd were stationed behind the palisade of stakes to defend against any who sought to get through there.

I may not have had archers to whittle down the numbers of Danes on their right flank but I did have slingers, mostly boys but there were also some men who were more used to a sling than they were fighting in the shield wall. My other surprise was javelins.

Abbot Ælfnoð had told me that he had read how the ancient Romans had used javelins called pila to weaken an advancing enemy line and so I had trained

some of the fyrd in their use. We didn't have any
pilum like those used by the Romans but we had
made hundreds of light spears over the winter.
Whilst the slingers attacked the Vikings' right we
would unleash a hail of javelins into their main body.

My aim was to weaken their numbers sufficiently
so that by the time we engaged shield to shield we
would seriously outnumber them. I had managed to
muster fourteen hundred in all but those first forty
longships could hold well over a thousand warriors
and the men of the fyrd were no match for Vikings.

I took my place between Æscwin on my left and
Wealmær, the captain of my hearth warriors, on my
right and we waited. I placed my lime-wood shield,
banded in iron and with an iron boss, on the ground
leaning against my leg. It was heavy and there was
no point in tiring myself unnecessarily. All the
experienced warriors did the same. Only the young
hotheads stood ready to fight an enemy who were
still aboard their ships.

Eafer handed me my helmet and gave me a drink
of water from a flagon before taking his own place
behind me in the second rank. The helmet was new
and was a present from Hilda. It was made from a
single piece of steel hammered into shape. In
addition to a nose guard it had cheek pieces which
protected the majority of my face and it had a
chainmail avantail to protect my neck and throat. She
had the armourer who made it decorate each cheek
piece and the front of the helmet with the prancing
horse of Cent in gold. No one who saw it could

mistake me for anyone other than the Ealdorman of Cent.

The keels of fifteen drekar and twenty five of the smaller snekkjur ground onto the stony beach in front of us and disgorged their crews of howling Vikings. They tried to run at us up the sloping shingle beach. I smiled. They would be tired long before they reached us. The small stones slipped between their feet slowing their progress and making them slip back a foot for every yard they advanced.

The slingers ran into position and a hail of stones hit the Danes on the right of their line. Few were killed but stones hitting helmets dazed or knocked their wearers out. However, the greatest damage was done by breaking bones, both in the arm and leg. Volley after volley tore into the Vikings and those on the right edged towards the centre to get away from the bombardment.

Some of the Danes broke away from the main body and headed towards their tormentors. However, heavily armed Danes slipping and sliding on shingle were never going to catch nimble boys clad only in tunics and trousers. As soon as the pursuing Danes gave up, the slingers returned and the hail of stones re-commenced.

At that moment the leading Vikings reached the salt pans. Some headed across them intending to attempt to tear down the wall of stakes but most crowded into the gaps between them and charged our various shield walls. I gave the signal and a single note on a hunting horn sounded. Seconds later the sky grew dark as the first volley of javelins arced over our heads and into the advancing Vikings.

The enemy were unprepared and most still had their shields at their sides. The iron tipped missiles tore into legs, throats and torsos. Some of those with good quality mail byrnies survived being hit in the chest but they were still bruised and winded. Before the enemy could recover and bring their shields across their bodies the second volley hit them. Most were ready for the third volley and most of the javelins struck shields but nevertheless some hit exposed legs and a few managed to find the gap between the helmet brim and the top of the shield.

By now the first few ranks of the Vikings were in chaos. Dead and wounded men hampered the progress of those behind and they were unable to form a shield wall. It was the moment I'd been waiting for. At a rough guess we had killed or incapacitated nearly a fifth of the enemy, including many of their leaders and those in the vanguard. These were always their best warriors.

The hunting horn blared out again and I led the advance through the gaps between the salt pans. We struck the disorganised enemy before they could re-form and now the advantage lay with us. Our first rank consisted of thegns and hearth warriors whilst the second contained other members of my nobles' warbands. All were trained fighters, unlike the fyrd who made up the next four ranks.

We advanced through the Vikings, cutting them down and killing the wounded as we passed them. A wounded man lying on the ground could be more dangerous than a man facing you. Many a good warrior had died from a thrust up under the hem of his byrnie from below.

We tried to maintain a straight line but it was difficult as some of us met more resistance than others. I had easily defeated my first two opponents but then I came face to face with a man at least a foot taller than me who carried a long two-bladed battleaxe. A blow from such a heavy weapon could cleave my shield in half leaving me defenceless, even if it didn't shatter my left arm as well. My only hope was to kill him before he could bring his axe down.

As he raised his weapon I dodged to one side and, at the same time, thrust my sword up under his armpit. I felt the resistance as the point went through skin, muscle and flesh to strike bone but it didn't stop the huge Viking. He merely grunted as he brought down the axe. In desperation I thrust harder using every ounce of strength I had. I felt the tip of my sword slide along the humerus and into the joint between arm and shoulder. I must have cut something vital because his arm went limp and he lost the use of his left hand. The axe swung away as I tugged my sword out and thrust it up under his jaw.

The giant's corpse hadn't hit the ground before my next adversary confronted me. This time it was a callow youth with a wispy excuse for a beard. He can't have been more than fifteen and I quickly disposed of him. I was breathing heavily by this stage and salty sweat ran into my eyes. As I blinked to clear my vision I was conscious that Æscwin and Wealmær had re-joined me.

'You bloody fool,' my brother hissed at me. 'You went forward of the shield wall; you could have been killed.'

'You bloody fool, lord,' I reprimanded him with a grin.

He barely had time to snort his derision in reply before the next Danes were upon us. It was ten minutes before I had time to pause and take stock. In that time we had killed another four of the invaders. Then I saw two things at once: Håkon not five yards away and a banner fluttering a few yards behind him, Wulfhere's banner.

For a moment I was undecided which of them to aim for, which was nearly my undoing. Danes had attacked both Æscwin and Wealmær. I was busy thrusting my sword into the neck of my brother's attacker when a boy came at me with a spear. It was Wealmær's job to defend my right side but the warrior guarding his right had been killed and my captain was fully engaged defending himself.

Thankfully the young Dane was inexperienced and the spear point hit the avantail protecting the side of neck instead of entering the exposed areas of my face. It snagged in the links of the chainmail and my helmet twisted so that the cheek guard obstructed my vision. I lashed out blindly with my sword and I was fortunate enough to hit the leather jerkin the lad was wearing. The edge was still sharp enough to cut through the leather but it only made a shallow cut in his side.

By the time that I'd angrily pushed my helmet back into place Wealmær had killed both his opponent and the wounded boy. Someone had stepped into the gap left by the dead warrior on the other side of my captain and the line was restored.

The Vikings withdrew a few paces and reformed. This time when they attacked it was a case of pushing shield against shield whilst trying to find a gap in which to strike at the man facing you. I had taken the opportunity to sheath my sword and draw my seax. It was much more useful in close quarter fighting than an unwieldy sword.

I pushed at the shield in front of me whilst trying to find a chink into which to insert my seax. The eyes of my opponent glared at me with hatred and I glared back.

'This time I'll make sure of your death, you Saxon pig.'

I realised with a start that the eyes belonged to Håkon. For an instant I was distracted and he took advantage of that moment to hook the top of my shield with a small axe and pull it forward and down. The man behind him thrust a spear at my exposed face and I barely had time to duck down. I felt the point score along the top of my helmet and I cursed. Hilda would not be pleased that her expensive present had been ruined.

With my head ducked down I could see Håkon's shin as he pushed his kneecap against the bottom of my shield. I slashed across in front of the lower part of my shield and felt it connect with the bottom of his thigh below the hem of his byrnie. He grunted in surprise and then the pain hit him. His leg collapsed under him just as the spearman made another stab at

89

my face. Håkon let go of his axe and I was able to bring my shield up just in time to deflect the point of the spear.

Håkon staggered back, struggling to stay on his feet, and cannoned into the spearman. I brought my seax around and cut deeply into his neck. Like me, he was wearing an avantail and that absorbed most of the blow but it badly bruised his throat. He choked, struggling for breath, and I saw my chance. A seax doesn't have a sharp point like a sword; it has a cutting and chopping blade with a rounded end. However, if one shoved hard enough into a mouth and up into the soft palate it could penetrate well into the head, perhaps even into the brain.

It was enough at any rate. The leader of the Vikings from Lundenwic dropped dead at my feet, ripping the seax out of my hand as he did so. I was defenceless apart from my shield and I raised it expecting the spearman to thrust at me again, but nothing happened. I peered over the rim of my shield to see that Wealmær had already killed him.

Word quickly spread that Jarl Håkon had been slain and the strength of the attack lessened immediately. As the Vikings withdrew a few paces I could see Wulfhere's black banner a mere six or seven yards from where I stood. My own warriors had relaxed as soon as the Danes had stepped back. They were no doubt as exhausted as I was and they would be feeling the sting of minor flesh wounds for the first time. Nevertheless I wasn't about to let Wulfhere escape if I could help it.

Calling on my hearth warriors for one last effort I drew my sword and charged towards the banner, cutting down several unprepared Danes in my way before they realised what was happening. My men followed, some slower on the uptake than others. Consequently we drove into the enemy in an untidy wedge formation.

Wulfhere must have realised what was happening because as soon as I got close to the banner it retreated. My unexpected charge had been the final act needed to break the resolve of the Danes and now they streamed back across the shingle eager to regain the safety of their ships and the sea beyond. For a while I lost sight of the black banner. When I next glimpsed it its bearer was standing protectively in front of Wulfhere as he was hauled back aboard his ship.

With some of the crews pushing and others using their oars to pole them backwards, most of longships made it out into water deep enough for them to turn and head back out to sea; most but not all.

We captured one drakar and six snekkjur on the beach and most of the others had significantly depleted crews. Later we counted upwards of three hundred Danish corpses. There were, of course, no wounded Danes by the time my men had finished going amongst the fallen. We had suffered as well, naturally. One hundred and seventy of my men had been slain and another sixty were too wounded to ever fight again.

That evening Bjarne told me that he estimated that he had killed over two hundred of the crews manning the forty ships at the rear of the Viking fleet. They had eventually turned tail and headed back towards the Temes estuary. He had then waited off the beach for the rest of the longships carrying their defeated army and had managed to capture another seven ships, killing another one hundred and sixty men.

It was a great victory. The Danes had lost a third of their number and their leader was dead. They would think twice before attacking Cent again. However, Wulfhere's longship wasn't one of those engaged by Bjarne during their retreat and so it seemed that he'd escaped once again. I cursed. Despite our triumph I didn't feel much like celebrating at the feast that evening. I was too preoccupied wondering where Wulfhere would appear next and cause further mayhem.

Chapter Five

WESSEX

883

A month after the Battle of Sandtun I left Dofras again. I wanted to make sure that work on the king's new burhs was progressing on schedule and so I planned a tour of Wessex including Wintanceaster. Ælfred had sent for me so that I could tell him about Håkon and Wulfhere in person and I had decided that I would ask him for permission to take Oswine with me on the rest of my tour.

After the boy had departed to become a king's page he hadn't written to his mother, or to me. He didn't even need to engage the services of a scribe as the monks of Cantwareburh had taught him to read and write. He would never be of any use in a scriptorium but he could use a quill well enough to write a letter. His silence caused us some concern, especially Hilda.

In the year before he left I sensed a restlessness in Oswine and he began to distance himself from me. I suspected that, as he grew towards manhood, he resented the fact that he wouldn't succeed his father as Ealdorman of Cent. Had he been old enough when the previous ealdorman had died he would undoubtedly have taken his place. As it was, he was a boy of three at the time and I had been appointed instead.

When we took refuge in the marshes of Athelney five years ago he and I had grown close but he'd been very young at the time. Now that he was eleven he was undoubtedly starting to think about his future. As a page and a friend of the Ætheling Edward, Ælfred's only son, he could expect to become a member of his gesith - his close companions and hearth warriors - in due course but I suspected he was more ambitious than that.

His mother owned two vills in her own right and she could give one to her son, but perhaps becoming a thegn wasn't enough either. My eldest son, Æscwin, was a novice in the monastery at Cantwareburh. As a churchman it was impossible for him to succeed me when I died. However, my other son, Ywer, showed every indication, even at eight years old, of becoming a warrior like me. He was a good rider for his age and he could already use a small bow with some proficiency.

Much to Hilda's displeasure I decided to take Ywer with me as well as my eldest child, Cuthfleda. She was fifteen and I made the excuse that I would seek a suitable husband for her at Ælfred's court. I had no intention of doing so; she deserved better than to be shackled to one of the fawning self-servers that hung around the king.

However, I did plan to leave her at Wintanceaster. When we'd been fugitives on the Isle of Athelney she had become very close to Æthelflaed, King Ælfred's eldest child. Like my daughter, she was always more interested in hunting with a bow than doing what her lady mother wanted. Æthelflaed was twelve and I didn't suppose it would be too long before the king betrothed her to someone suitable. I hoped that Æthelflaed, once she had settled down as a wife, would act as a good influence on Cuthfleda. As I was to discover later, it was flawed logic.

I didn't plan to head for Wintanceaster immediately, despite the king's summons. I wanted to see what progress had been made in rebuilding Silcestre. It had been the first vill I had owned and it was the first home that Leofflæd and I had shared. Thus it had a place in my heart that other places couldn't rival, not even the mighty fortress of Dofras.

Hilda and I parted on moderately good terms. Although she wasn't happy about Ywer accompanying me, she was pleased to see the back of Cuthfleda. I couldn't blame her. If I found my daughter a handful, I could only imagine the problems that my wife had in controlling her. It didn't help that Cuthfleda was Leofflæd's daughter, of course. If reprimanded by her step-mother, Cuthfleda would draw unfavourable comparisons between Hilda and her mother.

I was tired of the acrimony between them and, much as I would miss my daughter's company, I could see that sending her away was the best solution to the problem. It didn't help that I was beginning to question my love for Hilda. The heady days of romance had long since passed and the recriminations I faced when I was away from her were beginning to affect our relationship. I didn't

95

exactly look forward to leaving but it would be true to say that I felt as if a weight had been lifted from my shoulders as I rode away from Dofras.

†††

Not only did I wish to see how re-building the settlement at Silcestre was progressing but I also wanted to see how the new reeve was settling in. One of those who formed part of my entourage was Sherwyn, the elder son of Redwald, the previous reeve. He had just turned fifteen and was training both as a warrior and as a scout. As his father's heir he now owned land in the vill and I needed to make sure that his inheritance was being looked after.

Of course, he was of age and he might decide to stay on in Silcestre as a ceorl and farm the land himself. However, I doubted it. He struck me as far more interested in being a warrior rather than grubbing a living from the land.

Another who had joined the group was Uhtric. He had replaced Eafer as my body servant when the latter become a member of my hearth warriors. Uhtric had loathed leaving his brother but they would have parted in any case. I was sending Leofwine to join the monastery at Cantwareburh to be educated and to build on the skills he already had as a healer. There was much he could learn from the infirmarian and the herbalist.

I was relieved to see that the gates of Silcestre had been replaced and, although one set of the four pairs of gates stood open, two of my warband who were stationed at the settlement were guarding the entrance. A wooden watchtower had been built adjacent to the gates to give warning of any hostile approach but I was dismayed to see that the young ceorl, whose turn it was to act as lookout, seemed to be asleep. We were halfway to the gates before he woke up and sounded the bell to announce the approach of armed men.

The gate sentries didn't close the gates in response to the alarm. Eomær, who was carrying my banner, had unfurled it to display the prancing white horse of Cent on a red background. I had no doubt that the reeve would punish the youth in the watchtower for his negligence and his stupidity without me having to say anything.

As I rode in I saw that the charred remains of the old hall and huts had been cleared away but work had yet to start on their replacements. Instead the inhabitants were living in tents and makeshift shelters.

The reeve, a man called Ecgberht, was waiting outside the new hall to greet me. He had obviously had the ceorls, villeins and slaves work on it first as it was nearly complete. The foundations were of simple stonework. Above this the walls consisted of a solid oak frame with wattle and daub infill. This was the simplest way to construct a wall. A woven lattice of wooden strips, usually hazel or willow, was daubed with a sticky material made of clay, animal dung and straw to make each panel weatherproof. It was a cheap and quick way to build but it required more maintenance than a solid timber wall.

The stout timbers that would support the roof were also in place and horizontal battens had been fixed in place to connect them. Reeds were being placed on top of the battens and tied down in layers to make the roof watertight. By this stage about half of the roof was complete. I was pleased to see that Ecgberht had made a square solid timber hole for the smoke to exit the hall. On top of this he had placed a small pyramid shaped roof made of timber to stop rain entering the smoke hole.

I was far less happy to see that so much effort had been devoted to rebuilding the hall before work on the huts had even started. The repair of the stone-built church had also been neglected. It would have been a simple matter to have made the church usable again. The stone walls still stood so it was only a matter of re-roofing it. Then the inhabitants would have had a place to shelter from the rain until their homes were re-built.

'Why have you concentrated almost all your efforts on the hall, Ecgberht?' I asked after I'd dismounted.

The reeve opened and closed his mouth like a landed trout whilst Uhtric came to take our two horses to the fenced enclosure, which held the animals until new stables could be built.

'So that you and your warriors had somewhere to stay, lord.' He eventually got out.

'We are used to sleeping rough,' I replied tersely. 'Surely the truth is that it's where you and your family normally live?'

'Er, yes, lord. Except when you visit, of course,' he said brightly.

'That is no excuse. It is plain to me that you have had everyone working to complete your own home whilst the needs of ceorls and their households were neglected. Had you even repaired the church – an easy task compared to constructing a hall from scratch – then the people that you are responsible for would have had somewhere dry to shelter.'

I didn't for one moment think that he would allow the inhabitants of Silcestre to join him and his servants in the small hall.

A crowd had gathered immediately after my arrival and now there were shouts of agreement from some of the braver individuals. Ecgberht glared around him, no doubt noting those who had dared criticise him for punishment later.

'Who appointed you as my reeve?' I asked.

'Your steward, lord,' he replied, now looking a little apprehensive.

'Really? On whose recommendation?'

'The reeve of Basingestoches, lord.'

'Oh! And what relationship is he to you?'

'He's my elder brother,' Ecgberht muttered, looking at the ground.

'Well, Ecgberht, you are no longer the Reeve of Silcestre. You and your family are to pack your belongings and return to Basingestoches today. You may tell your brother that when I arrive there tomorrow we will have a discussion that he's not likely to enjoy.'

The man's wife had been standing outside the nearly finished hall with three small children. She gave me a venomous look which I ignored before she stomped off to collect the family's belongings. I whispered in Wealmær's ear and he followed her into the hall to make sure she only took what was theirs. I was left with the problem of replacing Ecgberht. This time it would have to be someone I could rely on to look after the inhabitants properly.

Sometimes reeves were elected by the ceorls of a vill but it wasn't a practice that most thegns and other landowners liked very much. The man elected tended to side with his fellow ceorls and not be loyal first and foremost to his lord. However, I had no such worries here and I decided that the easiest way out of my dilemma was to call a witan of all ceorls.

Wulfhere's raid had killed nearly half the population of Silcestre. It would have been more if it wasn't for the stubborn defence that Redwald and most of his men had put up, which had allowed the rest to flee into the woods. Because most of the male ceorls had been killed, the official heads of families were now boys younger than fourteen and therefore not yet old enough to be classed as men.

Much of the work to rebuild the settlement had fallen on the younger women. I therefore took the unprecedented step of allowing the oldest female to represent the family where the senior male was not yet of age. Some of the surviving men didn't like it but there were few enough of them and they confined their disagreement to mutterings under their breath.

What I hadn't expected was that, of the three nominations made, two would be young women. The only male candidate was a greybeard but he was probably the best of the available menfolk. All three stood in turn and gave a short speech saying why they would make a good reeve. The greybeard confined himself to saying that he was the obvious choice as he was a man; a woman couldn't be a reeve. Perhaps he was right as far as the law went but an old man wasn't what Silcestre needed.

Both women made a good case, enumerating what needed to be done and in what order. However, one gave equal priority to looking after the land as well as the building work and she seemed to me to be the more level headed of the two. Surprisingly she was the younger, being in her early twenties.

I allowed all those present to vote but I reserved the right to make the final choice myself. Thankfully the younger woman won quite decisively and I appointed Friðuswiþ as Wessex's first female reeve. It was a brave choice and I was certain that it would appal Ælfred and most of his nobles. However, I didn't care. My first concern was the inhabitants of my vill.

✝✝✝

When we arrived at Wintanceaster it was raining so hard that the gates only came into sight when we were close to them. I hadn't dismissed my reeve at Basingestoches; instead I confined myself to berating him for nominating his brother when he must have

known that he was a self-serving fool. The reeve
tried to excuse his brother by blaming Ecgberht's
wife. There might have been some truth in that but, if
a man allows himself to be henpecked into doing
what is wrong by his wife, he doesn't deserve a
position of responsibility.

Once I had dried off and changed into fresh
clothes I was taken to Ælfred's private chambers. I
thought that the king looked tired, pale and wan. His
eyes had dark rings around them and they seemed
sunken into their sockets. Nevertheless he had lost
none of his old fire and vigour.

He wasn't pleased that I had taken so long to
answer his summons and he was even less pleased
when word had reached him about Friðuswiþ.

'You really cannot appoint a woman to be a reeve,'
he almost shouted at me after he had reprimanded
me for my tardiness.

I had rarely seen him so irate. It was only then
that I noticed the two people standing in the corner of
the room. The Lady Ealhswith evidently shared her
husband's outrage, judging by the expression on her
face. However, their daughter the Lady Æthelflaed,
was smiling at me. She evidently approved of
Friðuswiþ's appointment; however, she was only a
child and her opinion counted for naught.

I did wonder why she was there but I soon found
out. After Ælfred had finished reprimanding me I
explained that there were no suitable men left after
Wulfhere's raid. That slightly mollified him and he
dropped the matter. I suspect that he had little
alternative. Much as everyone might disapprove of a

102

female reeve, they would probably object to the king interfering in the appointment of whomsoever a noble wished as one of his officials even more.

'Well, that's not why you are here, Jørren,' the king said with a sigh. 'You are only too well aware of the situation in Mercia. One third of the kingdom is ruled by Danes more or less under the control of King Æðelstan, one third is a lawless wasteland governed by pagan Danes who spend their time fighting each other from what I can see, and only the western part is under the control of our allies, the Angles, led by Ealdorman Æðelred.

'My earnest desire is to unite Mercia, or what's left of it, with Wessex. Only that way can we resist the growing menace of the pagan Danes. I have therefore decided that I need to tie Æðelred to me by marriage.'

I could see the miserable expression on Æthelflaed's face and I guessed what was coming.

'You and Æðelred are close, or at least as close as any in Wessex, and I have therefore chosen you to lead a deputation to Glowecestre to negotiate his marriage to the Lady Æthelflaed. You can tell him that, as her dowry, I will give him Lundenwic,' the king said grandly.

I nearly burst out laughing in surprise but the king wasn't given to making jests; he was deadly serious. His eldest daughter was fourteen and the Lord of the Mercians was in his late thirties. I was reminded of my wife's first marriage to a man very much older than she was. It had been an extremely unhappy experience for her and I wondered whether this child would fare any better.

As for giving Æðelred Lundenwic, it wasn't Ælfred's to give away. Despite Håkon's defeat and death, the old Roman city was still ruled by the Danes. Even if it wasn't, it had never been part of Wessex, much as past Saxon kings had disputed that. It was originally part of the old Kingdom of Ēast Seaxna Rīce but it had become part of Mercia two centuries ago, long before Ēast Seaxna Rīce had been incorporated into Wessex. For Ælfred to say that he was giving it to the Mercian leader as his bride's dowry was patently absurd.

'What do you mean, cyning? How are you giving Lundenwic back to the Mercians?' I asked, trying not to sound derisory.

'Because you are going to advise him how capture it. He will have to find the men, of course, but I'm sure that you come up with a way of expelling the Danes with minimum casualties. In exchange he is to acknowledge me as his king. That is all the bride price I want.'

The king seemed to have a surprising faith in my strategic ability, which was flattering, but my knowledge of siege warfare wasn't much greater than anyone else's. However, I realised what this was all about. Ælfred had made no secret of the fact that he saw himself as bretwalda of the all the Anglo-Saxon peoples. His dream was to drive out the Danes and the Norsemen and become king of a united Englaland, as he called it – the land of the Angles. No doubt he would have preferred to have called it Saxony – the land of the Saxons – but that was already the name of the area lying between Frisia and the mainland of Danmǫrk; the land from where his people had crossed the sea many centuries before.

'And once we have captured it – a not insignificant task in itself – how are we going to keep it?' I asked, wondering if Ælfred had gone mad.

'That will be Æðelred's problem, but keep it he must if we are ever going to rid Englaland of the accursed Danes.'

As he said this Ælfred began to cough and quickly put a cloth to his mouth. Ealhswith uttered an alarmed squawk and put her arm around her husband's shoulders. She turned him away from me but not before I saw that the cloth had a bright red splodge on it – blood. I'd heard rumours that the king had a delicate stomach and could eat no meat, only broth, but this was the first time I'd seen him ill.

Ælfred stumbled into an inner chamber, assisted by both his wife and daughter. As she closed the door behind her Æthelflaed looked at me intently as if pleading with me to botch her betrothal somehow. The door shut and I was left alone with several conflicting thoughts racing through my mind. I was worried because the king was obviously ill but that could be temporary, although I didn't think so. Evidently I wouldn't be touring the burhs just yet. I hadn't had a chance to talk to Ælfred and his wife about Cuthfleda as yet but, hopefully, I would get the opportunity before I left Wintanceaster.

There remained the problem of Ywer. I was happy to take him around a peaceful Wessex; I was far less happy about taking him into Mercia with me. Furthermore I had hoped to be able to take Oswine on my tour but Hilda would be horrified if I asked him to accompany me now. At least I could go and see him and scold him for his failure to write to his mother.

I found him with Edward the Ætheling. They were training with wooden swords and wicker shields under the supervision of a giant of a warrior. I watched for a while and was impressed at how much the two boys had learned already. They could hardly take their place in the shield wall yet but they had grasped the basic principles of swordplay. Although Oswine was nearly two years older than Edward they were closely matched, Edward being big for his age. I had expected Oswine to allow Edward to win but he seemed to be doing his level best to land a heavy blow on Ælfred's elder son. To be fair, Edward was trying to do the same to my stepson.

Eventually the warrior, whose name I gathered was Bryhthelm, called a halt to the bout. Both boys had bruised the other in several places but neither had landed a crippling blow, for which I was thankful. The boys collapsed thankfully onto the ground, exhausted.

'Lord Jørren, I didn't see you there,' Oswine suddenly called, sitting up but making no attempt to stand, as he should have done in my presence. 'What are you doing here?'

'I came to speak to you, Oswine. If the Ætheling Edward will excuse you, I would like to talk to you in private.'

I was irritated that he had evidently stopped calling me father but it didn't annoy me as much as the supercilious look that Edward gave me as Oswine sauntered over to me. I turned abruptly and led the way to a quiet courtyard.

'You seem to be quite the favourite with Edward; well done. His friendship will stand you in good stead in the future,' I began.

'That's not why I'm his friend,' Oswine flashed back, looking angry.

'No, of course not,' I replied, trying to placate him. This was not how I had planned our conversation going. 'I didn't mean to imply that you were acting the toady. Look, Oswine, what has happened? You've stopped calling me father and you haven't written to your mother or me since you arrived here. She's worried about you.'

'Yes, well, tell her that I am doing well and making my own way in the world.'

'What do you mean? You don't have to make your own way; you are the heir to two fine vills and I intend to settle more land on you once you reach fourteen.'

'I don't want your charity!' he spat at me. 'You have robbed me of my inheritance. I should be the Ealdorman of Cent not you.'

I was shocked by his vehemence.

'What are you talking about? The appointment of ealdormen is the king's decision, as advised by the Witenagemot. It's not something that is inherited, although if a son is suitable I'll agree that it is normal for him to follow in his father's footsteps. However, in this case you were a three year old boy when your father died. You might recall that Ælfred himself was chosen to be king when his brother Æthelred died as his own children were too young.'

'Yes, and the Ætheling Æthelwold has never forgotten that he should have succeeded King Æthelred instead of Ælfred.'

I was stung by the boy's statement, partly because of his disrespect to the king but also because he seemed to be taking the part of Æthelwold against him. I wondered what was going on. Not only did I seem to have lost the affection of my stepson but he seemed to harbouring treasonous thoughts; but perhaps he was just drawing a comparison? I certainly hoped so.

'Come Oswine, Lord Jørren has better things to do than talk to you. Get back to your training; you're keeping Edward waiting.'

I could hardly believe it. The speaker was Eadda, my predecessor as Hereræswa; a man who had good reason to hate me. Evidently the king had tried to soften the blow of his demotion by putting him in charge of his son's military education.

No wonder Oswine had taken against me. Eadda would have been dripping poison in his ear and stoking the fires of jealousy and righteous indignation. It was all I could do to stop myself walking across and punching Eadda's smug face. I watched with dismay as the two of them disappeared, Eadda with a proprietary hand on Oswine's shoulder. It seemed that my stepson had joined the ranks of my enemies.

Chapter Six

THE ÍRALANES SÆ

Summer 883

It was the beginning of July when I left for Glowecestre. In the end I'd decided to take Ywer with me rather than leave him at Wintanceaster. There he would have been on his own and I didn't trust Oswine not to bully him and take his frustration out on my son, particularly as Ywer was likely to succeed me as Ealdorman of Cent in the fullness of time.

Thankfully Æthelflaed had been delighted about the proposal that Cuthfleda should become one of her ladies, as I knew she would be. They were kindred spirits and quickly became good friends. Ealhswith wasn't exactly happy at the prospect but gave in when Æthelflaed pleaded that she would have few enough friends when she went to live in Mercia.

We docked at the small port on the River Sæfern that served Glowecestre and hired horses to take me together with a small escort to Æðelred's capital, only to discover that he wasn't there. He'd gone north with an army to retake Cæstir from the Norsemen who had captured it. I was in a dilemma. I would look pathetic if I returned to Wintanceaster having failed in my mission.

On the other hand, I had set out on the Saint Cuthbert from Portcæstre with only three other longships as escort. We were a large enough fleet for the more or less peaceful waters around the coast of Wessex but I hesitated to venture north into the Íralandes Sæ. Not only were the native Welsh who lived along the coast hostile but the waters were infested with Norse pirates from Dyflin.

Perhaps I would have risked it readily enough had I not had my son with me. He had just turned nine and, much as I hated to admit it, Hilda had been right all along. I should have left him at Dofras. On the other hand, he was relishing both the adventure and having me all to himself. He and I hadn't spent that much time together before now and I cherished the growing bond between us.

I had hoped that Æðelred might be returning soon but he had only left three weeks before our arrival and, according to his steward, he had only just started besieging the place. As it was another of the old fortified Roman towns it could take months to recapture it. Reluctantly I decided that I had little choice but to venture north to see him.

My decision was made easier when I discovered that Æðelred needed to have provisions sent to Cæstir on a regular basis. As luck would have it, a convoy was due to sail in two days' time and I asked to accompany it. The addition of four fighting ships was most welcome and so we set sail in the company of seven heavily laden knarrs and three Mercian escort ships two days later.

The Mercian warships weren't sleek longships like ours; they were birlinns, heavier and smaller than snekkjur and with a stern higher than the prow.

Consequently they were slower. We had to reef our sails to keep pace with them and the knarrs when the wind was in the right direction and when it wasn't our rowers had an easy time of it because the knarrs had to tack to make progress. Our knarrs didn't have sufficient oars or the men to man them on the open sea; reserving rowing for manoeuvring in harbour. Viking knarrs were of a different design, intended to trade far and wide; they carried more men and could propel themselves using their oars at sea, albeit more slowly than the sleeker longships.

By nightfall we had scarcely left the estuary of the River Sæfern and spent the night in a sheltered cove on the coast of Somersaete. The next day we were helped by a stiff southerly breeze and managed to reach the south-western tip of Wealas before nightfall. Once again we sheltered in a cove for the night but this time we anchored close to the shore, rather than beach the ships.

It was too dangerous to light a fire on board and so we had to content ourselves with a meal of cold salted fish, bread and cheese. We did however have ale but no one was foolish enough to drink more than a couple of leather tankards. We broke our fast with the same fare and continued on our voyage.

Now it became more dangerous. The shoreline of Wealas receded to the east and the coast of Íralond was less than fifty miles to the west. The weather stayed fair and the southerly wind blew us along at around five knots. Normally I would be grateful for both but I would rather we were hidden in rain and alone so that we could unfurl the sail and sail at a full eight knots.

We saw no other sail until the early afternoon when three ships appeared over the horizon coming from the north-west. There was little doubt that they were Viking longships out of Dyflin. They headed for us at first but then sheared away after seeing how many there were of us. I was tempted to give the order to give chase; three Norse longships would be no match for my four with their archers but I had promised to help guard the convoy.

That night we continued on our course whilst we took turns to sleep. We were in the open sea with no danger of running into anything but it wasn't something that our crews liked doing. They preferred to hole up somewhere sheltered during the hours of darkness. Of course, the Vikings were used to sailing through the hours of darkness or they wouldn't have been able to undertake such long voyages from their homes.

Ywer's initial excitement had turned into boredom during the voyage and so I had allowed him to join the ship's boys. He was too small to be of much use and I was pleased to see that he had the common sense to keep out of the way when necessary. However, he was genuinely interested in how the ship worked and in the finer points of sailing. I had explained many of the skills needed by a seafarer but he seemed to grasp things better from boys nearer his own age; furthermore he could experience things first hand instead of listening to his father talking.

He would listen intently when one of the boys explained to him why they were trimming the sail and what effect the direction and strength of the wind had on the ship's progress through the water. He even managed to grasp the more difficult concepts like leeway and simple navigation. I was proud of him, even if I was a little irked that I hadn't been able to satisfy his curiosity myself.

We saw no more sails, apart from the odd fishing boat, until we neared the end of our journey. The coast of Wealas was shaped like a bull's horns but there was a large island called Monez which was separated from the northern horn by a narrow channel. Cæstir lay a few miles up the River Dēvā but to get there we either had to go around Monez or through the channel. The shipmaster, Wilfrið, didn't know these waters and so he took the sensible decision to go around the island. At least it seemed sensible until we ran into a fleet of Norse longships coming towards us from the north.

✝✝✝

They had to be Norsemen, coming from that direction. Vikings from Danmork had conquered the east and centre of Englaland but it was Norsemen from Norþweg who had settled in more far flung places including Íralond, the Isle of Mann and all along the west coast north of Cæstir. I'd even heard stories that they had ventured further afield, to Snæland and beyond.

This fleet either carried reinforcements or provisions for the Vikings besieged in Cæstir, perhaps both. Mann had been conquered by the Norse kings of Dyflin a decade ago and so it seemed likely that this was where these longships had come from. Had they been coming from Dyflin, then they would have appeared from the west.

'What can you make out?' I called up to the lookout who had first spotted the ships on the horizon.

'Difficult to say at this distance, father. I can't see any sails but I've counted seven white bow waves.'

I realised with a start that Ywer was standing his turn up the mast. It wasn't what I'd intended when I agreed that he could join the ship's boys. Climbing the rigging to get to the yardarm was dangerous enough; staying there sat on it with one arm around the top of the mast whilst the ship pitched and rolled was even more perilous. What seemed a gentle motion on deck was like a stone being whirled around in a sling up there.

However, I wasn't about to shame my son by calling him down and sending an older boy up to take his place. Whilst being anxious for his safety, I was also immensely proud of him. Normally a ship's boy would be over eleven years of age and most were older than that when they started; even then they wouldn't be expected to act as the lookout until they had been afloat for some time. The fact that Ywer had insisted on going up the mast only a week or so into his fist voyage spoke volumes for his strength of character – and for his foolhardiness.

'Can you see if they are sleek longships or knarrs, which are broader in the beam?'

There was a pause whilst Ywer studied the oncoming ships.

'I think that there are probably four of the broader type and three longships, father. At any rate the four seem to be going much slower than the other three who are now rowing much faster.'

'How do you know?'

'The white bow wave is larger, and not just because they are a little closer now.'

'Well done, Ywer. Come down now.'

I didn't want him up there if we were about to go into battle. However, I doubted that was the case. There were seven warships in our fleet and we would make short work of the Norse ships.

I had expected Ywer to come down immediately but he stayed up there. I was about to shout up to him once more when he called down again.

'The other four ships have changed course,' he yelled in an excited treble voice. 'They are now heading south-east.'

That made sense. The slow moving knarrs were heading for the mouth of the Dēvā whilst the longships pretended to threaten us to give the knarrs a chance to reach safety.

'Wilfrið, signal the Mercian birlinns to join two of my ships. They are to pretend to engage those three snekkjur whilst we and the Holy Spirit try and catch those merchant ships.'

The Holy Spirit was another skeid, a large longship like the Saint Cuthbert, although she was a little smaller and had four less oars a side.

We raced across the water, propelled by oars as well as by sail now. The excitement of the chase inspired the rowers and they put everything they had into it. When Ywer had first spotted the enemy ships on the horizon they were probably about four miles away. When we started the chase we were still some fifty miles away from the mouth of Dēvā, the river that led to Cæstir, and so I anticipated no difficulty in catching them long before that, especially as their oarsmen would be tired whereas ours were fresh.

However, once they had passed to the north of Monez, they didn't change course to the south-east, as I'd expected. Instead they headed due south down the east coast of the island.

'They're going to seek safety in the channel between Monez and the northern coast of Wealas,' Wilfrið called across to me. 'I'm wary of chasing them into there because of the sandbanks.'

I nodded. We had avoided the shorter route past Monez precisely because of the treacherous sandbanks. We needed to catch the knarrs before they made it to the south-east tip of Monez and the entrance to the channel.

The rearmost of the knarrs was now less than two miles ahead of us. The east coast of Monez was between fifteen and twenty miles long, or so Wilfrið thought. We had been forced to lower our sail when we turned into the wind and so it was now the muscle of our rowers against theirs.

At our respective rates of progress it would only be an hour and a half before we caught the laggard; however, I wasn't interested in it. I would leave the two rearmost knarrs for the Holy Spirit to scoop up. I wanted to catch the two ships in the lead and they were drawing away from the other two. In fact, we were only gaining on them by about a mile every hour. It would be a close run thing.

Our own rowers were tiring now but so were theirs. We drew level with the rearmost knarr and as we did so my archers sent two volleys of arrows into the rowing benches. Several Norsemen were killed or wounded and the ship lost speed rapidly. Our success drove my men to even greater efforts and a short while later we passed the next knarr, dealing out the same rain of death. Now the front two knarrs were no more than three hundred yards away.

It seemed that their rowers were exhausted because both knarrs slowed down. They lay fifty yards apart and I told Wilfrið to steer between the two of them so that we could attack both of them at the same time. I was foolishly overconfident because, as we drew level and prepared to rake them with our arrows, they launched a dozen spears at us. One or two fell short but the rest hit our leading oarsmen. Several were killed and others were wounded in the shoulder or thigh. The other rowers lost their rhythm and we slewed to the left, our prow crashing into one of the knarrs.

We were still making some five knots through the water at the moment of impact. We stove in the side of the knarr and it started to take in water immediately. I yelled for our oarsmen to back water and we drew away from the sinking ship before renewing the chase. By now the other knarr was three hundred yards or more away. The extra warriors we carried, mainly archers, dragged the dead and wounded clear and several took the casualties' places. Whilst the ship's boys tended to the wounded we picked up the pace again.

'We're taking in water, lord.'

The cry came from a rower in the bows. We may have sunk the knarr we struck but in doing so we had damaged the planking on our own prow. I rushed forward with Wilfrið to assess the damage. It wasn't disastrous but there was more water coming in than we could cope with by baling. We would need to beach her and effect repairs and I reluctantly gave the order to turn towards Monez. As we headed towards the shoreline I watched in despair as the Norse knarr drew away from us.

I glanced behind me and saw that at least the Holy Spirit had captured the other two knarrs. I'd have to be content with that.

†††

Whilst we removed the damaged length of planking and repaired them as best we could with what we could find ashore, I sent groups of men out to obtain pine pitch and wool from the local people so that we could caulk the bows once they were repaired.

At first I was worried that we might be attacked but, once the Welsh who lived on Monez realised that we came in peace and would pay for what we needed, they helped us, albeit grudgingly. It probably helped that they were Christians, although followers of the old Celtic Church rather than Rome.

It took us a week before the Saint Cuthbert was sea worthy again. The Holy Spirit had joined us on the first evening, bringing with her the two captured knarrs. They carried grain, root vegetables and salted meat intended for the embattled Viking garrison of Cæstir, so we ate well that week. We traded some of the cargo for what we needed from the Welsh, thus preserving the small chest of silver I had brought with me.

I thought that the two snekkjur I had left to help the Mercians fight off the three Norse longships might have come looking for us but we saw no sign of them. I found out why when we finally moored on the bank of the River Dēvā next to the encampment of Æðelred's besieging army. According to the thegn who commanded the Mercian birlinns they had both been sunk by the Norsemen. As the three birlinns seemed to have escaped unscathed I strongly suspected that the Mercians had abandoned my ships and made good their escape. However, I could prove nothing and, although I seethed inside, I had to swallow my anger. To even accuse the Mercian thegn of cowardice in front of Lord Æðelred would ruin my chances of a successful negotiation before we had even begun.

Chapter Seven

CÆSTIR

September 883

I hadn't anticipated being kept waiting to see Æðelred. After coming all that way, and having been instrumental in preventing a re-supply convoy from reaching the Norse in the old city, I had expected to be welcomed as soon as I'd arrived. As it was I was kept kicking my heels for two days before he sent for me.

'How many men have you brought me?'

No greeting, no polite conversation, not even a word of gratitude; just a bald statement which had no relevance to my mission as far as I could see.

'I'm sorry, Lord Æðelred, I don't follow you.'

'Ælfred has sent you to help me, I assume, so how many warriors have you brought with you?' he asked again.

'I'm here at the request of King Ælfred, yes, but my mission has nothing to do with your siege of Cæstir. In fact, it wasn't until we reached Glowecestre that I even knew that you were here.'

I placed emphasis on the word king as Æðelred's use of Ælfred's name without the courtesy of using his title had irked me. However, my answer seemed to dumbfound him.

'Oh! Then why are you here if not in answer to my request for Wessex's help to expel the Norsemen from Mercia?'

'When was the request sent?'

'Three weeks ago, before I left Glowecestre.'

'Well, I'm afraid it hadn't reached Wintanceaster before I left ten days ago.'

Æðelred paced up and down, chewing his lip. It had been nine years since I'd last seen him at the Battle of Berncestre and he'd changed considerably over that time. Gone was the young man with the ready smile. Then I had counted him as a friend, now he treated me as a stranger and the friendliness had been replaced by near hostility.

'Then what are you doing here?'

'I'm here, as I said, at the behest of King Ælfred to offer you the hand of his eldest daughter in marriage and, if that's agreeable to you, to negotiate the terms of the betrothal.'

'Betrothal?' he spat. 'I'm fighting to keep a hold on what's left of Mercia and he sends you to arrange my marriage? Is he mad?'

'I can assure you, Æðelred, that the King of Wessex is far from mad,' I shot back, my temper rising to match his. 'He was under the impression that you would welcome an alliance with the only kingdom left under Anglo-Saxon rule.' I took a deep breath to subdue my ire and added, 'if you give yourself time to think about it, I think you will conclude that it's an advantageous match for you and for Mercia.'

He glared at me for a moment and then sighed.

'I'm sure you're right. It's not the right moment to think of wedlock; but I concede that a formal alliance with Wessex would be sensible, depending on the terms, of course. However, I cannot afford the time to discuss it with you, my friend, until Cæstir is back in my hands and the north of Mercia is cleared of these Norsemen.'

I was surprised at the Lord of Mercia's somewhat mercurial character. It was a good indication that he was near the end of his tether and I worried for Æthelflaed if he was so quick to change his mood. Of course, his position, and that of the rump of Mercia that was left, was precarious to say the least. The Danes to the east were quiescent for now but that could change in an instant. The Welsh were a constant problem. They regarded the Anglo-Saxons as invaders of their ancient lands just as much as we regarded the Danes as conquerors of ours.

Thankfully Wealas was divided into several kingdoms and the two of those which bordered Mercia, Gwynedd and Powys, were at war with each other at the moment. However, Hwicce in the south was constantly being raided by the Welsh of Gwent, which lay across the River Sæfern.

The north of Mercia had been quiet up to now; the Danes in Northumbria hadn't ventured as far as the shire of Cæstir but the influx of the Norsemen had meant that Æðelred's northern border was under threat. If he couldn't regain control of northern Mercia it was likely that his whole realm could collapse. No wonder he was on edge.

'What are you doing to retake Cæstir, perhaps I can help in some small way?' I said in a more conciliatory tone.

He sat down heavily on the stool behind a small table littered with scrolls and regarded me thoughtfully.

'If you haven't brought me men, perhaps you can bring your mind to bear on the problem. You always were an innovative thinker, unlike most of my nobles.'

At that moment the tent flap opened to admit a man dressed in a highly polished silver byrnie and carrying an ornate helmet under his arm. His face was handsome in a slightly effeminate way and the lack of any facial hair added to the impression that he was overly concerned with his appearance. I took an instant dislike to him.

'Ah! This is my Hereræswa, Ealdorman Cynbald of Hwicce. Cynbald, this is Ealdorman Jørren of Cent, your counterpart in Wessex.'

Cynbald gave me a supercilious look and then nodded briefly to acknowledge me.

'Welcome, Lord Jørren,' he said. 'Have you come to offer us the benefit of your wisdom? That must be it because I see you have only brought a few warriors with you.'

It was said with a sneer and my dislike of the man deepened.

'It seems you might need it,' I replied, 'if you think to starve the Norse out. Thankfully we intercepted a fleet of supply ships a few days ago but it is easy for the garrison to be resupplied by water.'

'You intercepted them? I thought that was our ships?' Æðelred interjected.

'I was travelling with them to bolster numbers. When we encountered the enemy I and my other skeid chased the four knarrs, sinking one and capturing two. Meanwhile my two snekkjur engaged three Viking longships and were sunk whilst your three birlinns escorted your own knarrs to safety. I lost a lot of good men and two valuable ships to save your convoy.'

'Oh! That's not what I was told. Where are the two Viking knarrs you seized now?'

'With my two remaining ships moored downstream. I intend to use them to block the river to stop any more Viking fleets reaching Cæstir.'

'Good idea,' Æðelred exclaimed. 'Why didn't you think of that, Cynbald?'

The Mercian hereræswa gave me a venomous look but didn't reply; instead he changed the subject.

'We need to make an assault on the walls, cyning.'

'Cyning? There is no King of Mercia anymore. Does Ælfred know that you have styled yourself king?' I demanded.

'No, it was slip of the tongue, wasn't it, Cynbald,' Æðelred said, glaring at the man.

'Yes, of course, lord,' he replied, licking his lips nervously.

It had been an inadvertent mistake but only because it was made in front of me. It seemed that the Lord of Mercia had royal ambitions. I know that Ælfred would never stand for that. He saw himself as the last of the Anglo-Saxon kings and he would be determined to keep it that way.

'We've had this discussion before. I can't afford to lose the men involved in a straightforward attack on the walls.'

I coughed politely.

'Perhaps I might offer a suggestion?' I said smiling at both men. 'You could make a diversionary attack to draw men away from one of the gates and use a battering ram to gain entry for your main force.'

'That wouldn't work,' Cynbald said contemptuously. 'Rams can only move slowly and they would realise where the main attack was coming from in plenty of time to reinforce the gates.'

'Not if we attacked at night, preferably just before dawn.'

Both men looked at me quizzically. This time Cynbald didn't seem quite so eager to pour scorn on my idea.

'Very well, if there's a good chance we can end the siege now I'm willing to give Lord Jørren's plan my support,' Æðelred said at last. 'It's dangerous for us to remain here for too long. The two of you had better go away and work out the details; meanwhile let's put the boom across the river using those captured knarrs, just in case we have to resort to starving them out after all.'

✝✝✝

We crept close to a place where the old Roman wall had been repaired with timber. The night was clear and moonlight bathed the ground in a ghostly silver colour. I had agreed with Cynbald that my men would spearhead the diversionary attack with some of the Mercian fyrd whilst he led the main body against the gates to the west of the town.

The Vikings had foolishly used torches to light up the top of the wall. All that did was to rob their sentries of their night vision whilst doing little to illuminate the approaches to the wall. It wasn't until we were in the process of placing our scaling ladders against the palisade, which filled the gap between two sections of the stone wall, that the alarm was given.

By the time that reinforcements were pouring onto the walkway behind the palisade I had reached the top of the ladder and thrust my spear into the body of a Norseman who was vainly trying to reach my head with his axe. He fell back and I climbed over the pointed stakes at the top of the timber palisade and jumped down onto the walkway.

I barely had time to register that more of my warriors had joined me from other scaling ladders before I was confronted by two more Norsemen. One was armed with sword and shield and the other with a two-handed battleaxe. The walkway wasn't wide and the axeman would put his companion in as much danger as me if he swung his weapon, so I ignored him for now.

My spear was still embedded in the first man I'd killed but it was useless in close quarter fighting in any case. I swung my shield around from my back and drew my seax as the two men stepped closer. A seax was a better weapon than a sword in close quarter fighting as it was more manoeuvrable in a confined area.

The two Vikings hesitated for an instant and that was their undoing. I ran at them and, by the time that they had brought their weapons into play, I was too close to them for them to strike at me effectively. The axeman thrust the wicked point on top of his axe at my face but I ducked and it went over my head, one of the two axe blades gouging a line into the top of my helmet. The other man thrust his sword at me but I batted it away with my shield. I chopped my seax down onto the swordsman's thigh and he collapsed onto one knee with a howl of agony mixed with rage.

I smashed the rim of my shield down onto his helmet with such force that it knocked him unconscious. With his fellow Norseman out of the way the other man swung his axe down, aiming to cut deep into my right shoulder. It was a sensible move as my shield protected my other side but I was too quick for him. I twisted around just in time and the axe blade chopped through the leather covering and into the lime wood of which my shield was made. My shield had saved me but the force of the blow numbed my whole arm.

The Viking tugged to free his axe but it was too deeply embedded in the wood. I chopped at his side with my seax but his byrnie was well made. My blade severed a few iron links and even cut into the leather jerkin he wore under it but didn't do more than badly bruise the body it protected. However, it must have also driven the air from his lungs because he gasped and for a moment he ceased his attempts to free his axe.

Suddenly he let go of it and dragged a dagger free from the sheath at his waist. I staggered back involuntarily as soon as he ceased to tug at his axe and that saved my life. The point of the dagger whistled past my throat, nicking it enough to draw blood but not enough to do any real damage. The failure of his blade to connect put him off balance and I stepped forward, thrusting the point of my seax into his own throat as I did so. He gurgled and spat blood at me as he fell sideways off the walkway. I heaved the other Norseman, who was still unconscious, out of the way and he followed his companion down into the blackness below the parapet.

I looked around for my next opponent but the rest of the defenders were all engaged in fierce combat with the warriors from my ships who had joined me on top of the wall. The noise of battle was loud but I could just make out the thump of ram against wood as the Mercians attempted to break open the eastern gates. I saw that one of my men was being hard pressed by two Norsemen and so I stabbed one of his opponents in the back. He died before he hit the walkway. His companion was distracted and my man finished him off before nodding his thanks to me. I didn't like stabbing men from behind, even the pagan Norse, but I didn't have time for moral scruples when the lives of my men were at stake.

I looked around for more Vikings to kill but it was all over. We were left in possession of the western side of the wall that encircled Cæstir. We were inside the fortifications whereas, by the sound of the continuing thumps from the other side of the settlement, the Mercians hadn't yet managed to break in. I smiled to myself. Æðelred wouldn't be pleased if we managed to capture Cæstir before him and Cynbald would be even more furious. However, I decided that we ought to go and help the Mercians to break in instead. It was the diplomatic thing to do, but I could tell that my men were not best pleased when I forbade them to start sacking the place. Instead I led them along the walkway towards the eastern gates.

The Mercians finally broke through the gates before we got there but their shouts of triumph and elation changed to ones of fear and anger almost immediately afterwards. Moments later I discovered why as we arrived on the scene. The Norsemen had built a concave palisade inside the gates so that the jubilant Mercians had rushed into a killing zone. The Vikings were hurling axes, spears and rocks down onto the mass of Mercian warriors below them. The latter were trying to retreat to safety outside the walls but those still outside were unaware of the trap. They pressed forward, eager to take part in the looting and pillaging, thus preventing those inside from retreating.

I took in the scene of chaos and carnage below me in a split second and, despite the fact that my two hundred crewmen and warriors were outnumbered by at least two to one by the Norsemen manning the palisade and the outer walls around the killing area, we charged into them.

The walkway was narrow and so only three of us were able to attack the enemy directly. Those behind us could only push at our backs to add to our momentum. We cut down the first few surprised men but then the fighting got tougher as three Vikings formed a shield wall across the walkway. We ground to halt which allowed the rest of the Norsemen on top of the palisade to renew their attack on the Mercians below.

I was in despair when I saw Norsemen further along the curved palisade start to drop. Wolnoth and fifty of my men hadn't followed the rest when we advanced along the palisade and instead had taken the path along the parapet of the old stone wall where it joined the palisade. They had quickly disposed of the thirty or so Norsemen who held it and were now sending volley after volley into the enemy manning the palisade.

The hail of missiles down onto the Mercians ceased and that allowed them to re-organise themselves. They dragged their dead to one side and brought the battering ram up to attack the inner gate. Of course, I could only catch glimpses of what was going on elsewhere as I was engaged with the Vikings defending this end of the palisade.

My two companions and I had managed to kill the first rank of our opponents when the man fighting on my right hand side was killed. Another warrior stepped forward to take his place and I noted with surprise that it was Eafer. He had only become a warrior a few months ago. Before that he had been my body servant and he and I had formed a bond. I worried now that his inexperience in the shield wall would get him killed and so I suppose that I was too busy protecting him to worry about myself.

The last thing I remember is a spear striking me, breaking apart the links of my chainmail byrnie and driving through the leather jerkin underneath. There was a brief moment of intense agony and then oblivion.

✝✝✝

When I awoke all I was conscious of was the searing pain in my chest. I dimly heard someone say that I was awake and I was aware of water being dribbled into my mouth. Then I collapsed back into blissful oblivion again.

The next time I awoke I was still in considerable pain but I was more aware of my surroundings. I was lying on a bed of furs in a room. The ceiling had been painted white at some stage but now it was yellowed and peeling, revealing the brown plaster underneath. I turned my head and felt a sharp stabbing pain so I closed my eyes. When I opened them again I was looking at a wall on which a fresco had been drawn. The scene was badly damaged and had darkened over time but I could see enough to make out that it was a hunting scene with horsemen in tunics and strange looking dogs chasing their quarry. However, it wasn't a stag or a boar but a young girl who was naked.

I knew then that I was in a room in an old Roman villa but I didn't know whether I was dreaming or if this was some surreal reality. I fell asleep again and when I next regained consciousness Uhtric was kneeling by me doing something to my chest which was causing me extreme pain. I tried to push him away but my hand flopped uselessly back to the bed. I was as weak as a new born babe. I tried to tell the boy to stop whatever he was doing but my voice came out as a croak.

'He's awake,' I heard Uhtric call out and then I saw Wolnoth and several others of my gesith peering down at me, their ugly faces split wide open with inane grins.

'What's wrong with me,' I tried to say but I couldn't form the words properly.

'Lie still, lord,' Wolnoth said his face looking concerned now rather than joyful. 'You've been at death's door for the past fortnight. If it wasn't for Uhtric's skill as a healer you'd be six feet underground now.'

Uhtric finished sticking red hot needles into my flesh, or whatever he was doing, and gave me several sips of water. Now my mouth wasn't so dry I tried speaking again.

'What happened?' I croaked.

'A spear broke several ribs but they saved you from greater damage inside your body, lord,' the boy said. 'It took a long time before I managed to clean out all the bits of clothing and chainmail from the wound and by that time you had lost quite a lot of blood. Then the wound became infected and you hovered between this world and the next for days. We bathed you constantly in cold water to bring down your temperature but you remained feverish.

When it eventually broke I knew that you would survive but the loss of blood and your inability to eat has left you very weak.

'I've changed your dressing and applied a fresh poultice of honey. The wound is healing cleanly; no sign of fresh infection, thank the Lord.' Uhtric paused and gave me a severe look. 'Now you need rest and allow yourself to get better. I'll bring you some broth tomorrow and we'll see if you can keep it down.'

Being lectured by a mere boy, and a servant at that, had angered me and, had I been able to, I would have cuffed him about the ears for his impudence; then I realised the reality of my situation. I owed my life to him and it was evident that he had cared for me to the very best of his ability. I shouldn't be angry: I should be eternally grateful and I determined to make sure that he was properly rewarded once I was well again.

'And what of the Norse?' I asked Wolnoth.

'Just after you fell the Mercians broke through the inner gate and killed most of the remaining Vikings. Some got away and, despite Lord Æðelred's orders, several of the inhabitants were killed, raped or had their houses ransacked in the aftermath. He and Cynbald managed to restore order and they hanged six of those caught looting as a warning to others. Æðelred and Cynbald left almost as soon as the gates were repaired and the settlement was defensible against attack.

'He left a garrison of five hundred men here and has appointed a man called Durwyn as Ealdorman of Cæstir. He had taken this place as his hall and had

134

you moved from the camp to this room when the rest of the army left.'

I croaked a thank you but then I noticed that something was still troubling Wolnoth.

'What else? What are you keeping from me?' I managed to ask with some difficulty.

'It's your son, Ywer,' he replied looking extremely uncomfortable.

I wondered what he could mean. I'd left Ywer with the other ships' boys and a guard of ten men at our camp next to our two longships when we'd gone off to attack the walls.

'Someone attacked our camp during the assault on Cæstir,' he said, looking at the ground. 'Three men and four of the boys were killed and several others were wounded before they beat off the attackers but then they noticed that Ywer was missing. We've searched the whole area and found nothing except one of his shoes. It's a relief that his body wasn't discovered but I can only conclude that he's been abducted.'

I was silent for a long time, overcome by grief and worry. I needed to find my son and kill whoever had taken him but I was too weak to do anything. I cursed and raged against fate and my enemies but when I'd calmed down I asked the obvious question.

'Did you manage to capture and question any of the attackers?'

'Several were killed and some were wounded. Unfortunately the attackers managed to carry their wounded away with them. However, the funny thing is that the dead they left behind weren't Vikings; from

135

the way that they were dressed and the coins they carried it seems most likely that they were from Wessex.'

Chapter Eight

CÆSTIR & GWYNEDD

Winter 883/884

It was early December before I was well enough to leave my bed and start to regain some of the weight and muscle I'd lost. I had found the enforced idleness extremely irksome and I fear I took my frustration out on Uhtric. He put up with my tirades against him and my misfortunes with stoical indifference, at least on the surface.

When Wealmær told me that he'd found him crying in a ruined corner of the villa after one of my more vehement outbursts I realised how unfair I was being. I owed the boy more than I could ever repay and my treatment of him was unforgiveable. I swallowed my pride and apologised to him. I was rewarded with a bright smile and his assurance that all that mattered to him was my recovery.

At first all I could manage was a few short walks. My wound punished me every time I was careless and pulled the scar, but gradually my strength returned and the pain caused by movement grew less and less. By the time that the first snow covered the land in a blanket of white I was ready to start training with sword and bow again.

Both the Saint Cuthbert and the Holy Spirit had long since returned to Portcæstre with their crews. All that were left at Cæstir, apart from the Mercian garrison, were ten members of my gesith including my captain, Wealmær, Wolnoth and Eafer. Fortunately they had survived the fight on the walls without a scratch, much to my surprise and delight.

I had instructed Wealmær to send messages to both Hilda and to Ælfred as soon as I was well enough to do so. I informed them about my injury and subsequent recovery and told the king that I had been able to make the offer of the Lady Æthelflaed's hand to Lord Æðelred. I went on to explain that we hadn't been able to discuss the details before I was wounded and he left for the south. It wasn't the complete truth but it was a diplomatic explanation of why I hadn't completed my mission. I didn't tell either of them about my son's abduction. I wanted to find out more first. Of course, I should have realised that the wagging tongues of the crews of the two skeids would broadcast the news as soon as they reached Portcæstre.

Hilda's reply reached me just before Yuletide. She expressed concern at my injury, berated me for putting myself in danger yet again, and blamed me for taking my son with me and for then allowing him to disappear. It didn't improve my mood at the time.

The king's reply, which arrived shortly afterwards, was even less welcome. Whilst congratulating me on helping the Mercians recapture Cæstir, he told me that I had no business in getting involved in Mercian affairs yet again. He reminded me that the last time I had gone off to help Æðelred without his permission I had lost my position as Ealdorman of Berrocscīr. He forgot to mention that this was because everyone thought that I was dead. He made it sound as if my reckless action now had threatened my position as Ealdorman of Cent. It didn't; but he pointed out that a hereræswa who was laid up and who might never be able to take his place on the battlefield again was of no use to him.

He had therefore taken the decision to replace me with Drefan, Ealdorman of Wiltunscīr. I can't say that I was sorry. I found the constant need to chivvy my fellow nobles into spending money on the king's new burhs and to improve the old Roman roads that connected them wearisome. It was a chore I could well do without. Hilda would no doubt be pleased that I would be able to spend most of my time in Cent in future. Then the thought of her fussing over me like a broody hen whilst I convalesced put me in another foul mood. Thankfully the winter storms gave me the perfect excuse to stay at Cæstir until the spring without having to explain about Ywer. By then I hoped to have fully recovered and I could start the hunt for my son.

✝✝✝

Naturally I hadn't been idle over the winter. I paid agents to try and find a trace of my son and I obtained several scraps of information about sightings. Unfortunately they were conflicting and when followed up proved to be false. I even sent men into Danish Mercia but they found nothing. Of course, a nine year old boy could vanish without trace quite easily, especially if he was dead. However, I didn't think he was.

My suspicion that he'd been abducted during our assault on Cæstir was confirmed when the captain of one of the knarrs used to blockade the River Dēvā was brought to see me. The man was clearly nervous and kept wringing his hands.

'Don't be afraid. I shan't harm you if you tell me the truth. I'm told that you might know something about my son's disappearance?'

'Perhaps, lord.'

He hesitated and so I smiled at him encouragingly, much as I wanted to hit him and tell him to get on with it.

'Well, as you know we were one of the two ships forming the boom across the river. We were anchored with a chain between us which we could lower to allow ships to pass. A Saxon ship had arrived at dusk the evening prior to the attack and, although I thought it was strange for Saxons to be bringing supplies, we let it through.'

'Why did you think it strange?' I asked.

'Because the only Saxon ships we'd seen up until then were yours when you escorted us here.'

He hesitated.

'Something else?'

'Yes, it carried over a dozen warriors as well as sailors, which is unusual for a trading ship and it rode too high in the water to be carry anything much in the way of a cargo.'

'Go on.'

'Well, the same ship came back down the river and asked to be allowed through the boom again just after dawn. We could still hear the noise of battle so we didn't think much about it at the time; we just assumed that they were scared and wanted to get away from the fighting.'

'I see, this was before the Norse ships made their escape?'

'Yes, lord. They forced us to let them through. They said they would board us and slay every man if we didn't,' he said apprehensively.

'I understand; you did the right thing or you wouldn't still be alive to tell me about the Saxon knarr. Was there anything else you can tell me about this ship?'

'Yes, lord. That's why I came to your camp when I heard that you were asking about your son. I could see that there was a young boy on the aft deck who was struggling in the grip of one of the warriors. As they passed through the boom the man hit the boy on the head with the pommel of his dagger and the boy collapsed. I just thought the lad might possibly have been your son.....'

His voice trailed away when he saw the anguished expression on my face.

'Thank you. You've been most helpful,' I managed to get out at last.

He was about to leave when I stopped him.

'One last question: why has it taken you until now to come forward with this information?'

'I'm a trader, lord. My ship has only just returned to Cæstir for the winter.'

141

I nodded my understanding and handed him a purse full of silver pennies. The man might have concocted the story to get the reward but I didn't think so. He was too scared of me to lie.

I mulled over who might have taken my son and why. The conclusion I came to was that Eadda was probably behind it, although he wouldn't have dirtied his hands himself. It was just the sort of revenge he would exact for my supposed crime of robbing him of his place as hereræswa, as he saw it. Although I suspected that wasn't his only reason for hating me. It was just as likely to be jealousy of my success in leading Ælfred's army to victory when he had failed to do the same. No doubt he would be elated that I had also been removed, even if it was because of my incapacity and not because I was in disgrace. Why the king had chosen Eadda, a man in whom he had lost faith, to manage his elder son's military education was a mystery to me. No doubt there was some political reason.

I wondered what Eadda would have done with Ywer once he had his hands on him. Doubtless it would be something that would cause me further distress without exposing himself to punishment or having to pay me wergeld. I wracked my brains over what fate he had in store for Ywer but nothing occurred to me. At least I still had one son – Æscwin – although he couldn't be my heir as he'd taken a vow of poverty when he became a monk.

Suddenly I had a flash of inspiration. If Eadda had enrolled him in a monastery as a novice he wouldn't be able to leave. Eventually he would become a monk and I would lose my heir, leaving a clear path for Oswine to inherit as my stepson. It all tied together, knowing how close Eadda and Oswine had become. It was flawed thinking, of course. Oswine's hostility had infuriated me and I had already decided to remove him from my will.

The more I thought about it, the more I thought that dumping Ywer in a monastery was the most likely explanation. Eadda could avoid soiling his hands with murder and, once the boy took his vows, however unwillingly, he was effectively lost to me. The Church wouldn't give him up again, even if I could find him.

If my logic was correct, all I had to do now was find which monastery housed Ywer and rescue him. Unfortunately that wasn't likely to be a simple task. I doubted that he would be lodged in one in Wessex or Anglian Mercia – too close to home. It was more likely to be in Alba, Wealas, Íralond or even on the Continent. The more I thought about it Wealas seemed the most likely. The border was close to where Ywer had been abducted and I suspected that his captor would want to get rid of him as quickly as possible.

The first thing I needed to do was to find out which monasteries lay in the north of Wealas. Unfortunately the man newly consecrated as the Abbot of Cæstir wasn't much help. He had been the prior of Eveshomme in Hwicce, Cynbald's shire, before being chosen to replace the previous abbot, who'd been martyred by the Norse. He knew nothing of the area but he gave his permission for me to talk to his monks.

Thankfully several of them had fled the Norse attack on their small monastery and a few of these had some knowledge of their fellow monks in Gwynedd, even though the latter were of the Celtic branch of Christianity.

'There are many monasteries in Gwynedd, lord,' the oldest of the monks told me when I met him and three of his fellow monks in the hut that served as their refectory. 'Most of them are quite small. I'm sure that they would welcome any new novice and, as almost none speak English and your son doesn't speak their language, he wouldn't be able to tell them who he was.'

I shook my head.

'He speaks some Latin so presumably he could protest.'

The monk nodded and smiled for an instant but then he looked dubious.

'It depends, lord. If the monks were members of the Celtic Church it's true that they are scholars and many speak both Latin and Greek. However, if they are Culdees that's unlikely to be the case.'

'Culdees?' I queried.

'Yes, Culdees means spouses of God. They are an ascetic Christian sect in Alba and Íralond as well as Wealas. They form communities of hermits or anchorites who live in total seclusion from normal society, seeking only sanctity through prayer. Although they are called monks they don't take vows but if your son has been left with them his chances of escaping are remote, especially if he's in one of the communities who live on an island.'

'I see. I hadn't heard of these Culdees before. It does seem the ideal place to hide someone. Where are their monasteries in Gwynedd?'

'They would call them communities rather than monasteries and there are quite a number of them, mostly quite small. However, I'm not sure where they all are.'

'If your son was abducted by boat then perhaps you might start with the ones within easy reach of the sea?' one of the other monks suggested, with a nervous look at the elder one.

When the senior monk nodded his approval the younger one continued.

'There are two on small islands, the rest I know about are in remote spots on the mainland. That doesn't mean that there aren't any on the coast of the mainland, of course. One is on one of two islands named after Saint Tudwal. They lie off the south coast off the Llŷn Peninsula. The other is just beyond the tip of the peninsula and is called Ynys Enlli.'

'Thank you; you've been extremely helpful.'

'We're only too pleased to have been of assistance,' the senior monk replied. 'I'll pray that you find your son safe and well. However, you mustn't harm the Culdees, if indeed they have him. They are holy men.'

I gave the monk a purse of silver and left. I wasn't too sure about not harming the Culdees. If they had treated Ywer badly then I intended to extract an eye for an eye.

†††

I was impatient to leave and rescue my son, if indeed he was on one of the two islands the monk had mentioned. However, it was nearly Yuletide and no one would put to sea at that time of the year. I resigned myself to spending the winter at Legacæstir. I was getting fitter and I could now wield a sword but not with any skill. My chest felt as if it was on fire every time I swung my blade or lunged with it.

Uhtric kept scolding me for trying to do too much too soon and, although I didn't want to admit it, I knew that it was good advice. I had promised to show him my gratitude for saving my life and so I gave him a book called the Lacnunga, a collection of herbal remedies for various ailments and diseases. I had paid the master of the scriptorium to make a special copy for me from the one held in the monastic library.

The infirmarian, who had supervised Uhtric's care of me until he was satisfied that the boy knew what he was doing, told me that he had found many of the treatments to be effective but he cautioned against too much bloodletting, which many of the remedies seemed to rely on to an excessive degree. Much of the book was written in Latin, although most medications suggested for common conditions were in the Mercian dialect of English. I had the monks translate the most useful of those recipes which were in Latin to English as Uhtric had, at best, a

146

rudimentary knowledge of the ancient Roman language.

I also freed him of his duties as my servant so he could concentrate on looking after the health of my men. I would need a replacement for him but having a physician in my household was more important than my comfort; appointing another body servant would have to wait for now.

By taking it easy and building up my strength gradually I found that I was almost fully fit by the end of February. Although the beginning of March was still early for ships to brave the seas because of the continuing likelihood of winter storms, I was too eager to visit the two islands to wait any longer.

If Ywer wasn't there I had no idea where to look next. Perhaps I'd have to torture Eadda to find out? That would no doubt cost me my shire and my vills, if not my life when Ælfred found out, so I prayed that it wouldn't be necessary. Perhaps I was pinning my faith on the Culdean theory too much but I had a strong inkling that we'd find him.

My next problem was finding a ship. I would have given half of the silver I had left in the chest I'd brought with me to have hired a longship but there were none available. There wasn't even a birlinn, so I had to content myself with a knarr. It was risky as we wouldn't be a match for even the smaller snekkja if we encountered one but it was early in the year and we wouldn't be sailing out of sight of land. It was a risk I was prepared to take. However, none of the knarr captains I approached were willing to take the same gamble. They only traversed the Íralandes Sæ in convoy.

Eventually I thought of the captain who had told me that he had seen my son being abducted on a birlinn. His knarr was still ashore having her bottom scraped clean of weed and her hull re-caulked. When I promised him a hundred shillings to take me to the two islands he reluctantly agreed. Three days later the knarr was back in the water and we were ready to leave.

It was only then that I realised that we had no one who could speak the particular dialect of the Brythonic tongue spoken in Wealas. I ground my teeth in frustration and sent my men into the settlement to find someone who could translate. Cæstir's proximity to Gwynedd meant that there were several who had originally come from Wealas; however none were prepared to risk travelling along the Llŷn Peninsula. I suspected that most of them were fugitives in some way; either from justice or from a family feud.

Eventually Eafer came back with an urchin who could speak both languages proficiently. At first I was reminded of how I'd first met Uhtric and his brother but then I realised that this was no boy. She was dressed in a loose tunic which concealed her breasts and her hair had been cut like a boy's but something about the way she stood and looked at me gave her gender away. She wasn't that old, probably thirteen or fourteen. I was impatient to set off and, as she was the only one we'd found so far who willing to come with us, I reluctantly agreed to take her.

After a bath and now dressed in a clean linen shift and a simple woollen outer dress called a peplos the girl, whose name was Othilia, looked quite different. The grime and the filthy homespun clothes had concealed a very pretty young woman. Eafer wasn't the only one giving her lustful looks. I groaned and hoped that she wouldn't prove to be trouble.

✝✝✝

The captain was worried about running into a storm, and with good reason. I had intended to land on Ynys Enlli first but when we got there the wind coming from the north-west was so strong we were forced to stand well out to sea or risk being driven onto the shore. We made for the other island which lay in the lee of the Llŷn Peninsula instead.

Once in calmer waters we let out the reefs in the sail and, as we rounded the southern tip of the peninsula, the islands of Saint Tudwal hove into view. As the monk had told me, there were two islands; the higher one to the west appeared to be uninhabited but I could see several strange looking beehive shapes on the western island. As we approached we saw people rushing towards the north-west corner of the island. At first I thought that there was nowhere to land as the island was surrounded by cliffs and rocks but, as we circumnavigated it, we found a small cove where the monks had congregated.

There was a wooden landing stage in the cove where two fishing boats were moored. From there steep steps led up to the top of the cliff. The monks were gesticulating at us, clearly indicating that we weren't welcome. I would have liked to have landed and questioned them but there wasn't room in the cove for the knarr and I realised that, if we couldn't land, then neither could a birlinn.

Of course, they could have used one of the fishing boats to ferry Ywer ashore but I doubted it. The monks would doubtless have reacted as angrily to the birlinn as they had to our arrival. Furthermore I couldn't see anyone ashore as young as my son. In fact there were no boys at all. We turned around, re-trimmed the sail and headed back towards Ynys Enlli. My heart was heavy; the other island was now my only hope of finding my son quickly.

The gale was still blowing as we beached the knarr in the middle of the long sandy shoreline which ran the length of the bay at the southern end of the peninsula. The area appeared to be deserted but nevertheless I put out guards as soon as it got dark.

The next morning the wind was as strong as ever and so I resigned myself to spending another day there. I sent Eomær and Eafer out with Wolnoth to see if they could find a hare or some other type of game to supplement the dried fish, bread and cheese we had brought with us. They came back at around noon with a small deer. Venison should hang for some time to allow the flavour to develop and for it to become tender. However, even tough venison is a welcome change after eating dried fish.

The next morning the wind had died down to stiff breeze and we sailed westwards propelled by the wind from the north-east. The waves grew larger and the wind stronger as we entered the channel between the end of the peninsula and Ynys Enlli.

'We'll never be able to land on the island in this weather,' the captain shouted in my ear above the sound of the wind and the crashing of the prow as it hit each wave.

'We might as well go around the island and find the best landing place as we're here,' I replied, trying to keep my disappointment to myself.

He shrugged and told the sailors to take in a reef as we ploughed further into the open water of the Íralandes Sæ. I had hoped to find a sandy beach, or at least one of shingle, where we could beach the ship once the weather improved but Ynys Enlli was enclosed by steep cliffs for the most part. Where the land did come down to meet the sea there were jagged rocks which would prevent us from reaching the shore. Even if there was the odd gap into which we could sail, there was the probability of danger lurking just under the surface. It wasn't a risk the captain was prepared to take and I didn't blame him.

I had nearly given up hope of finding anywhere when I spotted three small fishing boats pulled up high onto the shingle at the head of a narrow inlet. However, I could see white water breaking in several places as the waves rolled in and out of the inlet. They disclosed the presence of a reef just under the water. Doubtless the monks knew where the rocks were but we didn't and our ship was much larger than their small craft.

I had just about given up as we headed back to where we had spent the previous night when I spotted several figures standing up to their waists in water some distance from the shore. They were trying to spear fish and as I watched, one of them pulled a wooden trident out of the sea with something silver wriggling on the barbed points. When they saw our knarr they quickly waded ashore and stood on the shingle beach gesticulating furiously at us.

There were rocks between where they had been fishing and the shore, which would prevent us beaching our ship. However, it looked as if we might be able to get close enough with our shallow draft to allow us to slip over the side and wade ashore. After all, if the birlinn had come here, this was the only place that they could have put Ywer ashore. The captain was reluctant to venture further inshore at first but my offer to double the fee I was paying him persuaded him that the risk was worth it.

I lowered myself over the side and found myself waist deep in water but then the swell reached my chest before the wave retreated and I was merely knee deep in the water. The sea was bitterly cold but I did my best to ignore my chattering teeth. The ship's keel ground on the shingle under the water and the captain ordered his sailors to row back into deeper water. By then I had been joined by Wolnoth, Eomær and the girl, Othilia, but the rest of my men had to stay on board as the water was now too deep to disembark. I heard Wealmær arguing with the captain but the man refused to go any closer in.

'Stay there until we return,' I called across the water and Wealmær nodded.

As we waded ashore I heard the splash as the stone anchor was thrown overboard. Facing us were the monks who had been fishing and now several more joined them. They were dressed in simple woollen tunics tied at the waist with lengths of rope. The only sign that they were monks was the wooden cross they all wore suspended by a leather thong around their necks. The one who appeared to be their leader shouted something and I asked Othilia what he'd said.

'He wants to know what you are doing here?' she replied. 'This is holy land; only monks may walk upon its soil.'

'Tell him that I will stay with my feet in the sea if he tells me what I want to know,' I told her holding my hands clear of my body to show that I wasn't holding any weapons.

'He says that they are anchorites who live simple lives of meditation and prayer. They can't help you. They know nothing of the world.'

'Inform him that my nine-year-old son was abducted and I have reason to believe that he was brought here to be a novice.'

'He says that, if he was, then here he must remain. They serve God and none of them will ever return to the sinful world,' she translated.

'Then he is here?' I asked, my hopes rising.

She asked the monk something but he shook his head.

'Ask him if a nine year old boy came here in late September or early October.'

'He says they can't help you; he said that we're to go back whence we came.'

The monk who acted as their spokesmen had spoken firmly but I noticed that one or two of his companions were whispering urgently to each other.

'I think that he's lying,' I told Othilia. 'Ask him to swear before God that no boy was brought to the island six months ago.'

When she had translated this the monk looked uncomfortable but he still shook his head. He shouted something and I asked her what he'd said.

'Go back to your ship and sail away. There's nothing here for you.'

'Tell him to swear in the name of God the Father and of Jesus Christ that my son was not brought here and I'll go.'

The man hung his head for an instant, then raised it and called out something defiantly.

'He admits that a boy was brought here a few months ago but he is now a Culdee,' she said. 'Having joined their community he cannot leave it.'

My hand went to the hilt of my sword but Wolnoth put his hand on my arm.

'Lord, these are holy men. We cannot offer them violence, it would be a terrible sin.'

I looked at him and Eomær. I could see that they were in awe of these monks and, loyal as they were to me, they were superstitious men and believed that to harm these saintly men would mean spending eternity in the fires of hell.

'Very well, but I'm not leaving here without Ywer. Stay here.'

I started to wade the rest of the way ashore and the monks retreated. I would scour the whole island if I had to and, now I was certain Ywer was here, I would take him by force if necessary.

'Father!'

The cry from above startled me. I looked up and saw a boy standing on top of the cliff to the left of the narrow shingle beach.

'Ywer! Thank the Lord that you're safe. Can you come down?'

Just then two monks appeared behind him and he looked anxiously at them and then at the sheer drop below where he was standing. The two monks were yelling at him and in a second or two they would have grabbed hold of him. With one final desperate look behind him he turned and jumped.

The sea below the cliff was littered with jagged rocks but God must have been watching over him. He hit clear water between the rocks and disappeared below the surface. I turned and started to wade back to the knarr. Wealmær had seen what had happened and was already shouting for the crew to pull up the anchor and man the oars.

I watched as the ship headed for the spot where Ywer had disappeared below the waves hoping to see his head bob up but there was no sign of him, just the waves crashing against the rocks.

The captain had grabbed Wealmær's arm and was remonstrating with him but the latter was having none of it. Wealmær pulled out his seax and held it to the captain's throat. The rowers edged the ship carefully between the rocks but it seemed to me that my son must have already drowned. I had all but given up hope when his head broke the surface and he trod water. He was too far away for me to see but I imagined him drawing in great lungfuls of air and spitting out seawater.

I thanked God with all my heart that he had survived that crazy leap from a height of at least a hundred feet. Thankfully he had had the sense to enter the water feet first with his arms by his side. The water was deep at that point but he told me later that, even so, his plummeting body had still reached the bottom before he could strike out for the surface.

I'd insisted that he learned to swim before our voyage but his skill was rudimentary to say the least. Every stroke he made forward was negated by the sea washing him back again. The ship hove to a safe distance from the rocks and I saw Eafer, stripped to his braies, dive into the sea with a rope tied to his waist. He was a fair swimmer and the tide helped him. Ywer disappeared under the surface again as a larger than normal wave washed over him but he came back up spluttering. Then Eafer reached him and grabbed him around the chest. A few minutes later the two had been pulled back aboard the ship.

The curses of the Culdees followed us as we sailed back to Cæstir but I couldn't have cared less. My son was safe, although – as I was about to discover – he wasn't unscarred.

Chapter Nine

MERCIA & WESSEX

Spring / Summer 884

Now that I'd found Ywer I was anxious to return home as soon as possible. Initially I had thought of hiring horses but the way through Mercia could be parlous for a small group such as ours. The Welsh were raiding western Mercia and the only road further east lay close to the part of old Mercia that was now termed the Danelaw. Despite the threat of Viking pirates in the Íralandes Sǽ buying places on a knarr travelling south in convoy seemed the safest way to travel.

There was another reason why we couldn't travel overland. Ywer wouldn't be able to ride. His experience on Ynys Enlli had been far from a pleasant one. The monks had thought him simple because he didn't understand what he was told to do, so they beat him. Perhaps they thought he was being deliberately obtuse. My son had spirit and he fought back. Of course, that just made the beatings worse. When Uhtric examined him he found scars and two broken bones - one in his left leg and one in his left foot. Both had mended badly.

'Your son will limp for the rest of his life unless I break the bones again and reset them,' Uhtric had said.

I explained this to Ywer and he refused at first, anticipating the pain that was to come, but eventually he accepted that it was the only way forward if he was to become a warrior. Uhtric gave him something to make him sleep whilst he broke his left fibula and one of his metatarsals. He set the fibula first and splinted it to hold it in place whilst the two parts joined together, then broke the outer metatarsal which had set crookedly. He bound it up and insisted that Ywer stay in bed with his foot in a brace until it had mended.

Ywer found being immobilised frustrating, to put it mildly. It was thanks to Othilia that he stayed put. She asked him to teach her to read and write and the two of them could be found with their heads together, often laughing at something or other, whenever Ywer was awake. I found her devotion to my son poignant. There was nothing sexual about their relationship - after all Ywer wouldn't be ten for another six months. It was more like the relationship between brother and elder sister.

It was late March before the first convoy arrived and then we had to wait until all the knarrs had been unloaded and had taken on new cargoes, mainly leather goods, bales of wool and urns full of mead produced by the monks over the winter. Whilst we waited I pondered what to do with Othilia. I should really have let her go back to the streets where she'd come from but I felt a sense of obligation to her for her care of Ywer.

My son's bones hadn't fully mended when he was carried onto the knarr on a stretcher and he wouldn't be parted from Othilia. I found, much to my surprise, that I was pleased that she was coming with us. However, the lecherous looks she attracted from some of the sailors worried me. Her hair had grown and the peplos she wore did little to hide her slim figure. If I'd been worried for her safety on the short journey around the Llŷn Peninsula, the long voyage back to Hamwic, the nearest trading port to Wintanceaster, would be much more dangerous for her.

At first the sailors gave her a wide berth. Although I was well aware that some of my warriors had had lecherous thoughts initially, Othilia's care of Ywer had earned her a place in our small band and they became protective of her instead. Although they had warned the sailors off, one of them still tried to force himself on her in the middle of the night.

For most of its length the coast of Wealas was a dangerous place to go ashore. Either the shoreline was rocky or, where there was a beach, the Welsh lived close by. Consequently the convoy normally spent the hours of darkness anchored in a sheltered bay. My warriors, the crew and I slept on deck but the captain had erected an oiled wool awning in the bows to give Othilia some privacy. She shared this space with Ywer on his stretcher.

Although a stretch of water separated us from the shore, the Welsh had been known to paddle out in their strange craft made of leather stretched over a wicker frame and attack anchored ships. Therefore each knarr kept men on watch throughout the night.

On the third night one of the knarr's crew was on watch with Rinan. The sailor told him that he needed to piss and disappeared towards the bows. Shortly afterwards there was a scuffle from that direction. Rinan went to investigate and found Ywer unconscious and the sailor dead. Othilia had a small dagger in her hand which she waved threateningly at Rinan when he appeared inside the makeshift shelter. He held up his hands and said who he was. The girl dropped the dagger and started to wail, clutching Ywer to her breast, thinking he was dead.

I arrived a minute or so later followed by the captain, my men and several curious sailors. I told Rinan to keep the rest away whilst the captain and I found out what had happened. The captain was angry that one of his sailors had been killed but he was nowhere near as furious as I was. Thankfully Ywer suffered no more than a splitting headache but he could so easily have been killed.

I criticized the captain for not controlling his men better. He responded by blaming Othilia for being on board. He maintained that her presence was too much of a temptation and had ended up costing him one of his most experienced crewmen. He went on to demand that she be put ashore then and there but I wouldn't hear of it. Much to my surprise I realised that I wanted her to stay, not so much to look after Ywer but because I couldn't bear the thought of being parted from her. I wouldn't admit it to myself then but I'd fallen in love with her.

If I'd been honest I would have admitted to myself that a gulf had grown between Hilda and me. We were no longer in love the way we had been. As it was, I tried to deny my feelings for the girl and clung to the belief that my relationship with Hilda would grow strong again once I returned home. I was fooling myself but it was what I wanted to believe.

I had paid the captain to take me all the way to Hamwic but when we docked at Glowecestre he refused to take us any further. I forced him to pay me back half of the silver I'd paid for our passage and decided that we would either have to find another ship or travel overland. That would mean buying horses and a cart for Ywer to travel in, something I was loathe to do. It would be expensive and less comfortable for my son. However, as I was here, I decided to go and see Æðelred first. I had no idea what had happened about his betrothal and, if it hadn't already been arranged by another, I might be able to complete my original mission and thus placate Ælfred.

†††

'Tell me if I have understood the proposal correctly,' Æðelred thundered. 'Ælfred wants me to marry a child and in return he'll allow me to take back Lundenwic? Furthermore he expects me to become his vassal! Is that his idea of a joke?'

I shifted uncomfortably from one foot to the other.

'That's about the size of it, Lord Æðelred,' I confirmed. 'He believes, quite correctly in my view, that this would be the first step in recovering that part of Mercia which is now within the Danelaw.

Only by uniting the forces of Mercia and Wessex can we do that.'

'Be that as it may, I am not about to bend the knee to Wessex. It's unacceptable to me, as it would be to every Mercian noble.'

I wasn't surprised. Æðelred's position as Lord of Mercia was precarious. He wasn't related to the old royal house and so he depended on the support of his nobles for his position as their leader. I didn't envy him. Wessex and Mercia had been enemies for centuries and few would countenance subjugation to Ælfred, despite Mercia's perilous situation.

Cynbald had stood silently during our conversation, staring at me all the while as if I had brought something disgusting into the hall on my shoes. Now he broke eye contact with me and whispered something in Æðelred's ear.

'If King Ælfred will give us his army to help me take Lundenwic, then I will accept the betrothal. However, I will only agree to a mutually beneficial alliance between two equal partners. There can be no suggestion that Mercia is in some way inferior to Wessex.'

I tried to negotiate better terms but Æðelred wouldn't give an inch.

'Very well, Lord Æðelred; I'll convey your reply to my king.'

I inclined my head slightly and left the chamber. I was lost in thought, wondering how Ælfred would react and so I didn't notice the two men pacing up and down in the outer room until one of them hailed me. I looked round and was surprised to see Cissa and Hyrpa. The latter was one of the priests that Ælfred liked to surround himself with. He was a close confidant of Bishop Asser and so no friend of mine. Cissa was the Ealdorman of Berrocscīr and we could hardly be called friends.

I had been the ealdorman before him but I was taken prisoner in Mercia by the Danes whilst on a mission to see Burghred, the last King of Mercia. I had escaped with Æðelred's help but I had to lie low for a while before I could return to Wessex. In the meantime Ælfred was told that I was dead and he had appointed Cissa to replace me. Inevitably our relationship after that had been awkward. However, once I'd been given Cent I no longer harboured a grudge but I got the impression that Cissa was still wary of me.

'Cissa, Hyrpa? This is a surprise. What brings you to Glowecestre?'

'The same mission that you were given last year and so signally failed to accomplish,' the priest replied nastily.

'I wasn't speaking to you, priest. You forget yourself. Be silent in the presence of nobles unless your opinion is asked for.'

Hyrpa glowered at me and was about to say something further but Cissa put a warning hand on his arm and he subsided.

'You seem to make enemies wherever you go, Lord Jørren,' Cissa said with a wry smile. 'But what Father Hyrpa says is correct. We have come to negotiate the betrothal of the Lady Æthelflaed to Lord Æðelred.'

'Then I fear that you have had a wasted journey. I sustained an injury during the capture of Cæstir which delayed matters but I have just finished negotiating the betrothal with Æðelred.'

'I see,' Cissa said thoughtfully.

'It doesn't matter,' Hyrpa insisted. 'The king has replaced this man with us. We must be the ones to agree the terms of the Lady Æthelflaed's matrimony.'

'Don't be an idiot,' Cissa snapped. 'What do you think the Mercians would make of a second embassy from Wessex when the betrothal has already been agreed?'

I didn't like to point out that the terms fell a long way short of what the king was expecting and I was by no means certain that he would agree to them. However, if I told Cissa about the arrangement that Æðelred had offered there was a real danger that he might try and renegotiate. I couldn't see that going down very well at all and Æðelred could well renege on the betrothal. If that happened Cissa and I would end up in disgrace. So I kept quiet.

Cissa paced up and down for a moment or so and then appeared to reach a decision.

'Look, Jørren. I'll look a fool if I return having not even seen the Lord of the Mercians. I suggest that we return and report to the king together. What do you say?'

I saw no reason not to accept, apart from having to endure Hyrpa's obnoxious company, so I agreed. As Cissa had come here on one of the longships out of Portcæstre, travelling with him would save me the expense of hiring a knarr.

164

Ywer was still bed-bound whilst his bones set and so my group sailed on the smaller snekkje that had escorted Cissa's ship, the Holy Spirit. It suited me. I wouldn't have to endure Hyrpa's snide comments, nor would I have to explain Othilia's presence to him and to Cissa.

The voyage back to Portcæstre was uneventful. There was a shortage of horses to convey both groups up to Wintanceaster and, in any case, Ywer couldn't have ridden. Uhtric proclaimed himself pleased with the way that the bones had knitted together but he wanted to give it another week before he took the splints off. He said that the muscles of Ywer's leg would have wasted away in any case and it would take time and careful exercise before he was fully fit again. I left the three of them in Portcæstre together with most of my men. Only Wealmær, Eomær and Rinan accompanied me. I charged my men, and Wolnoth and Eafer in particular, with looking after Othilia.

As we took the road north the fine weather we had enjoyed since leaving Cæstir came to an abrupt end and it started to drizzle. I was already apprehensive about my audience with the king and the rain just added to my depression.

✝✝✝

As luck would have it Eadda was the first person I encountered as Cissa and I entered the outer chamber of the main hall. Cissa looked at me curiously when I asked him to give me a moment but nevertheless he went and waited by the central hearth, rubbing his hands to get some warmth back into them after our ride from Portcæstre.

Eadda looked at me warily as I put a hand on his shoulder and guided him out of earshot of the others waiting for an audience with the king.

'I'm glad I've seen you, Eadda. I have a message for you.'

'A message?' he queried, looking puzzled.

'Yes, it's from the Abbot of Ynys Enlli. He says that unfortunately he wasn't able to house the new novice any longer and he has now returned him whence he came.'

If I had any doubts about Eadda's involvement in the plot to kidnap my son they disappeared at that moment. He swallowed nervously and looked extremely uncomfortable.

'What's that got to do with me?' he tried to bluster.

'Oh, don't think I don't know who sent men to abduct Ywer. If I were you I would sleep with one eye open and watch my back from now on.'

'Are you threatening me?'

'Oh yes, most definitely. I will not rest until your corpse is dead and buried.'

At the time I said it I merely wanted to put him in fear of his life. I'm no assassin and, much as I wanted to, I didn't propose to actually kill him. Of course, later events forced me to change my mind.

Feeling very much happier I re-joined Cissa, leaving Eadda spluttering and cursing. Even the prospect of an uncomfortable interview with Ælfred couldn't dampen my cheerfulness. However, when

Oswine appeared to summon the next group to enter the audience chamber my good humour vanished. Eadda caught the boy's eye and nodded over towards me. Oswine followed his gaze and scowled. I may have got Ywer back but it seemed that Oswine was lost to me forever.

On the way from Portcæstre I had explained the nature of Æðelred's terms for the betrothal to Cissa. At first he was angry and berated me for not allowing him to try and change them. However, I managed to convince him that what the Lord of the Mercians had offered was better than no betrothal at all. Nevertheless, we were both wary of Ælfred's reaction.

I was relieved to see that the king was alone, apart from the usual guards and a couple of priests. Thankfully Hyrpa had taken the coward's way out and disassociated himself from the agreement, disappearing into the church to pray as soon as we entered Wintanceaster.

'Cyning, we're happy to report that Lord Æðelred is most eager to become betrothed to the Lady Æthelflaed,' I began, surprising even myself at how easily the lie tripped off my tongue.

'You saw him together?' Ælfred said, looking surprised.

'It was good fortune and God's will that we arrived at Glowecestre at the same time,' Cissa said disingenuously.

'Go on.'

'However, the Lord of the Mercians has asked for certain changes to the agreement you propose, cyning,' I said, swallowing a little nervously. 'Instead of becoming your vassal he proposes an alliance between you.'

'An alliance of equals, cyning,' Cissa added unhelpfully.

'Equals? How can we be equals? I'm the anointed King of Wessex and he's a mere ealdorman,' Ælfred burst out.

'No, you misunderstand cyning,' I intervened hastily, glaring at Cissa. 'He is proposing an alliance between Mercia and Wessex to our mutual benefit.'

'The Mercian Witenaġemot would never agree to subjugation by Wessex,' Cissa added by way of explanation.

I groaned, expecting this to add fuel to the fire but Ælfred nodded thoughtfully.

'Yes, I can understand that. Perhaps I was asking too much too soon. Very well, but he'd better understand that he is very much the junior partner. For public consumption we can say it is an alliance but he must privately accept my leadership as bretwalda.'

I nodded. I had a feeling that Æðelred would be able to accept that.

'What of Lundenwic? It's important that it is returned to Mercian hands to prevent the Danes from using the Temes as a route into the heart of Wessex.'

'As it also leads into the soft underbelly of Anglian Mercia he accepts that it must be retaken, cyning, but he proposes a joint attack to minimise casualties.'

Ælfred sucked his teeth at that.

'My intention was merely to concede that it is Mercian, not part of ancient Ēast Seaxna Rīce and therefore part of Wessex. Is that not enough?'

I assumed that the question was rhetorical and didn't reply. Thankfully Cissa also held his tongue.

'Very well. You may raise the fyrds of Cent and Berrocscīr to aid him.'

It wasn't at all what I was hoping for. Æðelred expected the army of Wessex to aid him, not just the fyrd of a few shires.

'But cyning,' I objected. 'Can we not also rely on help from Sūþrīgescīr and Suth-Seaxe at least? After all I will need to march through Sūþrīgescīr to reach the crossing over the Temes at Stanes and Suth-Seaxe is nearer to Lundenwic than either of our two shires.'

'Very well, you may ask for their help but I will not force them to aid you. You're the ones who promised the Mercians help, not me.'

'Who will command the forces of Wessex, cyning,' Cissa asked.

I had expected to be put in command as the more experienced of the two of us but Ælfred surprised us by nominating Drefan, the hereræswa and Ealdorman of Wiltunscīr. Neither his own shire nor the army of Wessex were involved; it was almost as if he didn't trust me and, much as I liked and respected Drefan, it seemed like a slap in the face.

†††

Both Cissa and I were due to leave Wintanceaster the next day and so the king threw a banquet that evening to thank us for arranging his daughter's betrothal. As a feast it was somewhat muted. I noted that Ælfred ate nothing apart from some vegetable broth and the rest of us were served fairly ordinary food.

Rumours continued to circulate about his poor health but no one knew exactly what he was suffering from. I hoped that he would live many years yet because Edward was still a child and I could see trouble brewing over the succession. Æthelhelm, the elder of Ælfred's two nephews, wasn't interested in the throne but his younger brother, Æthelwold, had never made a secret of the fact that he felt that he had more right to wear the crown than his uncle. He would never stand idly by and let Edward succeed, whatever his age.

If the kingdom was contested between Edward's supporters and those of Æthelhelm, the Danes could invade again and this time they would defeat the divided kingdom with ease. Of course that wasn't my only worry. Edward had made it clear he detested me for some reason and if he became king I worried about my prospects. Thankfully, despite his poor health, for the moment Ælfred ruled with an iron hand and a great deal of guile.

I was glad that I had the opportunity to speak to Cuthfleda before the feast. As I'd hoped, she and the Lady Æthelflaed had become close. That hadn't endeared her to the other ladies assigned to be companions to the king's daughter but that didn't bother her overmuch. She described them as a load of brainless sheep, much given to gossip and only interested in making eyes at every eligible man at court in the hope of securing a good marriage.

The king retired to his bed early and I was about to do the same when Oswine sought me out.

'Will you return to Dofras overland?' he asked me without preamble.

'To Dofras? No, I've asked Bjarne if I can return by sea. He's lending me a snekkja. Why?'

My stepson chewed his lower lip nervously and glanced around him to make sure we weren't being watched.

'That's what I suspected. Be careful on the way to Portcæstre.'

I pressed him for more information. It was obvious that he knew of some plot but he wouldn't say more and left hurriedly without saying goodbye. I thought it all very odd but the message was clear. Danger lurked along the way.

Another surprise awaited me as we mounted ready to depart. A page came running to find me saying that a messenger had arrived from my wife. I dismounted and followed the boy to where Lyndon was waiting. He was one of my gesith but he'd returned to Dofras with the fleet after the fall of Cæster and my injury.

'Lord, the Lady Hilda sent me,' he said handing me a letter. 'It's good to see you fully recovered,' he added with a smile. 'We were all worried about you.'

I smiled back. Lyndon had been one of my warband for the past decade and a half. He'd first joined me aged twelve and a trainee scout and he'd served me loyally ever since. Instead of breaking the seal and opening the letter I asked him what it said.

'Since you left, lord, Jerrik has married and Cei has become betrothed. The Lady Hilda felt that she should concede her place as the mistress of the fortress to Jerrik's bride and allow the couple to move into the chambers that you and your family used to occupy. Cei plans to move from the warriors' hall into the accommodation vacated by Jerrik and the Lady Hilda and your children have moved back to your hall at Cantwareburh.'

He said all of this in something of a rush as if the news would come as less of a shock to me if imparted quickly. In fact I wasn't surprised. I should have moved out of Dofras when I ceased to be the Sæ Hereræswa. However, I always preferred the fortress overlooking the Sūð-sæ to the ealdorman's hall above Cantwareburh. It was too exposed to attack, being a mere six miles from the entrance to the estuary of the River Temes. Furthermore, I knew that the hall held too many memories of her unhappy first marriage for Hilda.

I could have stuck to my original plan and sailed to Dofras before riding inland to Cantwareburh but I changed my mind and decided to travel all the way by road instead. If I travelled via Cicæstre where Heardwig, the Ealdorman of Suth-Seaxe, was based and then north to Guilforde to meet Dudda of Sūþrīgescīr, I could hopefully enlist their aid for the attack on Lundenwic.

I know that strictly speaking that was Drefan's role as hereræswa but I felt that the requests would come better from me. Heardwig was a Jute like me and I knew Dudda well. Both shires neighboured Cent and we had cooperated in the past. There was another reason I decided to make the approach myself. Drefan was a West Saxon and Wessex had conquered the smaller eastern kingdoms less than fifty years ago. Consequently we still tended to look on them with a certain degree of suspicion.

Furthermore, I only had three of my warriors with me and so it would have been foolhardy to have ridden the twenty five miles to Portcæstre with such a small escort knowing that we were likely to be ambushed. Of course, Ywer, Othilia and the rest of my men were still at Portcæstre so I sent Lyndon to tell them to meet me at Cicæster. They could sail there as it was at the head of a sea inlet.

It took the four of us less than a day to reach Heardwig' hall and he made us very welcome. He was an old man now but his son, also called Heardwig but with the sobriquet Geonga, meaning young. The ealdorman was cautious when I asked for his aid to capture Lundenwic but his son was eager. Suth-Seaxe had a long shoreline and, although there had been no major incursions for some time, occasionally Vikings raided the coastal settlements. Usually no more than one or two longships were involved and they were gone before Heardwig' warriors could confront them. Therefore Heardwig Geonga saw a major conflict as a chance to earn glory as well as a decent amount of plunder.

In the end the ealdorman agreed that his son could lead as many thegns and hearth warriors as he could get to volunteer. It was less than I was hoping for but it was better than nothing.

A few hours after dawn the Saint Cuthbert arrived with my other warriors on board. I was pleased to see that Uhtric had removed my son's splints and Ywer was now able to walk with the aid of a crutch.

I greeted everyone and introduced Ywer to Heardwig and his son. I noticed that my eyes weren't the only pair to dwell on Othilia; Heardwig Geonga seemed captivated and stared at her until reproved quietly by his father.

'Can my son ride?' I asked Uhtric dubiously.

'No, lord. He needs to build up the muscles in his left leg before he can control a horse properly. Besides I'm a poor rider and Othilia has never ridden before.'

I groaned inwardly. I had hoped to reach Guilforde, a distance of some fifty miles away, in one day. If we had to travel at the pace of a wagon it would take twice as long at the very least. However, there was nothing for it.

We had barely set out when Lyndon came up to ride alongside me.

'Lord, you should know that there were men waiting in ambush a few miles west of Portcæstre,' he said quietly.

I hadn't said anything to warn him as I was confident that Eadda's men wouldn't interfere with normal travellers. It was me they wanted. Of course, Lyndon had been a scout as a boy and he knew what to look out for. The ambushers may have been hidden but they didn't escape his notice. It confirmed the warning that Oswine had given me and I bemoaned our estrangement. I needed to do something to win back his affection but that would have to wait.

We reached Guilforde without incident and I received a rather better reaction from Dudda. Lundenwic lay across the Tames from Sudwerca, which was Sūþrīgescīr's major port. He suffered from the Danes, who not only launched minor raids across the river into his shire, but also from the forced diversion of merchant shipping heading for Sudwerca to the wharfs on the north bank.

'I will gladly help you if you can promise me that the Mercians won't interfere with trade once Lundenwic is in Æðelred's hands.'

I had no authority to promise any such thing but I didn't think that the Lord of the Mercians would want to alienate Ælfred by attacking knarrs heading for Sudwerca; so I gave him my word. He promised me three hundred warriors, which was more or less the same number that the thegns of Cent and I could raise without calling out the fyrd. I only wanted trained warriors for this campaign. What I'd failed to remember was that I wouldn't be leading it and so it wasn't my decision to make.

Chapter Ten

WESSEX

Autumn 884

My return to my family wasn't as joyous an occasion as I'd anticipated. Hilda was delighted by our safe return but her mood changed when she saw Othilia. She glanced between the two of us, trying to work out our relationship. Perhaps the warmth of my voice when I introduced Othilia as Ywer's nurse may have given her an inkling as to my feelings.

My son had exercised every morning and evening during the journey and he was able to walk without the crutch now, albeit with a slight limp. Uhtric was pleased at how well the bones had knitted back together and, after he had measured both legs, he told me that Ywer should be able to walk and run without a problem once the muscles were back to normal.

I trusted Uhtric's judgement implicitly but Hilda insisted on taking Ywer down to see the infirmarian in the monastery and, as it was good excuse to see Ywer's elder brother, Æscwin, I decided to accompany her. In any case I was duty bound to pay my respects to the archbishop now that I was back. However, none of that was at the forefront of my mind at the moment.

I had left my eldest brother, also called Æscwin, in charge of Cent in my absence. He was the shire reeve as well as Thegn of Cilleham, the vill where I was born. However, he had fallen ill during the winter and, according to the last message Hilda had received, he was still bed-ridden. I therefore intended to ride over to see him as soon as my business in Cantwareburh was finished.

My son Æscwin was now thirteen and, although he would still be a novice for another year, he had become the herbalist's assistant; an unusual honour for one so young. Uhtric asked to come with me so that he could see Leofwine, who was hoping to follow in his brother's footsteps and become a physician. I had sent him to the monastery, not as a novice, but to the school that the monks ran. In addition to helping the infirmarian I wanted him to improve his rudimentary skills at reading and writing in addition to learning Latin and Greek.

Uhtric had already become invaluable as a healer but I wanted to enrol him as well so he could learn the same skills. Once both boys were trained as physicians my intention was to keep one with my warband and to send the other to Dofras to look after the men who manned our longships.

'What are you going to do with Ywer's little nurse now that he's better,' Hilda asked snidely as we rode down to the settlement which lay below my hall.

'I'm not sure. Obviously I can't just abandon her after all she has done to nurse Ywer back to health. Do you have any ideas?' I asked amiably.

Hilda grunted and stared at me. Her displeasure was palpable but I was determined not to argue with her. If I allowed Othilia's fate to become a bone of contention between us I knew that I would have to send her away.

'She could join the nuns,' my wife suggested with an edge of malice.

'She's not religiously inclined; besides she and Uhtric make a good team. Perhaps we should keep her to nurse the sick and injured?'

'Very well, but she must marry Uhtric in that case.'

The boy had just turned fifteen. It was unusual for a boy to marry at that age but not unheard of. However, such early marriages were normally amongst those nobly born and for political reasons. Ceorls didn't marry until they were old enough to support a family.

'Isn't that a matter for them to decide?' I asked mildly. 'As far as I'm aware there is no romantic attachment between them.'

'That doesn't matter. If that girl is to stay then I want her married off. At the moment she's a disturbing influence with most of the garrison lusting after her. Don't think I haven't seen the lecherous looks she attracts from the highest born to the lowest.'

She gave me an angry glance and I tried to hide the guilt that I felt. As far as I was aware my feelings towards Othilia weren't reciprocated in the least. In fact, I wasn't aware of her having a soft spot for anyone, except for Ywer of course.

Thankfully we reached the bridge over the River Stour before I had a chance to reply. We clattered over the narrow timber bridge and the two sentries saluted me. At the far end of the bridge lay the ancient West Gate. Although Cantwareburh had been an important Roman town, lying as it did on Casingc Stræt and at the junction of the roads which fanned out from it to Dofras and the other ports in Cent, it had been abandoned after the Romans had left. It was only when Saint Augustine converted King Æthelbehrt of Cent to Christianity and established his monastery in the old town that it became important again.

The current settlement was surrounded by a ditch and a mixture of stone walls and a palisade where the old walls had vanished, much as was the case at Cæster, Eforwic and the Danish occupied part of Lundenwic. The West Gate had been rebuilt in stone at some stage in the past and now formed an imposing entrance to the narrow streets which lay beyond. The stench of urine, offal, faeces and rotting matter was the same as in any large settlement but it never failed to disgust me. I tried to ignore it but Hilda held a scented cloth to her nose.

We rode along the main thoroughfare until we reached the market square – the place where the old forum had been centuries before. We turned left and entered the monastery grounds through a stone-built gateway. As befitted the home of the senior representative of the Church in Englaland, the monastery was large and impressive. In addition to the main church dedicated to Saints Peter and Paul there was a second, timber one which held the tombs of the kings of Cent until the last king, Baldred, was defeated in 825 and it became part of Wessex.

We had to dismount inside the gate and boys came running to take our horses. We had been accompanied by Uhtric and Ywer but I left them at the stables whilst Hilda and I made our way to the archbishop's hall adjacent to the main church. We were escorted by a taciturn monk who had merely bowed to us and indicated that we should follow him without saying a word. The hall was built of timber and was no different to any other noble's hall, other than the woven cloths depicting the life of Christ that adorned the interior walls.

Archbishop Ethelred was now an old man, worn out by his disputes with the king over their respective authority in ecclesiastical matters. Ælfred preferred the advice of the wretched Bishop Asser and the priests he surrounded himself with to that of his archbishop and consequently Ethelred's authority of the Church in Anglo-Saxon Englaland had declined over the past fifteen years. Nevertheless he was still an important man in Cent and I wanted to keep his support.

'Ah, Lord Jørren,' he said, getting up with difficulty from the chair behind the desk where he'd been reading a scroll.

The monk who'd accompanied us rushed to help him but the archbishop waved him away as if he was an annoying fly.

'I see you've met Brother Edgar. He fusses over me like a mother hen. He's deaf and dumb so at least I don't have to listen to lectures about looking after myself.'

The archbishop chuckled to himself. I gathered that Edgar was the archbishop's personal servant and meeting us at the gate had just been a coincidence. The monk rushed to bring stools for Hilda and me to sit on and Ethelred resumed his chair. We made polite conversation for a while and I had to listen to the odd criticism of the king. Apparently raids on the northern coast of Cent were becoming more commonplace and Ethelred asked me what I proposed to do about it.

I'd already been told this by Hilda and I intended to visit the area as soon as I'd visited my sick brother. I had it in mind to build an outpost at Witenestaple midway between the Isle of Sceapig and Meregate. Witenestaple was a mere five miles from my hall: a short ride on horseback in an emergency. If I manned it with twenty mounted warriors they could patrol the north coast and ride to warn me of any raid. I explained this to Ethelred who nodded approvingly.

'If possible, my wife and I would like to have a brief meeting with my son, the novice Æscwin, lord archbishop. My other son, Ywer, is recovering from broken bones so perhaps he could see the infirmarian whilst we're here? There is also a boy called Leofwine being educated in the monastery. His brother is my physician and if possible he would like to see him as well.'

'Of course, but it will soon be time for Sext so you had better make haste.'

The service known as Sext took place at around midday and we had deliberately arrived just after Terce, the service held at nine o'clock in the morning so I was a little puzzled. The time of day was not something that was important to a warrior, however everything in a monastery was governed by it. King Ælfred had introduced candles marked with the hours of the day so that worship could occur at the right time but that was a fairly new innovation; I wondered how monks and priests had managed before that.

We returned to collect Ywer and Uhtric and then had to retrace our steps as both the infirmary and herb garden lay beyond the archbishop's hall and the main church. We found Æscwin easily enough but apparently Leofwine was in the scriptorium this morning, not in the infirmary. Uhtric went off with Brother Edgar but came back looking despondent. Leofwine had been in the scriptorium learning to write Latin but the monk in charge had forbidden Uhtric to enter and had sent him away with a flea in his ear.

By this stage Hilda and I had finished talking to Æscwin. He was well and had little to say except how well his studies were progressing, what herbs could be used to treat what ailments and some gossip about his fellow novices. He might have been my son but we had little in common. I was therefore glad of the excuse to take our leave and follow Edgar back to the scriptorium.

It was a timber building which was quite dark inside after the bright daylight. I waited for my eyes to adjust and then I could see monks bent over desks copying out scrolls and books by the light of a few candles. I wondered that they didn't go blind working in such conditions and the truth was that many did.

A few novices in homespun brown tunics that reached below their knees and bare legs sat in one corner together with a dozen boys of various ages dressed in a variety of the more normal trousers and short tunics that identified them as lay scholars. The monk in charge was listening to each boy read out a passage from the Bible in Latin. Every time a boy made a mistake the monk hit him about the head with a thin switch.

My eyes had now adjusted sufficiently and I went to walk towards the group of boys but one of the other monks barred my way.

'No one is allowed in here except for monks,' he told me belligerently.

'Then what are those boys doing here?' I asked quietly. 'They aren't even novices are they?'

'They're scholars!'

'Yes, and I'm paying for one of them to attend here; paying quite handsomely I might add. I doubt if Archbishop Ethelred or Abbot Ælfnoð would mind me having a word with the boy. Would you like me to go and ask them?'

The mention of his superiors' names made the monk hesitate but then his face hardened.

'You can't intimidate me, whoever you are. The rules are there to be observed.'

At that moment the bell for Sext ran out and everyone stopped what they were doing and made for the door.

'Ah, good. Off you go then,' I said to the obstreperous monk. 'Leofwine isn't a novice so I think he can be excused from attending church whilst he and I talk.'

I turned on my heel and walked outside leaving the man spluttering in my wake.

'They'll beat me for that, lord,' Leofwine told me after he and his brother had finished greeting each other. 'And for missing Sext, whatever the excuse.'

'Do you get beaten a lot?'

'All the time. I hate it here!' he said fiercely.

I didn't believe in mollycoddling boys. It was a harsh world and they needed to be prepared for it but Hilda wasn't the only one horrified when Leofwine told us about his treatment. It made Ywer's life on Ynys Enlli seem idyllic. The main difference was that his persecutors were careful not to break any bones. It wasn't just the monks that tormented him - that was bad enough – but his fellow scholars, mainly the sons of rich merchants and thegns, looked down on him for his humble origins and made his life even more miserable. I was amazed that the boy hadn't been broken by the experience. It said a lot for his resilience and his strength of character that he hadn't.

'Come with me,' I said and we marched off to the entrance to the church.

Sext was a short service and a few minutes after our arrival the doors opened and the abbot led the exodus.

'Abbot Ælfnoð, may I have a word?'

'Of course, Lord Jørren, it's a pleasure to see you. I was sorry to hear about your injury and I prayed

184

night and day for your recovery,' he said as we walked towards the smaller hall which served as his residence and the monastery's administrative centre.

It was said smoothly but it lacked sincerity.

'I'm not happy with the way this boy has been treated during his time here. Tell Father Abbot what you told me, Leofwine,' I told him once the rest of us were seated.

The boy looked frightened out of his wits but he recited his tale of woe clearly and without stumbling. I was proud of him.

'I see. Well, I'm well aware that life here is harsh but it does seem that Leofwine has been singled out for harsher treatment than is normal. I'm not sure what to do about it though. It's no use punishing the monks responsible, let alone the boy's fellow scholars. That would only make his life worse and it would cause great resentment in our community.'

'Very well. In that case I'm removing him. The additional funds I donate to the monastery over and above the tithe that I'm legally obliged to pay the Church will cease immediately, as will the fee for his education.'

The abbot opened and closed his mouth like a stranded fish but before he could object I turned and left.

'Well done,' Hilda said quietly as we made our way back to the stables. 'I would have been disappointed if you had left him there, but won't this stir up trouble with the Church?'

'Perhaps but the abbot is weak and the archbishop is frail. This place needs someone with a bit of moral fibre to sort it out. It may be a cruel thing to say but the sooner Ethelred and Ælfnoð die and can be replaced the better.'

✝✝✝

It seemed that the hard line I'd taken over the treatment of Leogsige had rehabilitated me in Hilda's estimation. The problem of Othilia remained but for the moment my wife seemed content to accept her as a servant in our hall. In any case I had other things to worry about.

As September wore on we began to lay in stores for the winter. The harvest on this side of the Norþsæ had been reasonable but Frankia and Frisia had a wet summer and the crops rotted in the fields. None of that would have affected us in Wessex except for the fact that the Vikings who habitually raided Frankia and Frisia, or who had settled there, decided to leave and sail across the sea to attack both Ēast Seaxna Rīce and Cent in some strength.

The first I knew of the new threat was when the outpost I was establishing at Witenestaple sent a rider with the news that a fleet of some fifty Danish longships had sailed past them quite close inshore. At first I thought that they were heading for the Isle of Sceapig. It lay mere yards off the mainland and provided a sheltered anchorage as well as food in the shape of sheep. It was an island and so it was difficult for the shepherds to flee and take their flocks to safety.

However, the next reports I received disabused me of that idea. They had sailed up the River Midweg as far as Hrofescæster and were setting up camp. Hrofescæster had a particularly poignant memory for me. It was where Cei and I had spent the first night after we ran away as boys to rescue my brother Alric from the Great Heathen Army. We had been attacked that night and had barely escaped with our lives. However, we had managed to kill all four of the robbers, more by luck than skill, and had become fugitives. The incident was two decades in the past but it still coloured my attitude to the place. Nevertheless, it guarded the crossing over the Midweg and so I had built a burh there to defend the bridge.

It appeared that these new Danish invaders from Frankia wanted to sail up the river to plunder and perhaps seize all of central Cent. To do so they had to either destroy the bridge or unship their masts and row each of their ships under it. The burh stood on a promontory surrounded on three sides by the river and the Danes would have to capture it to do either.

Hrofescæster lay some thirty miles away: a four hour ride along Casingc Stræt on a good horse. Although I believed my scouts I needed to see for myself what was going on and to estimate the scale of the incursion we were dealing with. I took twenty of my gesith with me mounted on our swiftest horses. We set off at dawn the next day and reached a ridge to the south of the burh from where we could look down at the Viking encampment. I counted no less than fifty three masts belonging to longships drawn up on the mudbanks. Most were the smaller snekkjer but about a dozen were the larger drekka. I therefore estimated the enemy numbers to be around two thousand - far more than I could deal with on my own.

I sent members of my gesith to spread the word to the thegns of Cent. They were to muster at Sidyngbourn, some eight miles away from the Danish encampment as soon as possible. Thankfully the harvest was all but in and I was hoping to raise well over a thousand men.

I sent Lyndon to Jerrik in Dofras with a request that he prepare his longships to sail around the coast and into the Midweg to prevent the Danes from escaping by sea. From there he was to travel on by sea to Portcæstre to alert Bjarne and then on to Wintanceaster to inform Ælfred. I could ask Dudda and Cynegils to call out their fyrds but it would be better if it came from the king.

There was nothing more I could do at that juncture and so, leaving five of my scouts to keep an eye on the Danes, I travelled inland to see how my brother was faring.

✝✝✝

I was surprised to see Alric emerge from the hall as I rode through the gates in the palisade around Cilleham. He was the middle brother between Æscwin and me and we had been inseparable as young boys. After I'd rescued him from the Danes two decades ago he had married Guthild, the daughter of Merewald, the previous Ealdorman of Wintanceaster. She had inherited four vills in the shire and one in Cent. The latter was in the west of the shire, a long way from both Cantwareburh and Dofras, which he only visited it occasionally. Consequently I'd only seen him occasionally after that.

I jumped down from my horse and we embraced. Although we didn't often have the opportunity to get together I was still close to him.

'How is he?' I asked as we entered Æscwin's hall together.

'Not good, I fear. The priest says that he has the wasting sickness.'

Æscwin's wife, Audrey, stood waiting to greet me just inside the door with her children, two daughters and a sour faced boy called Anson. The girls were six and eight and seemed in awe of me. In contrast Audrey and Anson stared at me resentfully as they nodded to acknowledge me. The boy was nine or ten I suppose: too young to inherit the vill at any rate. His mother would run it for him until he was fourteen.

Audrey had never made any secret of her jealousy. Her husband was my eldest brother and yet I was the ealdorman. Cilleham was a small vill and Æscwin only a minor thegn. Money was tight and the only men that my brother could afford to maintain as his hearth warriors were three greybeards that were good for little except sitting around the fire telling far-fetched tales of long forgotten battles.

I had brought Uhtric and Leofwine with me so that they could examine my brother. That didn't please the local priest but when I told him that Uhtric's skill had saved my life and that young Leofwine had trained under the infirmarian at Cantwareburh he was mollified.

Æscwin had been both tall and broad-shouldered. Beside him I had looked like a dwarf and I wasn't a small man. However, all that had changed. He was a shrunken shadow of his former self. He was only five years older than me but he looked twice my age. His sallow complexion, sunken features and thin wisps of hair appalled me. I knew that even the skill of my two young physicians wouldn't be enough to save him; indeed I was surprised that he was still alive.

His eyes brightened when he saw me and he grasped my hand in his own. The skin felt hot and paper thin.

'Take care of Audrey and my children,' he croaked through parched lips.

I nodded and promised that I would as Uhtric came to dribble some water into my brother's mouth. He and Leofwine examined him but Uhtric shook his head.

'He's too weak, lord. From the many cuts on his arms and legs I would guess that he had been bled far too much; that's robbed him of whatever strength he might have had to fight the sickness,' he whispered to me, glancing at the priest who stood at the bottom of the bed, his eyes closed and his hands together as he prayed.

'Is there nothing we can do for him?'

'The blood flows sluggishly in his veins. All we can do is make him comfortable and wait for the end. I wouldn't expect him to last the night.'

'Could he have survived if he hadn't been bled so much?'

'Perhaps, it's impossible to be certain. What I do know is that it hasn't helped.'

I nodded and glanced venomously at the priest who continued to mutter prayers blissfully unaware of the animosity I bore towards him.

Audrey and the children came to the bedside and I left them to sit with my brother whilst Alric and I went outside into the fresh air.

'How are Guthild and the children these days?' I asked.

'They are well; you must come and see for yourself the next time you're in Wintanceaster. After all we only live twenty miles away.'

I noted that he hadn't included Hilda in the invitation. He was well aware of my wife's aversion to travelling any distance.

'Yes, I will. However, that's not likely to be for a while,' and I told him about the Danish siege of Hrofescæster.

'In that case I should return home before the king calls out the fyrd.'

He looked agitated, fearful of being away from home at a time of crisis but loathe to leave Cilleham whilst our brother still breathed.

'Stay until tomorrow at least. I fear that Æscwin is unlikely to last the night, so Uhtric tells me. I'm sure

Guthild is quite capable of mustering your ceorls and getting your hearth warriors to prepare. '

He nodded and we embraced again before I went back into the hall to speak to Audrey.

'I hate to have to say this at a time like this, lady, but a large Danish army is attacking Hrofescæster.'

I could see that the name meant little to her. She was the daughter of the thegn of a neighbouring vill and she had never been further than Cantwareburh, a mere five miles away.

'It's a large burh in Cent half a day's ride away,' I explained.

'And you expect me to muster my ceorls and send them off to fight at a time like this?' she exploded.

'I know it's hard with Æscwin so ill but I can't make exceptions. We're going to need every man who can fight. Who is your senior warrior? If you prefer I can ask him to warn everyone.'

'No, I'll do it. Those useless old men are too ancient to fight. They'd be slaughtered. It's best that they don't know until it's too late.'

As Uhtric had predicted, my brother died in the early hours of the morning. The priest conducted the funeral the next day so that Alric could attend before he had to leave. I too took my leave and rode away with sadness in my heart. I may not have been close to Æscwin but he was still my eldest brother. Death in battle was one thing but seeing him die like that was awful. It was a sobering reminder of one's own mortality.

†††

I wasn't happy about leaving Hilda and the children in my hall above Cantwareburh. Although it was on top of a hill and protected by a fifteen foot high palisade, it wouldn't keep out a large group of marauding Danes. I decided that as soon as the present crisis was over I'd build a new hall within the precincts of the burh below.

I left ten of my warband, together with twenty members of the fyrd, to guard my present hall and set off with my gesith and the rest of my personal warband for Sidyngbourn. When we arrived my men set up camp beside the river and I settled in to wait for the rest of the army to arrive.

I'd still done nothing about finding a new body servant and so I was surprised when a boy came in to serve me some broth, bread and a tankard of mead. His face was hidden by a hood, which made me suspicious; why would he want to wear his hood up inside the tent? Then he pushed it back to reveal the grinning face of Othilia. I was stunned. She was dressed in a loose tunic, trousers and men's shoes, which concealed her female form, and the cowl had hidden her auburn hair as well as her face.

'What on earth are you doing here,' I demanded a trifle more brusquely than I had intended.

She looked a little taken aback.

'I'm sorry, lord. I would prefer to serve you here than be subjected to the Lady Hilda's vindictiveness. However, if you wish me to return to Cantwareburh I will endeavour to find a means to do so,' she said stiffly.

I passed a weary hand over my eyes and sat down on the only chair in the tent.

'What do you mean vindictiveness? Hasn't the Lady Hilda always treated you well? She was the one that allowed you to stay as a servant in my hall, after all.'

'Only so that she could wreak her petty revenge for the looks you kept giving me,' she shot back.

'What sort of looks?' I asked warily.

I thought that I had managed to keep my interest in the girl hidden from everyone.

'Perhaps I'm wrong, lord, but I thought that you cared for me, might even be a little bit in love with me.'

'And I thought I was being circumspect,' I said with a smile. 'If you noticed then I suppose that my wife must have done so as well. I thought it was just because you were pretty and she was jealous.'

'No, she definitely thinks that I'm your mistress from the vile accusations she made,' she said forcefully.

'Thank you for the refreshments, they are very welcome, but I'd like you to leave for now. I need time to think.'

She turned to go.

'Wait! Who else knows that you're here?'

'No one, lord. I rode here in the back of one of the wagons with the supplies and kept out of everyone's way. Only Uhtric and Leofwine know because that's who I scrounged the food and mead from.'

194

'Very well. Try and keep it that way. Sleep in their tent for now and we'd better find a boy's name for you. Let me think. Yes, Gebeor will do.'

'That means drinking companion,' she said with quizzical look. 'Very well, lord. From now on I'll be Gebeor.'

She giggled and gave me a cheeky look that managed to be lustful as well before leaving the tent, pulling up her cowl as she did so. I was left with my mind in a whirl. What sort of a mess was I getting myself into?

The next few days passed quickly. Gebeor, as I schooled myself to call her, even in my mind, came and went, bringing my food when I ate alone, tidying up after me, cleaning my armour and running messages. The sentries outside the tent didn't question her and if anyone suspected who she really was they didn't spread any rumours which I heard about. After that first night Leofwine cut Othilia's hair into a more masculine style and she kept her face slightly grubby to hide the absence of the incipient facial hair any boy her age would have sported.

She flirted with me and I responded but I never let my loins rule my head; all the same I wanted her desperately and I was left frustrated every time she departed.

Gebeor never said anything to me about the incident but Uhtric told me one day that one of the fyrd, a hulking great fellow from Sceapig, had taken a fancy to her, thinking she was a handsome boy, and had tried to sodomise her. She had kicked him hard where it hurt most and then, as he lay howling in agony on the ground, she had slit his nose with her knife. It was the punishment meted out to adulterers and it would mark him for life.

I didn't want the sodomite to try to revenge himself on her and so I had a quiet word with his thegn. The man was sent back to his settlement in disgrace that same day.

Slowly contingents trickled into the encampment and finally Ælfred himself arrived.

'How many men do we have in total?' he asked Drefan at the war council held in his tent that evening.

'Just over four thousand, cyning, including eight hundred and fifty nobles and their warbands.'

It wasn't a lot with which to take on two thousand Vikings. Of the three thousand or so armed ceorls in the fyrd, many would be totally without experience of combat whereas all but a handful of the youngest Danes would have killed at least one man before. Most would be experienced fighters.

'We need to await the arrival of the fleet, cyning,' I pointed out. 'Even if we win here, they can just sail away and attack somewhere else.'

'That makes sense,' Drefan said, giving me a smile.

I had few enough friends amongst Ælfred's inner circle but my replacement as hereræswa was one of them.

'What you probably don't know is that there is an even larger Viking fleet which has attacked East Anglia,' Ælfred told us gloomily.

'Guðrum's kingdom,' I said in surprise. 'But the inhabitants are now mainly Danes, or at least Angles who live under Danish domination.'

'Æðelstan!' Asser almost shouted. 'His name is now King Æðelstan.'

It was the name that Guðrum had taken when he was baptised as a Christian but everyone who had fought him when he was one of the leaders of the Great Heathen Army still called him by his pagan name.

'Yes, quite right bishop, Æðelstan's kingdom of East Anglia,' Ælfred said scowling at me. 'If my agents there are correct, some forty ships have landed a force of around one and a half thousand near the mouth of the River Stour at Herewic.'

'Surely Æðelstan and his Danes can deal with them?' Dudda of Sūþrīgescīr asked, putting heavy emphasis on Æðelstan and giving me a wink out of the eye hidden from the king.

'They can drive them out, or so one would hope, but if they are allowed to sail away then they could either reinforce the Danes here or raid elsewhere along our shores,' Drefan patiently explained.

'So we need to use our fleet both to bottle up the enemy here in the Midweg but also those in the Stour?' I asked.

'Precisely!' Ælfred agreed.

'But that means splitting our fleet, cyning, and that risks them being defeated.'

'I'm sure that the fleet that the king created with your help, Lord Jørren, can overcome a few Danish longships, even if they are divided in two.'

I looked at the speaker in amazement. It was Eadda, the man who had abducted my son and then tried to have me killed in an ambush.

'You forget, Eadda, that the Danes have more longships than we do and we can't always crew every ship we do have with the available manpower. Besides, we train to weaken them with arrow attacks from a distance out at sea. If we engage in close quarter combat in the confines of a river estuary they can board us and then they have the advantage.'

'That sounds like a sorry list of excuses to me,' he sneered.

'That's enough Eadda,' Ælfred snapped. 'Lord Jørren doesn't have to defend the capabilities of my fleet; he's not the Sæ Hereræswa. Try to remember that you're not a member of this council; you're here to look after my son whilst he learns something about warfare.'

Eadda's face changed colour to a nice shade of red but he subsided after giving me a nasty look. Edward stood by his side looking upset that his father had publicly rebuked his mentor.

'I accept that we must wait for the arrival of the fleet to block the exit from the Midweg to the Temes but I still want to discuss how best to attack the Danish encampment,' the king continued. 'What do we know about it?'

He looked at Drefan for an answer but he pointed out that my scouts had carried out the most detailed reconnaissance. He could have said the only reconnaissance as he'd accepted my report without checking for himself. It was flattering I suppose but it wasn't the action of a prudent leader. I would have insisted on seeing for myself.

'Well, cyning. Perhaps I can best explain by drawing a map on the dirt floor of your tent,' I suggested. 'The burh sits here surrounded by the river to the north, west and east. The Danes have erected a palisade here, across the neck of land on the fourth side.'

I drew a line to the south of where I had drawn the walls around the settlement.

'The distance between the two lines of fortification is two hundred yards, in other words outside the range of arrows. The burh's defences consist of the palisade all the way around it and a ditch eight feet deep to the south. It's connected to the river at both ends but the ditch is normally dry. However, the defenders have opened the sluice gates and so now the burh is protected by a moat to the south as well.

'The Danes have established two camps: the larger one behind their palisade to the south and a smaller one at the northern end of the bridge that crosses the Midweg on the road that leads to Lundenwic.

'They are constructing an earthen rampart to protect their major camp from attack from the east but they haven't bothered to do the same to the encampment at the far end of the bridge.'

'So if we capture that camp we can resupply the burh via the bridge?' Heardwig of Suth-Seaxe queried.

'Exactly so,' Ælfred said with a brief smile. 'Have you anything else to add, Lord Jørren?'

'Only that the Danes used their ships to land men on the west bank. We would have to do the same, but obviously out of sight of both camps and any piquets they may have put out, if we want to catch them unaware.'

'Thank you for a concise and clear report. Where do you suggest we embark and disembark the warriors who are to attack the Danes camp at the end of the bridge?'

'There is a watch ship anchored at the confluence of the Midweg and the Temes but it seems content to allow traffic to pass to and from Lundenwic. If we embark men at Witenestaple they can sail to the north of the Isle of Sceapig and land beyond the entrance to the Midweg. It is mainly marshland but there is a small fishing hamlet and a causeway that leads inland. From the landing point it's ten miles to the Danes' camp; a four or five hour march for men at night.'

'At night?' Drefan queried. 'Won't men get lost?'

'We need to travel at night so as to be in position for a dawn attack. I don't think you need worry Lord Drefan. I'm assured that there is only the one causeway through the marshes and then there is a clear track across pasture land which joins Casingc Stræt not far from the end of the bridge.'

The council broke up shortly after that but Ælfred called me over as I was about to leave.

'I want you to meet Brother Plegmund. He's my senior scribe at the moment.'

I knew of Plegmund as I'd seen him around and about at the king's hall but I had never spoken to him.

I was aware that he was a scholar of some note and that he had been a hermit at some point. Rumour had it that he followed the rule of Saint Benedict zealously but that he was a leader by example rather than a martinet in such matters.

'Brother Plegmund,' I said nodding my head in acknowledgement.

He smiled in return and then surprised me.

'I understand that you are not altogether happy with the present regime at Cantwareburh, at least as far as the novices and boy scholars are concerned.'

'You are remarkably well informed brother.'

'Indeed. I have reason to be,' he said enigmatically.

'You may not have heard yet, but Abbot Ælfnoð has had a seizure and has been forced to take to his bed. The archbishop has written to me asking for my permission to appoint the prior in his place. You know him I think?'

'Yes, a man cut from the same cloth as Ælfnoð. Both have grown indolent in old age and I fear that he will be even worse than the old abbot. He's too weak a character to keep his senior monks in check and the lives of the junior monks, novices and scholars will become even more miserable.'

'Quite. That's why I intend to send Plegmund to take over the management of the monastery. I would like you to provide him with an escort of a few warriors just to ensure that he doesn't encounter any opposition. You know how touchy Ethelred is when he thinks I'm interfering in Church business.'

'Very well, cyning. I'll send Wolnoth and a few of my most devout hearth warriors to make sure that there's no trouble. I'll make it clear to them that they are to act with discretion and to follow Abbot Plegmund's instructions.'

Plegmund smiled at my use of his new title and I left the tent feeling elated that at last the monastery would be in good hands. I couldn't deny that Ælfnoð had been helpful to me in the past but as the years went by he'd thought more and more about his own comforts and less and less about his responsibilities.

My good mood didn't last long. When I got back to my tent I looked for Othilia but she wasn't there. I thought that was odd as it was past the time when she normally brought me something to eat and drink. Suddenly I heard an altercation outside. I recognised the voice of Leofwine demanding to see me and the sentry, who plainly didn't recognise him, telling him to wait whilst he checked with me. I saved him the trouble and went outside.

'What's the problem Leofwine?'

'It's Oth... - umm – Gebeor, lord. He's been stabbed. My brother is tending to him now but it doesn't look good.'

The boy was trying to hold back his tears and my heart sank.

'Where's Gebeor now?'

'Outside our tent, lord,' Leofwine muttered.

'Take me there,'

With that I was off running after Leofwine who darted in and out amongst the leather and wool tents like a hare evading a dog.

'I'm afraid you're too late lord,' Uhtric said as he rose to his feet beside the still form of Othilia. 'She has just breathed her last.'

I knelt beside the body of the girl and wept. Later I would try and take comfort from the fact that she had been taken from me before I could commit the sin of fornication with her. She had made it plain that she was willing enough but I had managed to resist the temptation to take her to my bed up until then. Although, had she not been killed, I'm not sure I could have managed to do so indefinitely.

I had held out partly because I felt that I would betraying Hilda and our marriage vows and partly because I knew that Ælfred would never condone adultery. I would have risked losing his favour and my enemies could then have brought me down if I'd succumbed and he'd found out.

For now I felt a deep sense of loss and a burning desire to revenge myself on whoever had killed her.

'Did you see who stabbed her?'

'Yes, it was that hulking brute who teaches swordsmanship to Edward the Ætheling and his companions.'

'You're certain?'

'Positive. I've watched them practice under his guidance. I though he was going to kill us when we heard her scream and we came out of the tent. He stood there bloody seax in hand over her poor body. He took a step towards us but then we heard voices and he hesitated. The next moment he was gone.'

'He's Eadda's man. He must have ordered him to kill Othilia, but why?'

'Perhaps he found out that she was a girl and thought she was your mistress, lord,' he suggested diffidently with his eyes on the ground.

'Well, she wasn't!' I growled savagely. 'But she was my body servant and anyone who harms one of my people harms me.'

I paced up and down, lost in thought for a moment, then I noticed that a crowd was gathering.

'Take him inside the tent,' I ordered Uhtric and his brother. 'Then we are going to see the king.'

He was ensconced with Drefan but I insisted on seeing him when the sentry barred my way.

'Let Lord Jørren in,' Ælfred called when he heard my voice.

'What is it, Jørren and why have you brought these two boys with you?'

'They are my physicians, cyning, and they are witnesses to the murder of my body servant, Gebeor, a short while ago.'

'Murder? Here in my camp? Have you apprehended the killer?'

'No, but they have identified him.'

'Who? Who would dare commit murder in my encampment?'

'It is the man who teaches your son swordsmanship, cyning. We both saw him standing over the body with a bloody seax in his hand,' Uhtric said clearly, standing up straight.

'You're sure?'

'Quite sure, cyning,' Leofwine said, backing up his brother.

'Drefan, arrange for Bryhthelm to be arrested and questioned. '

'Yes, cyning.'

Drefan left the tent and spoke to the sentry before returning.

'Why would Bryhthelm do such a thing?' Ælfred asked. 'Did he have a motive?'

'He's Eadda's man, cyning. I'm as certain as I can be that he was carrying out Eadda's orders.'

'But you don't have any proof? I know that he still resents his dismissal as hereræswa and your appointment to replace him but that was nearly a decade ago.'

'He's never forgotten nor forgiven, cyning. I have every reason to think that he was the man responsible for the abduction of my son Ywer and for consigning him to a life with the Culdees on Ynys Enlli.'

'You haven't told me about this!'

'No, because I can only prove that the kidnappers were Saxons.'

'And Ywer? Is he still there?'

'No, I managed to rescue him, thank the Lord God.'

It was only then that I realised something.

'The person who acted as my translator during negotiations with the Culdee monks was Oth... Gebeor. Perhaps that was another reason for his death?'

'You were about to call him by another name, why?' Ælfred demanded accusingly.

'He changed his name when he joined me as my body servant,' I lied smoothly. 'The Welsh are not popular in Mercia or Wessex.'

Thankfully the king seemed to accept my explanation but I decided to get Othilia buried quietly as soon as possible. I didn't want anyone preparing the corpse and finding out her secret.

'You have no proof that Eadda was behind either Ywer's kidnapping or your body servant's killing from what you say.'

'No firm evidence, no cyning. Let's hope that this man Bryhthelm can be persuaded to talk.'

✝✝✝

He refused to say a word. In the end Ælfred found him guilty and fined him the blood price for killing a ceorl – two hundred shillings. Perhaps he hoped that Eadda would pay it for him but he didn't. Bryhthelm had nowhere near enough to pay the fine himself and so he, his wife and daughter were sold into slavery.

The last I heard of him he'd been bought by an Irish slave-trader and taken to Dyflin but his wife and daughter had become slaves on a vill in Hamtunscīr. At the time I thought nothing more about it but I later learned that their new master was Eadda. At least the man had the decency to look after his creature's family, even if he had abandoned him to his fate. However, that did nothing to change my determination that Eadda had to die for all the distress he had caused me and my family.

We buried Othilia the next day. It was only when she was dead that I realised the depth of my love for her. I tried to tell myself that it was probably for the best as an adulterous relationship would have only led to my ruin. It didn't help.

Thankfully I had other things to occupy my mind. That afternoon our fleet was sighted off Witenestaple and I was forced to concentrate on the task in hand. Whilst Ælfred and Drefan took the main body of the army to threaten the main Danish encampment I was to lead the men of Cent in the attack on the camp by the bridge.

Chapter Eleven

HROFESCÆSTER

Early October 884

The small harbour at Witenestaple was crowded. Quite apart from the fishing boats several longships, including the Saint Cuthbert and the Holy Spirit, had tied up alongside so that Jerrik and his senior captains could disembark and join me for a council of war. There was a long spit of shingle that ran out from the beach and the rest of the fleet had been run aground along the sheltered side of the spit and on the beach to the west of it.

Bjarne wasn't there of course. He was taking the longships from Portcæstre to the coast of East Anglia to assist Guðrum against the other Danish fleet from the Continent.

'Splitting the fleet was a mad idea,' Jerrik grumbled after we'd greeted each other.

I agreed but I couldn't be seen to criticise the king and so I ignored his comment.

'How many longships have you brought with you?' I asked.

'Every ship that was available at Dofras; ten skeids and twelve Snekkjur. How many do the Danes have at Hrofescæster?'

'Fifty.'

He looked at me in amazement.

'How are we meant to defeat a fleet that size?'

'Well, twelve of them are drawn up on the west bank, which is where I get my estimate of between four and five hundred Danes camped at the end of the bridge from. I hope that my thousand men will be enough to overwhelm them and capture or burn all their longships.'

'That still leaves nearly twice as many ships as I have on the east bank.'

'True, but they can't all exit the Midweg at once. If you harass them with archers as they emerge you should be able to whittle their numbers down quite considerably. After that, shadow them and pick off as many more as you can. The Temes estuary is wide enough for you to manoeuvre and stop them boarding you.'

Jerrik grunted a reluctant acceptance of what I'd said as my warriors and the Cent fyrd started to embark.

It was still daylight and, not wanting to risk the ships getting lost or bumping each other in the dark, I planned to reach the fishing hamlet before dusk. However, getting everyone on board took longer than I'd anticipated.

It started to rain just as we set out. In one way it was good news because those Danes not on guard duty would be sheltering in their tents but it also meant that it would be difficult to set fire to the longships drawn up on the mud banks along this side of the river. I would need to change my plans.

I had put Cináed in charge of the fifty men detailed to eliminate the sentinels on the ships. His orders were to set the cordage and the rigging alight and then cast the longships adrift. Instead I told him to hole the hulls below the waterline and then push them into the middle of the river. Hopefully that way they would impede some of the craft from the far bank; that's always assuming that many of the Danes would flee rather than fight Ælfred's army.

Because we were late setting off it and because the rain brought the darkness before I was expecting, I worried that our ships would have difficulty in finding our destination. However, each ship carried a lantern mounted on the stern, shielded so that the light only showed directly aft. Thus each ship was able to follow the one in front to the landing stage.

At first everything went according to plan. We landed each contingent from our ships on the wooden landing stage, although it took an age because there was only room for two ships to tie up at a time. All the while men were getting wetter and wetter and they moaned loudly until they were told to shut up. It wouldn't have mattered as no one could have heard us at any distance in that downpour and the enemy were ten miles away in any case.

By the time that we were ready to set out I judged that about three hours had passed since dusk. We had about ten hours left before we needed to be in position. It would probably take five hours to travel to the Danish encampment at night so we should still have plenty of time before commencing our attack. However, I wanted the men to get some sleep, otherwise they would be exhausted before the fighting started.

Furthermore, Cináed would need at least an hour to approach stealthily and deal with those left to watch the ships. I wanted him to time casting the longships adrift just as we attacked.

There was so much that could go wrong. Cináed's men could bungle silencing the men and ships' boys on watch, one of the other sentries could give the alarm, or some of my men might not have woken up in time to join in the attack, making it an uncoordinated shambles.

Thankfully the rain petered out after an hour or so, although by that time everyone was soaked to the skin. We spent an uncomfortable few hours waiting for dawn. Although the idea was for everyone to get some sleep, I doubt that few did. I certainly didn't and time seemed to pass very slowly.

In the end it was an alert sentry over on the other side of the river who spotted Cináed's men slaughtering the sentries guarding the ships by the light of their camp fires. The blast of the warning horn drifted over the water a good hour before first light and, given the overcast sky, it was still so dark that I could hardly see my hand in front of my face.

For one fleeting moment I thought of giving the order to attack but it would have been madness. We would have been just as likely to kill each other as the enemy. I decided to wait and passed the word to remain in position along the line.

Thankfully Cináed had the good sense to melt away into the darkness. The Danes would find the ship's watch slaughtered and so they would know that something was up, but it couldn't be helped.

With any luck they would think it was a just a party of raiders trying to steal their ships.

There was turmoil in the camp for some time. The Danes lit torches and that enabled us to see where they were searching. Thankfully they concentrated on the area near the river bank and came nowhere near where we were hidden. Just before dawn they gave up the search and got fires going on which to cook.

Dawn was slow in making an appearance. The dark grey clouds kept the Sun's light at bay for a while. When the blackness turned to grey and pale muted colours began to infuse everything I gave the signal and we rose out of the ground all around the Danes' camp.

They were not as unprepared for our attack as I'd originally planned but there was a long moment when they got to their feet and just stared at us in amazement. Then pandemonium broke out as they rushed hither and thither to gather armour, helmets and weapons from their tents. By this time we had reached the edge of the camp and the first isolated Danes were hacked down.

I slashed my seax across the throat of a Dane who emerged from his tent and he fell back on top of another who was trying to get past him. I jabbed my seax at where I thought his body was and was rewarded by a yelp of pain. I glanced about for my next opponent and caught a glimpse of another battle going on near where the longships were beached. Presumably Cináed was attacking the replacement watch on the ships. I had no time to see how he was doing before a large Dane clad in a rust stained byrnie and wielding a large battleaxe barred my path.

Perhaps the fact that I was grieving over the loss of Othilia made me reckless but I charged into the Dane, thrusting the boss of my shield into his helmeted face before jamming the point of my seax into the side of his knee. I felt the axe blade strike my back but there was little force in the blow and my chainmail didn't split. The blow did injure me however and I arched my spine as the pain hit me.

The big Dane's leg buckled under him and he fell back with me on top of him. He couldn't use the axe but he managed to drag his dagger out of its sheath. The pain in my back was such that I was unable to move. I could see the point of the dagger coming towards my eyes but there was nothing I could do to protect myself.

Out of the corner of my eye I saw a sword as it was plunged into the Dane's neck. Blood spurted out from one of his carotid arteries and his body went limp. My saviour was Eomær and I started to thank him. However, when he went to help me up I screamed from the pain in my back. That was the last thing I remembered.

✝✝✝

When I woke up I was lying on a bed in a room I didn't recognise. The agonising pain in my back had been replaced by a dull ache but when I went to shift my position it intensified.

'Don't try and move, lord,' Uhtric chided me. 'You've broken several bones in the rear of your ribcage. One of them appears to have punctured something inside of you. The bones will heal but you need to keep still to give whatever damage has been done inside your chest a chance to repair itself.'

I groaned in frustration. The last thing I wanted at the moment was to be immobilised.

'Did we beat the Danes?' I asked anxiously.

'Oh, yes. Quite decisively. There were only enough left on our side of the river to crew two longships.'

The speaker wasn't Uhtric but my captain, Wealmær.

'Cináed didn't have a chance to fire the Vikings' ships but he managed to cast most of them adrift after he'd killed those who defended them,' he continued. 'The main body found themselves surrounded but they refused to surrender. They fought like demons. Some managed to fight their way clear but the rest were killed or wounded. We slew the badly wounded, of course, and took the rest prisoner. Once their wounds have healed we should have a hundred and fifty or so for the slave traders.

'We suffered casualties as well, losing nearly two hundred of the fyrd and nineteen of our warband. Thankfully none of your gesith suffered more than the odd flesh wound.'

'And Hrofescæster? Is it safe? Did the king manage to defeat the main body of the Danes?'

'Yes, lord. He didn't even have to fight them. As soon as he started to advance towards their camp they made for their longships and beat a hasty retreat towards the confluence with the Temes.'

'Do you know what happened when they ran into Jerrik's fleet?'

'The rumours are that our ships kept their distance and peppered the Viking craft with arrows, killing enough to slow them down. Both wind and tide were against them and our men did enough damage to slow them even further. Some Danes went alongside other Viking ships and climbed aboard, abandoning their own ships. That gave them enough numbers to crew the ships that escaped. It's said that Jerrik took seven longships as a result; all without suffering a single casualty.'

'So the rest got away to raid and pillage my shire elsewhere?'

'No, lord,' Wealmær said emphatically, shaking his head. 'I heard that, when last seen from the lookout post at Witenestaple, the Vikings were heading back towards the Continent as fast as they could go whilst Jerrik's ships continued to harass them like a pack of sheepdogs herding a flock.'

'Thank you, Wealmær. If the rumours are true, then we have managed to win a great victory and doubtless the Vikings in Frankia will look for easier pickings the next time there is a famine abroad.'

'I hope so, lord. The king was asking after your health. He was heard to say that Wessex owed you and all Centish men a debt of gratitude for yesterday's victory. He's allowed us to keep the plunder we won. It hasn't gone down well with the rest of the army, of course, but they did practically nothing, other than go for a stroll downhill. He also allowed us a share of the Danes' horse herd. Apparently they weren't stolen here but were shipped over with their army.'

I drifted off to sleep, content in the knowledge that my shire was safe. My last conscious thought was to wonder if Bjarne had enjoyed the same success against the Danes who'd invaded East Anglia.

†††

It was six weeks before Uhtric pronounced himself satisfied that my bones had mended sufficiently for me to resume normal activities. He'd kept me in bed for the first three weeks, saying that he was still worried that the jagged ends of my broken ribs could still do as much damage to my innards as a Viking sword. I'd grumbled and given him a hard time of it, which he bore stoically, but deep down I knew he was right.

Ælfred himself came to see me the day after Wealmær had visited. He was accompanied by Drefan and the other ealdormen who had been present at the muster. All were sincere in their congratulations and I felt that at long last I had been accepted by my peers. It gave me a warm feeling. I would have enjoyed basking in their praise more had not the depression following the death of Othilia still hung over me like a dark cloud.

'I was very sorry to hear what happened to Othilia, lord,' Wolnoth said on his return from Cantwareburh.

Abbot Ælfnoð had died, most conveniently, the day after Plegmund's arrival, and the monks had grudgingly accepted him as their new abbot. Archbishop Ethelred, contrary to expectation, seemed pleased by Plegmund's appointment and so Wolnoth and his men had returned to Hrofescæster after a brief visit to his family and to pay his respects to my wife.

'Lady Hilda seemed vexed that Othilia had run away, lord,' he told me. 'Of course, I didn't know then that she'd been murdered.

'She took on the guise of a boy and became my body servant.'

I saw the look on his face and bit back the angry retort that came unbidden to my lips.

'No, we weren't lovers,' I said calmly, 'despite what you may have heard, but I did love her in a way. I still miss her.'

I was dissembling of course but the more I told myself that what I'd just said was true, the more I believed it.

'You need a new body servant, lord,' Wolnoth said briskly.

'That's true; Uhtric has better things to do than look after me now I'm well on the road to recovery. Any suggestions?'

'Well there were a few Danish boys amongst the captives. We held onto them when the rest were shipped off to be sold. If you fancy taming another viper you could pick one of them.'

I smiled at that. Several of my men had started life as Danish captives. Once they could be persuaded to

217

give me their oath they made good warriors and were loyal to a fault.

'Very well, I'll come and look them over this afternoon.'

Uhtric tutted in disapproval when I told him but the pain in my back had all but gone and he reluctantly agreed that a walk would probably do me good.

There were a dozen young Danes who pro tem served my gesith, cooking, cleaning armour and looking after our horses. One couldn't say that they were exactly happy about it but most had accepted their fate. If they still had family, it was across the sea and, if they ran away there was nowhere for them to go. Cent was a long way from Eastern Mercia and the Danelaw and, having lived on the Continent previously, they had no idea how to get there.

Some appeared to have accepted their lot without much difficulty and some had the scars to show that they had to be beaten into submission. They were all aged between eleven and fourteen. Most had been ship's boys but a few of the older ones had started to train as warriors. They were wasted as servants and I determined to hand most of them over to Jerrik to serve at sea.

One boy did catch my eye, however. He had startlingly red hair and his eyes flashed defiance although he had the good sense to keep his unbroken pride in check. He wore a permanent scowl and didn't have any sign of facial hair as yet. I put his age at twelve or thirteen. I later discovered that he was only eleven but big for his age.

'What's your name boy?' I asked him in Danish.

He looked surprised, probably because I could speak his language like a native, rather than with an English accent.

'Arne,' he replied, studying me with interest.

'You call him lord,' Wolnoth growled at him.

'Arne, lord,' he said staring me straight in the eye.

There had been the faintest of pauses between the two words and he used the title herskir, which meant master or ruler, rather than the more usual herre. I had the nasty feeling that I was being mocked.

'I don't like herskir,' I told the boy. 'Call me jarl,'

'But that is what warriors call their leader,' he said, looking surprised.

'Don't you want to be a warrior?'

'Yes, of course; but I'm a thrall, a slave,'

'Bjarne, the commander of our longships, and Cei, the captain of one of our mightiest fortresses, were slaves at one point.   But you have to earn your freedom and any advancement thereafter. It's a hard road.'

I watched him as he mulled over what I'd said.

'Of course, you can stay with the rest and become a ship's boy on one of our longships instead.'

The life of a ship's boy, especially one who was a slave, was hard.

'I'll serve you, jarl,' he said, the scowl disappearing from his face for the first time.

'Good,' I said and then turned to Wolnoth. 'Get him washed and see if you can find him a clean tunic, trousers and some shoes to wear.'

Wolnoth was about to leave with Arne when I added one more thing.

'And thank you for the suggestion about finding a new body servant.'

'The last one was murdered so watch your step, boy,' Wolnoth told Arne whilst winking at me.

I knew he was just teasing the young Dane but his words hit me like a knife twisting in my guts. For a while I had ceased to dwell on Othilia's death. Now the realisation that I would never see her again enveloped me like a black cloud. I kept telling myself that time was a great healer but it didn't help.

✝✝✝

It was another week before Uhtric pronounced himself satisfied that I was fit enough to ride a horse again. The strappings had been removed some time ago and I hadn't been in any pain for several weeks. I had remained at Hrofescæster in the house of the burh's reeve whilst I was convalescing and I gave his wife a small purse of silver for her trouble.

Ælfred and the rest of the army had long since departed, of course. Tidings of the Danes who had invaded East Anglia had reached us several weeks after the king had left. It seemed that Bjarne had cornered sixteen Viking ships near Herewic. He defeated them, sinking nine and capturing the rest for the loss of one of our ships. It was a great victory but unfortunately he ran into a larger Viking fleet as he was making his way south again.

Wilfrið, the captain of the Saint Cuthbert, came to Hrofescæster to tell me what had happened.

'We had twenty six ships against the enemy's thirty or more but ours weren't fully manned.' He said as he sat on a stool beside my bed. 'We'd lost both sailors and warriors in the first engagement and, of course, we had to spread the rest between our ships and the seven we'd captured. The wind was against us and so we were forced to row. Every ship we had was undermanned and so we were unable to stay clear of the Viking ships; consequently several of our ships were boarded.

'The Saint Cuthbert was larger than any of the enemy and we managed to beat off anyone trying to board us. However, Bjarne was hit by a spear which killed him instantly. I took command and told the horn blower to sound the withdrawal. Several of us managed to fight our way clear but the rest were captured or sunk.'

I was stunned. Bjarne had been one of my closest companions since I'd taken him prisoner at the Battle of Meretum. Initially he'd been put to work as a spit boy, a dreadful occupation at which boys seldom survived for long. I'd rescued him and he'd served me for many years. He'd been a ship's boy for several years and had mastered the art of sailing before I knew him and he'd been invaluable in teaching me the ways of the sea. Without his expertise I'd have been at a grave disadvantage when Ælfred had appointed me as his Sæ Hereræswa. I mourned his loss more than anyone since my first wife and that got me thinking gloomily about all my other hearth

221

warriors who had died in battle. However, there was no point in dwelling on the past; I forced my thoughts back to the present.

'How many of our ships survived?'

'Only seven, however we gave a good account of ourselves and the last I heard the remnants of the Viking fleet were heading back across the Norþ-sǽ to Frisia.'

It was devastating news. We had defeated the invaders but our fleet was crippled and its commander was dead.

I wasn't altogether surprised when a messenger arrived from the king asking me to come and see him as soon as I was fit enough to do so. I could guess what he wanted. Bjarne had been appointed as Sǽ Hererǽswa despite the fact that he wasn't a noble; not even a landholder of any description. He had been accepted by the Witenaġemot, albeit with some reluctance and not a little opposition, but only because of Ælfred's support and my recommendation that he was the best man for the task. The fact that he had been a Swéoþeod seafarer had helped. The nobles and senior clerics of Wessex may have loathed the Vikings but they respected their seafaring skills.

Jerrik, his deputy, was a different prospect. He was a Jute and a ceorl who had learned to sail and to fight at sea from Bjarne and myself. Saxons tended to look down on Jutes and even the poorest thegn thought himself far superior to the wealthiest ceorl. Jerrik had been appointed as Bjarne's deputy without opposition because that appointment wasn't subject to the agreement of the Witenaġemot. However, they would never approve of him as the Sæ Heræswa. In any case I suspected that the prospect of the senior command would terrify Jerrik; he'd been reluctant enough to accept when I asked him to become Bjarne's second-in-command.

I had only ceased to be Sæ Heræswa myself when Ælfred made me the Heræswa of Wessex in place of Eadda. Of course, he'd eventually needed to deprive me of the post and appoint Drefan when I'd been badly wounded at Cæstir. I was now thirty two and, although hopefully far away from my dotage, I felt I had enough to do with my duties as ealdorman of a large shire, especially as I had yet to appoint and train a new shire reeve to assist me.

Of course, I could have been quite wrong and the reason that Ælfred wanted to see me was for some entirely different reason; but I didn't think so.

†††

What Ælfred told me surprised me. Yes, he did ask me to take over as Sæ Heræswa again but there was more to it. Most of the Danish warriors captured at Hrofescæster had refused to talk and had been sold as slaves but a few had been more forthcoming. In return they had been allowed to join the permanent crews of our longships.

They had been split up amongst the rest of the sailors and warriors allocated to each ship. The king was too wise to allow them to stay together and perhaps plot to break the oaths of loyalty they had sworn to him; not that I thought that was likely.

One's honour was as important to most Vikings as his life was – perhaps more so.

The surprise lay in what they had revealed.

'We knew that the famine on the Continent had driven them across the Sūð-sæ,' the king told me. 'What we didn't know was who had organised them into two sizeable armies and selected the targets for their attack. There was no one jarl or leader as far as we could discover but someone had to be the one who had united the disparate groups of Danes into the two fleets.'

'So it wasn't Rollo, cyning?'

A Danish jarl called Rollo was emerging as the leader of the Vikings – both Norse and Danes – who had captured Rouen and who had settled his followers in the surrounding area.

'No, I never thought that was likely. After all, these Vikings invaded East Anglia as well as Cent and King Æthelstan is known to be an ally of Rollo.'

I had to think for a moment before I realised that he was referring to Guðrum who had taken the name of Æthelstan when he became a Christian.

'Then who was the leader of the invasion?'

'It seems that the person who organised the attack on Hrofescæster was Wulfhere and his fellow traitor, Tunbehrt, led the incursion into East Anglia.'

I was stunned. I knew that Tunbehrt had returned to Frisia – in fact I was the person who arranged his passage for him – but I thought Wulfhere was still in the Danelaw somewhere.

'How did a couple of treasonous Saxons manage to put together such a large army?'

'Wulfhere must have had help from someone in the Danelaw. As for Tunbehrt, he married the daughter of Jarl Asbjorn, one of the most powerful Vikings in Frisia and so I suppose his father-in-law must have helped him to raise the army who sacked Herewic and the surrounding area. I don't suppose that Tunbehrt and Asbjorn ever meant to do more than pillage and secure food for their starving families back in Frisia but Wulfhere had a different agenda.

'If he'd managed to seize Hrofescæster it appears that he would have used it as a base to plunder the valley of the River Midweg. He'd promised his followers land all over Cent so this was no mere raid but a deliberate attempt to take and hold the whole peninsula.'

'Do you know where Wulfhere is now?'

'According to the captive Danes, his base is at Honfleur, a small port at the mouth of the River Seine. I want you to raid Honfleur and make sure that you kill Wulfhere this time. It won't be easy as they say that the settlement is defended by a high palisade; however I'm sure that you can find a way in. You've let him slip through your fingers once before, don't let it happen again.'

I looked at the king in surprise. My task when I went into the Danelaw two years ago had been to locate Wulfhere, not kill him. He was being unfair but it was pointless protesting; kings tend to have a way of convincing themselves that anything that goes wrong is always another's fault.

'Very well, cyning. I'll put a raiding party together and hope to leave before winter sets in,' I said in as neutral a tone as I could manage.

I left the king's hall fuming quietly. Not only had Ælfred been unfair. He'd give me an appointment I didn't want and now he expected me to set out to attack Wulfhere in his lair overseas. Without a shire reeve in Cent there was no one to leave in charge in my absence. Who would be responsible for collecting taxes and the revenue due to me personally from my vills, enforcing law and order, giving judgement in the shire court or arranging the defence of the shire in case of raids or, Heaven forbid, another serious attack?

✝✝✝

I had brought only a small escort with me. I would need many more experienced warriors I could trust if I was to infiltrate Wulfhere's base and kill him without starting a major conflict on Frankish soil. Although the Vikings were enemies of King Carloman of West Frankia, he had reached an accommodation with them and any blatant attack on his kingdom could embroil Wessex in a conflict with the Franks. I wasn't about to incur Ælfred's wrath on that score.

I sent messengers to Cantwareburh to summon most of my warband to meet me at Portcæstre. In the meantime I would have to head there myself but not before I'd made a decision on who I wanted to become the new shire reeve. It needed to be a thegn respected by his fellows and he had to be a man of

226

experience, capable of unbiased judgement and honest. That eliminated quite a few. Then I had an idea.

Although my brother Alric was lord of four vills in Hamtunscīr he was also thegn of Tunbrige, an important settlement which stood on high ground near the highest navigable point on the River Midweg. The management of the vill was in the hands of the reeve but if I could persuade Alric to move there permanently I could ask Ælfred to approve his appointment as shire reeve. However, even if he was happy to do so, I doubted that his wife, Guthild, would want to move her family out of her home near Wintanceaster.

I mulled over my options for some time and slept only fitfully that night. By the time that dawn broke I'd decided that I had little to lose by going to see Alric and Guthild. After morning mass and a bite to eat I set off for my brother's hall accompanied by just Wealmær, Wolnoth and two boys who had been training as scouts ever since their father was killed by Wulfhere – Sherwyn and Rowe.

Redwald's sons were now fourteen and twelve respectively, the same sort of age as Alric and Guthild's two children – a boy called Ajs and a girl named Ecgwynna. Both Sherwyn and Rowe were personable boys and I hoped that they might get on well with Alric's children. If so, they might serve as allies in my bid to persuade their parents to move to Tunbrige.

My ploy in taking the two boys with me was only partially successful. I had sent them ahead to warn

Alric and Guthild of my visit and I gathered that Ecgwynna, who was thirteen, had made shy doe eyes at Sherwyn as soon as she saw him. Unfortunately this only served to annoy her brother, who was the same age as Sherwyn, when he saw that her interest was reciprocated.

Alric and Guthild were pleased to see me but puzzled by my unexpected visit. Over the meal that evening I explained what Ælfred had asked me to do. I kept my voice low because I didn't want any word of my expedition across the sea to reach Wulfhere and I knew from experience that slaves and servants have sharp ears. I wouldn't put it past Wulfhere to have spies in Wessex, perhaps even in my brother's hall.

'Do you want me to come with you?' Alric said, his eyes alight with excitement.

Guthild dug her elbow into his ribs and glared at him. His enthusiasm faded and he looked crestfallen. I wasn't surprised at their respective reactions. Of course, my brother had leapt to the wrong conclusion but it confirmed that it was Guthild who I needed to win over.

'No, you are needed here, with your family, but I do have a favour to ask.'

I paused to allow them to speculate about what it might be.

'Ever since Æscwin's death I have been without a shire reeve and I have been worrying over who should replace him. The person who I ask the king to appoint would, in most respects, be acting as ealdorman as I will be away a lot building up the fleet again and patrolling our shores.'

I took a bite of venison and chewed it slowly to let what I had said sink in. Alric was perfectly content with his lot but I knew that Guthild, much as she loved my brother, resented the fact that her status as an ealdorman's daughter had become diminished when she married a coerl. Alric was a thegn now, and a wealthy one at that, but only because of the lands that Guthild had inherited from her late father. Becoming shire reeve would be a step up in rank for her as well as for my brother.

'You have a prosperous vill at Tunbrige,' I said when I'd finished chewing the somewhat tough piece of meat.

'You're asking me to replace Æscwin?' Alric asked incredulously.

'I'm asking you to at least discuss it with Guthild. I realise I'm asking a lot. It would mean uprooting your family so you may want to discuss it with your children as well.'

'They'll do as they're told,' Guthild responded sharply.

Her response was a relief. I inferred from it that she wasn't averse to the idea. I went to bed that night in a happier frame of mind.

The next day I could tell immediately that Alric and Guthild were in favour of the move. However, Ajs was vehemently opposed to it. It didn't change anything, of course, but it rather soured the atmosphere. I took Alric to one side for a quiet word.

'What are your plans for Ajs? He's just turned fourteen and it's time he began his training to be a warrior.'

229

'He's a good rider and one of my hearth warriors is teaching him to use spear, sword and shield,' Alric replied, a little defensively.

'I didn't mean to criticise, brother. He's your heir but he has few boys his age here – or I suspect in Tunbrige - with whom he can train. Send him to me and I'll teach him to become a warrior and a leader.'

'I'll need to discuss it with Guthild,' he said doubtfully. 'I'm sure you're right, and it's time he left the somewhat cloying life he leads here.'

By that I took it that Ajs was rather doted on by his mother. I don't know what transpired between Alric and his wife but I suspected that my brother had put his foot down – a somewhat rare occurrence – because he told me that Ajs would be leaving with me. The sour look that Guthild gave him at the midday meal indicated that she wasn't entirely in favour of the idea. I had a feeling that Alric would suffer her displeasure for some time to come.

It was only 20 miles from my brother's hall to Portcæstre and so we set out just after noon. The two boys rode ahead as scouts and I told Ajs to ride with them and watch what they did. He looked rather scornful, as if there was nothing of value that he could learn from Sherwyn and his brother, but he did as he was told.

Later I asked Sherwyn how it had gone.

'He started by being somewhat aloof. He ignored me, although I can't think what I've done to offend him, but he seemed happy to listen to my brother after a while. Rowe pointed out signs that might indicate an ambush, like the absence of bird song. He also chatted away to Ajs about hunting and tracking and he seemed quite interested.'

I was pleased by that. I was convinced that my nephew had all the right qualities to make a warrior; all he needed was education and motivation.

That night we stayed in the fort at Portcæstre and I gathered my captains together to formally tell them that I was their new commander. I added that I would be taking a small patrol across the Sūð-sæ to confirm that the Vikings had returned to their bases in Frankia.

The end of October was late to be out at sea - the storm season would soon be upon us - but it was worth the risk if it enabled me to catch Wulfhere in Honfleur.

Chapter Twelve

THE COAST OF FRANKIA

November 884

I left Portcæstre on the Saint Cuthbert accompanied by the Holy Spirit. We docked at Dofras to load my warband onto the two longships and onto a third skeid we had named the Resurrection. The latter was the largest of the prizes we had taken from the Danes at Hrofescæster. It seemed an apt name for a longship that we'd converted from a Viking raider into one of Ælfred's warships. The only changes we'd actually made were to replace the serpent's head on the prow with a large cross and to dye the sail dark brown to hide the raven symbol on a red and white striped background that identified her as Danish. I was also taking a knarr with us onto which we loaded four horses for the scouts to use.

Whilst the small fleet was being prepared for the crossing I took the opportunity to ride to Cantwareburh. I had written to Hilda from Wintanceaster to tell her that I was well and about my new appointment but I wanted to see her in person to tell her that I would be away for a short while.

At first my reception was somewhat frosty. No one had told her of Othilia's death but she had assumed, correctly as it happened, that the girl had run off to join me. I couldn't blame her for assuming that I'd allowed her to become my mistress whilst in camp outside Hrofescæster. That had so nearly become true.

'Where is that wretched girl,' she had stormed at me once she had greeted me, rather formally, outside the hall and we'd retreated to our chamber.

'Dead, as it happens,' I replied tersely, assuming correctly that she meant Othilia.

'Dead?' Hilda's jaw dropped in surprise. 'How?'

'She came with Uhtric and Leofwine to help them look after the wounded and was stabbed to death outside their tent one night.'

'Murdered you mean? Why? By whom?'

'By Bryhthelm, one of Eadda's men; a warrior who was employed to teach weapon skills to the Ætheling Edward and your son Oswine, amongst others.'

'Why on earth would he kill a servant girl?'

'Because she was part of my household, I assume. Perhaps his intention was to rob me of my two physicians as well. Who knows? He didn't talk when questioned and the king fined him wergeld for her murder, which he was unable to pay. Bryhthelm is now a slave in Íralond and his family are in bond to Eadda.'

Hilda shuddered and thankfully dropped the subject. Being reminded about Othilia's death had depressed me but I tried to put a brave face on it. I stayed the night with Hilda before returning to Dofras the next morning. She had been in the mood for making love and, although I wasn't very keen at first - still being depressed about Othilia - her ministrations soon changed my mind.

Each ship had a full crew of sailors including four ship's boys but I also sent Ajs to join the Holy Spirit and Sherwyn to the Resurrection, keeping Rowe on the Saint Cuthbert. My two scouts were good at their job on land but I wanted to broaden their experience. I also thought that a bit of hard work amongst Ajs's social inferiors might knock some of the aloofness out of him.

It was raining as we cleared the harbour and headed out into a distinctly choppy sea. We headed due south and with a strong wind from the west the waves caught us broadside on, rolling the longship to and fro. It was uncomfortable and more than a few of my warriors who were unused to being afloat soon learned the advisedness of spewing over the leeward side.

I was amused to see that Rowe was relishing the sensation of wind and water in his face and the lively movement of the ship and I wondered how my nephew was faring over on the Resurrection. Being built in Danmǫrk, she had a shallower draft than our ships and consequently wallowed more.

As we reached the middle of the crossing the wind increased so we were forced to take in two reefs in the sail. I watched as the ship's boys struggled to control the heavy, flapping woollen sail and sent two of the men to help them. Once it was lowered the rowers kept the ship head to wind and the movement became more comfortable. I was pleased to see that Rowe quickly caught on to what was required and, with the other boys, quickly tied the reefing knots in place across the sail. That done, two men sweated the yardarm up again whilst the boys paid out the sheets tied to the bottom corners of the sail.

We set sail again, the reefs making our passage through the heavy seas more comfortable. Otherwise the crossing was uneventful. We saw no other sails, although visibility was such that another craft could have passed us a mile away and we wouldn't have seen it. It was too rough for a lookout to climb the rigging, and even more difficult for him to maintain a perch on the yardarm. The top of the mast was dancing around so violently that it wouldn't have been long before anyone up there would have been sent hurtling into the sea like a stone out of a sling.

Instead the lookout stood in the bows with one hand on the forestay and the other arm around the carved figurehead of Saint Cuthbert. It was Rowe's turn to be on watch when the blurred grey outline of the Frankish coast emerged ahead of us.

'Land ho!' he yelled in his piping treble voice.

The sound was whipped away by the rain laden wind before it reached me in the stern but I saw him gesticulate urgently and made my way to the bows. The land couldn't have been more than half a mile away and I didn't know this coastline. Wary of rocks lying offshore, I turned to signal Wilfrið and he ordered the steersman to bear away. The ship's boys ran to trim the sail and we altered course to run along the shoreline.

I needed to find a deserted cove where we could beach the ships for the night. I had no idea whether we had struck land north or south of Honfleur; that would be for the scouts to find out in the morning.

✝✝✝

In the end we had to wait for a day in a cove with a beach of golden sand that we had been fortunate enough to find. We had passed what looked like a fishing hamlet five miles north but I hoped that it was far enough away for us to remain undiscovered. Surprise was a vital element in my plan to take Honfleur and kill Wulfhere.

The horses were in a poor way after such a rough crossing and they needed time to recover. They had been transported in slings so no legs were broken but they were extremely stressed by the experience. We unloaded them using the slings and then led them ashore through knee-deep water. The marram grass that grew on the dunes above the beach was no good for grazing and so they were led up to an area of grass and shrubs a few hundred yards inland. We set up camp in a sizeable hollow and posted sentries to the north, south and east.

We had a job to light a fire but eventually we got one going. After that it was easy to light several more so that all two hundred and fifty of us could get warm. Our clothes remained sodden as the continuous rain soaked them again as soon as they began to steam in the heat of the spitting flames.

At least we had some heat. The ships' boys and the sailors I had left to guard the ships didn't even have that luxury.

I woke at dawn the next day to see a watery sun rise over the flat land to the east. The rain had ceased during the night and the wind had eased to a moderate breeze. Once a few of my men had finished eating I sent them down to the ships to relieve those left on watch so that they could come and get some hot food inside them.

The sun soon dispersed the early morning mist but it wasn't exactly hot in November. Therefore we had to gather more firewood before we could dry out our clothes. My byrnie, helmet and weapons had travelled in an oiled leather sack but nevertheless rust had appeared on them and Arne was kept busy using sand in a sack to burnish them.

The horses had recovered overnight and I was relieved that they all appeared to be uninjured when examined. However, they needed gentle exercise before they would be safe to ride for any distance. Sherwyn, Rowe and two other young scouts led them using halters whilst the horses walked then trotted beside them. By midday they appeared fit enough to ride.

I sent one pair of scouts up the coast and another pair in the opposite direction to find Honfleur. Rinan and Rowe, who had gone south, were the first to return some two hours before dusk.

'We found a small hamlet with three longships moored in the harbour,' Rinan told me, brimming with pride at having been the one to find Wulfhere. 'There's a hall and several huts but no palisade.'

I was surprised as Ælfred had definitely been told by the captive Danes that Honfleur was defended by one. Perhaps they had been mistaken, or else wanted to mislead us for some reason.

'Did you see any sign of a banner?' I asked.

'Yes, lord,' Rinan said, nodding eagerly. 'One was flying outside the hall. It was red embroidered with what looked like a yellow serpent.'

I tried to hide my disappointment.

'That's not Wulfhere's banner, unless he's changed it,'

'Oh! Sorry, lord.'

'Don't worry; it's not your fault. Hopefully Eomær and Sherwyn have had more luck.'

They had. They came riding in just as twilight darkened the land on exhausted horses.

'The first vill we came to was at the mouth of a small river. It's quite large but there were no longships; just a dozen fishing boats drawn up onto the sand,' Eomær told me.

I knew that Honfleur lay on the south side of the estuary of a river called the Seine, which ran all the way to a place called Paris, a major settlement the size of Lundenwic. It didn't sound as if this river could be the Seine. I presumed that they had found a fishing hamlet inhabited by Franks.

'We had to cross the river but we had to go a long way inland before we found a ford. We rode back until we hit the coast again and continued north.'

Eomær paused for breath and Sherwyn gave him an impatient look.

'We found it, lord,' the boy said excitedly. 'I recognised the banner, a running horse on a black background.'

'I was just coming to that,' Eomær said, looking peeved. 'We found a port surrounded by a palisade at the mouth of the next river with, as Sherwyn said, a black banner above the gate.'

'Excellent; well done the two of you. What else did you manage to find out?'

'It lies at the junction of two estuaries, a large one which must be the Seine you told us about and a smaller one. There is a palisade around the settlement which lies on the south bank of the smaller river. We could see a jetty but nothing was moored to it.'

My heart sank. Did that mean that Wulfhere was off raiding somewhere?

'There were two longships a little way from the settlement. They had been dragged up high onto a beach and were supported by props.'

I breathed a sigh of relief. It seemed that Wulfhere was there after all and was busy preparing his ships for the winter.

'Did you manage to make an estimate of the number of warriors in the place?' I asked.

'We were conscious of the fact that the day was well advanced and if we wanted to get back before dark we didn't have very long. There was small hall which I presumed was the home of the renegade Wulfhere and a larger hall which would be where his warriors lived. If so it could probably hold fifty or perhaps sixty men; but there were several huts and we could see a number of women and children. Judging by the size of the longships they would take perhaps seventy men to crew them and obviously some would stay to guard the place when the ships were away. If I was asked to hazard a guess I would say perhaps a hundred men in all.'

'I counted a dozen huts in addition to stables, kennels, store huts and a brewhouse,' Sherwyn added.

If the hall held sixty men there were probably ninety in all, allowing for a man and one son of fighting age in each hut. We outnumbered them three to one but that was negated by the fact that they would be behind a palisade. Besides, I didn't intend to lose men by making a direct assault using scaling ladders.

At least we now knew where the enemy was. I would need to see the place for myself before I could hope to come up with any sort of plan, and we would need to move our base closer. I tried to sleep that night but my mind kept pouring over all the various ways that we might be able to get inside the defences. It wasn't until the early hours of the morning that I fell into a fitful sleep and consequently felt like death warmed up when Arne came to wake me with a hot goblet of spiced mead.

✝✝✝

I crept forward with Eomær, Wealmær and Wolnoth to the top of the hill overlooking Honfleur. From there I could study the fortifications and the area around the port. The tributary that led to Honfleur from the estuary of the River Seine was reasonably wide at the beginning but downstream from the settlement it ran into marshland and virtually disappeared. As Eomær had said, there were no ships moored at the short jetty but there was a sizeable fishing boat capable of holding perhaps ten men.

On the other side of the river from Honfleur there was a small fort. I could just make out a chain running into the water from there. Presumably the other end was secured inside the palisade somewhere. Its purpose was clearly to prevent craft entering the area of the waterfront, where there was no palisade.

As I watched, ten men clambered into the boat and two men rowed the rest across to the fort. Eight more men were waiting on the far bank and the boat returned with them. This process was repeated three times. Evidently the garrison that guarded the far end of the chain boom had changed over. Moreover I now knew that the fort was manned by twenty four warriors.

An idea began to formulate itself but I needed to see Wulfhere's two boats before I could be certain that it had a chance of working. We couldn't see the beach from where we were so we edged back to where we had tethered our horses and then made our way around the side of the hill.

Suddenly Eomær, who was leading stopped and crouched down. We did likewise and he got down on his belly before slithering back to me.

'There's a shepherd boy with two dogs just below the crest on this side,' he whispered in my ear. 'His flock are scattered over the hillside above the beach.'

I debated what to do. I wanted to see the position of the ships for myself and judge how far they were from the settlement. More importantly I needed to assess how well defended they were. I didn't like killing unless it was necessary but the dogs would have to be silenced.

Wealmær and Wolnoth strung their bows and nocked an arrow in readiness.

'Go!' I told Eomær and he sprang up and headed straight for the boy.

At the same time the other two released and the two dogs died without making a sound. The shepherd, who looked to be about fifteen, jumped to his feet and looked around in alarm. He seemed paralysed for a moment then he spotted Eomær heading for him. He turned and ran headlong downhill.

Eomær was fast but this lad was faster. I reluctantly nodded to the two archers and they drew back their bowstrings and took careful aim. Just at that moment the boy tripped over something and tumbled headlong downhill. Before he could regain his feet Eomær was upon him and knocked him out with the pommel of his dagger.

I looked around anxiously but we were hidden from both Honfleur and the beach. We went down to join Eomær and crept forward to the ridgeline from where we could look down on Wulfhere's two longships. Just at that moment the shepherd groaned and sat up. Either he had a very thick skull or Eomær hadn't hit him hard enough.

Wolnoth ran back up the hill and tore of a piece of the boy's grubby tunic and stuffed it in his mouth. Instead of trousers he wore lengths of wool wound around his legs to keep the cold out. Over his coarse woollen tunic he wore a jerkin fashioned from a sheepskin. Wolnoth unwound the cloth binding from his right leg and tied both his hands and feet with it.

Satisfied that the shepherd was immobilised, I returned to my examination of the ships. They had been dragged up the beach far enough so that the high tide wouldn't reach them, even in a storm, and four huts had been built near them.

They had been stripped of all rigging, other cordage, masts and spars. A few men and several boys were hacking out the old caulking from between the planks of the hull whilst others were cleaning the area under the waterline of seaweed, barnacles and the like. Evidently they had only recently been taken out of the water. Once cleaned they would no doubt be covered over for the winter and then re-caulked and fitted out again in March the following year.

Two boys were collecting up oars and taking them into the largest of the huts, which was presumably the store. I assumed that the other huts would house those detailed to guard the ships over the winter. Judging by their size, there wouldn't be more than a dozen on watch at any given time.

The beach was on the same level as the settlement and, as far as I could see, there was nothing much in the way. The ships would certainly be in sight of the watchtower which stood beside the one landward pair of gates in the palisade. I had what I'd come for and we edged our way back over the skyline.

'What about the shepherd?' Wealmær asked prodding the boy with his foot.

'We can't let him go,' I replied thoughtfully. 'Although he's a Frank by the way he's dressed he might still warn Wulfhere that we're in the vicinity.'

In truth, I thought it unlikely. The Viking invaders preyed on the locals and forced them to provide them with food and slaves. Wulfhere's men would be the same. The last thing a Frank would do was to help them. Nevertheless I wasn't prepared to take the risk.

'Bring him with us. Eomær, you'll have to ride double with him so you take the strongest horse.'

Once back in camp I tried to question the boy but he spoke nothing but the local dialect. I assumed this to be Franconian but I noted that the boy's ears pricked up when mass was celebrated by Father Abrecan, the priest who had come with us to minister to the men's spiritual needs. I asked him to speak to the boy in Latin.

It turned out that the local language was something called Sermo Vulgaris, a colloquial version that had developed from the Latin spoken by the Gauls. There were enough words in common for the shepherd, whose name was Tescelin, to converse with Abrecan, at least up to a point. When he heard that we intended to eliminate the nest of pirates in Honfleur he appeared eager to help.

It took some time but Tescelin confirmed that there were about a hundred men in Honfleur. He thought that about forty of them were Saxons and another forty or so were Danes. The remainder were renegade Franks. He had been inside the place with his father when they took the annual tax to Wulfhere in the form of sheep. There were about ten women, probably the wives of some of the warriors, and two dozen children of various ages. There were also a number of slaves – mostly girls who seemed to be passed around between the single men. There were also a few male slaves.

I asked Abrecan, whose Latin was better than mine, to thank Tescelin and relay my promise to release him as soon as our business in Frankia was done. I then briefed everyone on my plan.

Chapter Thirteen

HONFLEUR, FRANKIA

Mid-November 884

I waited impatiently for dawn to break. The best plans are simple but mine was anything but. I had decided on a three pronged attack led by myself, Wealmær and Wolnoth respectively. The key was timing and there was no way I could co-ordinate the three aspects of the plan. I had to rely on the common sense of the other two and on luck.

The first fingers of sunlight crept over the land as I stood in the bows of the Saint Cuthbert anxiously looking between Wulfhere's beached ships and at the fort in turn. My ships had to move into position in the dark and that was hazardous enough in itself. The entrance to the Seine estuary was wide but there were sandbanks and mud banks on both sides of the navigable channel.

The approach to the fort was particularly difficult, according to Tescelin, whose uncle was a fisherman. For that reason I had chosen the Resurrection to land the group to attack the fort. It had the shallowest draft but, even so, the crew had to cast the lead to check the depth of water as they inched their way towards the shore. If they ran aground or were spotted my plan would be in ruins.

I had used the knarr to land the twenty men under Wolnoth's command to kill the watch on the two beached longships. His was a more straightforward task as the approach to the beach from the north was clear of obstacles. However, he would still have to judge when to turn out of the main channel carefully if he was to avoid the line of mudbanks between the main channel and the southern channel.

Beside me Ajs was on duty as lookout. I planned to leave him on board when we attacked. He was the least experienced of all those on this expedition and I really didn't want to face Guthild's wrath if anything happened to him.

The Holy Spirit lay a hundred yards abeam of us. Like ours, her rowers were occasionally dipping their oars in the sea to keep her on station. The sea was calm with just a gentle swell and the wind from the east was no more than a light breeze. Nevertheless it was icy cold and I had a feeling that winter wasn't far away.

The first rays of the sun broke the line of the horizon and the tension I felt in my guts mounted. The coastline to the north and south of us came into view and I could hear the faint sounds of yelling coming across the water. Still I waited.

As the gloom lifted I could see the Resurrection to the north-east of us. It had evidently cleared the mud banks without grounding and men carrying scaling ladders were heading for the fort. I breathed a sigh of relief. At least the first part of my plan was in progress. Suddenly a bell sounded and men rushed to man the parapet of the fort.

Someone in Honfleur had seen what was happening and another, deeper, bell rang out. Almost

at the same time a small fire sprang up from the area
of Wulfhere's ships. It meant that the second stage
had gone without a hitch. Still I had to wait.

After ten minutes of fierce fighting the fort fell and
several of my men rushed to untie the chain from the
post to which it was secured.

'That's it! Now row, row as if your life depended
on it,' I yelled. 'Row as if all the demons of Hell are on
your tail!'

I could see Ajs out of the corner of my eye looking
at me in amazement, but his eyes betrayed his
excitement.

'Don't forget, you're to stay on board with the
ship's boys when we disembark,' I reminded him
sternly.

He nodded, disappointment etched on his face.
His hand went to the hilt of the seax I had given him
as a present and I could tell that he was itching to
prove himself a man. I had also given him a leather
tunic sewn all over with metal scales and a simple pot
helmet but they were for his protection against stray
missiles, not for combat.

He went to join Sherwyn, Rowe and the other boys
as they prepared to jump ashore with the mooring
lines. We had entered the tributary off the Seine now
and headed for the jetty. Before the settlement
blocked my view I had seen a horde of people -
women and older children as well as men – heading
for the burning ships. They were carrying buckets
and anything that could hold water but not weapons,
other than the swords and seaxes the warriors
habitually wore. It meant that there would be fewer

left to fight in Honfleur and the less women and children there were the better.

We bumped against the wooden jetty and, before the boys had secured the ship alongside, I jumped ashore along with the rest of the crew. We were faced by two score of men who had formed a shield wall but, as the warriors from the Holy Spirit joined us, it must have become apparent to them how outnumbered they were. A volley of arrows convinced them that flight was better than certain death, despite the fact that most had been protected by their shields, and they broke and ran.

We split up into groups to hunt the enemy down. I headed for the smaller hall with a few of my hearth warriors. I hoped that was where I'd find Wulfhere but it was deserted. I checked the warriors' hall next but that too was empty, apart from a few women and young girls. I assured them as best I could that they would come to no harm and sent my men out to search for Wulfhere. In retrospect it was stupid of me as it left me on my own.

As I rounded the corner of a hut I'd just searched I came face to face with a Frank armed with two swords. Evidently this was one of the local warriors who had turned against his own people to gain plunder with Wulfhere. He reacted more quickly than I did and the point of one of his swords darted towards my throat as the second blade made a cut at my legs.

I lowered my shield to deflect the second sword whilst jerking my head to one side. The point of the first sword lodged in the chain mail links of my avantail and my head was twisted to one side so that I lost sight of the Frank. I jumped backwards, just missing the second of his swords as he thrust it towards my unprotected eyes. The man was quick and I was fighting for my life.

As he made another cut at me, this time at my right arm, I twisted my whole body so that my shield took the blow instead. As he aimed another thrust at me with his other blade I smashed the boss of my shield into his face. He was wearing a pot helmet with cheek pieces but no nose guard. The metal boss flattened his nose and broke several of his teeth, leaving his face a bloody mess.

He stepped back, shaking his head to try and see properly. That gave me my chance and I brought the rim of my shield down on his leather clad feet, breaking several toes. At the same time I lunged with my sword aiming at his neck. However, he doubled up in pain and the point skidded off the top of his helmet instead.

Had he been able to take advantage at that point he could have killed me without difficulty. My shield was too low to be of any use and my chest and neck were vulnerable. Thankfully he was incapacitated at that moment. A second later I swung my sword at his neck with all the strength I could muster. It cut through the iron links of his avantail and the leather hood he wore underneath. The blow jarred my arm and I almost lost my grip on the hilt. However, it penetrated his neck enough to grievously wound him. He sunk to his knees and, taking a fresh grip on my sword, I repeated the blow. This time, with nothing except sinew, flesh and bone to impede it, it sliced clean through his neck and the Frank's head bounced away to come to rest against the side of a hut.

I stuck my sword point first into the ground and leant on it, heaving in great lungfuls of air. For the first time in my life I realised that, at thirty three years old, I was no longer a young man. I wasn't elderly by any means; many nobles who didn't die in battle lived into their late forties or even into their fifties. However, I was slowing down and everything was a little more of an effort now.

Within half an hour the last of the defenders had been slain but there was no sign of the man I sought. I could only conclude that Wulfhere had gone to supervise the firefighters on the beach. I felt completely miserable. Unless he'd been killed fighting against Wolnoth and his men - something I thought rather unlikely; Wulfhere wasn't one to lead from the front - he'd evaded me yet again. Just at that moment Cináed appeared on horseback. I had given him, Acwel, Lyndon and Eomær our four horses and told them to watch for any who tried to flee into the hinterland. Perhaps all wasn't yet lost.

'There were three men on horseback who led those who came put out the fires,' he told me, gasping for breath. 'They fled as soon as they realised that Honfleur was under attack and headed east. Acwel and the others are in pursuit but I thought you'd want to know.'

I was as certain as I could be that one of the three horseman was Wulfhere. I was about to order Cináed to give me his horse when Sherwyn, Ajs and Rowe appeared. The three of them had found the stables and were mounted on good horses. They had brought a fourth for me thinking to accompany me over to see what had happened at the beach. It was fortuitous and I was about to order them to hand their mounts to warriors when they set off at a canter.

Sherwyn and Rowe had evidently overheard what Acwel had told me and assumed that the man who'd killed their father was getting away. Ajs had simply followed them. Swearing ineffectually at their retreating backs, I heaved myself into the saddle of the fourth horse and set off after them, Cináed falling in beside me.

✝✝✝

I could just see Acwel and the others in the distance before they disappeared into some trees. The three boys were a good mile or more behind them but, being lighter, they were slowly catching the scouts up. Cináed and I were a quarter of a mile further back.

We were following a good track. It had been churned up by horses and carts in the past but the cold temperature meant that the ground was now firm. I was tempted to increase the pace to a gallop but horses can't keep that up for very long. Thankfully the three boys didn't seem to be pushing their horses too hard either.

In my eagerness to follow the others I hadn't been paying attention to my surroundings. The morning had started sunny but clouds had soon covered the sun. Now they got blacker and blacker. The first few drops of sleet on my face therefore caught me by surprise.

Thankfully we entered the woods at that point and the trees, bare as they were, gave us a little protection from the wet flakes. The track we were following curved to the right and so I couldn't see the boys ahead of us. It straightened out as we left the wood and emerged into flat pasture land filled by grazing sheep. Off to my left I could see the Seine in the distance. The track was now running parallel to the river.

The sheep had been scattered by the other three groups of riders and inevitably we did the same. An old shepherd and a boy stood nearby with a large dog. They yelled what were presumably curses at us and the dog added his vociferous disapproval. We ignored them and cantered on.

When I estimated that we had covered ten miles or so I slowed to a trot. Horses can canter for perhaps an hour but by then they are exhausted and need a rest. It galled me because my instinct was to try and catch those ahead of us up but I knew that would only result in us killing our mounts.

The sleet died away but the bitingly cold wind remained. The first person we came across was Ajs. The boys had continued to canter long past the point when it was sensible to slow down and my nephew's horse was spent. The boy was standing despondently beside it as its flanks heaved, drawing in great breaths. Thankfully he hadn't ridden it to death.

'Stay here and don't try to ride it. Eventually it should recover but you'll have to lead it back to Honfleur at first. If you think the horse can stand it, alternate riding and walking.'

'I understand uncle; thank you.'

We trotted on and an hour later we caught up with Sherwyn and Rowe. They had dismounted and strung their bows. I got down and made my way undercover of the shrubs by the side of the track to where they stood.

'Lord, Acwel and the others have caught up with Wulfhere and his two companions but the latter attacked our men so that Wulfhere could make his escape.'

I could see the two renegade Saxons desperately trying to hold off my men and swore obscenely as I spotted Wulfhere disappearing over a rise in the track some two hundred yards away. Just as that moment Acwel forced one of the two enemy back and Sherwyn took the opportunity to send an arrow his way. It was a rushed shot but it caught the man in his thigh. He gasped with shock and Acwel sliced his sword across his neck. Meanwhile the other two scouts had dispatched the second of Wulfhere's men.

'Come on,' I yelled and kicked my horse back into a canter.

With the others strung out behind me I chased after Wulfhere but, by the time I'd reached the ridge where I'd last seen him he'd disappeared. The track stretched for at least a mile in front of me but it was deserted. I had no idea how my quarry had managed to vanish. There were no woods nearby, just scrubland and the odd lone tree.

✝✝✝

Eomær was the first to reach me. He slowed his horse to a walk and studied the ground carefully as he went.

'He turned off here,' he called, pointing along a fold in the ground which deepened as it went.

'Well spotted,' I said with a grin.

We turned off the track and followed the trail. The ground was soft and the hoof prints of his horse weren't difficult to follow once we had left the stony ground beside the track. The fold in the ground deepened as we progressed, turning into a defile lined with scrub. It explained why we hadn't seen him from the top of the ridge.

After a mile or more the defile flattened out again and we could see the glimmer of the River Seine through some trees ahead of us. I had been told that there were several Viking camps along the Seine and I suspected he was heading towards one of them. If he reached it before we caught him we'd have to give up the chase. Even if the camp housed the crew of just one Snekkja we would be heavily outnumbered. There were just six of us who were trained warriors, counting Sherwyn, and I wasn't about to risk the lives of my nephew or Rowe.

Then we had a stroke of luck. Eomær had dismounted to study the hoof prints before punching the air.

'His horse is lame,' Eomær said excitedly.

Cináed jumped off his horse and knelt beside him. 'He's right!' he said, thumping Eomær on the back.

If Wulfhere's horse was lame he wouldn't be able to move at more than a walking pace. Any man with a sense of compassion for the beast would have dismounted and left it, but it seemed that Wulfhere was still mounted on the lame animal. Whatever the reason for the lameness, continuing to ride it would just make its limp worse.

Half a mile further on we found the horse's corpse. Presumably Wulfhere had cut its throat in a fit of rage. He was now on foot and I risked pushing our own steeds into a canter. The river was now quite close, although I couldn't see any sign of habitation on this bank.

A few minutes later we caught up with Wulfhere. He was within a couple of hundred yards of the river and we could see the smoke of several fires curling above the trees further along the bank. Another five minutes and the renegade Saxon would have reached safety.

Whilst Acwel and Eomær rode around him to prevent escape, the rest of us dismounted. Cináed strung his bow.

'There's no point in risking anyone's life for this piece of garbage, lord. Let me bring him down.'

Wulfhere had adopted a fighting pose, crouching with sword in one hand and his seax in the other. He was dressed in a thick woollen tunic and a wolf-skin cloak. Of course, he hadn't expected to have to fight when he'd gone to investigate the blazing longships.

256

However, he'd had the sense to take his weapons. Now his eyes darted this way and that, trying to work out from which direction the attack would come.

'No, he may be a traitor but he's still from a noble house; one of the oldest in Wessex. I'll fight him so that he may at least die with dignity,' I told him, getting off my horse.

'You're too honourable for your own good,' Cináed muttered with a scowl, adding 'lord', after a pause.

No doubt he thought me a fool but I had wanted to kill this man for years. However, I didn't have the chance. With a roar of rage Sherwyn and Rowe sprinted past me and faced up to Wulfhere. Each was armed with a seax and a dagger. I was appalled. They were still boys and didn't stand a chance, or so I thought.

'He's ours, lord. He killed our father and we demand the right to our revenge,' Sherwyn said before I could order him back in line.

He made a feint at Wulfhere's head and, whilst the man dodged aside, Rowe rolled on the ground and hacked at the back of their opponent's leg with his seax. Evidently he had managed to cut his hamstring because Wulfhere sank to one knee with a scream.

He swung his sword at Sherwyn's legs and tried to stab Rowe's prone body with his seax at the same time. I realised then that Wulfhere was no warrior. Neither boy had any difficulty in evading the blades. He should have merely held off Sherwyn and concentrated on killing Rowe first as he was the more vulnerable one.

Rowe rolled out of reach as Wulfhere made another attempt to stab him. That unbalanced the kneeling man and I expected Sherwyn to step in and stab him in the neck; he didn't. Instead he thrust his seax into Wulfhere's right biceps, causing him to drop his sword. I realised that the two boys were playing with him. This man had killed their father and they intended to make him suffer before they slew him.

Wulfhere waved his seax ineffectually at Sherwyn as Rowe got to his feet and darted in, stabbing his dagger into the man's thigh. He must have severed the femoral artery because blood didn't just seep out it spurted, coating Rowe in gore.

The two boys moved away and watched as Wulfhere's lifeblood soaked the ground on which he lay. They evidently intended to let him lie there until he expired but enough was enough. I stepped in and thrust the point of my sword into his chest. It pierced the heart and Wulfhere, once the proud Ealdorman of Wiltunscīr, died in a pool of his own blood, faeces and urine. It wasn't a nice way to die.

✝✝✝

When we returned to Honfleur I discovered that my men had killed the wounded pirates, and the few who'd surrendered. It was probably for the best but I wouldn't have ordered the killing of uninjured captives had I been there. When we left we took their women and children with us to sell as slaves back in Wessex.

There were also fifteen young women and eight boys who had been enslaved by Wulfhere. I freed them and the ten girls and three boys who were Franks were left to walk back to their old homes.

I offered the other five girls, who ranged in age from fifteen to twenty, places in my household as paid servants. They accepted without hesitation. I had no doubt that most of them would end up as the wives of my warriors. That left the six boys. They were a mixture of Danes who had been taken prisoner when Wulfhere captured Honfleur from the Danish jarl who had held it before him, and Saxons. It wasn't unusual for Danes to quarrel amongst themselves and I wasn't surprised that Wulfhere had taken his base on the Continent by force. The two Saxon slaves were more of a mystery until they explained that they'd been ship's boys on one of the longships captured during the abortive invasion of Cent and East Anglia.

I offered to enrol all six of them: the Danes for training as warriors and the Saxons to serve in the fleet. All of them eagerly accepted.

There were also a dozen horses in the stables. There wasn't room for all of them on the knarr and so I picked the best six and made a present of the rest to Tescelin. They represented a fortune to a poor shepherd and he gabbled his thanks. At least I assumed that he was thanking me as I didn't understand a word he said. The expression on his face said it all though.

The ships were overladen with people, horses and the chests of silver we had found in Wulfhere's hall. Those items that were clearly looted from churches and monasteries would be handed over to Abbot Plegmund. The rest would be shared out; half would go to swell my coffers and Ælfred would no doubt expect a gift, but my men would also be well rewarded.

Thankfully the weather for the crossing to Cent was benign and we reached Dofras without incident. I picked out a brooch made of gold and encrusted with rubies and emeralds as a present for Hilda and set out on the last leg of the journey back to Cantwareburh in a happy frame of mind. Wulfhere was dead, Ajs had stopped behaving like a spoilt brat and I had no doubt that he would become a fine young man and a good warrior in due course. The significant increase in my personal wealth also helped.

I trusted that the Year of our Lord eight hundred and eighty five would prove to be a lot less exciting that the year just drawing to a close.

Chapter Fourteen

WESSEX

Spring 885

The wolf stood on the top of the crag eyeing me warily. It had been a harsh winter for animals and humans alike. The snows had come shortly after I returned to Cantwareburh. Jerrik was now at Portcæstre with the western fleet, depleted as it was. I wanted to return to Dofras now that I was Sæ Hereræswa once more but two things stopped me. Hilda refused to move, and the roads became impassable before I managed to convince her that I needed to base myself there. It wasn't a good start to what would prove to be a difficult few months.

Food was running short, even though Hilda had been prudent in filling the storage huts before winter set in. The cold and icy landscape yielded little in the form of prey for the wolves that normally stayed well clear of humans and so they were forced to seek our livestock in order to survive. Most cattle and pigs spent the winter under cover but the sheep were left in outside pens to cope as best they might.

After a wolf had killed a boy who had tried to drive off a pack of the beasts who were slaughtering his family's flock inside a pen, I decided to lead a hunt to rid the area of them. Normally we'd have used dogs to follow the trail but the snow was too deep. However, my scouts had no trouble in following the pack's trail from the blood splattered pen. The air was still and there had been no fresh fall of snow to obliterate their paw prints.

We ran them to earth some six miles to the east of the pen. Even our horses had a hard time plodding through the snow. It came up higher than the wolves' bellies and consequently they were exhausted and could run no further. There were six of them – two dogs and four she-wolves. None were young; no doubt the previous spring's cubs were the first to die. Our horses were still scared of them and so we dismounted before circling them, keeping our hunting spears pointing towards them.

This wasn't a hunt for sport; the aim was to kill as quickly and safely as possible. Eomær and Rinan took off their gauntlets and strung their bows. It wasn't easy to use a bow in such cold conditions but it was the best way of thinning the wolves' numbers. They aimed at the pair that appeared to be the alphas and once they fell the other four howled in despair.

Suddenly three of them rushed us. One, the remaining dog, used the last of his strength to leap in the air and came down on my chest. I fell backwards, my spear falling from my hands as the wolf's teeth snapped together inches from my face. I scarcely noticed its stinking breath as I fought to push it away from me.

I don't know how long I managed to keep it's fangs from ripping out my throat. It seemed like an age but it was probably no more than a second or two before Acwel jabbed his spear into its left flank and Lyndon thrust his into its throat from the other side. The wolf collapsed on top of me, its blood soaking me. Even the lining of my cloak was coated in the stuff.

The beast's claws had ripped my padded leather jerkin and woollen tunic to shreds and had torn into the flesh underneath. Acwel and Lyndon pulled the wolf off me and helped me to my feet. Arne came running up, as efficient as ever, and handed me a cloth to wipe the worst of the gore off me. He helped me remove my shredded clothes and washed and bandaged my chest. I didn't have a change of clothing so I had to put my bloodstained and torn clothes back on. I held my cloak together across my front to keep out the worst of the cold but I was still chilled to the bone by that stage.

'One of the she-wolves got away,' Wealmær told me once I had remounted with Arne's help. 'I've sent Cináed, Sherwyn and Rowe to track it.'

Most of the countryside around Cantwareburh was rolling pasture land interspersed with small woods and patches of arable land around each vill. However, there were areas of rocky outcrops and that was where the last wolf appeared to be heading. The three scouts had followed it up onto the top of a crag and trapped it there.

I looked up and watched her as she desperately looked around for a way to escape. There wasn't one so she turned and disappeared from my sight. I could see Cináed and Sherwyn on either side of where the wolf had been standing. Rowe had to be the one behind her and evidently she had decided to attack him as the smallest of her enemies. I dismounted and ran as fast as I could through the thick snow up the path to the top of the crag, ignoring the cold eating into me.

By the time I got there it was all over. Rowe had bravely faced the charging she-wolf with his spear held in front of him. The beast had run onto the spear and had kept trying to get at Rowe even with the point deep inside her. He was knocked back by the animal's momentum and had slipped in the snow, falling onto his back. Thankfully the beast was dead by that time and he suffered no more injury than a bruised backside.

I was shivering uncontrollably and so, leaving the others to bring the six dead wolves back on Arne's horse, I set off with my servant riding double in front of me. That kept the wind off my chest and his body heat warmed me back to some semblance of normality.

Hilda fussed over me but in reality the wounds made by the wolf's claws weren't too serious and they healed up in a couple of weeks. It was the cold that had proved more dangerous. I decided to make a sleeveless over-tunic and a cloak from the pelts; the meat wouldn't go to waste either. It would feed the hunting dogs for some time to come.

✝✝✝

The weather changed in the middle of February. The snow melted and torrential rain washed what was left of it away. Everywhere became coated in cloying mud and the roads remained impassable. Conditions improved at the end of the month when we had ten days of unbroken sunshine. At that time of year the sun wasn't hot but eventually the ground dried up and it was possible to start preparations for sowing crops; weeding and ploughing the fields.

The roads were usable again by early March and shortly afterwards a messenger arrived from the king.

To my faithful and esteemed Lord Jørren, Ealdorman of Cent and Sæ Hereræswa, greetings.

The time has come to unite what remains of Mercia with Wessex. I have sent a message to Ealdorman Æðelred informing him that I wish him to take my beloved daughter Æthelflaed to be his wife and so cement the alliance between us. We can then proceed to retake Lundenwic and so begin our campaign to defeat the heathen Danes and free the Anglo-Saxon kingdoms.

To this end I wish you to prepare a suitable number of longships to go to Glowecestre and escort Lord Æðelred to Hamwic and thence to Wintanceaster for the wedding ceremony. You are then to escort the married couple back to Glowecestre.

Time is of the essence as we must also prepare for our joint enterprise to recapture Lundenwic. I would like you to come to Wintanceaster as soon as you are able and I will brief you more fully.

Ælfredus Rex

I re-read the letter with a sinking heart. I had hoped to spend the year with my family dealing with various issues that needed my attention in Cent, not to mention the massive challenge of re-building the navy. It seemed it was not to be. Instead I was to play nursemaid to a young girl and her betrothed.

My first reaction was to wonder why Æðelred wasn't going to make his own way to Wintanceaster. His ships weren't as large as the longships but he had had enough of them to brave the sea passage around the peninsula of Dumnonia and into the Sūð-sæ.

It was Hilda who told me I was being naïve.

'He wants to demonstrate that he is a king whereas his future son-in-law is merely a noble who governs a fragment of what once was the mighty kingdom of Mercia. It's a statement of his superiority.'

'Well, Æðelred won't like it. He considers himself a king in waiting. I have little doubt that his aim is to use Wessex to help him re-conquer the Five Boroughs and the other Danish parts of Mercia so that he can mount the Mercian throne as Ælfred's equal.'

'And do you think that Ælfred will ever let that happen?' she asked.

'No, I suppose not.'

I groaned inwardly; I was faced with as difficult a task as any I had yet tackled, although of a political, not military nature.

✝✝✝

I decided to travel overland to Wintanceaster to ascertain how my various vills in Cent and elsewhere had fared after such a harsh winter. I wasn't anticipating any trouble and the land was peaceful after the conflict of past years but nevertheless I decided to take ten of my gesith with me in addition to Arne, as well as Leofwine to deal with any minor ailments, Ywer and Ajs for the experience and the two brothers, Sherwyn and Rowe.

They had asked to come with me as far as Silcestre as they had inherited land there from their father, Redwald. Not only did they want to see how their inheritance was faring but they had money from their share of the spoils from Honfleur to invest in more equipment, livestock and perhaps even purchase more slaves to work their land.

I visited other vills I owned in Cent on the way. I had asked Alric to check on those which weren't near our route but it still took a week to reach Silcestre. Friðuswiþ, the female reeve, had completed the restoration of all the buildings destroyed during Wulfhere's raid two and a half years ago and had built new ones. Two of these were extra storehouses and another was a dovecote to provide some fresh meat to supplement the smoked and salted mutton, ham, and beef.

Ceorls, bondsmen, slaves and their families subsisted mainly on a diet of vegetables with meat only as an occasional treat but elderly animals were slaughtered in the late autumn and preserved, either by smoking or by using salt, ready for feast days like Yuletide.

I was pleased with the progress that Friðuswiþ had made and I was even more impressed when I saw that she had improved the defences by blocking off two of the four old Roman gates and building towers beside the remaining two. These were of timber and not stone, like the walls, but they would provide a place for archers to fire down on anyone trying to destroy the two sets of remaining gates.

We stayed until noon the next day so that Sherwyn and his brother could finish their business with the reeve and the senior bondsman who looked after their land. The one thing the vill lacked was a mill and, as there was a mound which was difficult to plough, the brothers decided to use it to build a windmill. Not only would that increase their income but it would save everyone having to take their grain to Basingestoches to have it ground.

Basingestoches was another of the vills I owned outside of Cent and we travelled there next. From there it was only a twenty mile ride to Wintanceaster and we arrived mid-afternoon the following day. I had barely climbed out of the saddle when a page came running up.

'King Ælfred demands your presence immediately,' he told me in a high piping voice. I didn't like the impertinent way the boy had addressed me nor the fact that he didn't call me 'lord.'

'What's your name, whelp?' I asked angrily.

The boy looked startled for an instant but then the insolent look on his face returned.

'Sexmund, son of Eadda,' he replied arrogantly.

So this was Eadda's one and only child. I had thought him still a small boy but he looked to be about eleven or twelve.

'Well, Sexmund, son of Thegn Eadda, I'm an ealdorman and you call me lord; do you understand.'

'Yes,' he replied, his eyes flashing angrily. After a pause he added 'lord.'

'Are you sure that the king needs to see me so urgently that he doesn't want me to brush the dust from my clothes and make myself presentable first?'

'I was told he wanted to see you as soon as you finally arrived,... lord.'

The word finally explained the urgency of the summons. Ælfred was doubtless annoyed that it had taken me two weeks to answer his invitation. The boy had communicated the king's irritability in his message to me. A page more attuned to the niceties of the royal court would have phrased it more diplomatically. Ælfred might be impatient but nothing could be so urgent that I needed to rush to see him without first changing my clothes.

Thankfully the chamberlain appeared at that moment and escorted me to the guest chamber that had been allocated to me. Arne followed with the panniers containing my spare clothes whilst Wolnoth, who commanded my escort, took the men away to the warriors' hall, handing our horses over to the stable boys.

I washed the grime from my face and hands in the bucket provided for that purpose and put on a clean scarlet tunic, richly embroidered at the edges with gold and silver thread, and blue trousers. I thought it made me look like a popinjay but they had been a present from Hilda and she had insisted that I pack them.

Despite the supposed urgency I was kept waiting outside the king's private chambers for some time before being shown in. As I entered Edward the Ætheling brushed past me with a scowl on his face. Evidently he and his father had argued about something and I doubted that that would have improved Ælfred's mood.

'You should have been here a week ago,' the king barked at me as I entered the room.

He wasn't alone. The Lady Ealhswith stood beside him, glaring at me, whilst Ealdorman Drefan and Lady Æthelflaed gave me sympathetic looks.

'The roads were impassable until a couple of weeks ago, cyning, and, as you will know only too well, it has been an unusually harsh winter. I therefore visited as many of my vills as I could along the way to check that my people had survived. Thankfully most had except for the elderly; many of them perished.'

I regarded him coolly after I'd finished speaking and he glowered at me.

'Don't be impertinent!' Ealhswith reproved me.

'If what I said was impertinent and not factual, then I apologise, cyning,' I said, ignoring her and addressing my reply to the king.

Then I let my anger get the better of me.

'If anyone is impertinent in this place it's that little brat of Eadda's, Sexmund. He's not just arrogant, he's deliberately insolent. He doesn't deserve to be one of your pages,' I spat out venomously. 'Why on earth are you showing that man favour by including his son in your household when you know that he was behind the kidnapping of my son and the murder of my body servant?'

'How dare you speak to the king like that!' Ealhswith said, scandalised.

Ælfred held up his hand and she subsided, simmering.

'Lord Jørren has a point, even if he could have expressed it more tactfully. Although he has no proof, he has grounds for his suspicions about Eadda.'

The king looked at the floor as if seeking inspiration for a moment. It was a mosaic laid by the Romans centuries before. It had been damaged in places and had been repaired using pieces of stone inexpertly cut. However, you could still make out the scene depicted: a fight between a man with a trident and net and another wearing a strange full face helmet and wielding a weapon that looked a little like a seax. In the background were what looked like faces - a lot of them. I assumed that the two warriors were fighting in an arena.

'You need to understand that Eadda, although only a thegn, is the lord of many vills and is therefore wealthy. He also has the ear of several of my ealdormen. Some of them secretly support Æthelwold's claim to his father's throne. They regard me, even now, as a usurper. I'm not well,' Ælfred confessed. 'If anything should happen to me, they would seek to elect Æthelwold as the next king. If that came about then I wouldn't give a silver penny for my son's chances of survival.'

He didn't mention his other nephew, Æthelhelm, Æthelwold's elder brother. We both knew that he

271

had no aspirations towards the throne. He was lord of half a dozen vills left to him in his father's will and he seemed content to lead the life of a thegn.

'Which is why you appointed Eadda as your son's military tutor; to bind him closely to Edward and ensure that he would be loyal to him?' I surmised.

Ælfred nodded.

'My son will need all the support he can get when the time comes. You understand now why I can't afford to alienate Eadda.'

'Does my support count for nothing then, cyning?' I asked quietly. 'For I'm certain that your action in creating a bond between Eadda and Edward has enabled him to drip poison about me in the ætheling's ear. Consequently Edward hates me and Eadda has even succeeded in turning my own stepson against me. Is this calculated to make me support Edward when the Witenaġemot comes to elect the next king?'

I thought that I might have gone too far. Ealhswith certainly thought so, judging by the shocked expression on her face, but before she could say anything Drefan intervened.

'I'm sure that Lord Jørren didn't mean to imply that he would ever be disloyal to Edward, cyning.'

'Loyalty is a two way thing,' I pointed out. 'If Edward deprives me of Cent, as Eadda is trying to persuade him to do, then my support would count for naught.'

'Edward isn't a fool,' Ælfred said. 'He's still very young but he must realise that you are one of Wessex's most valuable military commanders.'

'Have you asked him what he thinks of me? Has he told you that he would keep me on as one of his closest advisors? No. You may think your son has a wise head on his shoulders, cyning, but by trying to bind Eadda to him you are clouding his judgement. I suspect that Eadda's aim is to get Edward to appoint him as his hereræswa. We all know what a disaster that would prove to be.'

'My son would never be so stupid,' Ealhswith proclaimed. 'We don't agree on many things, Lord Jørren, but about Eadda's military abilities – or lack of them - we are in accord.'

'Perhaps I was unwise to appoint him,' Ælfred said thoughtfully. 'However, to deprive him of the role would create uproar amongst his friends. I simply can't afford disharmony within Wessex at a time when I am trying to create unity between Wessex and Mercia.'

'Eadda is no youngster, cyning. Perhaps the Lord will call him to his side in Heaven and solve the problem for us?'

Everyone in the room looked horrified; all except Æthelflaed who half-smiled at what I'd said.

'You can't possibly wish the man ill,' Ælfred told me reprovingly.

'Of course not, cyning,' I replied briskly. 'Now I think you wanted to discuss arrangements for Lord Æðelred's journey to Wintanceaster for the marriage ceremony?'

†††

I stood on the small aft deck of the Saint Cuthbert beside the steersman and Wilfrið, its captain. We were accompanied by five other longships, just in case we encountered Vikings out of Dyflin, but so far the sea had remained remarkably empty. Behind me stood Edward the Ætheling, Eadda and my stepson, Oswine. Edward had stormed out of the meeting with his parents and sister back in Wintanceaster because he wasn't happy about being sent to accompany Lord Æðelred back for the wedding. He thought the task beneath him.

Ælfred was less than wise in insisting that the boy obey him. Sending a truculent thirteen year old on a diplomatic mission was idiotic. Even worse, making Eadda and I spend several days cheek by jowl in the confines of a longship was even more likely to end in disaster, and so it proved.

We camped on a beach for the first two nights and the two of us managed to avoid one another. On board during the day we ignored each other. Only on one occasion did I hear Eadda say something behind my back which made Edward snigger. I didn't have to hear what was whispered to know that it was something derogatory about me. I was pleased, however, that Oswine didn't join in the stifled giggles.

On the third day we rounded the southern point of Dumnonia and headed north-east up the west coast. We were under sail and the stiff breeze was pushing us along at a good pace. Halfway through the afternoon the sky darkened out to sea and the wind from the west became stronger. Wilfrið prudently

274

decided to put a reef in the sail but Edward challenged him.

'Why are you shortening sail, old man? I want to get to Glowecestre and back again with all speed. I've better things to do than spend any longer than necessary on this tub of a ship.'

'You know nothing about sailing, Lord Edward, so leave it to those who do,' Wilfrið retorted sharply.

The shipmaster was never one to suffer fools gladly and calling him an old man had infuriated him. However, the man's disrespectful tone had angered the ætheling and his hand went to the hilt of the seax he wore at his waist. I was about to step in when thankfully Eadda had the common sense to calm the boy down. I don't know what he whispered to him but Edward reluctantly let go of his seax and stared sulkily out to sea. I prayed that Ælfred lived a long life because I could see catastrophe ahead if this petulant brat ever ruled Wessex.

The wind increased in strength and veered so that it was now coming from the north-east. That meant we were heading directly into it. The ship's boys got the sail down and stowed the heavy wet woollen cloth on deck. As we rowed into the waves, water broke over the prow and cascaded over everyone. There wasn't much shelter on a longship and we were all soaked to the skin in minutes. Even worse, the bilges were filling with water.

'Right everyone who isn't rowing, start bailing with whatever you can find,' I ordered.

Everyone grabbed helmets, buckets and anything else that would serve and started to scoop the seawater up and hurl it over the side. Everyone that is except Eadda and his two charges.

'Do you want to end up in a watery grave,' I yelled over the wind at the three of them. 'No? Then start bailing!'

Oswine immediately ran to help but the other two just glared at me.

'You don't expect the king's son to work like a common seaman, do you?' Eadda snarled back.

I got up from where I was scooping up water and pushed my face close to his.

'I expect him to lead by example, just as his father would if he was here. What sort of tutor are you if you teach him to look down his nose at his fellows? Men follow a leader because they respect him, not because he wears a crown on his head. The sooner this little princeling learns that the better. Under your tutelage he won't succeed Ælfred, Æthelwold will. Now I'm sure that none of us want that, do we? So get off your arses and bail!'

Eadda glared at me but he did what he was told and Edward, after giving me a rather strange look that I could best describe as speculative, followed suit.

The wind eased after a few hours and then backed to the west but by that time the day was almost over. We were somewhere in the middle of the sea between the south coast of Wealas and the northern shore of Dumnonia. Thankfully the other longships had managed to stay with us but we would never reach a suitable beach before nightfall.

We raised the sail again and headed east until we could see land ahead. By this time the light was fading and we had to be content with anchoring as close to the rocky shoreline as we dared. Everyone was exhausted and so I let them sleep whilst I took the first watch myself.

I needed a shit and so I made my way to the bows. Normally we had to wait until we were ashore for the night before emptying our bowels but we kept a wooden bucket on board for that purpose, just in case. It was something we had learned from the Vikings who made many long voyages out of sight of land.

I had done what I had to do and had just dropped the bucket into the sea to wash it out when I heard a noise behind me. I turned around but all I could see were recumbent, snoring figures. I turned back and was hauling the bucket back on board via the rope tied to its handle when I sensed rather than heard someone close behind me. Instinctively I ducked and twisted around. A figure in a cloak with a hood stood above me gripping a dagger which glinted in the faint moonlight.

I kicked out and my foot connected with my assailant's right knee. I had no idea how much I'd hurt him but he emitted a muffled howl. Rising to my feet, I punched at where I calculated my assailant's jaw to be hidden within the confines of his hood. My fist hit something and the man's head snapped back. Once on my feet I grabbed the hand holding the dagger and we struggled. The hood dropped back and I recognised Eadda's face.

'You die now, you bastard!' he muttered as he brought his knee up into my groin.

The pain was excruciating and I let go of his right hand. I saw his dagger heading for my unprotected throat but there was nothing I could do about. Then suddenly he slumped and fell towards me. More in instinct that anything I dropped to my knee and his unconscious body fell onto my back. Still in great pain I managed to heave myself upright with one hand on the gunwale and I felt the weight slide off me. I sank down in relief, nursing my injured groin.

I felt someone kneel down beside me and ask 'are you alright, father?' in a concerned voice. At first I thought it was Ywer, who was acting as one of the ship's boys, but this voice sounded as if it belonged to a boy entering puberty. I opened my eyes and gazed into Oswine's worried face.

'I knew he was up to something when he got up in the middle of the night and drew his dagger, so I followed him.'

'Thank God you did,' I replied, trying to smile through the pain. 'What did you hit him with?'

Oswine held up a large axe that we kept on board. It was there to cut free the grapnel lines of a ship trying to board us or to cut through the rigging of a collapsed mast. Tonight, however, it had saved my life.

'I only hit him with the flat of the blade. I didn't want to kill him, just stop him hurting you,' he said in a plaintive voice.

'Thank you Oswine, I'm forever in your debt. By the way, where is Eadda?'

'He went overboard when you tried to stand up. I tried to grab him but failed.'

He had attempted to save Eadda so he had nothing to feel guilty about. I was glad that his conscience was clear. I didn't want him obsessing over what had happened. I was even happier that Eadda was gone.

'Are you sure that he drowned?'

'He was unconscious or worse after I hit him with the axe and he can't swim, even if he came round when he hit the water.'

He peered over the side but shook his head. It seemed likely that Eadda had sunk to the bottom of the sea without ever coming round. By this time the acute pain had subsided to a dull ache and I was able to stand without my stepson's help. I looked around the ship and, as far as I could tell, everyone else was still fast asleep.

'What do we say?' Oswine suddenly whispered.

'Say?'

'About Eadda's death?'

'Nothing. He just disappeared over the side sometime during the night. Perhaps he stood on the gunwale to take a piss and slipped?'

I heard Oswine chuckle quietly at the image this conjured up.

'I'm sorry I believed his lies about you, father. I should have known better. As time wore on I realised that he accused you of false crimes because of his hatred of you; I now know that the truth is very different.'

'Don't apologise; I blame him, not you. It's good to have you back,' I said with a smile. 'However, I remain concerned about the damage he's done to my reputation in Edward's eyes.'

✝✝✝

Naturally there was consternation on board when it was discovered that Eadda had disappeared. Edward was frantic with worry and he insisted that we sail up and down that part of the coast in search of him. I tried to convince him that no one could have survived for long in the cold sea even if he could swim, which Eadda couldn't.

'You, you wanted him gone! You threw him over the side,' he accused me.

'Be very careful what you say, Lord Edward,' Father Tidwold cautioned him. 'What proof do you have for your allegation?'

Tidwold was one of the priests that Ælfred surrounded himself with and he had been chosen to act as the boy's confessor and spiritual guide. He was one of three clerics who accompanied the delegation to escort Æðelred. I didn't know him well but he struck me as a sensible man, even if he was one of Bishop Asser's close associates.

'Proof? What more proof do I need? Jørren always hated Eadda and unfairly accused him of abducting that brat!'

He pointed at Ywer, who stepped towards the ætheling and raised his fist as if to strike him.

'Everybody calm down,' I thundered and the angry glare in my son's eyes died away. 'You will treat me with the respect I deserve as one of your father's senior nobles and the Sæ Hereræswa of Wessex.'

I waited for Edward to apologise but he didn't.

'It's true that Eadda hated me, mainly because I succeeded in defeating the Danes where he had failed. It's also true that I held him responsible for abducting Ywer and for the killing of my body servant but I could prove nothing and so I accepted that there was little that I could do. You have no grounds for accusing me of causing Eadda's death. When we return to Wintanceaster I will inform the king of his disappearance and also of your accusation against me. He will decide the truth of the matter, not you. I also intend to complain about your inappropriate behaviour towards me.'

I expected an angry retort but the ætheling pursed his lips and appeared to think about what I had just said. After a short while he nodded and went to stand in the bows. After a minute or two Oswine joined him and the two became engrossed in earnest conversation.

'I apologise on behalf of my charge, Lord Jørren.'

I turned to see Father Tidwold at my elbow.

'Edward is young and I agree that he is hot-headed. That is something he is going to have to curb if he wants to be king in due course,' he continued. 'However, it does seem to be strange that Eadda just disappeared like that. Rumours abound, of course. It's hardly surprising; the enmity between you was well known.'

'Perhaps but, although I held the man responsible for taking my son and marooning him on a rock with the Culdees as well as sending his man to kill my servant, I would never stoop to his cold blooded murder.'

'No,' the priest said thoughtfully, 'I don't think you would. However, it might be a different story if he attacked you and you defended yourself.'

I realised then that either the priest was very astute or he had been awake and seen what had occurred last night.

'Even if that were true and even if I had a witness, do you think that it would help me? It might exonerate me but people would still say I killed Eadda and it would reinforce Edward's hatred of me. Furthermore Eadda has a son who already dislikes me. I would never pay him wergeld for his father's death and that would just start a blood feud. No, it's better if people think that he was clumsy and fell overboard of his own accord.'

'Very well. Perhaps you're right. Let's say no more about it. I will try and make Edward see sense and keep his own counsel but I'm not sure he'll listen.'

'He needs to realise the realities of life, father. He's not the only ætheling and many would support Æthelwold's claim to succeed Ælfred. Edward will not help his cause if he's seen as rash and irrational.'

'You're right, of course. I'll do my best to make him understand that.'

In complete contrast to yesterday, today it was sunny with a gentle breeze to waft us on our way. There was still a sizeable swell – the aftermath of the storm – and the motion of the Saint Cuthbert caused quite a few to spew over the side. Amongst them was

Edward. I saw Oswine comforting his friend and I hoped that the combined efforts of my stepson and Father Tidwold might make him see me in a better light.

We finally reached the mouth of the River Sæfern and beached the ships on the east bank for the night. I needed to stretch my legs and set off on my own up through the dunes. There was a wood nearby and I had just finished emptying my bowels when I heard a twig snap.

I buckled my belt around my tunic and quietly unsheathed both my sword and my seax. I waited behind a tree to see who was trying to creep up on me but relaxed when I saw it was Edward. The boy had both a seax and a dagger hanging from his belt but neither had been drawn.

He jumped when I stepped in front of him, having put my weapons away first.

'Lord Jørren,' he said nervously. 'You startled me.'

'I thought that someone was trying to creep up on me, I'm sorry if I made you jump.'

'I was following you,' he confessed, 'but only because I wanted a word in private.'

'I'm glad that you want to talk. It was never my wish for us to be enemies.'

'Perhaps I've been unfair to you. Oswine has tried to convince me that what Eadda said about you was mostly lies.'

'I'm pleased to hear it. Eadda was a man consumed by jealousy, I fear. He never forgave me for taking his place as Hereræswa and proving myself to be a better commander than he ever was.'

'Father Tidwold has also tried to talk some sense into me,' he added.

I couldn't see his features clearly in the gloom under the trees but I sensed a rueful smile had crossed his face.

'He says that I must learn to cultivate my nobles not alienate them, if I wish to be a good king.'

'He's correct, up to a point. You need to put the needs of Wessex above your own personal inclinations but I wouldn't want to see you become duplicitous. There is a difference between the application of common sense and deceitful cunning.'

'I can see that I have a lot to learn,' he said with a sigh. 'Can we start again and put the past behind us? Will you give me your oath to be my man when I come to the throne?'

'I will gladly give you my support now and my oath if you are elected king by Witenaġemot in the fullness of time. You will appreciate that I can't give it now just in case Æthelwold is selected instead of you.'

I sensed him stiffen.

'You think that my uncle would make a better king than me?' he asked incredulously.

'No, I don't. Like Eadda he's consumed by hatred, in his case for your father, and that makes him bitter. It clouds his judgement. However, as Ealdorman of Cent I am bound to follow whoever wears the crown.'

'Yes, I can see that. Very well, I accept your position but I must confess I'm disappointed. I hope that we can work together from now on to ensure that the Witenaġemot makes the right decision.'

We walked back together talking about the forthcoming wedding – which he didn't approve of – and Mercia's unhappy situation. He felt that Wessex should help expel the Danes from Mercia but only on the condition that Æðelred acknowledged his father as king of both realms. He was wary of Mercia becoming powerful again and rivalling Wessex as the most powerful of the Anglo-Saxon kingdoms. I was impressed by Edward's grasp of the political situation at the tender age of eleven. Perhaps he had the makings of a good ruler after all.

When we parted back on the beach I sat for a while mulling over what had just transpired. On reflection I was surprised by Edward's sudden volte face in his attitude towards me and suspicious of the reasons behind it. Even if Oswine and Tidwold had managed to convince him that I wasn't as black as Eadda had painted me, to seek me out and make amends so soon after his mentor's death didn't seem altogether natural. Edward might be hot-tempered but I didn't think he was mercurial. In fact he seemed more level headed, given time to think things over, than I had imagined.

On refelction I came to the conclusion that Tidwold and my stepson had convinced him that he needed my support. That explained his sudden change of heart but his true feelings towards me remained uncertain. I needed to be circumspect in my dealings with him; there was always the possibility that, despite what he'd told me, he could well turn against me once his position as king was secure.

†††

The voyage back to Hamwic, which was where we disembarked because it was closer to Wintanceaster than Portcæstre, was uneventful. Æðelred elected to travel on one of his own ships and Edward decided to accompany his future brother-in-law. Despite our apparent rapprochement I was far happier not to have him on board. I was sorry to be deprived of Oswine's company, however, as I would have liked to have built on the incipient bond between us. On balance it suited me not to have to interact with Æðelred in the close confines of a longship. I was not a natural diplomat and could not have deceived him about Ælfred's covert strategy to bring Mercia under his rule.

The wedding ceremony took place on a typical April day – sunshine one minute and showers the next. I wore my garish finery again but I was outshone by many of those present. King Ælfred was the most sombrely dressed of us all, apart from the priests, of course. Æðelred wore a purple tunic made of the finest wool and embroidered at the ends of the short sleeves, collar and hem with gold wire. Small gems had been fastened in place amongst the embroidery with more gold wire. His trousers were dark green which clashed with the purple and he wore red leather shoes on his feet. He wore a sword belt around his waist which was studded with jewels in gold settings. The hilt of his sword was similarly encrusted with gems which made it useless as a weapon. Frankly I thought he looked ridiculous.

In contrast to her flamboyant groom Æthelflaed wore a simple white linen under-tunic with a plain cream woollen peplos. The circlet over her headscarf was made of gold, as were the brooches holding her peplos together at the shoulder. That was the only jewellery she wore. Even the belt around her waist was plain black leather.

The ceremony was conducted by Bishop Asser and his homily on the respective rights and duties of a Christian man and his wife seemed to go on for eternity. As far as I could see the rights belonged to Æðelred and the duties to Æthelflaed. I'm not sure that she saw it that way.

I was pleased to see that my daughter had been chosen as her chief attendant. Cuthfleda was carrying the new sword which would be presented to the groom as part of the ceremony. In return Æðelred would present the pretentious sword he was wearing to Cuthfleda, acting on behalf of the bride. Æthelflaed would be expected to keep this safe so she could present it to the couple's eldest son when he reached maturity at the age of fourteen, always provided they had a son, of course.

After the exchange of swords and of rings the bishop proclaimed the couple to be man and wife and everyone filed out of the church in order. First the supposedly happy couple, then Ælfred and Ealhswith, Bishop Asser and his priests then the nobles of Wessex and Mercia, all jostling for position. I thought it undignified and held back. Thus I found myself

287

walking beside a morose Edward. He said nothing until we got to the door and stepped out into the pouring rain.

'What do you make of our esteemed new ally?' he asked me in a soft voice.

'Well, he's a trifle old for your sister, I suppose,' I began, assuming he was referring to Æðelred.

It was true; he was over twice her age but that wasn't unusual amongst the nobles. Hilda's first marriage had been to an old man – Oswine's father - when she was even younger than Æthelflaed.

'That wasn't what I meant,' he muttered. 'I was talking about Mercia. What good will they be as our allies when the east and north of Mercia is ruled by a hotchpotch of Danes and the rest is being attacked by the Welsh in the west?'

'Your father plans to help Æðelred get rid of the threat from the Welsh this summer so that they are free to capture Lundenwic. That is the lynchpin to recovering the rest of Mercia.'

'But that's foolhardy. Mercia and Wessex have always been enemies. As I think I've told you before, I'm concerned that after we help make Mercia strong again she will become a rival for leadership of the Anglo-Saxon people.'

It wasn't quite as simple as that of course, and I didn't think that poor broken Mercia would ever regain its previous status. However, I didn't have the chance to reply before we reached the hall where the wedding feast was to be held and we made our way to our respective places.

The feast itself was relatively uneventful. Men got sozzled and the womenfolk retired before they were pawed by the drunks and fights could break out with between them and their husbands or fathers. Æthelflaed was made ready for her new husband in the bridal bed by Cuthfleda and her other ladies before a somewhat inebriated Æðelred was carried into the bedchamber, undressed and put into the bridal bed by the Mercian nobles. I felt sorry for his bride. I had always liked Æthelflaed and admired her spirit. Æðelred would expect to dominate her and she was never going to be the compliant, dutiful wife he expected her to be. There would inevitably be a battle of wills which he was bound to win.

Still, it wasn't my concern. I was looking forward to returning to Hilda and my family and forgetting all about Mercia and its problems. I should have known that was a pipe dream. I was shaken out of my complacency the next morning when Ælfred sent for me and Drefan.

'I want you to gather a small army of experienced warriors. The fleet is to take you to land on the south coast of Gwent and push up north-eastwards to link up with the Mercians. Between you I want the Welsh in the south of that benighted country crushed so that Æðelred is free to concentrate on the capture of Lundenwic next spring.'

My family and the quiet life would have to wait it seemed.

Chapter Fifteen

GWENT

Summer/ Autumn 885

I had spent the three weeks after our meeting with Ælfred finding the men to crew the ten longships and fifteen knarrs that would carry Drefan, his six hundred warriors and fifty horses around the coast to the mouth of a river called Afon Wysg by the local inhabitants.

I had wanted to take Ywer with me, and he was eager to go, but Hilda put her foot down. After what had happened last time we went away she wasn't about to let him go anywhere near Wealas again. He stayed, sulking morosely until the day I left.

I had fondly imagined that my involvement in this campaign would end when we landed Drefan and his army but he soon disabused me of that idea.

'The king wants us to travel by ship up the Afon Wysg as far as a place called Abergafenni, the fortress of the King of Gwent,' he told me. 'We are to unite with the Mercians and capture the fortress, slaying everyone in it. Apparently it's not going to be an easy task. It used to be a Roman fort which they erected on a spur with steep sides above the river - a naturally defensible site that offers clear views across the surrounding landscape.

'I'm told that the river should be navigable as far as Abergafenni in the spring when the water is higher than it is in the summer. However, we have only the word of a priest who comes from the area for this and he is no sailor.'

It didn't sound promising. My fear, apart from grounding in the shallower sections, was an attack from the river banks whilst we were rowing up stream. We would be strung out and the ships' archers would be unable to support each other. We would also have to carry enough provisions for both the crews and Drefan's warriors. We both agreed that the Welsh, apart from those left behind to harass us, were likely to flee in the face of our advance taking their livestock with them. It was still too early in the year for the crops to be ripe and such grain stores as there were would most likely be set on fire before we reached them.

I was therefore in a somewhat pessimistic frame of mind when we set out on the voyage around Dumnonia before heading north for the southern coast of Wealas.

✝✝✝

There was a settlement at the mouth of the Afon Wysg; a primitive fishing hamlet with a dozen hovels. Incongruously there was a sizeable timber church nearby with yet more hovels built around it. I was on the Saint Cuthbert, the first ship to enter the river. Drefan was on the Holy Spirit somewhere behind me and so I took charge.

We beached the longship and a knarr, which was carrying several of our horses, in the mud and I jumped down off the ship into the shallow water, my boots sinking into the sludge below the surface. I struggled ashore with difficulty followed by several of my men. Meanwhile the crew of the knarr started to winch four of the horses ashore in a sling.

The hamlet stank of fish and there were signs that a catch had been recently gutted. However, the place was deserted. We went and checked the church and the other buildings but they too had been abandoned. I learned later that the monastery had been founded by a minor fifth century king called Saint Gwynllyw. It was now the seat of the Bishop of Gwent.

I thought it was a mean place to site the heart of a diocese, even a Celtic one. Anything valuable, including food, had been removed which slightly worried me as it could mean that the local Welsh had plenty of warning about our coming. However, it might also be that they had little to take away to safety in the first place.

Above the primitive buildings stood an ancient hill fort. Drefan joined me after I'd finished checking both hamlet and monastery and asked me to send four men up each side of the river to scout for any Welshmen who might be waiting to ambush us. Acwel, Lyndon, Sherwyn and Rowe took the west bank whilst Eomær and three others investigated the east bank. Firm ground lay beyond a reed bed, consequently the knarr's crew had even more difficulty in unloading four horses on that side of the river. I didn't envy the scouts their task in such miserable conditions but they just seemed to be happy to be on board a horse rather than a ship.

Acwel and Sherwyn rode up to the old hillfort but came back to report that it was as empty as the rest of the place. They set off along the river bank whilst I struggled back through the sludge and was hauled aboard. Thankfully the tide was coming in and so we merely had to wait a short while before we floated free of the mud. I wouldn't have wanted to push the longship back into the river.

The rain eased to a fine drizzle but the visibility didn't improve much. It wasn't possible to use the sails in the confines of the river but the oarsmen had an easy time of it as the current swept us along. It was getting quite late when we rounded a bend to find Acwel and his companions waiting for us on the river bank. Although the tide had come in there was still an expanse of brown mud between the ship and the bank so I asked Acwel to shout across to me.

'There is a large settlement around the next bend,' he called. 'There's the remains of what looks like an amphitheatre and beyond that a large fort. There's a wharf and several storage huts as well.'

'It sounds like the old Roman legionary fort of Isca Augusta,' Father Tidwold said at my elbow.

He had asked to come with us and the king had readily agreed. There were several other priests with the army but none I trusted as much as Tidwold and so I had invited him to join me on the Saint Cuthbert.

'Isca Augusta?' I queried.

'Yes, from what little I know I believe that it is named after the Roman name for the river and the title of the legion who were stationed here for a long time – the Second Augusta. Slowly the men who manned it were called away to serve on the Continent and it became a sort of depot. Even the stone of the walls and buildings were carted away by ship for use elsewhere. What you see now is but a shell of what it used to be.'

As we rounded the bend the place came into view. Through the gloom I could make out the circular amphitheatre and what appeared to be part of the old fortress. The stone gateway still stood, although part of the parapet had fallen away. A stone wall abutted it for a hundred feet or so but the rest of the visible defences appeared to be no more than a ditch and a steep earthen ramp. At one corner stood the forlorn remains of a stone tower.

As Acwel had told me, there was a wooden jetty with store huts nearby but the area appeared to be deserted. At least I saw nothing moving except a mangy dog. It was a different story over at the fort. Conditions were still murky but it was no more than a hundred and fifty yards away and I could see a horde of wildly gesticulating warriors on top of the ramparts.

They did nothing to oppose our landing, which was just as well. There was only room for three ships alongside the jetty at any one time and it took until dusk to get everyone ashore with their equipment. The horses took longest to offload. Although we could use ramps rather than hoists, the animals were very skittish and each one had to be coaxed slowly down onto the jetty.

We set up camp in the area of the amphitheatre. We put the horses in the middle and blocked off the exits. There was grass for them to graze and it would be difficult for the Welsh to drive them off from there if they launched a night-time raid.

The ships were anchored in a long line in the middle of the river with a watch on board each one. Those amongst the rowers who were trained warriors joined the rest of Drefan's men sleeping on the grass covered steps of the amphitheatre or just outside it. The rest of us – the skypfyrd who made up the majority of the rowers, the ship's boys and my gesith camped along the banks of the river.

Naturally we had put out sentries and a piquet to watch the fort's gates. As the night progressed the cloud dispersed and by the time I lay down to get a little sleep the area was bathed in pale moonlight. It seemed only a few minutes before I was woken up but it was probably more like a few hours.

'The hereræswa sent me, lord. He says that gates opened a few minutes ago to let a party of Welshmen out. At first he thought that they meant to attack the amphitheatre but they've disappeared in the other direction. We don't know where they are at the moment but Lord Drefan thought that they might be making for the ships.'

The man who'd woken me was one of my thegns from Cent. I thanked him and went to rouse my men quietly. If the ships were the target, the Welsh were presumably planning to attack us from upstream. I walked along the bank in that direction and heard faint splashes in the silence of the night. The moon

295

had gone behind a cloud but when it emerged I could quite plainly see a small fleet of strange oval craft being paddled towards the nearest of the anchored ships. Each one held between six and eight men and they would be there within the next minute or so. There was no time for subtleness.

'Arne, where are you?' I yelled.

'Here, lord,' he replied from a few yards away.

'Good, have you got your horn with you?'

One of my servant's tasks in battle was to relay orders using his hunting horn.

'Of course, lord.'

'Then blow on the damn thing and keep blowing as if your life depended on it.'

As the first notes sounded several arrows were fired at the Welsh boats from archers on the longship further upstream. An alert sentry must have roused the on-board watch before I'd seen the Welsh craft.

Several of the attackers were hit and fell into the water, upsetting two of the boats as they did so. Finding themselves discovered, the Welshmen beat a hasty retreat. A few more of their men were hit before they disappeared.

'Wealmær, where are you?'

'Here, lord.'

'Come on then, I want to intercept that lot before they make it back to the fort. Kill as many as you like but I want some prisoners for interrogation. Do you understand?'

He nodded and, accompanied by the rest of my hearth warrior, we set off as fast as we dared over the rough ground in a north-easterly direction. It is never easy to move at night, still less make an attack, but my hearth warriors were amongst the most experienced fighters anywhere. Many had trained as scouts and knew how to move over ground without making a noise. I was making for a point halfway between the fort's gates and the point from where I thought the enemy must have launched their craft.

After a few minutes I could see men pulling the oval boats ashore in the pale moonlight before they headed back towards the fort. We crouched low so that they didn't see us, then moved off towards a low hillock.

'String your bows,' I called quietly.

I waited until the leading Welshmen had reached the point closest to us.

'Ready, pick your target, fire.' I shouted. 'Carry on until they are out of range.'

Volley after volley sped towards the startled enemy. It was difficult to make out individual targets but they were massed together and several were hit in the first two volleys, then they recovered from the shock and either dropped to the ground or started running towards the gates.

I saw one of them crawling away and so I told my men to cease firing and ran after him. Perhaps he hadn't realised that the shower of missiles had stopped and he kept on moving like a snake. It didn't take me long to catch him and I hit him hard on the top of his head with the pommel of my seax.

Just at that moment the gates opened and hundreds of Welshmen erupted from the fort. I didn't have long so I heaved the unconscious man over my shoulder and made my way back to my men as quickly as I could. They sent another couple of volleys towards the advancing horde and then we withdrew, two of my men relieving me of my burden.

The enemy halted once they were certain that their raiding party was safe and, as we made our way back to the encampment, I heard the gates shut with a loud bang.

✝✝✝

Drefan called a meeting of the senior commanders the next morning. Only nobles and their warbands had been brought along to do the fighting on land and there were three other ealdormen apart from Drefan and myself: Hildenrinc of Dornsæte, Nerian of Somersaete and Eadred of Dyfneintscīr.

'Good morning, gentlemen. If last night proved anything it was that we cannot afford to leave this place in the hands of the Welsh. We have to take it and slaughter all those inside before we can move on towards Abergafenni.'

'Slaughter all, Drefan?' Nerian queried. 'Including women and children?'

'Ideally I would like to take them as slaves but we cannot afford to encumber ourselves with captives.'

'There is space on one of the knarrs,' I pointed out. 'That is, if you leave some of the horses ashore to scout along the river banks.'

'They still need guarding and feeding and we have only just enough provisions as it is.'

'Then give them the bare minimum in the way of food; it's better to go hungry than be killed. As for guards, the crew of the knarr transporting them, supplemented by a few of my skypfyrd, will be enough to ensure they don't cause any problems. We can send them back once we've captured the fort.'

Drefan frowned at me. Evidently he didn't like being contradicted but, much as I liked him, I wasn't going to be drawn into the needless slaughter of women and children. Besides, this expedition was costing me a lot more than the king had promised me and selling my share of the slaves would go some way towards mitigating that.

'Very well,' he said reluctantly, 'but Welsh women and even some of their older children have been known to join their men in fighting. The lives of any that do are forfeit.'

He looked around the small tent challenging anyone to contradict him; none did. He had a point.

'Good. Let's move on to the assault itself.'

A long discussion followed in which I took little interest. My only involvement would be the archers from my longships, who would be required to counter any archers the defenders might have and to keep the rest of the enemy's heads down below the top of the rampart.

At dawn the priests dispensed mass to those about to assault the old fort. Drefan had asked them to pray for fine weather because rain would make the mud slope of the ramparts slippery. Their prayers worked, or perhaps it was just good luck, but the night was cold and clear and there were only fluffy white clouds in the sky the next morning.

I had two hundred warriors from my warband on board the longships and all were more or less proficient with a bow. I led them into position in front of Drefan's first wave and we advanced slowly towards the western side of the fort. This was where the ditch was shallowest and the ramp lowest. The ground at the bottom of the ditch was rocky, which explained why that was the case.

Practically all the Welsh lined the defences facing us. I tried to count them and reckoned that there were between three and four hundred. As Drefan had predicted, a few were women and perhaps a third of them were boys under the age of fourteen. The men appeared to be either youths or old men, which made me wonder where the rest were.

As I pondered the mystery I had a nasty thought and rushed back to speak to Drefan. He was mounted on a superb grey horse, not because he was going anywhere, but because it gave him a better view.

'There are no men between twenty and forty years old up on the rampart,' I yelled up at him, trying to catch my breath.

'So what?'

'Where are they? I suspect they are waiting for us to attack and then they'll catch us in the flank, possibly from that wood over there.'

I pointed to the trees some three hundred yards away. He appeared undecided and for a horrible moment I thought that he was going to dismiss my warning.

'At least send some scouts to check,' I said, trying not to sound desperate.

'Very well. Send half a dozen of your men to check but I'm not holding up the assault.'

He turned away from me and nodded at the man beside him. He put his horn to his lips and blew three blasts.

Cursing I ran back to where my archers were. They had already started to advance and I called on them to halt. They came to a shambling stop, confused and wondering what the hell was happening.

'Wolnoth, take five scouts and go and check that wood to the north of us. Be careful because it may well contain the bulk of the enemy of fighting age. You'll have to do it on foot because there's no time to collect horses from the amphitheatre.'

He nodded and calling out the names of five of my best scouts he ran off towards the wood with the others hot on his heels.

'Why have you stopped?' Drefan bellowed at me.

He had ridden through the ranks of his men and mine and now towered over me, red in the face.

I pointed to my scouts.

'My archers aren't moving another step until they've reported back,' I said firmly.

Drefan jumped off his horse and came and thrust his face close to mine.

'You seem to forget, Lord Jørren, that I command here, not you. Now get them moving again or I'll have you escorted back to your ship and your captain can take over.'

'Pardon me, lord, but none of us are going to obey any orders except those given to us by Lord Jørren,' Wealmær said respectfully but resolutely.

Drefan's hand went to the hilt of his sword and for a moment I thought that he was going to do something stupid. My men were loyal to a fault and, had he drawn his sword, I knew that they would have cut him down before I could stop them. However, just at that moment Rinan tugged my arm and pointed.

'Look, lord. You were right.'

Both Drefan and I looked in that direction to see a horde of Welshmen emerge from the trees. My scouts were only halfway to the trees but whoever commanded the enemy had obviously realised that their ruse had been rumbled and had decided to charge before we could re-organise ourselves.

'Shit!' Drefan swore. 'You were right, damn it. Get your archers facing that way whilst I get my men into a shield wall.'

'Wait!' I yelled and pointed towards the fort where the defenders had disappeared, only to re-emerge from the gate, heading our way.

Drefan seemed paralyzed with shock so I took charge.

'You get your men to form a shield wall and face the lot from the trees and my men will deal with the fort's defenders.'

He nodded and disappeared.

'Right, listen to me. We'll thin them out with a couple of volley of arrows and then, on my signal, form a shield wall.'

We were lucky in that it took the Welsh time to get through the gate and form up ready to charge. By that time we had moved around to face east. We waited until they were a hundred and fifty yards away before releasing the first volley. It was fired at high trajectory and so the arrows came down throughout the oncoming mass. I suppose that the two hundred arrows caused perhaps fifty casualties but when the next volley was released, this time straight at those in the lead, they were no more than a hundred yards away. Not all those in the front rank were hit, and some were struck by two or three arrows, but another forty were killed or wounded.

It was enough to cause the charge to falter. Perhaps a quarter of the enemy were out of the fight and I hoped that the rest would now retreat. They didn't. Someone started to yell at them and encourage them to continue the charge. The third volley should have discouraged them but, having re-discovered their courage, they were now baying for our blood.

'Form a shield wall,' I called, praying that I'd not left it too late. Arne echoed the order on his horn and my men dropped their bows, swung their shields around from their backs and drew their swords. Unfortunately none had spears or axes; it was too difficult to carry them in addition to a bow and a quiver full of arrows.

I stepped back into the line between Wealmær and Cináed just in time before the first Welshman reached me; except it wasn't a man, it was a screaming, fanatical young woman. I hesitated, which might have been fatal, but then Cináed stabbed out with his sword and twisted it in her guts. Her eyes opened in shock and she collapsed.

Many a man has been killed because he ignored a wounded foe on the ground. A prone man – or woman, even a seriously wounded one, can easily hamstring you or thrust their dagger up between your thighs and into your groin. I wasn't taking that chance and I thrust down with my sword into her throat.

The headlong charge had been repulsed and the defenders from the fort withdrew to re-group. That gave me a chance to look off to my left. Wulnoth and his companions, hampered as they were by mail byrnies, helmets, weapons and shields, weren't far ahead of the leading Welshmen. In another minute they would be caught. They were a mere forty yards from Drefan's shield wall but that didn't help.

'Lyndon,' I called to the warrior who was at the left hand end of my line. 'See if you can bring down those closest to Wulnoth.'

It seemed to be an age before Lyndon and a few warriors who were closest to him had retrieved their bows and nocked an arrow in place. By then the leading Welshmen had caught up with the rearmost scout. The bowstrings thrummed just as a blow to his helmet knocked my scout to the ground. The man who had knocked my scout down was hit, along with a few others. A second volley took out the next four pursuers and by that time Wulnoth and four of his men had reached the safety of Drefan's shield wall.

Suddenly the scout who'd been caught sprung to his feet, shook his head and sprinted to safety.

A great cheer went up but a few seconds later the main body of Welshmen tore into Drefan's warriors. Emboldened by the arrival of reinforcements, the fort's defenders cavorted and gave us a nice view of a line of buttocks before charging us once more. This time we were better prepared. We were arranged in four lines, the first three ranks of fifty formed the shield wall but the fourth rank brought their bows into play once more.

Two volleys of arrows struck the enemy from above before they reached our shield wall and that robbed the charge of its impetus. This time it was relatively easy to beat off the attack and fifteen minutes later, whilst we inhaled deeply to get our breath back, the surviving hundred and fifty or so defenders fled back into the fort.

Now that the immediate danger had passed, I looked over to see how Drefan was faring. He had some six hundred men and, although he was being attacked by rather more than that, his men were seasoned fighters and the shield wall remained unbroken. In contrast, the Welsh had lost perhaps a third of their number. I could see a few of the enemy in the rear begin to slink off and I decided to end it.

'Form up into a wedge,' I yelled.

My men were weary but they hastened to obey.

'Right, let's show the others what the men of Cent are made of.'

With a great cheer we set off to strike the Welsh in the left flank. That was what finally broke them and within a short time they gave up and fled the field.

We were too tired to chase them on foot and our horses were still in the amphitheatre several hundred yards away. It was a lesson for the future. I sat down wearily on a rock and sent Arne off to tell Drefan where I was. He came back some time later but he looked dejected.

'He's badly wounded, lord. Uhtric and Leofwine are trying to save his life but they say he's lost a great deal of blood and they're not hopeful.'

I was stunned. It was the last thing I'd expected to be told. Unlike me, Drefan normally had the good sense to stay out of the front line. It didn't sound good and I bitterly regretted that our last words to each other had been spoken in anger.

✝✝✝

Drefan died the night we captured Isca Augusta. Uhtric said that he had lost too much blood for him to save his life. It didn't stop two of the priests accusing him and his brother of incompetence but Father Tidwold agreed that Drefan was beyond hope.

He'd been really unlucky. He had been watching the battle from the rear of the shield wall with the other ealdormen and a dozen of his gesith, all mounted, when one of the enemy had thrown a spear towards him. Perhaps his big grey stallion had made him a target or perhaps it was just bad luck. The spear had struck him in the upper chest and had enough momentum to puncture his byrnie and his leather under tunic before lodging in his flesh.

Perhaps the wound wouldn't have been fatal but the spear had a barbed point and Drefan had been foolish enough to try to pull it out. In doing so he had evidently nicked an artery. Uhtric had cauterised the wound once he'd cut the spearhead out but it was too late. He was deathly white by that stage and looked like a corpse even before he breathed his last. I was with him but he had never regained consciousness after the wound was cauterised.

I sent his body back to Wessex on the same knarr as the slaves as well as the more seriously wounded. Leofwine went with the latter to tend to their wounds. I sent one of the longships manned by the more lightly wounded with the knarr to act as escort.

We had lost forty three men and another seventy were wounded. It had seriously weakened our small army but the enemy dead numbered nearly three hundred. There were no Welsh wounded; they had been killed when my men plundered the battlefield.

We stayed at Isca Augusta another day burying our dead. The Welsh were left where they fell as food for the animals and the carrion crows. My fellow ealdormen elected me to replace Drefan as commander on land as well as of the ships and just after dawn we slowly rowed our way north. I deployed scouts along the banks of the river just to make sure that we wouldn't be ambushed.

For the first ten miles we encountered no problems, then we hit some shallows and it wasn't possible to proceed further by ship.

'The river is deep enough again after these shallows,' Eomær reported, and so I went with him to see for myself.

Sure enough after a hundred yards or so the shallows ended. However, a few miles further on there were more shallows so, even if we cut logs and used them as rollers to transport each ship into the deeper water, we would only face the same problem again further on. Each porterage over the shallows would cost us time – a lot of time; time we couldn't afford if we were to meet up with the Mercians one week from now.

There was nothing for it. We would have to return to Isca Augusta and leave the ships there, protected by the fort. The skypfyrd would stay under Wolnoth's command to man the fort and defend the ships. The problem now was transporting all the provisions needed to feed the army without the knarrs.

Having wasted a day we set out again on foot. I allocated ten of the horses for the scouts and the remainder were pressed into service as pack animals to carry the bare essentials. The rest of us would have to walk. I doubted that my fellow ealdormen liked it but they didn't say anything. I just hoped that Æðelred would be able to feed us when we got to Abergafenni; if not we would end up eating the horses.

The river meandered all over the place so it was obvious that it would be much shorter if we could find a track or road leading north instead of following the river. I now regretted sending all the Welsh captives away. Perhaps one of them could have been persuaded to act as a guide. Instead of setting out blindly I decided to wait another day and send out scouts to see if they could locate a road heading north.

My fellow ealdormen and some of the thegns protested at the delay but eventually I made them see sense. The area to the north of Isca Augusta was a wasteland of open moorland and dense forests where we risked getting lost or held up by difficult terrain. Far better to find a road heading in the right direction which we could follow. With that as the point of reference the scouts could operate more effectively as well.

The first pair of scouts came back without finding anything other than animal tracks but shortly afterwards Eomær and Rinan returned having discovered a road of sorts which headed north from the fishing hamlet at the mouth of the Afon Wysg. By the end of the day we had pitched camp four miles inland from the hamlet.

The next three days were uneventful; we followed the track northwards with the scouts coming across nothing other than deserted settlements but then we had some luck. Two of the youngest scouts saw a shepherd with a flock of sheep down in a valley. The man tried to drive the sheep out of sight but one of the scouts followed him at a distance whilst the other returned to report. When we camped that night we dined on mutton.

We still had a hundred or so sheep left. They slowed us down but it was worth it; my worries over having enough provisions were at an end – for now at any rate.

In the middle of the following day Acwel and Lyndon came riding back at a canter full of excitement. Morale amongst the army had been sinking with each mile we marched into what seemed to be an endless deserted landscape. Their elation was therefore understandable. They had found the river again.

We camped on its banks that night and ate the last of the mutton. If my calculations were anything like accurate, Abergafenni couldn't be far away. All we had to do now was to follow the river.

I awoke the next morning to find that the fine weather had come to an end. Not only was it raining but the temperature had dropped significantly during the night and there was sleet mixed in with the rain. I sent out six scouts this time with orders to follow the left bank. If we were close to our target then they might encounter a Welsh patrol. I thought it unlikely though. We were slightly late for our rendezvous with the Mercians and by now I expected them to have the place under siege.

It turned out that Abergafenni was only three miles from where we had camped. The bad news was that there was no sign of the Mercians.

✝✝✝

As we marched along the river we saw a fortress come into view some four hundred yards from the far bank. Somewhat to my surprise we came across a paved road leading to a crossing place over the river and on to the south gate of the fort. As I was to discover later, this was an old Roman road that led to the east of the route we had taken but which ended up at Isca Augusta. Our misfortune was not discovering it as it petered out several miles from the first fort we'd captured.

However, my mind was on other things. The road crossed the river via a bed of shingle. Unfortunately the crossing was defended; initially by a hundred men but as we drew near a horde of reinforcements rushed out of the fortress to bolster the defenders numbers tenfold. I had no doubt that we could force a crossing but it would cost me a lot of men to do so.

'Cináed, take the scouts and ride back the way we came until you're out of sight of the enemy, then go into those woods to the south west of us and see if you can find another crossing further up river.'

'Yes, lord.'

Whilst they were away I formed up the warbands belonging to the other ealdormen so that it appeared as if they were about to attempt a crossing. The last thing I wanted was for the Welsh to think that we were searching for another way over the river. That done, I sent my own warband and the rest of the archers forward. I had left twenty with Wolnoth and another ten had departed with the longship escorting the knarr carrying the captives and the wounded but that still left me with a hundred and seventy, plenty for what I had in mind.

'Wealmær,' I said, turning to my captain, 'take command of the archers. I want them to fire at high trajectory as far as they can into the rear of the enemy.'

'Why not into the front ranks? They'll be their best fighters and they'll be easier to hit.'

'Because then they'll retreat out of range. If they do that they may think about other crossing points. I want to keep their attention on us.'

Wealmær had been with me for the past twenty years. He'd been a young scout serving Edmund of Bebbanburg, who had died in the rout after the first battle for Eforwic, when I first met him. I felt betrayed by Edmund just before the battle and had left him in anger, taking four of his scouts with me. I'd felt guilty about deserting him when I heard about his death but there was nothing we could have done to change the outcome.

Wealmær had been with me ever since. Tragically his three friends had been killed in various battles over the intervening years. He'd always shown promise as a leader and men followed him, which is why I'd made him my captain, but he was unimaginative, always preferring the orthodox ways of fighting.

After the first couple of volleys the Welsh in the middle and rear crowded forward yelling revenge for the hail of death raining down on them. The wet conditions reduced the bows' range and power but nevertheless our arrows inflicted scores of casualties on the enemy.

After another couple of volleys the Welshmen in the rear realised their error and retreated out of range. From there they continued to shout insults and obscenities at us. Of course, we didn't know what they were saying but it was unlikely to be anything nice.

Following a blast on the horn carried by Arne, Wealmær ordered the archers to concentrate on the first few ranks instead. A few had chainmail or leather armour and all carried small shields but nevertheless several were killed and wounded by the initial volley. This enraged the rest and they charged en masse across the river. It wasn't what I'd expected and for a moment I was caught out.

The archers let fly once more and then I rode forward and told Wealmær to withdraw. The archers retreated and merged into the shield wall, dropping their bows, hauling their shields around from their backs and drawing their swords.

I had drawn my warriors up, not in a straight line, but in a shallow crescent. Had the Welsh managed to break the line it would have been disastrous but my men held firm and the enemy horde broke apart on the solid line of shields facing them. Nearly a hundred must have been killed or wounded in the next five minutes. In return they killed one of our men and gave a few more flesh wounds; that was it. They retreated back across the river with their tails between their legs.

I looked down on a scene of utter carnage. Bodies were strewn all over the far bank, more were rising and falling in the shallow water running over the crossing and they lay in heaps in front of the shield wall. A significant number weren't dead but they were seriously wounded. My men advanced to the river's edge systematically killing the wounded and robbing them of weapons and anything else worth taking. Needless to say this caused howls of rage from those watching from over the river but they did nothing about it.

'There is another crossing point a mile or so upstream, lord,' Cináed reported. 'The river flows around a small island of shingle, sand and scrub. It fills most of the river between the two banks but there is water between it and each bank.'

'How deep is the water?'

'Thigh deep and fast flowing, but each channel is no more than ten feet wide.'

We spent the rest of the day erecting a barricade on our side of the river to make the enemy think that we were frightened of another attack. We left our campfires burning when we left a couple of hours after dark and made our way in groups of fifty to the crossing point up stream. By midnight we were all in position on the south bank.

I led the horsemen across first. Thanks to the sheep we hadn't actually needed to slaughter any of the horses for meat on the way north and so I was able to deploy forty men as a screen to protect the crossing whilst the others erected ropes across the two deep channels. Once that was done those on foot started crossing in single file. By dawn everyone was on the north bank.

We moved along the bank towards Abergafenni with the scouts in front. At first we traversed open country but after a little while we entered a wood. Thankfully the trees were widely spaced and, although the undergrowth slowed us down, we were able to keep formation through it. When we emerged into open country once more dawn was breaking and we could see the old Roman fort in front of us.

We were approaching the western wall as the river looped south at that point before heading east again. No one appeared to be on lookout from that wall and we could see perhaps a thousand or more Welshmen gathered at the ford on the old Roman road ready to launch an attack over the river. What they didn't know was that the barricade on the south bank wasn't manned.

The south gates stood wide open; it was too good an opportunity to miss.

'Lord Nerian, you and Wealmær take the horsemen and gallop for the open gates. Seize them and close them. Hold them against all comers until we can join you.'

'With pleasure, Jørren,' he replied with a wolfish grin and seconds later he led fifty men on horseback towards the gates at a gallop.

In contrast to yesterday, today was fine and clear, if somewhat chilly. Each bowman had at least one dry string so that the enemy would now feel the full force and range of our arrows. The Welsh had spotted us by now. Those in the middle of crossing the river stopped, some still on the bank turned and ran back towards the fort, still more turned to face us, but the great majority milled about not knowing what to do.

Someone wearing a red cloak and an ornately decorated helmet was trying to restore some

semblance of order. I assumed that he must be Hywel
ap Rhys, the King of Gwent. I had been told that he
was over sixty but, if so, he was still a fine figure of a
man. I prayed that I would still be able to lead an
army into battle at that age, should I be spared to live
that long.

My scouts and the mounted warriors of my gesith
had gone with Nerian so I was the only one on
horseback with the main body, apart from Arne who
carried the signalling horn. I resisted my initial
impulse to charge into the milling throng of
Welshmen in an effort to kill Hywel; instead I called
for the archers.

I led them forward at a slow jog. When we were a
hundred and fifty yards from the enemy I halted
them. By now their leaders had restored some
semblance of order amongst the Welsh but there
were still groups making their way away from us.
They were obviously heading back to the safety of the
fort but they found the gates shut against them. I
hoped that was because Nerian and Wealmær had
succeeded in securing them. Even if they had done
so, there was no guarantee that they could continue
to hold the gates against whoever had been left in the
fort.

The first volley of arrows soared into the sky and
dropped like a black cloud into the mass of
Welshmen. I had deliberately chosen to use high
trajectory because many of the bowmen wouldn't
have their breathing under control yet. The second
volley went the same way. With a howl of rage the

Welsh erupted into a headlong rush towards the archers.

I glanced behind me to check that the bulk of my army had formed a shield wall. Most had but some were still coming up into position. I had to risk one more volley; this time it would be aimed at the front rank.

One hundred and seventy arrows tore into the leading wave of Welshmen, bringing down about sixty of them. Those behind tripped over the dead and wounded and chaos ensued. The archers had done their job; they had delayed the enemy and eliminated perhaps a sixth of the numbers we faced. Once more they moved back into the shield wall and exchanged bows for swords and shields.

The Welsh quickly recovered and came on again, yelling their anger and no doubt their promise to slaughter us. I did a swift calculation from the back of my horse just behind the fourth rank of my men and reckoned that they outnumbered us by two to one.

The first Welshmen to reach us were easily disposed of but then a great wave of the enemy crashed into the front rank, forcing them back. The three rows behind them shoved their shields against the backs of the men in front of them and the rearward push was halted. Now the killing began.

Those in my front rank used swords, seaxes and short axes to hack at the attackers whilst those in the second row thrust spears through the small gaps between the interlocked shields of the front row to stab at the enemy.

This time we didn't have such an easy time of it. The Welsh had learned the trick of one man pulling down the top of one of our big round shields so that the man beside him could hack at the exposed neck and shoulders of the shield bearer. Thankfully we had trained to counter this. As soon as a Welshman grabbed the top of the shield with both hands, the man to the right of the shield bearer either chopped off the hands of the Welshman gripping the shield or stabbed him, thus forcing him to let go.

After what seemed like an age of fierce fighting, but was probably no more than a few minutes in reality, the Welsh withdrew. They left behind a pile of their dead and dying. Perhaps a hundred and fifty men had fallen on their side in those few minutes. We hadn't emerged entirely unscathed; perhaps twenty or thirty of my men had fallen but only half had been killed. The rest were passed back through the shield wall for Uhtred and the three priests to treat.

I could see Hywel in deep discussion with a group of men mounted on shaggy ponies, presumably his chieftains. After a while one of them, a youth of no more than fifteen, approached us bearing a branch from a tree. It should have had leaves on it to denote a wish to negotiate but this was November and the only leaves formed a golden carpet in the woods.

He was accompanied by another man on foot. This one was wearing a knee length homespun tunic with bare legs ending in leather sandals. His hair was shaved at the front and incongruously, bearing in mind the rest of his appearance, he wore a large golden crucifix dangling from a leather thong around his neck.

'This is Owain ap Hywel, Regis Filius of Hywel ap Rhys Rex,' he said in poor Latin. 'I'm Bishop Maelgwn of Gwent. We wish to speak to your lord.'

'I'm Jørren, Ealdorman of Cent in the Kingdom of Wessex, and I command here,' I replied in rather better Latin.

Maelgwn looked surprised, probably because Cent was a long way from Gwent, before translating for the benefit of Owain, who he'd said was the king's son. The boy said something back whilst scowling fiercely at me.

'Prince Owain wishes to know why you have come here from so far away to carry out an unprovoked attack on the poor people of Gwent, killing and murdering all in your path. He asks if this is at the behest of Ælfred, who he thought was a good Christian.'

'Wessex is an ally of Mercia, whose lands you have mercilessly plundered for years. This is in retribution for those raids.'

After another long exchange between the prince and the bishop Maelgwn eventually replied.

'Whoever raided Mercia it wasn't men from Gwent. King Hywel would never have permitted it. You have therefore led an unprovoked attack on this kingdom and Prince Owain demands that you pay us five thousand shillings in compensation.'

'We're wasting time,' I replied harshly. 'We both know that men from Gwent have raided Mercia for years. Surrender both Hywel ap Rhys for judgement

by Æðelred, Lord of Mercia, and the fort of
Abergafenni and I'll let you depart without any
further bloodshed. Reject my terms and you had
better move out of the way so that we can finish what
we have begun.'

Bishop Maelgwn looked so shocked that he forgot
to translate until Owain demanded to know what I'd
said. When he did so the young prince's hand went to
his sword but a sharp word from the bishop checked
his impulse to attack me. He whirled his pony around
and dug his heels into the beast's flanks so savagely
that it reared up before galloping back to the lines of
Welshmen as if the hounds of Hell were at his heels.
The bishop followed at a more sedate pace.

A heated discussion followed between father and
son. Apart from that, quiet had descended on the
battlefield; then the sound of fighting came from the
south gate. Whoever was left inside the fort had
evidently launched an attack on Nerian and my men.

The Welsh formed up again but made no move to
attack us. Then two hundred or so set off for the
gates. When they got there they started to attack the
wooden gates with axes.

'Archers follow me,' I yelled and set off for our left
flank.

From there it was perhaps four hundred yards to
the mass of men outside the gates; beyond the
distance that most of my archers could fire an arrow.
So I ordered the whole line to advance. This caused
consternation amongst the Welsh and a lot of
discussion amongst their leaders. However, they
made no move to attack us.

320

When we were two hundred and fifty yards away I halted the line and ordered the archers to commence firing. Once more a black cloud of arrows poured down on the Welsh. Some fell short but most struck a man. It required three volleys before sense prevailed and those trying to chop down the stout gates withdrew.

Seeing this, the main body reacted by charging towards us. It was uncoordinated and I doubt that anyone had given an order; it was just a reaction to yet another humiliation for their side.

'Archers ready another arrow,' I yelled. 'Nerian, open the gates.'

The archers brought down the maddened enemy leading the charge as the gates creaked open. My bowmen sent three more volleys into the charging horde whilst the rest of my men charged them in the flank. Chaos ensued and the Welsh wheeled around to face this new threat. That left the way to the open gates clear and I ordered Arne to blow three blasts on his horn. It was the signal for my men to break off the fight and head for the fort. About half of them managed to do so and they hastened through the gates.

Seeing the fort now occupied by so many of my warriors disheartedned the Welsh and many of them broke off the fight and fled. However, the rest stayed and fought. By now my archers had exchanged their bows for shields and swords and I led them into the disorganised enemy in a wedge formation.

I fended off a spear aimed at my face with my shield and cut down a bewildered man who was still facing the rest of my warriors. After that everything became a blur. I was moving and striking out of pure instinct and I've no idea how many men I killed or wounded until I stopped through sheer exhaustion. It was only then that I realised that the rest of the Welshmen had broken off the fight and had retreated to reform.

I took the opportunity to order the rest of my men who were still outside the fort to join the others inside. The Welsh howled in rage as they saw us disappearing through the gateway but by then it was too late for them to do anything about it. I brought up the rear and the gates clanged shut just as the first of the enemy reached them.

The archers raced up to the parapet and began firing arrow after arrow into the maddened Welshmen before the latter had the sense to withdraw. They left behind a lot more bodies. I calculated that since we had arrived at Abergafenni Hywel's army had lost almost half of their number. Whether Æðelred turned up now with the Mercian army seemed immaterial. Gwent was no longer in any position to threaten Mercia when Æðelred and his army were away besieging Lundenwic.

The following day the remnants of Hywel's army marched away, taking their dead and wounded with them. Their losses had severely weakened Gwent and so reduced their ability to raid into Mercia. Furthermore, the various Welsh kingdoms were always fighting amongst themselves and a weak Gwent would be at the mercy of the Kingdoms of Powys to the north and Glywysing to the West.

Consequently Powys, which also bordered Mercia, would be too busy taking advantage of the situation within Wealas to cause Æðelred any anxiety for some time to come.

Chapter Sixteen

CENT

Autumn 885 to Spring 886

'Æðelred finally arrived three days later,' I told a stony faced Ælfred.

The news of Drefan's death hadn't gone down well. It was almost as if the king thought that I had a hand in it. By the time that the Mercians arrived we had buried our dead and dealt with our wounded as best we could.

There was a great deal of food stored in the fort, as well as plunder in the form of weapons, silver and gold. We'd loaded all of it onto carts, together with the wounded, and the convoy was ready to leave when Æðelred arrived. He wasn't best pleased that we had taken anything worth having but, as I'd pointed out to him, my men had done all the fighting and they deserved the rewards. He had to content himself with raiding the area around the fortress and taking the meagre pickings to be found there. Needless to say, it didn't endear me to him.

It took us four days to return to Isca Augusta. The Roman road was much better than the one we'd followed up to Abergafenni but it gradually deteriorated the further south we went until it petered out entirely seven miles north of Isca Augusta. It wasn't surprising the scouts hadn't found it. We loaded the ships and ten days later we docked at Hamwic. I had decided to go there first, rather than directly to Portcæstre, where the longships were based, because that was where I would find the merchants to buy our spoils.

We arrived back at Portcæstre the following day and everyone got drunk at the feast I threw that night to celebrate our victory. It was with a sore head that I set out the next day to report to the king. Perhaps I should have postponed doing so until I felt better but Ælfred would know that we had returned and any delay would put him in a bad mood.

Not that he was exactly pleased with our victory; I think the loss of Drefan had hit him hard and he no doubt thought that it was a poor exchange for helping Mercia.

'I suppose that you should be congratulated,' he said eventually, making it sound as if he'd uttered even that faint praise with reluctance. 'However, replacing Drefan gives me a problem.'

If I thought that he was going to ask me to take on the mantle once more he soon disabused me of that idea.

'You are the obvious choice, of course, but I can't ask you to give up Cent.'

'Give up Cent?' I asked in surprise.

'Yes, whoever the next hereræswa is, I can't have him living at the other end of the kingdom. It needs to be someone whose counsel I can readily obtain. It always seems to take you weeks to get here whenever I send for you. Besides you've enough to do building up the fleet again, and there are rumours of plague in Cent. You'll need to take measures to quarantine your shire if they are true.'

There were often small outbreaks of the plague from time to time but there hadn't been a serious epidemic within living memory so I didn't worry about it. Besides the king said it was only a rumour.

I presented him with his share of the proceeds from the campaign and left Wintanceaster shortly afterwards. I didn't think that the king had looked at all well and the gossip in his hall was that he'd had several bouts of illness recently.

As we rode through the gates a hunting party came the other way. Evidently they had had some success as servants led three ponies, each carrying the carcass of a deer. Consequently the hunters were in a jubilant mood. They were led by Edward with Oswine riding at his right hand. This didn't surprise me but the person on his other side did. It was Sexmund, son of the late and unlamented Eadda. Edward acknowledged me with a nod but Sexmund glared at me with hatred.

Oswine stopped to have a word and, after exchanging the usual pleasantries, I asked him about Sexmund. He frowned before replying.

'That little bastard has managed to worm his way into Edward's gesith. I think Edward feels sorry for him after the death of his father.'

'It doesn't sound as if you care for him overmuch?'

'I don't! He hates me because I'm your stepson and he's trying to turn Edward against me. He's convinced that you were responsible for his father's disappearance at sea.'

'Can't Edward see what he's doing?'

'Oh, he's not doing it in an obvious way. Sexmund is sly and he's clever.'

He took his leave of me and rode through the gates after the rest of the hunting party. I thought about what he'd said but I dismissed it. Sexmund was nothing more than a young boy. What harm could he do to me and my family? I'd forgotten that I killed my first man when I was just thirteen, the same age as Sexmund now.

✝✝✝

I returned to Dofras by sea and was delighted to find Hilda and the children had moved there after all.

'I didn't think you wanted to live in the fortress,' I said once we were alone.

'I didn't,' she replied tartly, 'but plague came to Cantwareburh. I suppose you've heard that Ethelred is dead?'

I hadn't. I was surprised that Ælfred hadn't told me, especially as the archbishop had been a thorn in his side for as long as I could remember. He'd mentioned rumours about the plague, of course. Obviously it had been far worse an outbreak than I had expected. I later discovered that news about the extent of the plague in eastern Cent and the death of Ethelred, amongst many others, hadn't reached Wintanceaster until after I'd left.

'The monks have elected Plegmund as the new Archbishop,' she went on.

One of the things that caused the estrangement between king and archbishop had been the right of the ecclesiastical community to elect abbots and bishops. Ælfred wasn't the first king to demand that he had to approve their nomination, which meant in practice that the choice lay in his hands. Plegmund had been nominated by the king as abbot, of course, so presumably he would approve of him as archbishop. In any case he couldn't be enthroned until after he'd travelled to Rome to receive his pallium from the Pope.

'Is the plague still rife in Cent?' I queried.

'No, it seems to be dying out. The last report I heard was that there had only been two deaths in the past week,' Hilda replied.

It struck me that there was something she wasn't telling me. She wouldn't meet my eye and kept wringing her hands.

'There's something else,' she added, giving me an anxious glance.

'What is it? Why are you so nervous about telling me?'

'It's Alric.'

Still she hesitated.

'My brother? What is it? Has he contracted the plague?' I asked, horrified at the thought.

She nodded.

'Not just him. Guthild and Ajs are dead too, along with half the vill. Thank God your neice, Ecgwynna, survived.'

I felt as if I had been kicked hard in my stomach. I sat down on a stool and put my head in my hands. At first I couldn't take it in: not Alric – the brother who I'd rescued from the Danes and who I'd been closest to as a child. Both my brothers were now dead and I suddenly felt very old.

I stayed in my chamber for two days, mourning my loss. However, the death of Alric didn't just mean personal loss; he was also the shire reeve and there were many matters that now needed my attention; not least the question of inheritance of land. Several thegns and many land-owning ceorls had perished during the sudden epidemic. It was the arrival of Ecgwynna who roused me from my torpor, however.

My niece had come to see me and had brought Alric's will. When I read it I gathered that Ajs had died first and then Guthild. When my brother first fell ill he was still well enough to make a new will.

He was a wealthy thegn owning several vills and he didn't want Ecgwynna, should she survive, being married off to some man who was attracted to her wealth and cared nothing for her. He therefore made me her guardian with the stipulation that I find a suitable husband for her. He left the dowry to be given to the groom at my discretion but the majority of my late brother's estate was to be transferred to Ecgwynna upon marriage and be held in her name, not that of her husband. He made one other bequest, leaving a significant sum of money to the Church on condition that they said masses for his soul and that of his wife and son every day for a year.

The last time I'd seen Ecgwynna she had been a young girl of thirteen whose body was still that of a child. That had changed over the past year and she had become a young woman. At fourteen many girls got betrothed, if not married, but I agreed with Hilda that my niece needed time to grieve before we could even discuss her marriage.

I enacted my brother's will, drawing up the necessary deeds. These would be lodged with other land transfer deeds at the monastery at Cantwareburh. I decided to take them myself as I wanted to see Plegmund and to assess the havoc wrought by the plague. Hilda had told me that the epidemic had all but died out, nevertheless I didn't want to risk anyone's lives unnecessarily and so I only took Arne with me.

The boy had been captured at Hrofescæster along with many Danes but he was of Norse origin. He was the youngest of four sons born to a poor bóndi who owned a small farm in the north of Frankia. That much I knew, but not how he'd come to speak Danish so well or how he came to join them in their ill-fated attempt to invade Cent. The ride to Cantwareburh and back would give me an opportunity to get to know him better.

The route from Dofras to Cantwareburh was the final stretch of the old Roman road known as Casingc Stræt. For most of the way it was still paved with cobblestones and only the odd section had vanished, deteriorating into a muddy track. I had been improving these sections as part of Ælfred's defensive plan of burhs and interconnecting roads and, although they weren't constructed in the same manner as the Roman roads, they had a stone base with gravel on top. Even at a walk a mounted man could make the journey between the two places in under four hours. At a gentle canter it could be covered in an hour and a half.

We set out after mass and a quick bite to eat. I was riding Scur and my horse seemed to be as pleased to be outside the fortress as I was. It was a hot day for early September and we rode under a clear blue sky dotted with small white clouds. Hilda had been nervous about my travelling with just a boy as escort so I had agreed to wear my byrnie and take my helmet and shield as well as my sword and seax. Arne didn't normally carry any weapons, apart from his knife, but today I allowed him to wear a seax hanging from his belt.

After a while I found that wearing a byrnie, a leather jerkin under it and a woollen tunic under that was making me sweat so I dismounted and took off the byrnie and jerkin, handing them to Arne to put into a sack and tie behind his saddle. When we set off again he started to talk about the land we were riding through. He said that it was far more varied and interesting than where he came from.

'I know your family comes for Northern Frankia, Arne, but not how you ended up with the Danes at Hrofescæster,' I said in Danish.

Although Arne was picking up the variety of English we spoke in Cent quite quickly, I felt that he would be more comfortable in Danish. I could have asked him in Norse but my Norse wasn't much better than his English. Danish and Norse were similar and a Dane and Norseman who only spoke their own tongue could converse after a fashion but there were many differences between the two languages. For example sword was sverð in Danish but swerdą in Norse.

'It was difficult for our farm to provide enough food for all of us to eat,' he explained. 'In addition to my parents, there were my three brothers and two sisters. We therefore relied on raiding to survive. Two years ago the summer was wet and the crops failed. Everywhere on the Continent was in the same position so food was even scarcer than normal. We did manage to take a little plunder from the Franks but prices for what food there was were high and we still starved.

'My father told me and my younger brother, Leif, that we could no longer stay. We were the smallest and not able to work as hard as our two elder brothers. He also made our sister, Estrid, marry a widowed neighbour of ours who was in his fifties in order to get rid of her. She was just thirteen.

'Leif and I made our way to the nearest port seeking work. Luckily there was a Frisian there seeking crews for several longships he was building for a Danish jarl. We signed up with him as ship's boys.'

It sounded plausible. The Frisians were known to build the best ships; in fact I planned to travel over to Frisia as soon as I could to commission some new longships for Ælfred's fleet.

'The rest you know. Leif and I were guarding our longship on the west bank of the River Midweg when your men came and attacked us. My brother and I were taken captive. I presume that he's now a ship's boy on one of your ships but I can't be certain.'

He was silent and looked downcast at the memory, no doubt wondering if his brother was still alive. I could understand his feelings having just lost Alric. We rode in silence for a while and then he seemed to cheer up and look about him again.

'Most Norse I've come across have fair or brown hair, I've rarely seen one with hair as red as yours,' I said glancing at the bright red hair that hung down to his shoulders.

'That's because my mother was a thrall from Ireland before my father freed her and then married her,' he said with a grin. 'She has hair that's an even brighter shade of red than mine.'

We reached Cantwareburh just as the church bell in the monastery was ringing out calling the monks to the noon service known as Sext. I suspected that Plegmund would probably attend Sext and so we rode into the courtyard of a tavern and handed our horses over to the ostler. Arne went to follow him into the stables to care for them but I tossed the ostler a silver penny and told him to feed and water them before inviting Arne to join me for something to eat.

He looked startled but did as he was bid. I suppose it was unusual for a servant, and one who was a slave at that, to sit and eat with an ealdorman but I detested eating on my own. Besides, I liked the lad and wanted to hear more about his life in Frankia.

'We lived in a region called Norðmanndi,' he told me. 'It means land of the northmen. My father was born in Norþweg but I've never been there. He said it was a barren land of fjords and mountains where farming is difficult. He told me that was why the Norse became Vikings, plundering the richer lands across the sea. Even in Norðmanndi life was hard, Odin knows what it must have been like in the frozen north.'

I looked at him sharply. He'd been brought up as a pagan, of course, but I'd insisted that he become a Christian when he joined me. He'd been baptised and taught the rudiments of Christianity but it seemed his heathen beliefs still had a hold on him.

'Sorry lord. I meant nothing by it. I've accepted the White Christ, truly,' he said contritely.

'And you renounce Odin, Thor and the Norse so-called pantheon of false gods?'

'Yes, lord. Look,' he said showing me a wooden crucifix that he wore on a leather thong around his neck. 'I've thrown away my Mjolnir.'

The Mjolnir was the likeness of Thor's hammer that pagans wore as a talisman instead of a crucifix.

At that moment a pretty serving girl came with a flagon of ale for each of us and a platter of bread, cheese and apples. She gave Arne a lingering glance and the boy blushed, his face even redder than his hair.

'I think she's interested in you,' I teased him.

'Do you think so?' he asked me hopefully, his eyes following the girl's retreating back.

'Look, I don't need you whilst I visit the archbishop. Why don't you stay here and find out?'

After that Arne wasn't interested in talking about Frankia. As he munched his way through the food and quaffed the ale his eyes continually sought out the girl. She wasn't the only one serving the customers but she was the only one near his age. I guessed she might be fifteen or sixteen and was likely to be experienced in the ways of lovemaking, if the look she'd given Arne was anything to go by. Judging by his reaction I was willing to bet that he was still a virgin.

I gave Arne a small purse of silver pence with which to pay for our meal and left to go and see the archbishop. Plegmund was pleased to see me and seemed to have settled in well to his new role. He gave me a detailed account of the effect that the plague had wrought on the local population. He estimated that perhaps a quarter had died of it, which meant that labour was scarce and prices had risen. However, things were now returning to normal much quicker than he'd anticipated.

He invited me to stay the night but I politely declined, saying that I needed to visit my hall on the hill. When I returned to the tavern I found that my body servant seemed a little different. He had gained in confidence and the purse I had left him was lighter than it should have been if he'd just paid for the food and ale. I smiled to myself when the pretty serving girl came out to watch us, or rather him, leave.

We rode up to my hall above the settlement in companionable silence. I didn't ask how his afternoon had gone and he didn't boast about his first time. It confirmed my opinion that Arne was a decent young man. I made the decision then to train him as a warrior.

'There were four men here yesterday asking about you, lord,' the reeve told me just after we'd dismounted.

He seemed agitated and I guessed that they hadn't been the sort of men who I'd normally associate with.

'Tell me about them.'

'Their leader asked if I knew where you were, but of course I didn't. I had a nasty feeling that, if two of your warband hadn't been on guard outside the hall, he would have been more aggressive in his questioning. He looked a big, ugly brute.'

'Describe him to me.'

The reeve did so. As soon as he mentioned that the man spoke in the dialect of Wessex, had a scarred face and stood head and shoulders above his fellows I had a horrid feeling I knew who he was.

'Tell me about the men with him.'

'They didn't say anything to me but they muttered to themselves in a strange language I'd never heard before. It wasn't Danish or Norse.'

He nodded over to where Arne was unloading the panniers containing my clothes from the horses.

'Two of them had hair the same colour as your servant's, only not as red.'

That confirmed my suspicions. Bryhthelm had somehow escaped from slavery in Íralond and the men with him were Irish.

✝✝✝

My first thought was to take men from the few who defended my hall at Cantwareburh but they were old warriors or ones who had been wounded and could no longer serve in the shield wall. None of them were proficient scouts. So I sent a messenger to Dofras to summon six of my gesith. They appeared at dawn the next day having ridden through the early hours of the morning. Arne roused me from my sleep to let me know they had arrived and I put on a robe to go and brief them.

I told them about Bryrhthelm and the three Irish mercenaries and explained my plan to them before sending them off to the warriors' hall to get a few hours' sleep.

We attended mass the next morning and I prayed fervently that my plan would work. After a quick meal of bread and cheese washed down with weak ale we set off. Wolnoth, Acwel and Lyndon went first, followed by Arne and myself ten minutes later. Finally Cináed, Eomær and Rinan brought up the rear. Both parts of my escort disappeared into the trees at the side of the road as soon as we left the hall. My aim was to capture the men who stalked me so that I could question them. I needed to know for certain who they were working for.

The day wasn't nearly as pleasant as the previous day; the sky was overcast and there was a cold wind from the east. I had put on the over-tunic and a cloak made from wolf pelts which concealed the fact that I was wearing my byrnie underneath. It was cold but I was soon sweating with all that on. I hoped it wouldn't be too long before Bryhthelm made his move and I could shed some of my layers. Before we left I had found a chain mail byrnie in a chest that was more or less the right size for Arne to wear under his cloak. It was rusty but it would serve to protect him.

The road south undulated a little at first but the last quarter of the route ran through hilly country. That was where I was expecting to be ambushed. I wasn't disappointed.

The first we knew of the attack were two arrows that came at us from the undergrowth to the right of the road. They weren't intended to kill us, merely to unhorse us. One struck Arne's mare in the chest and it sank to its knees before rolling over. He jumped from the saddle just in time to avoid being trapped under the dead animal.

The other arrow hit Scur in the shoulder. It was only a flesh wound but nevertheless he was in pain and I had difficulty in controlling him. I gave up and, once his forelegs hit the ground after rearing up, I hastily dismounted. Arne drew his seax and I my sword, swinging my shield around from my back at the same time.

'Well, well; look who we have here,' Bryhthelm drawled as he stepped into sight, followed by his three henchmen. 'No less a person than the mighty Lord Jørren, Ealdorman of Cent and Sæ Hereræswa of Wessex, not to mention murderer of Lord Eadda.'

He was carrying an axe in his right hand and a shield on his left arm. Two of the Irishmen covered us with their bows whilst the third held the reins of their horses.

'What's the matter, Jørren? Cat got your tongue?'

The fact that I remained silent whilst warily watching him seemed to annoy him.

'Who's that with you? Not another little whore dressed up to look like a boy. Or perhaps you like boys in your bed as well as young girls? I enjoyed killing the last one but sadly there was no time to rape her first. We've plenty of time now though. Perhaps I'll rape this one whilst you watch, then kill you.'

Arne swore at the man in a language I wasn't familiar with; presumably his mother had taught him Irish because the three men with Bryhthelm looked surprised and one of them replied angrily in the same tongue. I sensed that Arne was about to enter into a slanging match so I told him to shut up. I was happy for our enemies to talk as long as they liked but I didn't want to provoke one of the bowmen to let fly another arrow.

The road wasn't busy, probably because people were still wary of the plague. We had passed a few merchants, the odd farmer with produce to sell and a pair of monks during our journey but the road would normally have been crowded at this time of day. However, as we faced each other a man and two boys herding sheep to market came over the brow of the hill to the south of us.

"Get out of here if you know what's good for you,' Bryhthelm yelled at them and the two Irishmen with bows trained them on the shepherds to encourage them to obey.

A second later all three Irishmen fell to the ground, each with two arrows protruding from the bodies. Bryhthelm stood there, stunned by what had just happened. A few seconds later Wulnoth and the other five scouts stepped from the trees. They went to disarm Bryhthelm but I ordered them to leave him to me.

'You owe me a blood debt, Bryhthelm, but before I exact it tell me who paid you to kill me.'

'Go to hell, Jørren.'

Scarcely had he uttered the words when he charged at me, raising his axe over his head as he did so. It was large and heavy. Had it landed on my shield it would probably have split it in two. Instead I side stepped and he stumbled past me, missing his footing when the axe didn't connect as he'd expected. I brought my sword around and it cut quite deeply into the soft flesh at the back of his thighs.

It wasn't a fatal wound but I expected it to incapacitate him. It didn't. With a roar of rage he came at me again, albeit more slowly this time, hampered by his wounded legs. Once more I moved nimbly out of his way and this time I brought my sword down on his helmet as he stumbled past me. It should have stunned him but he whirled around much more quickly than I thought him capable of and jabbed a dagger at my chest.

It was a savage thrust and carried all the force behind it that the big man could muster. The point went through my wolf-skin tunic, parted the links of my byrnie and cut into the leather jerkin underneath.

It nicked my flesh but that was all. The layers I was wearing saved me from serious injury.

His face was close to mine as he tried to push the dagger in further and he spat in my face. I pushed him away and as he raised his axe in his other hand I stepped in close and smashed the pommel of my sword into his face, breaking several teeth as well as his nose. He yelped in pain and stumbled clear.

I followed him and, whilst he was still blinded by pain and blood, brought my blade down hard, severing his right hand at the wrist. It was over. I was tempted to hang him from the nearest tree, along with his companions to serve as a warning to others but I wanted to know who had sent him.

Half an hour later my men had buried the three Irishmen in shallow graves in the woods, got a fire going and cauterised the stump of Bryhthelm's arm and the wounds in his thighs. He'd passed out from the pain, which was probably a mercy for him.

We took him back to Dofras where I put him in a dank room with only the sound of the waves crashing against the rocks below for company. I sent Uhtred and Leofwine to tend to his wounds, just to make sure that he wouldn't die on me. I let him have water but otherwise starved him in the hope that he would betray whoever sent him, but he remained obstinately silent. So I left him to rot.

✝✝✝

A month passed and I let the prisoner have a little stale bread, just enough to keep him alive, but still he remained silent. Winter came but thankfully this year it was merely wet and we had little snow. In early March I set out to visit Fresia. I had commissioned several new longships to be built at Hamwic, Portcæstre and Dofras but I needed still more to replace those lost during the Danish incursion eighteen months previously. The Fresians were reputed to build the best ships, both in terms of speed through the water and strength, and they had built many of the Danish longships.

I was back by the end of the month having commissioned four new ships. I visited Bryhthelm in his prison the day after my return and I was shocked in the change in him. Gone was the muscular giant of a warrior. Instead he was gaunt, scrawny and filthy.

'Enough!' he said hoarsely as soon as I entered his chamber. 'I give in. I'll tell you what you want to know.'

I smiled grimly. I hadn't liked starving even a creature like Bryhthelm but I had to have proof about who had sent him to kill me.

'Good. Get him washed and fed, not too much mind; his stomach can't take it, then bring him up to the hall.'

I sat with Cei on one side of me and Wealmær on the other as he was brought in. He had to be supported; he was still too weak to walk unaided but at least he was clean and both his hair and his beard had been washed and combed.

'Well, who sent you?' I demanded.

'First promise me that you'll release me if I tell you.'

'No, that would be seen as weakness. All I can promise you is that I will let the king decide your fate, otherwise you'll go back to your prison and rot there unfed until you die of starvation.'

He hung his head for a while before replying.

'Very well. I was paid by Eadda's son to kill you. He arranged with a merchant from Hamwic to buy my freedom and to recruit the three mercenaries you found me with.'

'Sexmund?'

'Yes, lord. Sexmund, although I think his mother must have also had a hand in it. After all, she controls the money until the boy reaches the age of fourteen.'

'Thank you. You could have saved yourself months of misery had you told me this earlier.'

'Will you let me go now, lord?'

'No, I want you to repeat what you have just told me to the king. We will set out by sea for Wintanceaster tomorrow.'

However, fate intervened and I never did take Bryhthelm to face the king. That afternoon a messenger arrived to say that Edward the Ætheling was on his way to visit me. Doubtless he would have that little weasel Sexmund with him. This could be interesting.

✝✝✝

Unlike the previous times we had encountered one another, Edward was all smiles and affability when we met this time. I was standing at the foot of the steps outside my hall within the high Roman walls of the fortress at Dofras when he arrived accompanied by his gesith, a score of his father's warriors and two score clerics, servants and hangers on. He greeted Hilda with deference and made a fuss of Ywer, Kjestin and even five year old Æbbe. However, the attention he gave my children was as nothing compared to Ecgwynna. Both Hilda and I could tell that the young ætheling was captivated the moment he laid eyes on my niece. The fact that she was the elder by two years didn't seem to matter.

'It seems that young Edward has learned diplomacy if not common sense.'

I turned to see Father Tidwold at my elbow.

'Don't be deceived by his friendly demeanour, he isn't your friend. In private he mocks you, egged on by that whelp Sexmund. Oswine has tried to convince him of your importance as a noble and military commander but all that's done is to create a gulf between the two of them. Don't get me wrong, I don't think the boy is naturally malicious; he's just not very good at choosing who he listens to.'

I found Tidwold's counsel intriguing and I would have questioned him more closely but Edward was standing looking at the interior of my hall and I went to join him as his host.

'This is a fine hall, Lord Jørren; nearly as grand as my father's.'

'It isn't really mine, Lord Edward. My hall as ealdorman is at Cantwareburh but this is more convenient for me as the Sæ Hereræswa. I'm afraid that my wife prefers the timber walls there to the cold stone here.'

'They are the best constructed stone walls I've seen.'

'That's because they were built by the Romans; we don't have their skill as masons I fear.'

'If the fortress isn't your home, whose is it?'

'The man who commands here is Cei. Let me introduce you.'

'Cei is an unusual name for a Saxon, or even a Jute,' Edward remarked after I'd introduced him to Cei.

'My family originally came from Wealas, lord,' Cei replied, 'although I was born in Cent, at Cilleham.'

'Cilleham? Isn't that where you were born, Lord Jørren?'

'It is. My nephew is now the thegn there.'

'Tell me, Edward, what brings you to Dofras?' I asked, steering the conversation away from Cei's antecedents.

'It was my father's idea,' he said as if he had something distasteful in his mouth. 'He thinks I should get to know the kingdom which will eventually be mine.'

We sat down to eat just as the sun was setting. Edward sat next to Hilda with Ecgwynna on his other side. It was a mistake. He completely ignored my wife, who sat huffily pecking at the food, and talked to my niece throughout the meal. I could understand why Hilda was upset but I was annoyed when all she gave me were monosyllabic answers, so I gave up trying to talk to her and spent the evening talking to Cei's wife, who sat on my left.

345

Oswine and Sexmund sat with the ætheling's other companions on another table. I had allowed Ywer to sit beside his step brother and the two seemed to be getting on well. Sexmund, on the other hand, looked as if he'd eaten something disgusting and sat with a sour look on his face watching Edward and Ecgwynna. For some reason he seemed to be jealous.

When the meal was over I turned to Edward and asked if he would help me decide a case of attempted murder and possible treason. This immediately piqued his interest.

I nodded to Wealmær and he opened the door to the hall to admit Bryhthelm accompanied by two of my warriors. I watched Sexmund closely and grunted in satisfaction when I saw his face pale.

'You recognise Bryhthelm, of course, Lord Edward. He used to be your tutor in swordsmanship before he murdered my body servant and was sold into slavery.'

'Yes, of course,' Edward replied distractedly. 'But what's he doing here. The last I heard he he'd been shipped off to Íralond.'

'Perhaps he'd like to tell you himself?'

I looked at Bryhthelm pointedly and he licked his lips nervously.

'I was bought out of slavery and brought back to Wessex, lord,' he said hesitantly.

'Who paid for your freedom and why?' Edward demanded.

'I didn't know at first, a merchant arrived to negotiate my freedom. He brought me back to

346

Hamwic together with three Irish mercenaries, gave me fresh clothes and told us to go to a tavern called the Silver Chailce in Wintanceaster and ask for Leif. He gave me a few silver pennies and we did as he'd asked. I was nervous about entering Wintanceaster but no one challenged me.'

Whilst Bryhthelm was talking I was watching Sexmund. He was sweating and looking increasingly uncomfortable.

'When I asked for Leif we were shown to a table and told to wait,' the man continued. 'We were fed and given ale but it was an hour before this man calling himself Leif appeared. It wasn't his name, the man who joined us was the reeve from the late Thegn Eadda's largest vill. He had someone with him, a boy, but the lad kept his face hidden in his hood and didn't speak.'

When Bryhthelm said this Sexmund visibly relaxed and a sly smile crossed his face.

'The reeve passed a purse across the table to each of us. Mine contained a hundred silver pennies and, by their comparative size, I think that the others were each given about half that sum. He told us that he would pay us the same again if we killed Lord Jørren. It was then that the boy spoke for the first time. He said he would double it if we brought him Lord Jørren's severed head.'

Sexmund had been drinking from his goblet when Bryhthelm said this; he spluttered and put it down, looking ashen faced.

'Did you recognise the voice, Bryhthelm?' I asked quietly.

'Yes, lord. It was Eadda's son, Sexmund. I'd watched him grew up and I'd know that voice anywhere.'

Sexmund suddenly leapt to his feet with his eating knife in his hand. I thought he was going to cut Bryhthelm's throat before he could say anymore but he headed in my direction instead. It wasn't our custom to wear swords in my hall, especially when eating and drinking. Drunken arguments could so easily end in an unintended death. The only armed men were the two sentries at the door, the two guarding the prisoner and Rinan, the one standing behind me.

Everyone except for Rinan and me were taken by surprise. Sexmund's eating knife was six inches long – more like the size of a dagger - and there was no doubt in my mind that he would kill me if he reached me. I had put down my own knife when I got up to question Bryhthelm and the boy would have stabbed me before I could pick it up.

Thankfully Rinan was ready. He'd been told that Sexmund might try and kill Bryhthelm. The attack on me was a surprise; nevertheless, Rinan reacted with commendable speed. His arm went back and the spear flew from his hand, striking Sexmund in the centre of his chest just as he reached the other side of the table from me.

He fell backwards and lay in a spreading pool of blood. For an instant there was a stunned silence, then all hell broke loose. Women started to scream. Men stood up and benches crashed over. The other sentries rushed to where the body lay and Bryhthelm seized the opportunity to make his escape.

He dashed for the door but Eomer, who was one of the men guarding him, ran after him, barging people out of the way. Bryhthelm was trying to tug open the door when Eomær threw the hand axe he carried on his belt. It struck the fleeing man in the centre of his back, smashing his spine and driving the broken ends of his rear ribs into vital organs. He fell to the ground and Eomær tugged his axe free from the corpse.

It was a pity because Bryhthelm hadn't quite finished telling me all I wanted to know. I would have dearly loved to have known the identity of the merchant who freed him and hired the Irish mercenaries. I also wanted to know who had told him that I would be returning to Dofras on the day he ambushed me. I supposed that I'd never know now.

I banged on the table to restore order and servants came to carry the two corpses away. I apologised to Edward for the uproar; it wasn't quite how I had intended the evening to go. He was shocked, not so much by the killings, but by the fact that Sexmund, his close friend, had tried to procure my death.

'I trusted him implicitly,' he told me later.

'A king must learn who to trust,' I advised him, 'certainly not those whose honeyed words are intended to flatter. Judge men by their deeds.'

'I've learned a valuable lesson, Lord Jørren, and I have you to thank for that. I was wrong to believe Eadda's vitriol and wrong to allow his sycophantic son to get close to me.'

✝✝✝

I was out riding with Ywer and Kjestin when the messenger came. Kjestin was nearly as good a rider as her brother and she reminded me of her elder sister, Cuthfleda, in many ways. I thought of her mother every time I looked at Kjestin. It didn't mean that I was unhappy being married to Hilda; it was just that she didn't understand what drove those of us who were natural warriors.

The twins were now eleven and Ywer was pestering me to be allowed to train properly as a warrior. Instead I'd decided to send him to the monastery to improve his education years. Fourteen was soon enough to become a fledgling fighter. Needless to say, he didn't see it that way.

The messenger awaited our return to Dofras. I'd been expecting the summons but I hoped that it would be later in the year. There was still so much I needed to do, both as ealdorman and as sæ hereræswa. I hadn't even appointed anyone as shire reeve to look after things whilst I was away.

The messenger was one of Ælfred's gesith and he brought news as well as the king's letter. Drefan's elder brother, Eadred, Ealdorman of Dornsæte, was to be the new hereræswa. I liked and respected Eadred and he was a good choice. His appointment would have to be confirmed officially at the next meeting of the Witenaġemot but I couldn't see that being a problem.

350

The next appointment did surprise me, however. A thegn called Æthelhelm had been appointed to succeed the childless Drefan as Ealdorman of Wiltunscīr. I didn't really know the man but what I did know wasn't encouraging. He was said to be young, vain, arrogant and one of those men who thought he knew everything but who was, in reality, quite stupid.

I wondered what made Ælfred select him, then I remembered that he was lord of more than a score of vills and was consequently extremely wealthy. Constructing and manning burhs, improving roads and re-building the fleet all cost money. Ælfred could never be accused of corruption but there was no denying that financial considerations played a part in his choice of Æthelhelm.

I took the king's letter and read it quietly. It said what I'd expected. The time had come to assist the Mercians to retake Lundenwic. I was to gather my own forces and those of Sūþrīgescīr and Suth-Seaxe and muster at Stanes, twenty five miles to the west of Lundenwic. Æðelred and the army of Mercia would meet us there on the twentieth of April.

Chapter Seventeen

Lundenwic

April 886

I stood on the quayside at Sudwerca on the south bank of the River Temes and gazed across at Lundenwic on the far side. The settlement was divided into two distinct parts: the old Roman city immediately in front of me and the sprawling collection of hovels, halls and huts of one kind or another across the River Flēot to the west of it. The latter had sprung up haphazardly because our pagan ancestors had been frightened of the ghosts who were said to roam the old city.

The Romans had built a bridge across the Temes between the old city and Sudwerca. It must have been an impressive structure in its heyday and I marvelled at the skills of the people who had made it. It was constructed of stone and was just wide enough for two carts to pass each other. Father Tidwold had told me that it had been made wide enough for a body of Roman soldiers to march across it eight abreast, eight being the number in a contubernium, the smallest unit.

Now, however, it had fallen into disrepair. I could clearly see that there had been seventeen arches originally, the one in the centre being three times as wide as the rest to allow shipping to pass through it, although they would have had to lower their masts to do so. The central arch had collapsed, as had two of the others. The debris from the missing roadway and from other areas where sections of the parapet had fallen away, made navigation through the bridge hazardous and most river traffic waited until near high tide before attempting it.

The fallen stonework could have been cleared away easily enough and the bridge could have been repaired in timber but the north bank was in Danish hands and the south bank belonged to Wessex, so it suited everybody to leave it as it was. Instead ferries of various sizes conveyed traffic across the river between an area called Lambehitha Moor to the west of Sudwerca and the settlement of Lundenwic at the junction of the Temes and the Flēot.

Although the inhabitants of the latter were mainly Anglo-Saxons, they were part of Danish dominated Mercia and were subjects of the jarl who now ruled the old city, a Dane called Erik Berkse – meaning brutal or cruel, an epithet he thoroughly deserved if the stories about his vicious nature were to be believed. He was said to have a thousand followers and, judging by the number of longships anchored in the river and moored along the waterfront, it was a fair estimate.

I had been in the city area of Lundenwic myself and, in preparation for the assault on it, I'd tried to find out more about the layout. I knew it had seven gates; four on the western wall, two on the north wall and one to the north east. The Danes had repaired the Roman stone walls with stout timber palisade where sections had collapsed but the south wall

353

along the river had numerous gaps in it. Some were made intentionally to allow access between warehouses on shore and the quayside.

The old legionary fort lay in the north-west corner of the city and this was almost completely intact. Like all Roman forts it was laid out with two roads running through it from north to south and east to west. Two of the cities gates led into the fort with two more gates giving access into the city. Erik Barkse had based himself in the building which had been the house of the Roman governor and later that of the kings of Mercia. I'd been told that the walls had been repaired with wattle and daub and the tiled roof was now thatched but it was still more luxurious than any royal hall.

The fort would give Æðelred and me the greatest problem. Even if we could capture the city – and that was a big if – the fort was the key to controlling it. Unless we could drive the Danes out of it they could sally out at any time and attack us.

I turned Scur westwards and then dug my heels into his flanks. He changed pace to a gentle canter and I rode through the gathering dusk to rejoin my men before they camped for the night.

†††

We weren't the first contingent to reach the muster point at Stanes on the south bank of the Temes. Unsurprisingly the army of Sūþrīgescīr, who had the least distance to travel, had arrived the day before. Stanes was the furthest west the territory controlled by the Danes extended along the Temes. From there to its source the north bank lay in that part of Mercia ruled by Æðelred. That didn't mean that there weren't Danes about – the border was fluid – but the settlements all paid their taxes and owed allegiance to the Lord of the Mercians.

There had been a small Danish settlement on the opposite bank to Stanes and the Jarl who owned it had charged a fee for those crossing the timber bridge over the Temes. In these relatively peaceful times there was trade between Wessex on the south bank and the Danes and Mercians across the river. However, one of the first things that Sūþrīgescīr's ealdorman, Dudda, had done was to lead a raid across the bridge and kill every Dane he could find on the far bank.

'Did any get away?' I asked, concerned that they would have warned the garrison at Lundenwic about the muster.

'I don't think so; we hunted down those who ran.'

I would have done things differently, crossing further upstream and surrounding the settlement before launching an attack to secure the bridge but there was no point in falling out with Dudda; what was done was done.

The next day Heardwig Geonga, the ealdorman of Suth-Seaxe's son, arrived with nearly four hundred men. Our force now numbered a thousand experienced warriors, the same as the Danes were reputed to have in Lundenwic. I hoped that Æðelred would be able to muster enough men so that we had sufficient between us to make capturing the walled city feasible.

The following day was the twentieth of April. We waited all day but the Mercians failed to appear. I was now getting nervous. We needed to make our assault swiftly before Erik could send for more men to reinforce his garrison. Then towards nightfall a column of men appeared but they came, not along the Mercian north bank, but from the south. It wasn't Æðelred but the new hereræswa, Eadred of Dyfneintscīr, with fifty of his own warband and another hundred men from Ælfred's personal warband. I didn't know whether to be pleased that the responsibility of command was no longer mine or not. The reinforcements were welcome, of course, but Eadred was something of an unknown factor when it came to warfare.

'Do we know where the Mercians are?' he asked me as soon as he arrived and had been briefed on the situation.

I shook my head. 'I've sent out patrols along the north bank of the Temes but there's no sign of them. It's possible that they have taken a different route and are coming from the north-west. I've scouts watching the main approaches, naturally, but there is no sign of them there either. Whichever way they're coming they're more than a day's march away.'

'Then all we can do is wait,' he concluded.

'But all the time Erik will be preparing for an attack. Whether he was warned by Danes from the settlement across the river or not, he must know of our presence here by now,' I pointed out.

'The king's instructions were quite clear. We are here to support Æðelred; he is to command. We can't do anything until he gets here.'

'Can't we at least send scouts to watch the approaches to Lundenwic so we know if Erik is being reinforced or laying in more provisions?' I asked.

Eadred thought about this for a while.

'No, if he doesn't know we're here yet that would risk warning him of our presence.'

I groaned inwardly, wishing that I'd already sent out scouts to watch the city. It seemed that Eadred was going to err on the side of caution. In my experience it was flair and swift action that won battles, not prudence.

✝✝✝

'Where are those men going?' Eadred asked me as a dozen horsemen trotted out of the encampment.

'Just a routine patrol,' I lied.

In fact I'd sent Wolnoth and Cináed out at the head of two groups of scouts to check the main Roman roads heading into Lundenwic from the Danelaw: Casingc Stræt, which came in from the area north of Verulamacæster and the Five Boroughs, and Earninga Stræt, which was the route that Danes coming from Guðrum's kingdom of East Anglia were would most likely to take.

Æðelred and five hundred warriors finally arrived two days later. I was surprised to see that he had brought his wife, the Lady Æthelflaed with him, although I was glad to see Cuthfleda again.

'I need to talk to you,' she whispered to me when we embraced.

However, that would have to wait as Æðelred immediately called a meeting with Eadred, Dudda, Heardwig and myself. When I entered the Lord of Mercia's hastily erected tent I was less than pleased to renew my acquaintance with the Mercian hereræswa, Cynbald. The man had not improved over the intervening years since I'd last seen him. If anything, he had grown even more disdainful and arrogant. I was glad that he hadn't been at Abergafenni the previous year.

'What do we know about Lundenwic? The strength of the garrison? Are they being reinforced?' he asked Eadred.

Just at that moment a Mercian sentry lifted the tent flap to admit Wealmær who looked worried.

'Ah! My captain looks as if he might have news about that, Lord Æðelred,' I said, beckoning him inside and hoping that I was correct.

'Yes, lord. Our scouts have returned to say that large bands of Danes are on the march south from the Danelaw towards Lundenwic. It looks as if Erik has got wind of our attack and is hastening to reinforce the city.'

'When you say from the Danelaw,' Æðelred barked, 'where exactly are these men coming from, where are they now and in what numbers?'

I could tell from his demeanour that Wealmær didn't appreciate being spoken to like a naughty child.

'It might be better to address your questions to the leaders of the scouts,' he replied stony faced and omitting the customary 'lord'.

He opened the flap again and Wolnoth and Cináed entered.

'We travelled north alongside Casingc Stræt as far as Verulamacæster. There were perhaps three hundred of the enemy setting up camp for the night,' Wolnoth told us. 'We travelled on towards Bedaforde and encountered another two hundred and fifty men a day's march further north. Having seen enough we returned here as fast as possible.'

'It was more or less the same story on Earninga Stræt,' Cináed reported. 'At first we spotted small groups of Danes on the road but then we saw a much larger group near Waras. They were flying a banner depicting a gold crown pierced by two arrows on a blue background.'

No one said anything. It was the flag that Guðrum had adopted when he became a Christian and Ælfred gave him the Kingdom of East Anglia. It represented the crown of Saint Edmund pierced by the arrows with which the Vikings had martyred him.

✝✝✝

We rode through the night. With the Mercians' horses we could mount six hundred men and we would need every one of them. I led three hundred Saxons and Cynbald the same number of Mercians. Under a full moon we followed muddy roads and tracks around the north of Lundenwic heading ever eastwards. When we reached the first Roman road Cynbald peeled off without a word of farewell and headed north along it. We continued for a further hour before reaching Earninga Stræt.

We stopped after two miles to rest the horses and for my men to get a few hours' sleep before daybreak. The sentries roused everyone once the first pale yellow fingers of dawn appeared over the horizon to the east and the scouts set off a mile ahead of the main body.

It wasn't long before they returned.

'There's a camp at the side of the road three miles ahead,' Wolnoth said. 'They're just stirring but I doubt that they'll be ready to move on for an hour or so yet. I counted thirty but there were a few tents as well; perhaps fifty in all plus a few thralls.'

'How many horses?'

'Only five.'

'Thank you, Wulnoth, well done. Now show me where this camp is.'

It was as he had said. They had stopped for the night in a hollow a hundred yards to the west of the road. A few thralls were collecting wood and piling it onto several campfires whilst others were preparing what looked like some type of porridge. The Danes themselves were putting on byrnies or leather jerkins, taking a piss on the outskirts of the encampment or disappearing in the nearby wood to empty their bowels.

As far as I could see there were just three bored looking sentries standing on the lip of the hollow. They seemed more interested in what was happening inside the camp than they were in guarding it. I'd seen enough.

Half an hour later I led fifty men into the camp on horseback whilst another hundred followed us in on foot. The other hundred and fifty rode to block the road north and south.

Chaos ensued. Some of the Danes just stared at us open mouthed whilst others rushed to collect spears, axes and shields. We rode through the camp without stopping, cutting down those within reach and ignoring the rest. Our job was to cause panic and mayhem. Wealmær followed up leading those on foot who systematically slaughtered the rest. Less than ten escaped and they were cut down by the horsemen outside the perimeter.

We stripped the bodies of weapons, armour and anything valuable and buried it all in the wood for collection on our return. I didn't want men encumbered by loot when we ran into Guðrum and the main body of Danes.

By the time we resumed our trek northwards it was two hours past sunrise. I calculated that Guðrum would have been on the road for an hour or so by then. That would mean that his scouts wouldn't be far ahead of us. In confirmation of that Wolnoth and Cináed came riding back at a gallop to say that they had spotted a line of ten scouts no more than two miles away.

We dismounted and the majority of the Saxon warriors accompanying me formed a shield wall. My own warband of ninety strung their bows and took up a position in a long line ahead of the shield wall. Then we waited.

When the Danish scouts appeared I ordered Rinan to unfurl my banner. Nerian, who was the only other ealdorman in my small army, commanded the shield wall and two of his men unfurled his own banner and Ælfred's banner of a golden dragon on a blood red background. He might not have been present in person but we were his army acting on his orders.

The Danish host came up the road and halted behind their scouts. They began to deploy into line but a shouted command stopped them. A minute later three men rode forward and halted half way between the two armies. I recognised the leader; it was Guðrum himself. Another was his standard bearer but the third man was dressed more like a king than Guðrum himself.

He wore a good quality byrnie which had been polished until it shone. He had six silver and two gold arm rings around his biceps and a red woollen cloak trimmed with fur over his shoulders. However, all that paled into insignificance compared to his helmet. It was of polished steel chased with intricate patterns in gold. On top there was a gold crest representing a snarling wolf about to leap onto its prey. It was all very impressive but the fact that it had no dents or marks on its fine surface told me that it had never been worn in battle. The man was all show and no substance.

'Greetings, Lord Jørren, Lord Nerian. What are you doing invading my kingdom? Has Ælfred declared war on me?' Guðrum asked in a mild voice.

'Good morning, cyning. We heard that you were on your way to reinforce Erik Barkse in Lundenwic. As King Ælfred has decided that it should be returned to its rightful owner, the Lord of the Mercians, it is you who will be declaring war if you advance any further down this road.'

'And you are going to stop me with this ragtag of an army? We outnumber you two to one. Now get out of my way.'

'This ragtag, as you put it, are all seasoned warriors, not like the farmboys who follow you.'

It was true. Once Guðrum's followers had been fierce Vikings but for the past eight years the survivors of the Battle of Ethundun, where we had finally defeated him, had settled in East Anglia and had turned from warriors into farmers. In that respect they were little better than our fyrd, although admittedly better armed.

'Even your nobles appear to be more like popinjays than warriors if this one is anything to go by,' I added scornfully.

The man's hand went to his sword hilt but Guðrum's hand restrained him.

'This is my son, Eohric. Don't let appearances deceive you. I venture to suggest that he's a better swordsman than you are, Jørren. I am not in the habit of repeating myself but unless you get out of my way, we will slaughter you.'

'I very much doubt that. I am loath to start a war in which Mercia and Wessex will invade East Anglia and ravage it, but I will if I must. As to slaughtering us, it is your men who will die. My archers will turn the odds into evens, at best, before the two shield walls can come to grips,' I continued. 'I'd advise you to turn around now, cyning, or risk losing your throne.'

Guðrum eyed the battered line of helmets and shields facing him. Their owners weren't the fyrd; they were hardened warriors. Moreover he knew the reputation of my archers.

'Very well, I will do as you ask, Lord Jørren, but not because I fear your puny army, but because I swore an oath to Ælfred.'

Eohric protested volubly but Guðrum ignored him. For a moment I thought that the hot headed young Dane was about to draw his sword and charge me but common sense prevailed and, after showering me with threats and curses, he followed his father back to their army.

'May Guðrum live a long life,' Nerian muttered when I returned to our lines. 'I have a feeling that young Eohric will give us a lot of trouble when he becomes king.'

My scouts trailed the East Anglians host as far as Waras and then, satisfied that they weren't trying to trick us by doubling back, we returned to Stanes.

✝✝✝

Apart from a couple of minor flesh wounds suffered during the first encounter, we had returned unscathed. Cynbald had enjoyed a similar success with the groups of Danes he'd encountered on Casingc Stræt; however, he'd suffered seventeen killed and a score wounded before he overcame them. When we reported to Æðelred he congratulated us but he drew an unflattering comparison between my success and that of his hereræswa, something which increased the enmity the man evidently felt towards me.

Æthelflaed and Cuthfleda were sitting in Æðelred's tent whilst we were talking. Ælfred's daughter flashed me a quick smile before returning to her embroidery and Cuthfleda came to greet me before returning to her own piece of embroidery. Both girls looked bored and I could tell at a glance that the piece that they were working on looked amateurish – and that was being kind.

Later the sentry outside my own tent said that there was someone to see me. I thought it would be one of my senior warriors but it was Cuthfleda.

'How does Æðelred treat his wife?' I asked after we had spent a few minutes catching up.

'Well enough, I suppose. He doesn't beat her or anything like that, although he insists on his marital rights, as he puts it, whether Æthelflaed is willing or not. However, he doesn't trust her out of his sight and he controls everything she does. That's why he brought her with him. She feels stifled, of course, and I've had to stop her running away once already.'

'Running away? Where would she go?'

'Back to her father I suppose. I don't think she thought it through; she says she just needs to get away.'

'Ælfred is hardly likely to welcome her. I'm sure he loves her as a daughter but she's a pawn in his plan to rule Mercia as well as Wessex.'

'Rule Mercia? I don't think Æðelred is likely to bend the knee to him. You know that Cynbald and one or two of the other Mercian ealdormen have been trying to persuade him to declare himself King of Mercia?'

'Yes, or at least I suspected it.'

'The fact that Æthelflaed is pregnant may help him make his mind up in that respect. If he has a son to succeed him he is more likely to risk Ælfred's wrath by seizing the vacant throne.'

Cuthfleda left me pondering over what she'd said. I'd heard rumours the Ælfred was thinking of calling himself King of the Anglo-Saxons. If Æðelred declared himself King of Mercia I could see a serious rift developing between the two of them.

✝✝✝

The combined forces of Wessex and Mercia crossed the bridge over the Temes the following morning and marched towards Lundenwic in the pouring rain. However, the miserable weather did nothing to dampen their spirits. The men were in a confident mood and Æðelred had agreed a plan in which he had confidence, even if that snake Cynbald had predicted that it was doomed to fail.

I watched them go and then set off along the south bank heading for Sudwerca and then Witenestaple. I was glad of the downpour. It meant that no one on the north bank of the river would see me and my ninety men riding eastwards. It was still raining, although not quite so hard, when we reached Witenestaple where Cei was waiting for me with three knarrs. He had been glad of the opportunity to get out of Defras for a while. Jerrik was busy patrolling the Temes estuary with our fleet to ensure that no reinforcements reached Lundenwic from either East Anglia or the Continent and so Cei seemed the obvious man to command the knarrs. His was a vital task; without those ships the plan would fail.

I was thankful for the continuing rain as it would keep sentries huddled anywhere that offered a little shelter rather than watching a river devoid of traffic. Normally it would be a bustling port but the fast spreading knowledge that it was about to be attacked was keeping merchants away for now.

My warriors stayed out of sight below the gunwales whilst the crew tied up alongside the deserted wharf that ran most of the length of the river bank along the southern boundary of the old Roman city. Thankfully it was high tide and the sides of the knarrs rode higher than the wharf. Consequently it was difficult for anyone standing ashore to see inside the ships.

As the last of the three knarrs tied up a man wearing a long robe and a cloak left the shelter of a hut and approached us accompanied by four men wearing helmets and carrying spears. I presumed that he was an official employed by the port reeve, or whatever the Danish equivalent was.

'How long are you staying and what cargo are you carrying?' he asked officiously in Danish.

'Not long,' Cei replied in English.

'You're Saxon,' the man asked in surprise.

'No, Welsh, but I speak better English than I do Danish.'

'Welsh? We don't get many of your sort here. What's your cargo,' he asked again.

'Death,' Cei replied, producing the seax he'd been holding behind his back and slicing the official's throat open from side to side.

At the same time the crew standing on the jetty killed the four guards. I stepped ashore and looked around, but there was no shout of alarm and, as far as I could see, no one had seen what had just occurred. We tipped the bodies into the river and my men scrambled onto the jetty.

Our shields normally displayed the rearing white horse of Cent but we had painted them black before leaving Stanes. My men had adopted the broad ribbons favoured by the Danes instead of the narrower type we normally wore from ankle to knee. Most of my men were clean shaven or wore long moustaches instead of beards, which would have betrayed us, so everyone wore cloaks with hoods over their helmets which hid most of their faces.

We made our way from the wharf up into the city, passing the ruins of a Roman temple on our left. The street we were following headed due north until it crossed the street leading from the old forum to the northernmost of the two gates in the eastern wall. The buildings were a mixture of ruins, Roman villas which had been repaired using timber, wattle and daub and straw for the roofs or new timber huts. Fallen masonry littered the city and had either been left where it had fallen or had been pushed to the sides of the streets to clear a way through for carts.

We came across a tavern from which came the sound of raucous laughter but the persistent rain had kept most people indoors. The only people we'd seen had been an old beggar, a boy running an errand and several half-starved waifs scavenging for food. All of them took one look at us and disappeared up an alley or into the ruins until we'd passed by. However, our luck couldn't hold.

The street turned a corner and headed north east; just around the bend we encountered a patrol. They were evidently the city watch - old and maimed warriors who were employed to keep order. There were a dozen of them and they barred the street as we approached.

'Who are you and what are you doing here,' the greybeard who appeared to be in charge challenged us.

'I'm Jarl Sigmund from East Anglia. We're the first of the reinforcements sent by King Guðrum,' I replied in Danish.

I'd used his pagan name. Most Danes in Lundenwic were still believers in the Norse pantheon and would never have called Guðrum by his baptismal name of Æðelstan; indeed, few did outside the court of King Ælfred.

'You're a welcome sight then, but I thought Guðrum was coming overland?'

'The cursed Saxons have blocked the roads and so we've had to make our way here by sea.'

The watch stood aside for us to pass but, as we did so, one of them spotted Lyndon's moustache, the tips of which reached his chin. Only Anglo-Saxons grew their facial hair like that. He cried a warning but my men reacted quickly before the watch realised the danger and lowered their spears. A minute later we dragged their corpses into a side alley and dumped them there.

I noticed shutters in the nearby huts had opened during the brief slaughter of the watch but they immediately shut again and no one inside the huts tried to raise the alarm. No doubt they would do so once we'd moved on but we couldn't enter every house and kill its occupants.

Five minutes later we heard the faint sounds of an outcry behind us. No doubt some of the bolder souls had ventured out of their huts and found the bodies. It was now even more urgent for us to reach our objective quickly.

We arrived at the crossroads where one street led to Ealdredes Geat, the gate in the north wall on this side of the fort. Ealdred was a Saxon name and therefore I presumed that the gateway had been repaired by a man of that name at some point. The other road ended at the southern gate of the fort itself.

The plan was to seize both gates. Our task was to open Ealdredes Geat to admit the rest of the army and hold the fort's southern gate to prevent the Danish garrison from rushing forth until we had sufficient men assembled to capture the fort. Forty five men weren't sufficient for either task but they were all I had.

I set off for Ealdredes Geat whilst one of my senior thegns from Cent, a man called Sigehelm, led the other group towards the south gate of the fort. Which party to lead had been a difficult choice for me to make. However, if Sigehelm failed it would make it difficult to prise the Danes out of the fort but if we didn't manage to let the army into the city the whole strategy would collapse. Ealdredes Geat was therefore the priority.

I went forward with Wealmær and Rinan to reconnoitre the gate. It lay two hundred yards to the west of the junction where the fort's western wall met the northern wall of the city. At one time there had been a square tower there but it had long since fallen down. The foundations were still there and the Danes had built a wooden watchtower in its place. It abutted the stone walls of the fort but the city wall was a palisade between the watch tower and Ealdredes Geat.

It was an impressive structure. The gateway itself was twelve feet high and eight feet wide. It was curved at the top and above the archway the stonework extended as high again. It stood between two square towers and they topped the archway by a further eight feet. The gates were made of massive timbers crossed braced and studded with iron nails. There were two large baulks of timber which were held in place by two iron brackets on each of the two gates. By the look of them, it would take four men to lift each timber out of the brackets.

There was a door at the base of each tower and I imagined that these would lead to stairs going up to the fighting platforms on the walls to either side of the gate and on top of the gate itself. A further flight would no doubt lead up to the top of each tower.

I looked up, the rainwater splashing over my face and making me blink. Thankfully I was in the shadows as one of the Danish sentries looked over the top of the parapet on top of the right hand tower at that moment and spat a globule of phlegm down onto the cobbled street below.

'Rinan, run and see if the doors at the base of the towers are locked. Make sure you're not seen.'

He slid along the front wall of the hut beside which we were hiding and disappeared. Five minutes later he re-appeared standing flat against the city wall. He slid along it and around to the first of the doors. He opened it slightly and closed it again. He ran across the gateway and tested the second door with the same result. Ten minutes later he re-joined us and we went back to join the rest of our group.

The idea was that Sigehelm and I would co-ordinate our attacks so that one assault didn't give the other gate's defenders any warning. When I was in position I sent Rowe to find the other group. When he left both he and Sigehelm would count to three hundred. Rowe would tell me how far he'd counted when he returned and I would carry on until I reached three hundred. Then we'd attack. It wasn't fool proof - for a start people count at different rates – but it was the best I could come up with.

'Two hundred and eleven, lord,' Rowe panted when he got back to me.

We had moved up to a position opposite Ealdredes Geat and I carried on counting up to three hundred before running across the intervening space to the right hand door. I had taken a dozen men with me and Wealmær had the same number for the attack on the left hand tower. The rest were led by Wolnoth. Their task was to remove the two locking bars and open the gates. Once that was done, Arne would blow his horn to tell Æðelred of our success. I prayed that Wolnoth's thirty men would be enough to then hold the gate until our army arrived.

I reached the door into the tower without any alarm being sounded. Inside it was pitch black, the only light entering via the door which was largely blocked by the men following me. I didn't have time to let my eyes adjust to the gloom and so I felt with my foot for the first step.

The first few were made of stone but then the steps changed to timber. I continued upwards until I came to a door to my left. This had to lead to the parapet on top of the archway. I turned to the man behind me.

'Cináed, you take five men and continue up to the top of the tower. Kill anyone you find up there and throw their bodies over the parapet. I know it's raining but string your bows and help me to clear the parapet along the city wall. Then aim at anyone attacking Wolnoth's shield wall from inside the city. Understand?'

'Yes, lord.'

When he and his men had gone on up the stairs I waited to give him enough time to reach the top and then opened the door. A hundred yards away someone had constructed a makeshift shelter consisting of a framework with a conical straw roof to keep off most of the rain. Under it sat three Danes. They got to their feet looking happy when I appeared and then they reached for their weapons when they realised that we weren't their relief sentries.

One, the youngest, threw his spear at me but it was badly aimed and I twisted to one side. It flew past me and hit the wall of the tower. It clattered down into the street below. Meanwhile the other two, both with shields and one with a sword, the other with a hand axe, advanced towards me. There was only room for two men abreast on the fighting platform so the youngest Dane brought up the rear. Eomær took the place to my right and we waited for the three to attack.

They had hesitated when they saw several more men emerge behind Eomær and me but then the Dane in the rear said something and they rushed us. Lyndon was standing behind me and he thrust his spear over the top of my shield and Eomær's. The Dane on the right was so intent on trying to thrust his sword into my eyes that he never saw the spear point coming. Lyndon thrust it into his neck and the man fell sideways off the parapet, landing on the cobbles sixteen feet below with a sickening thud.

The youngest Dane, a boy of no more than fourteen, stepped into the space left by his dead comrade and thrust his sword at me. I deflected it with my own sword but then the other Dane hooked his axe over the top of it and pulled my shield down. The boy tried to take advantage by thrusting the point of his sword at my neck, even though it was protected by an avantail. Lyndon thrust once more with his spear and it stuck in the boy's shoulder. He screeched in agony and frustration just as Eomær cut down the Dane with the axe. The parapet was ours, at least for the moment. No doubt there were other ways up to it but that didn't matter.

'Rinan, you and Eomær bring the boy along and see if you can staunch the bleeding. The lad's got spirit and I'd like to keep him alive if possible.'

They nodded and carried him into the tower. I stood there for a moment. There were sounds of fighting coming from the fort but the other tower and the wall beyond seemed quiet. I grunted in satisfaction; at least we had a gate into the city. I glanced down into the space inside the gate but it was still deserted. Unfortunately so was the area outside the walls. Where the hell was Æðelred?

✝✝✝

'Lord, Thegn Sigehelm has managed to capture the fort's gate but he is having trouble beating off the Danes,' Rowe told me when he returned.

The rain had stopped at last and everywhere reeked of damp as the summer sunshine turned the rainwater which had soaked the streets, buildings and men into a steamy vapour.

I looked around me. The Ealdredes Geat had been counter-attacked by a score of Danes but we had beaten them off easily and they hadn't reappeared as yet. I could see men coming along the ramparts, some from the west but many more from the east. That puzzled me until I realised that the larger group must be from the fort's garrison. Of course, there had to be access to the fighting platform around the city walls from the fort. That gave me an idea.

I was less concerned about the Danes coming from the west; the archers on top of the tower on that side of the gate should be able to keep them at bay. The ones coming from the fort were a different matter. Once they had plucked up the courage to rush the tower my archers could cause casualties but enough of them would reach safety and then it was just a matter of time before they recaptured that tower, the walkway over the archway and the second tower.

Once they had secured the eastern tower they could descend to street level and capture the gates. Then all we'd achieved would have been for nothing. We had to stop them reaching the tower in the first place. I also needed to tell the rest of the army to get a bloody move on.

At that moment Sherwyn and Rowe appeared. They had found two horses from somewhere; they were sorry looking nags but they would be quicker than a man on foot.

'Go and find Lord Æðelred. Tell him we have secured both gates but I'm not sure how much longer we can hold the Danes off. Tell him I need his horsemen here now!'

I couldn't understand why they weren't here already, then I had a nasty thought.

'Wait! If the Mercians are being difficult for some reason, find Lord Eadred and explain the situation to him.'

I didn't trust Æðelred, or rather I didn't trust Cynbald. Eadred had nine hundred men. If the Mercians didn't want to capture Lundenwic, then we'd do it on our own and it would belong to Wessex instead of Mercia.

I took my dozen men up the stairs of the other tower and out onto the fighting platform. We were just in time. The Danes had made their rush and a score or more had reached the area where the archers above them couldn't see them. Unfortunately for them, we were ready and waiting. The ones who reached us were brave, but also young and inexperienced. The fighting was fierce but our experience and cool headedness prevailed. I lost two men but the Danes lost three times as many before they withdrew. The archers up above us culled several more before the enemy managed to retreat out of range.

'Lord, you're wounded.'

Rinan was right. I hadn't noticed in the excitement of the fight but I had a cut to my thigh that was weeping rather a lot of blood. It was galling but I had to wait whilst Uhtric came to wash and stitch up the cut in my leg. It was agonising and I passed out for a short while. When I came to I felt nauseous and the pain was worse, if anything. However, I didn't have the luxury of time to feel sorry for myself. I got to my feet with assistance and started to issue orders.

I left thirty men under Wolnoth's command to hold the gate and led the rest to the southern gate of the fort. When we got there the gates were firmly shut and I could see a fierce battle taking place on the ramparts on either side of the gateway.

'Archers, careful where you aim. Don't hit our men but concentrate on the Danes in the middle and rear to take the pressure off Sigehelm's warriors.'

It took a little while as the archers restrung their bows with dry bowstrings then the arrows began to fly. The Danes soon learned to keep their heads down and thankfully that hampered their ability to attack the warriors defending the top of the gateway.

At that moment I felt an agonising pain. The Danes had few archers but one of them had risked bobbing up to fire in our direction. Unfortunately it hit me just above the rim of my shield, driving through chainmail, leather and under tunic to lodge in my shoulder. I tried to ignore it but my shield grew increasingly heavy and I let go of it.

Then disaster struck. Suddenly a hundred Danes erupted from the area between the south-eastern corner of the fort and the ruins of the old Roman amphitheatre. Evidently they had left the fort via the eastern gate in order to attack us in the flank. I ordered my archers to engage them and the leading ranks of the enemy fell dead or wounded. Three more volleys followed and the Danes retreated back through the gap between the fort and the amphitheatre.

I vaguely heard Wealmær give the order to form a shield wall and I saw a blurred image of a line two deep forming in the gap but I was finding it increasingly difficult to focus on what was happening. The combination of pain, exhaustion and the loss of blood made it difficult to concentrate. I must have passed out because the next thing I knew my men were cheering and thumping one another on the back. Someone had helped me to my feet and, when my vision cleared, I saw hundreds of horsemen sweep into the area in front of the fort's gate. The gates remained firmly shut however. Sigehelm might have managed to hang onto the parapet over the gateway but he wasn't able to open the gates.

'Lord Eadred,' I called when I spotted him. 'The men beyond the amphitheatre came out of the eastern gate. It might still be open.'

He waved in acknowledgement and he rode in that direction followed by hundreds of horsemen. By that time the men of Wessex who were on foot arrived and charged after the hereræswa. I had little doubt now that Lundenwic would fall to us, without any help from the Mercians it would seem. My job was done and I relaxed into blissful oblivion.

Chapter Eighteen

Lundenwic

April 886

I awoke to find myself in a room I didn't recognise with Uhtric and Leofwine doing something excruciatingly painful to my shoulder.

'Hold still, lord,' the elder one said. 'We've got to get every last bit of metal and material out of the wound.'

'Then give me something to dull the pain, damn you,' I gasped through gritted teeth.

Someone came and poured mead into my open mouth. When I looked to see who it was I was surprised to see Cuthfleda bending over me.

'What are you doing here?' I managed to say between swallows.

'I came to see how you are, father,' she said with a smile. 'I'm told you lost a lot of blood but you'll survive, God willing.'

Leofwine extracted another bit of detritus with his tweezers and Uhtric poured something into the wound which doubled the agony I was suffering. Then blackness overcame me once more.

When I woke up my mouth was parched and I called for something to drink. However, only a croak came out. Then I saw Cuthfleda bending over me.

'Ah, you're awake at last,' she said with satisfaction. 'I'll let Uhtric know.'

'Wait, drink,' I managed to utter.

My throat felt as if it was full of dry earth. My daughter dripped some water into it which made it feel a little better. The agony in my shoulder had faded to a dull ache but I could now feel the sting in my leg where I'd also been wounded.

'Uhtric said I wasn't to give you too much to drink or you'd be sick and pull the stitches in your shoulder.'

I nodded and she rushed out of the room. She returned some time later with Leofwine.

'Uhtric is busy dealing with our other wounded,' he explained.

Leofwine was now sixteen and his brother two years older. They were never going to be big men but they were unrecognisable as the two urchins I had found in Lundenwic four years ago.

He changed both dressings and told me that there was no sign of infection. Then he left me and Cuthfleda alone again.

'What happened?' I asked her. 'Why didn't Æðelred attack as soon as he saw we had secured the gates?'

'He went down with a fever the evening before,' she explained. 'That worm Cynbald maintained that Æðelred had to give the order and he refused to leave the camp without it. There was an argument, of course, but he remained adamant. The man's a coward!'

I had a feeling that, whether that was true or not, he had held off coming to our support in the hope that I'd be killed. It seemed improbable that he would risk not capturing the city because of his vindictiveness towards me but I couldn't think of another likely explanation.

'Why didn't Eadred come to our aid without the Mercians?'

She shrugged. 'He wanted to but, without the Mercians, I think he thought it was too risky. However, when Rowe turned up with your message he changed his mind. Cynbald tried to stop him leading his men to your rescue but Lady Æthelflaed intervened, saying that she would lead the Mercians into the city herself if he didn't get off his arse and go to your aid.'

I smiled at that. Æthelflaed was too much of a lady to curse normally; that she had done so then showed the depth of her feelings and her contempt for her husband's hereræswa.

'Eadred left at that point and, as you know, he led the men of Wessex into Lundenwic. There was another argument between Æthelflaed and Cynbald but the other ealdormen sided with her. I think they felt ashamed that Wessex was fighting for what had been a Mercian city whilst they stood idly by. Anyway the upshot was that eventually Cynbald agreed to follow Eadred's lead.

'I gather that it was all over by that time. Eadred had secured the fort and either killed or captured the garrison. All the Mercians had to do was scour the rest of the city for Danes. Inevitably that led to looting, rape and some of the city was burnt. Most of the residents were Danes but some were Saxons or Mercians. That didn't help them and they suffered just as much as the Danes.'

I felt disgusted. It was common for warriors to sack somewhere they had captured after a hard fight. In many ways it was a natural reaction after the loss of comrades, but the Mercians had done nothing and lost no one. It was my men who'd done most of the fighting.

Three days later I felt well enough to get out of bed and, although I was still weak, I managed to walk a little. The next day I was stronger and the day after that I felt well enough to go for a short walk outside, albeit with a limp. There was an air of excitement abroad and I soon discovered why. King Ælfred had been seen approaching the city.

The day after his arrival Ælfred called a meeting of the ealdormen present from both Wessex and Mercia. He had sent a message to me personally hoping that I would be fit enough to attend and congratulating me on my part in the capture of Lundenwic. Uhtric said that I was still too ill to go but I ignored him. I wasn't about to miss this for anything.

✝✝✝

Arne and Wealmær had to help me into the saddle. I was still feeling weak and my leg troubled me. My shoulder was still painful and my left arm was strapped to my chest to stop me using it and tearing the wound open. I had to be helped down from the saddle when we reached the former Roman Governor's house, which Ælfred had taken over as his hall. It was built on three sides around a central courtyard with a wall and a pair of entrance gates on the fourth side. Like most other Roman buildings, it had fallen into disrepair but, unlike them, this one had been repaired in stone – albeit inexpertly. The tiled roof had also been repaired, using tiles that didn't match.

I was told that it had been the hall of Erik Barkse and had been the scene of the only fighting the Mercians had seen when they captured it. Erik himself had been killed there and the mosaic floor of the large room being used for the meeting still displayed a dark reddish brown stain where the blood hadn't been completely washed away.

There wasn't room for everyone attending to sit but Ælfred's chamberlain escorted me to a chair at the front opposite a small dais on which there were four chairs. The only other seating in the room were two chairs beside mine. Eadred, Dudda and Heardwig Geonga came over to see how I was and to congratulate me on the success of my plan. When they moved to one side Sigehelm came to speak to me.

'It's not me who deserves congratulations, Sigehelm,' I told him, 'it's you and your men. Holding the gate to the fort called for bravery and determination. If it wasn't for you the attack would have failed. I'm going to ask the king to approve your appointment as Shire Reeve of Cent, that is if you'll accept.'

'Of course,' he replied with a broad smile. 'I'm honoured, lord.'

At that moment Æðelred entered accompanied by Lady Æthelflaed, Cuthfleda, Cynbald and six Mercian ealdormen. They walked through the nobles already there escorted by the chamberlain. When the Lord of the Mercians went to sit on one of the chairs on the dais the chamberlain politely indicated that he and his wife should sit in the chairs beside me instead. He wasn't best pleased but he wasn't about to make a scene in front of the nobles of Wessex.

'I'm pleased to see you are recovering,' he said to me as he sat down. 'Your daughter has kept us informed of your progress, of course,'

I thanked him, trying not to show surprise that he hadn't congratulated me on my part in the capture of the city. Cynbald said nothing. He looked everywhere except at me. He was plainly disgruntled at having to stand whilst I sat and I tried hard not to look smug.

The chamberlain tapped the staff he carried on the mosaic floor twice and I got to my feet as the king entered the chamber. Æthelflaed also stood and after a pause, which nearly verged on insolence, Æðelred also stood up. Ælfred looked better than when I'd last seen him. He was accompanied by Archbishop Plegmund, his son Edward and, to my surprise, the Lady Ealhswith.

After they were seated we three sat down again and a hush descended on the room. Ælfred's eyes scanned the room and he smiled at his daughter. Plegmund nodded towards me and Edward also acknowledged me, but Ealhswith glared at me with a look of distaste on her pinched face.

'Ealdormen of Wessex and Mercia, thank you for attending this witan. Before we start I call upon the Archbishop of Cantwareburh and Metropolitan of Wessex, Mercia and East Anglia to lead us in prayer.'

Officially Plegmund had been appointed by the Pope to oversee all the diocesan bishops of Englaland outside of Northumbria, where the Archbishop of York was the metropolitan, but I'd never heard the title used before. Ælfred was making the point that his archbishop was also responsible for ecclesiastic matters in the other two kingdoms. It presaged what was to come.

Unlike most churchman, Plegmund kept the prayers and the homily that followed mercifully short. Even so I sensed Æðelred fidgeting impatiently in the chair next to mine.

'Lord Archbishop, Lord Æðelred, Lady Æthelflaed, ealdormen of Wessex and Mercia, I have asked you here today for two reasons to congratulate those who have taken back Lundenwic from the heathen Danes and to decide on its future.'

At this a hubbub of conversation broke out amongst the Mercian nobles present and Æðelred looked stunned.

'Cyning,' he said getting to his feet. 'Lundenwic is a Mercian settlement; it's most important centre in fact. It has always been Mercian and I, as Lord of Mercia, will decide its future government.'

'That's not quite true, is it Lord Æðelred? I am told by Bishop Asser, who has done some research into this, that it was originally settled by the Middle Saxons and later became part of Essex, then ruled by the King of Cent. It was then captured by Mercia before you lost it to the Vikings. It would therefore seem that both Wessex and Mercia have a claim to it. As it was warriors from Wessex, notably Lord Jørren, Ealdorman of Cent, who captured this place and, from what I've been told, Mercia played no part in the attack, it would seem that it belongs to me by right of conquest.'

'Cyning, I was ill and unable to lead the assault, as you well know. We had an agreement that Lundenwic would be returned to Mercia after we had expelled the Danes!'

Æðelred had grown more heated as he spoke and he now sounded quite belligerent. Ælfred, in contrast, remained calm throughout their exchange.

'Yes, the agreement was that I would lend you warriors to support your attempt to retake the walled city. However, that isn't what happened. As I have already said, it was Wessex who retook Lundenwic and Mercian troops didn't even support them. Instead you looted the place and killed Angles and Saxons once the Danes had surrendered. Do you expect to be rewarded for failure? Failure to fight and failure to control your men and stop them killing innocent Christians?'

Æðelred was seething with indignation but he stayed silent and sat down. Cynbald, on the other hand, didn't have the sense to keep quiet.

'Lord Ælfred, you can't do this. Lundenwic is Mercian and you swore to help us recapture it.

You've done that, and we are grateful, but you have no right to claim it as yours,' he fumed.

'Ah, yes. Cynbald. Cynbald the hereræswa, or should I say Cynbald the coward. You should have been ready to support Lord Jørren when he opened the gates for you. But you didn't; you stayed in your camp letting the Danes kill good Wessex men needlessly. Even when Jørren sent a messenger pleading for your support you refused. Thankfully Eadred came to his senses and led my men into the city. It wasn't until my daughter, who showed a lot more courage than you did, threatened to lead the army of Mercia that you acted. By then it was all over and you would have done better to stay in camp. Instead you belatedly led your men in a campaign of rape and pillage.'

Ælfred's eyes were flashing dangerously, despite his calm outward demeanour but Cynbald couldn't see that he was digging his own grave.

'It wasn't like that. It might have been a trap. It would have been irresponsible of me to lead my men into the city on the word of a boy. Only Lord Æðelred had the authority to send his army into the city and he was indisposed.'

'I've heard quite enough. Not another word if you value your life.'

Cynbald opened and shut his mouth like a fish but he said nothing further.

'This is what I've decided,' Ælfred said after a pause so hushed that you could hear birdsong in the courtyard through the open windows. 'Lundenwic is the name given to the settlement on the other side of the River Flēot. To distinguish it from the old Roman city this place will now be renamed as Lundenburg. It is appropriate as it will become the major defensive burh in this area, controlling both the surrounding land and traffic on the Temes. The existing settlement is henceforth to be known as Ealdwic – the old settlement –and its inhabitants are to be encouraged to move inside the defences of Lundenburg.

'Whilst Lundenburg and Ealdwic will both become part of my realm, I am going to appoint Lord Æðelred as its first governor, provided he swears fealty to me for it.

'I have one other condition. The coward Cynbald is to be deprived of his lands and sent into exile.'

There was a stunned silence in the room before Æðelred got to his feet.

'And if I don't agree?'

'Then Mercia, or at least that part of it which you rule, must fend for itself. Before you decide you should be aware that I have been in communication with King Æðelstan of East Anglia after his misguided attempt to reinforce Jarl Erik. He is on his way here now under safe conduct and with only a small escort to explain himself. He too will swear fealty to me or suffer the consequences. If you refuse to agree my terms you will find yourself facing the Welsh in the West, East Anglia in the East and the Viking Kingdom of Northumbria in the north without any support from me. The choice is yours.'

†††

When Cuthfleda came to see how I was two days later I could see that she had been crying. I was feeling more like my old self by then. Although I still didn't have the use of my left arm I was able to walk moderate distances unaided; even my limp was scarcely noticeable now.

'Why are you upset?' I asked after we had sat down in the small garden of the villa which Wealmær had appropriated for my use after the fall of the city.

'Because that pig Æðelred has taken his anger at her father out on the Lady Æthelflaed. The night after that farce of a witan he beat her and then raped her.'

'Does Ælfred know?'

'Yes, I went and told him myself.'

'What did he say? Has he taken Æðelred to task over it?'

'No,' she said with disgust. 'He replied that it was a husband's right to treat his wife as he wished. She was his chattel and he couldn't interfere, much as he might wish to.'

'What he means is that he has achieved his aim of bringing Mercia under his governance and that a few bruises suffered by his eldest child as a consequence is a small price to pay,' I said bitterly.

There was nothing I could do but Ælfred had gone down in my estimation.

A few days later the Guðrum arrived in the newly renamed Lundenburg with an escort of thirty men. The chamberlain allocated them a tavern near the waterfront, an insalubrious area, as their accommodation and told Guðrum that King Ælfred would send for him when he was ready to receive him. Obviously it was all done to humiliate the King of East Anglia.

There was a delay of two weeks, during which time Ælfred summoned a full meeting of the Witenaġemot to be held in the main church in Lundenburg – the cathedral of St Paul. This was a much repaired timber building dating from the start of the seventh century which stood - if rumour was to be believed - on what had been the site of a Roman temple. It had been used by the pagan Vikings as a stable but it had now been cleaned and re-consecrated.

The carvings of Roman gods cavorting around the sides of the stone altar had been hidden behind a plain white linen cloth. A gold cross stood on the cloth together with two gold candlesticks. The only light came from these few candles and a few windows covered in thin cloth. Consequently the interior was gloomy, which matched the mood of those assembled there.

It was a long way for most of Wessex's nobles and senior churchmen to come and the Mercian nobles present were still angry about the way that their leader had been treated. Ælfred greeted Guðrum as his good friend King Æðelstan, which annoyed the Mercians even more.

It was significant that the senior nobles and clergy of both Wessex and Mercia had been invited to attend. It reinforced Ælfred's claim to suzerainty over Mercia. Once more Plegmund led us in prayer and treated us to a homily about humility. There was a great deal of minor business to attend to, including Sigehelm's formal appointment as my shire reeve, and it wasn't until the second day that we turned our attention to the matter of East Anglia.

I could tell that Guðrum was furious about the way he was being treated. After all, the original treaty after the Battle of Ethundun had recognised him as king of an independent East Anglia. But his probable involvement in the invasion of Cent two years ago and his attempt to join Erik Barkse had sealed his fate.

He was no longer a young man and he had his own problems keeping his throne. Vikings were ever minded to plough their own furrow and didn't take kindly to being controlled by a king. He therefore agreed to a new treaty whereby East Anglia became a client kingdom of Wessex in much the same way as Cent had many decades before. It was that or face invasion and the loss of his kingdom entirely.

On the final day of the Witenaġemot Ælfred made a speech about overcoming adversity and how Wessex had grown from the threat of extinction to greatness once more. He then stunned everyone by stating that he was no longer just the King of Wessex but in future his title would be King of the Anglo-Saxons.

I had known for some time that his dream was to unite all of Englaland under his rule. Now it seemed that he had taken the first steps along that road. However, Mercia was still a riven realm, divided into several parts only one of which was ruled by an Anglo-Saxon. Conquering the Five Boroughs of North

Eastern Mercia and the various independent jarldoms north of Lundenburg seemed an insurmountable task. And that was always providing there was no more large scale invasions from the Vikings of Danmørk.

Epilogue

Wessex

890 - 891

The four years after the capture of Lundenburg had been relatively peaceful ones for me. It took time to get over the injury to my left shoulder and it still hurt me if I overexerted it, but otherwise I felt fit and healthy, surprisingly so considering I would reach the grand age of forty next year.

News reached us in April that Guðrum had died and had been succeeded as King of East Anglia by his son Eohric. Ælfred had been in poor health for a time last year but he seemed to have recovered. Edward was now sixteen and by all account he was increasingly frustrated at not being given a proper role by his father. Oswine remained a member of his gesith but he now spent some of his time looking after his vill of Ægelesthrep. This had belonged to Hilda but she had given it to him when he became an adult at the age of fourteen. I think he still had greater ambitions but it was a wealthy vill and he concentrated on making it wealthier still.

I had intended to seek out the merchant who had bought Bryhthelm's freedom and recruited three mercenaries to kill me but, after I had recovered from my wounded shoulder, I decided that I had better things to do with my time. It belonged to my past and there it would remain.

We no longer lived at Dofras. After I was wounded I was no longer capable of acting as sǣ hererǣswa and the king had asked me to choose another to command the fleet. I had eventually chosen Cei and it proved to be a good choice. He was an excellent mariner and, despite his origins, he was respected by all those who served on Ælfred's ships, including Jerrik. I had finally decided that it didn't matter what the nobles thought, he was the right man for the role and Ælfred supported my choice. I left Dofras with some regret; I had always preferred it to my hall at Cantwareburh.

It was the visit of Edward the Ætheling to see his friend Oswine at Ægelesthrep that was to change all our lives, and the future of Englaland in due course. Oswine had spent Christmas with his mother and me but we didn't expect to see him again for some time. We were therefore surprised when a messenger arrived to say that Oswine was coming to visit us. We were even morer surprised when he said that he would be bringing Edward with him.

It promised to be a time for celebration as a family. My eldest son, Æscwin, had just become the prior at Cantwareburh and he was bringing Ywer back home after completing his studies. My second son had just turned fourteen and he would now start his training as a warrior. Furthermore his twin sister, Kjestin, was about to be betrothed to Odda, the eldest son of Ealdorman Eadred, the hererǣswa. Consequently Hilda was busy planning the biggest feast ever to be held in my hall.

I had improved the place since we'd moved back to it. I had demolished the old hall and built a new, larger one to replace it. The walls were made of wattle and daub in an oak frame but the foundations were made of stone. Instead of beaten earth the floor consisted of suspended timber planks supported on stone piers. There were two hearths, both made of stone, and there were four side chambers: one for Hilda and me, one for our children and two for guests. It would still be crowded when Oswine and Edward came, especially as the ætheling would presumably bring an entourage of clerics, servants and his gesith. They would have to camp outside the palisade.

I had also strengthened the defences. I had employed a mason from Frankia to build the hall's foundations and then he had stayed on to construct a stone gateway with a tower either side on the lines of the one I'd attacked in Lundenburg, but on a smaller scale. The palisade was still built of timber but I had made it more difficult to assault by digging a deep ditch eight feet deep below it. It was dry – there was no water to fill it as my hall sat on top of a hill and our water supply came from two wells – but the bottom was filled with sharpened stakes and caltrops.

My niece Ecgwynna now lived on her own at Tunbrige when she wasn't away visiting one of the other four vills she owned. She was now nineteen and I suspected that she might remain a spinster. I had tried to find her a suitable husband but she was adamant that she didn't want to marry any of the men I chose for her. I suspected that she was under the misapprehension that Edward would come back for her one day.

He was likely to be king after Ælfred died but there was another candidate - the king's nephew Æthelwold. Edward's parents would want him to make a politically advantageous marriage to strengthen his position when the time came. The daughter of a thegn, even the niece of an ealdorman, wouldn't be a contender.

At least that's what I thought. I had cause to revise my opinion when Edward arrived.

'I was hoping to renew my acquaintance with your pretty niece, Ecgwynna,' Edward said after the usual pleasantries had been disposed of.

'I'm afraid that she doesn't live in my hall any more, Lord Edward,' I replied after recovering from my surprise. 'She has her own vills to manage and she spends most of her time at Tunbrige.'

He looked disappointed and so I unwisely added, 'however, I'm sure she would be delighted to see you again. I'll send her an invitation to the feast.'

She was as pleased to see him again as he was her. I had no idea whether Edward had thought about her at all over the years since they had first met but I knew that Ecgwynna had pined for Edward. She was still a virgin but, if the rumours were true, Edward had turned out to be something of a womaniser.

At the feast it was obvious that there was still something between them. Hilda had put herself on one side of Edward and Ecgwynna on the other. If she was hoping he'd talk to her she was about to be disappointed; I don't think he said more than two words to her the whole evening.

He stayed for a week, which put something of a strain on our provisions, and spent as much time as possible in Ecgwynna's company.

'They appear to be very much in love,' Father Tidwold said to me one day, a troubled expression on his face.

He was now Edward's chaplain and spiritual mentor.

'Yes, there was a spark there when they first met four years ago but it seems to have ignited into a fire. I worry in case she succumbs and allows Edward to seduce her.'

'Oh, I think that it's too late for that, lord. I have reason to believe that they are already lovers.'

My heart sank. I held Ecgwynna in high regard and she deserved better than to have her reputation ruined by a casual affair. Tidwold seemed lost in thought and I was about to go and discuss the matter with Hilda when he gripped my arm.

'You should know that Edward is so besotted with your niece that he plans to wed her before he leaves. The marriage will have to remain secret until after Edward becomes king, of course, but he needs an impeccable witness.'

'You mean me?' I asked.

I was dumbfounded. Not only was it utter folly for his heir to marry without the king's permission but making me party to it could cost me dear once Ælfred found out.

'No! I won't be a party to this madness and I forbid the marriage.'

'You can't do that, lord,' Tidwold replied. 'Both are adults and, although Edward should seek his father's permission, as a courtesy, the wedding would still be lawful without it.'

In the end I compromised by allowing the marriage to go ahead in the small timber church within the hall complex but I refused to act as a witness. Instead Oswine and Ywer attended the brief ceremony.

Edward spent the night with his bride and then left the next day. Father Tidwold gave me the marriage certificate for safe keeping and I reluctantly accepted it. I put it at the bottom of one of my coffers which held important documents and hoped that it would never need to see the light of day again. My niece might have lost her virginity but I fully expected Edward to forget about her now that he had bedded her and then everything could return to the way it was.

My hopes were shattered three months later when Hilda came to tell me that Ecgwynna was pregnant. She gave birth to a boy six months later and she named him Æthelstan – meaning noble stone. I wrote to Edward to tell him that he was now a father but he didn't reply.

A few months later I had a letter from Ælfred. It seemed that Edward had unwisely told his parents the news and it had gone down as badly as I'd feared. Father Tidwold was banished and I heard later that he'd become a parish priest in an obscure vill in

Mercia. I was told to destroy the marriage certificate and to bring the baby to Wintanceaster.

I was in a quandary. Although I didn't think Ælfred was the type of man to murder a small baby I couldn't be certain that Æthelstan would be safe. At least he hadn't punished Ecgwynna. She could continue with her present life but she would never be allowed to see Edward again. That broke her heart.

I debated long and hard about what to do. In the end I decided that I had no option but to do as Ælfred commanded.

'Thank you for bringing my grandson to me, Lord Jørren, Ælfred said when I entered his chamber with the baby and its wet nurse. 'This is a sorry business. Edward has been a fool, risking his throne for a pretty face. You understand that the wedding never happened? This boy, Æthelstan, is a bastard as far as anyone outside this room is concerned.'

'I understand, cyning. What will happen to him?'

'He'll be sent to my daughter in Mercia. He'll be brought up in her household until he's old enough to become a novice monk.'

I breathed a sigh of relief; at least he was being allowed to live. When I left the king I found Edward waiting for me outside his chamber.

'You've given him my son?' he asked.

'Yes, Æthelstan is being sent to your sister in Mercia where he will become a monk in due course.'

Edward look thoroughly miserable and I felt sorry for him.

'I've been a fool and I'm sorry.'

There was nothing I could say to that. We embraced briefly and I returned to Cantwareburh thinking that would be the last I saw or heard of Æthelstan. How wrong I was.

Jørren will return in

The Way of the Raven

The story of the last great Danish invasion in Ælfred's lifetime

Due out in the late Autumn of 2020

Printed in Great Britain
by Amazon

84802832R00233